So, she was a servant, after all? She spoke well and carried herself such that for a moment Lord Dashford thought her more than that. Perhaps at one time she had been. Indeed, with a few good meals and a proper wardrobe, this young temptress would rival any London courtesan. Her skin was flawless. He allowed a few moments just to drink in the sight of her. Even his last mistress hadn't affected him quite this strongly.

Indeed, she promised to be a most welcome—and enjoyable—distraction from an otherwise bothersome evening. She was making little mewing sounds as his lips left hers, and he began raining slow kisses on other body parts. She responded by letting her own hands and lips explore his body. She was slow and tentative, reacting to each movement as if this were her first time.

Certainly, he'd had women before who'd feigned inexperience, but she was the most convincing by far. Except, of course, innocents were not generally to be found at night, wandering the garden, alone, inebriated, and in a state of undress . . .

Mistress by Mistake

SUSAN GEE HEINO

BERKLEY SENSATION, NEW YORK

THE BERKLEY PUBLISHING GROUP
Published by the Penguin Group
Penguin Group (USA) Inc.
375 Hudson Street, New York, New York 10014, USA
Penguin Group (Canada), 90 Eglinton Avenue East, Suite 700, Toronto, Ontario M4P 2Y3, Canada
(a division of Pearson Penguin Canada Inc.)
Penguin Books Ltd., 80 Strand, London WC2R 0RL, England
Penguin Group Ireland, 25 St. Stephen's Green, Dublin 2, Ireland (a division of Penguin Books Ltd.)
Penguin Group (Australia), 250 Camberwell Road, Camberwell, Victoria 3124, Australia
(a division of Pearson Australia Group Pty. Ltd.)
Penguin Books India Pvt. Ltd., 11 Community Centre, Panchsheel Park, New Delhi—110 017, India
Penguin Group (NZ), 67 Apollo Drive, Rosedale, North Shore 0632, New Zealand
(a division of Pearson New Zealand Ltd.)
Penguin Books (South Africa) (Pty.) Ltd., 24 Sturdee Avenue, Rosebank, Johannesburg 2196,
South Africa

Penguin Books Ltd., Registered Offices: 80 Strand, London WC2R 0RL, England

This is a work of fiction. Names, characters, places, and incidents either are the product of the author's imagination or are used fictitiously, and any resemblance to actual persons, living or dead, business establishments, events, or locales is entirely coincidental. The publisher does not have any control over and does not assume any responsibility for author or third-party websites or their content.

MISTRESS BY MISTAKE

A Berkley Sensation Book / published by arrangement with the author

PRINTING HISTORY
Berkley Sensation mass-market edition / December 2009

Copyright © 2009 by Susan Gee Heino.
Excerpt from *Damsel in Disguise* by Susan Gee Heino copyright © by Susan Gee Heino.
Interior text design by Kristin del Rosario.

ISBN: 978-0-425-23151-7

BERKLEY® SENSATION
Berkley Sensation Books are published by The Berkley Publishing Group,
a division of Penguin Group (USA) Inc.,
375 Hudson Street, New York, New York 10014.
BERKLEY® SENSATION and the "B" design are trademarks of Penguin Group (USA) Inc.

PRINTED IN THE UNITED STATES OF AMERICA

10 9 8 7 6 5 4 3 2 1

*Dedicated to my long-suffering
friends and family:
Melody Knopf, Ed and
Blanche Gee, Marilyn Heino,
Diane Gee Frasca, Ellen Gee Mangine,
and most especially my hero
Jack and my darlings, Joy and Jake.
Please know how much I truly
appreciate everything.
Really. I'm serious. For once.*

Acknowledgments

Q: How many creative people does it take to make a Mistress by Mistake?

A: This many—Central Ohio Fiction Writers, the Pixie Chicks, Donna MacMeans and the MR-Debut gals, my Cracker Barrel Brainstormers, a fabulous agent, Cori Deyoe, and a wonderful editor, Leis Pederson. Thanks to all of you!

Chapter One

✦

"Shame on you, Evaline Pinchley. You're positively drunk."

No, that hadn't been Aunt Bella's sharp derision, although it certainly sounded enough like her. Evaline had said it herself. She was quite surprised by this, actually. Who knew she had such talent? By heavens, she'd gotten the tone and the timbre just right. She sounded exactly like Aunt Bella. That made her giggle.

Poor, scheming Aunt Bella. Wouldn't she be upset tomorrow when she went down to breakfast with their elusive host only to find their nice little plans were completely and utterly ruined? Aunt Bella would likely turn a lovely shade of maroon, and that reprobate Lord Dashford would . . . well, Evaline really had no idea what the viscount would do. Despite the fact that Aunt Bella was convinced the man was desperate to marry Evaline, he'd barely given her a second look at their brief meeting earlier tonight.

At least, Evaline thought that must have been Dashford her aunt was gushing over. To be honest, Evaline had rather been woolgathering when the actual introduction was made, and she'd found Lord Dashford—when he finally deigned to appear—decidedly disappointing. The rumor mill certainly had him a much more dashing and romantic figure than the gentleman she met in the Hartwood drawing room tonight. Pity, but it was just as well. Evaline would see the inside of Hades before she'd let Papa's hard-earned fortune go to a dissipated opportunist like Dashford.

She would, however, enjoy seeing Aunt Bella stuttering and stammering for some excuse to give his lordship once the truth about Evaline's competence came out. Oh, but the woman deserved whatever apoplexy she brought upon herself. Just the thought of it made Evaline giggle again.

How odd! She hadn't giggled in ages, not since she was a girl. But she was no girl now, was she? No, she was a fully grown and fully competent adult, as a matter of fact. A full quarter of a century old now; adult and independent—finally. That, of course, was the whole point. Today Evaline reached her age of majority, while poor Aunt Bella was under the faulty impression that she could still control Evaline—and the fortune that went with her—for another five months.

Honestly, what sort of auntie could not be bothered to learn the actual date of her niece's birth? The sort who would throw perfectly worthless men at said niece from sunup 'til sundown and try to compromise the poor girl into marrying one of them simply to gain control of her enormous trust fund, that was the sort. Well, no more. Evaline was finally free of all that.

At least, she would be once Papa's man of business arrived with some funds for her. She'd been corresponding with the man for two weeks, and the timing should have been perfect. She hadn't counted on this dratted weather, though. Likely all the rain had held the man up. London to Warwickshire was quite a journey, but with luck he was not more than a day behind. Mr. Carrington knew how important this was, and no doubt word would come tomorrow announcing his clandestine arrival in the nearby village of Findutton-on-Avon, just as planned. Ah, then she would truly be free and independent.

She glanced around the garden, green and damp and bathed in patchy moonlight. Thank heavens the rain had let up. All around her was still; no one stirred but the fish in the reflecting pool and the crickets in the shrubs. Good thing, too. She'd left her room to come out here in nothing more than her frayed night rail and thin, tattered wrap. She must look a sight. Just one more thing she had against her guardians: they never saw reason to waste any of Evaline's generous allowance on updating her wardrobe. Oh, no, why should they when it was so much easier for Uncle Troy to just gamble it away?

But none of that mattered tonight. She was completely alone out here and bound and determined to enjoy her first breath of freedom since burying Papa all those cold years ago. It felt good to allow herself a few private indiscretions. She plopped down on a low stone bench and raised her half-empty bottle of Madeira up toward the ivory moon.

My, but it was a beautiful moon. This was a beautiful garden, too. And the night was a beautiful night. In fact, right at this moment, everything in Evaline's life seemed, well, beautiful.

Except, of course, for the annoying little fact that she was alone. Drat, but that really rankled. What good was it to have these beautiful surroundings, this perfect opportunity, and no one to share it with?

It irked her to no end that even after all Papa's warnings and all these years of fighting off Aunt Bella's procured suitors, the idea of romantic entanglement still seemed so appealing. Clearly it must be Grandmamma's influence. Papa had warned her about that—he never let her forget her tainted bloodline. Indeed, Evaline had learned at a young age that she could never trust her own passions.

She'd learned, instead, to restrain them, no matter what sweet words dripped from the lips of her flattering admirers. During nearly eight years as the ward of scheming Aunt Bella, this skill above all others had served her well. Miraculously, she avoided the pitfall of succumbing to the many men who, despite her mousy and threadbare appearance, had sought to woo her. They were all no different than this Lord Dashford: decadent, disgusting, and desperate. True, they were not generally so grand as an actual viscount, but they all had one thing in common. Every man she'd ever known was only interested in one thing: Papa's money.

Well, it was *her* money, as of today. And she'd be dashed before she'd share it with the likes of them!

She gulped down another full swallow and glared at the moon. Its gentle glow on the vacant seat beside her nearly made her cry. Bother. With as much Madeira as she'd drunk tonight, how could she possibly still feel so empty inside?

"Such a waste of perfectly good moonlight," she sighed to herself.

It wasn't herself who answered, though. "Oh, it doesn't appear wasted at all."

The girl was totally out of place but undeniably fetching. Dashford noticed her in the garden immediately, her worn white nightgown fairly glowing in the moonlight. Odd to find her out here like this, though. One of his mother's ruddy guests at this sham of a house party, perhaps? Or maybe a ghost? He'd not heard of this particular garden being haunted, but he couldn't disregard the notion. Something radiated from her and drew him. He simply couldn't take his eyes from her. Well, it was his garden, after all, so he decided if this was a specter, it was technically his possession, and therefore he was perfectly within his rights to keep staring. So he did. In fact, he moved closer.

But she was not a ghost. Her delectable little form was pleasantly corporeal. The young woman sat contentedly on a bench near the fountain, and even though Dashford's boots crunched lightly on the walkway as he came near, she didn't seem to notice. He realized why when she tipped her head back and downed a healthy swallow of wine right from the bottle. By God, she was drunk!

Probably not one of Mother's guests, then, but someone he'd gladly welcome into his garden all the more. Despite the gossip racing through London about his propensity for expensive ladies, it had been a good while since he'd found himself in this position—alone with a scantily clad female. It was a position he'd heartily embrace.

She was a happy reprieve for what, no doubt, awaited him inside. Mother—God bless her—had dredged up another heiress, and he'd walked right into a trap. What a fool he'd been to fall for the matriarch's emergency summons. As if a leaking roof was cause to come rushing back to Hartwood.

He should have known she had something sinister planned for him. Heiress, indeed.

Well, he'd avoided them all this evening. Eaten his dinner at the local inn, he had, then cloistered himself with his steward on the pretense of business. Lord, what a coward he was. His unfortunate friend Anthony Rastmoor had felt compelled to join the group after dinner, though. Too polite for his own good, the man was. Hell, he'd probably fawned over the heiress just as Mother expected. Well, let him. Rastmoor didn't have as much at stake as Dashford did.

On the other hand, Rastmoor didn't have a tarnished angel sitting on a moonlit bench in front of him, either. Absently she fondled the bottle in her hands, her fingers running slowly up and down its neck. Dashford found his throat suddenly dry and his trousers suddenly tight. Indeed, his friend Rastmoor—likely still stuck inside with the prudish heiress—should be doubly pitied just now.

The girl tipped her head again to drink, and the fabric of her gown pulled tight against her ample breasts. Her neck was delicate and well-defined, as was the rest of her. In the white moonlight there was little left to Dashford's imagination, yet somehow he found plenty to imagine.

She was small but fully endowed with all the gentle curves a man could ask for. In all the right places, too, it appeared. Her honey-colored hair was rather loosely piled atop her head; a few golden ringlets hung down past her shoulders. Altogether she was quite easy to look at and certainly most pleasant to find in one's private garden.

He moved closer, and she still did not seem to notice. He knew, of course, he should either announce his presence or leave her in peace, but he really hated to do either. Leaving was out of the question and, really, conversation was not exactly foremost on his mind just now.

But he had to say something, didn't he? What was the protocol for this situation? He jumped a bit when she solved his dilemma by speaking.

"Such a waste of perfectly good moonlight." She sighed into the air.

Now she jumped a bit when he answered. "Oh, it doesn't appear wasted at all."

Slowly she turned her face up toward him. Ah, moist green eyes under thick, dark lashes and quite an exquisite complexion, especially for someone of her obvious low circumstances. The fabric of her nightgown had been patched and restitched in several places. At least he could safely assume this was no heiress nor any other guest of his mother. The Dowager Lady Dashford was quite high in the instep, after all. Perhaps this vision was someone's companion, or a servant, even.

He had never been one to dally with servants, but something about this one set her apart from all the others. Perhaps it was the cultured lilt in her voice, or perhaps it was the very charming—and very inviting—smile she was giving him. Indeed, perhaps it was time he began dallying with servants. This one might just be worth it. Given all the effort and education he'd put into living up to the rumors he'd so carefully cultivated of late, he knew how to make it worthwhile for her.

EVALINE LET HER HEAD ROLL BACK ON HER NECK and found herself looking up into eyes that were every bit as bright and silvery as the moon itself. Well, this was quite a surprise! Where on earth did they come from?

"Hello," she said, proud of herself for remembering to be so polite.

The eyes, she came to discover, were part of a face. A very good face with everything from symmetry to an excellent complexion. And there was the most fetching hint of dark beard, which of course wouldn't have been nearly so fetching were this face belonging to someone of the female variety, but—fortunately for the face—it did indeed belong to someone male. Someone deliciously male and several years under sixty.

Her head felt decidedly heavy, but she managed to loll it down and then back up again. Yes, this was indeed someone male. And he was not nearly so bland and resistible as the Lord Dashford she had just met in the drawing room. He was so very non-bland, non-resistible, and non-sixty, in fact, she wondered if he was nothing more than an invention of the wine. Or the moonlight.

But he spoke.

"Hello to you," he said, and he sounded quite real. "And just why are you so disappointed in tonight's moon?"

"Oh, I'm not disappointed in the moon at all!" she replied, strangely overjoyed at his existence. "Just the fact that I'm terribly alone under it."

He was studying her closely, and she supposed she ought to feel some concern—or at least self-consciousness—but she was too busy studying him to feel much of anything besides this giddy lightheadedness. What a fine figure he was, so tall and broad shouldered. Without all his layers of clothing, he would probably look like one of those fine marble sculptures of Roman gods she'd seen depicted in books.

Oh, what he could do to her, a man with shoulders like that! Such strong arms and capable hands. Why, he seemed so solid and powerful, he could . . .

And there she was blank. Odd, but she had no clue what he might do to her if it didn't involve her struggling against him. Even with Grandmamma's courtesan blood flowing in her veins, she was uncertain. So much of these last seven years had been spent fending men off that Evaline never actually got around to figuring out what it might be like to lead one on. No doubt this one was as much a liar and scoundrel as the rest, but what if she decided not to be concerned about that? What exactly would he do to her if she, for once, said yes? The possibilities were mind-boggling.

"You're giggling," he stated.

"I am," she agreed, and the sound she made then sounded unfortunately more like a snort than a giggle. "But please don't take it personally."

"Would you care to share the joke?"

"I was just thinking—" She paused to consider. What had she been thinking? Oh yes, about his godlike shoulders and how she might wish to succumb to them.

"I guess I was wrong," she amended with another giggle. "I suppose you *could* have every reason to take it personally. Oh, but don't be offended. It had to do with your wonderful shoulders and how I wish you weren't wearing so many clothes."

Now he made an odd sound. "Funny, I was having rather a similar thought."

"Were you? I should think you'd be very much shocked."

"I should be, yes. But you'll find there's very little that shocks me of late."

"I will find that?"

"Should you like to?"

It was hard to make out his expression now. The moon was behind him, a glowing aura. It reminded her of the stained glass windows at the church she used to attend with Grandmamma years and years ago.

"You have a halo," she said. "It's most becoming on you."

"Does it make me appear angelic?"

She had to consider that for a moment. "Hmm. On you, sir, I suppose it could go either way."

He laughed. "Word has it I'm hardly an angel."

"Are you sure? I'm getting quite dizzy staring up at you like this."

He laughed, and it danced through her mind like music. A waltz, she decided. Yes, his laughter was a waltz. How funny that she would notice this now, when the last thing on earth she could do would be to stand up and dance.

Much to the joy of her swimming senses and foggy equilibrium, he moved to her side and sat on the bench. She could feel the heat from his body, and she could smell the clean scent of soap and linen on him. Better still, now she had but to tilt her head slightly for a closer view of his bright, simmering eyes. Ah, this was much better than craning her neck and fighting with the moonlight.

"Is this better?" he asked.

"Much," she admitted.

"I agree."

She sucked in a short gasp of air as he reached for her. How heavenly it would be to let him touch her! His hands were so elegant and manly. Would they be rough? Would they be gentle? Oh, she could hardly breathe for the anticipation.

Unfortunately, when his touch came, it was scarcely enough to learn anything. His hand only barely brushed hers. It was the wine bottle he was after. Drat.

He pulled the nearly empty bottle from her limp fingers and held it up to the light. "Have you taken care of all this yourself?"

"I have," she said with pride.

"Formidable."

"Thank you. Dissipation is rather a new hobby of mine, and I'm pleased you think I've made good headway so far."

"Excellent headway, indeed." He laughed. "But I'm curious. Are the entertainments here so very lacking that you must resort to private intoxication?"

Ah, so he hadn't yet had the pleasure of socializing with the sedate crowd gathered here at Lady Dashford's mostly geriatric house party.

"I take it you've only just arrived?" she asked.

"Indeed, and I plan to leave again at the earliest possible moment," he replied with conviction.

"A man of great intelligence, I see."

"I've found it helpful to be aware of my surroundings. So, you are a guest of her ladyship?"

"Guest? Well, that's a generous way to put it."

"What, a housebreaker, then?"

"Certainly not. Let's just say I'm here out of necessity; familial obligation, and all that rubbish."

"Oh. I see."

"I hope not," she said and laughed. "You might just be the noble sort who'd feel compelled to report me out here enjoying myself with you when I ought to be in there, tending to duty. She'll bring out the strap again for certain."

He looked positively scandalized. "Someone takes a strap to you? Here?"

That made her giggle. "No, not here, of course."

"Elsewhere, then?"

She thought about answering but decided against it. Her battles with Aunt Bella were nearly over and certainly not anything she wished to share with a stranger. She shrugged and leaned into him, reaching for the bottle. "Can I have my wine back, please?"

Her breasts brushed against him, and he held the bottle just far enough out of her reach that she was forced to maintain the pose. How warm and comfortable he was! Then the feeling got even better when he put one arm around her to keep her from sliding off the bench. Ah, delightful.

"Tell me, who has mistreated you?" he asked gently.

"Bother," she sighed, her body slumping against him. "I don't want to think about that now. I was feeling so good, and you've been so friendly and nice to talk to."

"Then, by all means, talk to me."

She stopped reaching for the bottle, and her hand fell against his chest. For a quick moment she wasn't sure what to do, then her fingers took over and she didn't have to think. They curled over the thick fabric of his coat and traced their way over to the row of buttons. What fascinating things, buttons. She squinted in careful study of them, then finally managed to get one undone. Victory! She smiled up at him.

"I'd rather *not* talk to you right now," she said and hoped he might understand what she meant, since she wasn't entirely sure she did.

He seemed to have a fair idea, though. The wine bottle hit the ground beside his feet as his fingers found something better to hold onto: *her*. She liked that.

"That's nice," she said, or at least tried to say as his thumb followed the curve of her jawline. His other hand was secure around her, barely cupping her right breast.

The man was so warm and solid beneath her touch. Not that she could actually feel him, since he had that wool coat, vest, and whatever layers of linen shirt were under that. Still, it was the closest she'd come to willfully touching a man's chest, and she was determined to enjoy it. Soon enough he'd probably become shocked by her forward behavior and send her on her way, but for now she was going to investigate all she could.

His grip on her was gradually tightening. She wasn't sure what that meant, but she was glad for it in the end. It kept her from swooning when his lips came down on hers.

He was kissing her! Well, this was nothing like the awkward busses she remembered from her one girlhood infatuation, or the slobbering clutches of some more recent suitors eager to compromise her into a forced—and profitable—marriage. No, this was far, far beyond any of that. This man held her against him and worked his perfectly symmetrical lips over hers, capturing them and sending shivers of pleasure through her. She felt a little sigh escape her, but thankfully, he didn't stop.

In fact, it seemed there was much more to kissing than just aimless groping and lips touching lips. There was work to be done by the tongue, too, it turned out. My, he tasted good. Not like the wine she'd been drinking; something different. Port, perhaps? Or maybe it was just him. She wasn't sure, but she was only too happy that he seemed in no hurry to block her from tasting him to her heart's content.

His tongue teased hers, and she reveled in the experience. She found the thin fabric of his shirt beneath his coat and was pleased to discover it was warm from his body heat. She could almost imagine her skin rubbing against his as their mouths played at this wonderful game back and forth. How pleasant it would be to give in to him completely. Would he let her? Did she dare invite him?

Unfortunately, whether she dared or not was irrelevant. The real issue, she realized, was that she honestly had no clue what to do next. Pooh. It never dawned on her that her ignorance of these matters would be such a hindrance. Apparently she had not taken after Grandmamma quite as much as Papa seemed to think. Whatever was she to do? It would simply be dreadful to lose this once-in-a-lifetime opportunity!

"What's the matter?" he asked.

She realized she'd not been paying attention. Bah, now she'd gone and ruined the whole thing by suddenly feeling all missish and awkward. Perhaps if they were indoors, with the usual furnishings and less moonlight, she would be more confident.

"I was wishing we were inside, in my own room, perhaps," she answered.

"Don't worry," he soothed. "This is a very private garden. We won't be interrupted."

As he spoke, his hand slid to the frayed ties that held her dressing gown. He undid them smoothly and didn't seem to care in the least that they were out of doors. His assurance was comforting. Perhaps all was not ruined. As long as he knew what to do, things would go just fine. He loosened the ties and slid her dressing gown and night rail down over one shoulder, covering her naked skin with kisses. Yes indeed, he knew exactly what to do.

"You have very lovely skin," he murmured, leaning close.

His lips were warm, and she felt the moisture from his hot breath. It was every bit as intoxicating as the wine. She arched her body against him to make it easier for his lips to skim over her, to explore her neck, her collarbone, and down toward her breasts. Indeed, she was quite certain she would expire completely if his lips did not find their way to her breasts. She helped him along by tugging at her garments, pulling the night rail and shift down low.

He chuckled—a deep rumbling sound that echoed inside her—and dipped his head obediently. One hand cupped her breast and set it free from the binding fabric. The air touched her nipple seconds before his lips did, and she gasped. Who could have ever imagined this would be so wondrous? He was clearly an expert. She would have to remember to thank him at some point, but she was a bit too distracted just now. His tongue was molding her nipple inside his mouth while one of his hands was trailing slowly up the inside of her thigh.

She scooted on the bench, twisting so that he could have better access. The moonlight shone on her pale legs as he pushed her night rail up higher and higher, and she watched in amazement. Oddly, any shyness or hesitation was gone. That must be due to the wine. Oh, blessed liquid! To think it could bring her to such a place as this. She should have tried it years ago.

Then again, this gentleman had to be given a goodly portion of the credit for her current bliss. His hands glided over her body. His kisses burned hot as flames, and she moaned aloud, begging to be marked by them. He held her gently but with a strength and firmness that convinced her she'd never been this safe.

"Is this what you want?" he asked softly, breathing the words against her ear.

"Yes, please," she said. Her voice was pitifully thin and ragged.

But he didn't seem bothered by that. In fact, he rewarded

her with sensations she could never have dreamed of. He touched her most private corner, the tender, throbbing dale between her legs. The flames rose higher and nearly overwhelmed her.

She shifted again; her legs parted of their own accord, and she clung to him for support. As his hand explored, she drifted into another world. All was light and sensation, and floodwaters of heated desire washed over her. She rocked against him, bringing further waves of pleasure that seemed to be building toward something.

And to think she had once worried this was something to be feared! Well, now she knew that was just silly. This was wonderful beyond description, and she wanted more. She wanted all of it, and she was determined to learn exactly what that was.

Angry that there should be any barrier between them, she ripped at his coat. He responded with husky laughter, complying with her demands and shedding his many layers, even as her own remaining clothing was torn aside. At last she could see him before her, bared to the waist and glittering like gold in the moonlight. Dark hairs wisped over his chest, collecting in a tantalizing mass that trailed in a thin line down, down into his trousers. A map, guiding the way toward buried treasure.

She laughed. He was more beautiful than she'd expected and much, much better than cold, unmoving stone. She knew she did not deserve such perfection, but she wasn't about to quibble now! This man held the key—whatever that was—to the growing urgency within her, and she'd be damned before she'd let him escape now. She reached for him, but he grasped her hands.

"Wait. Allow me to finish with you first," he said.

What on earth did that mean? She was quite certain she was trying to *help* him finish with her. Well, he was the expert, and she was just an inexperienced souse. Clearly she'd have to let him determine what happened next. She smiled and nodded.

"All right. You may finish with me."

He seemed pleased with that, and she was glad she could make him happy. He leaned her back, and she realized he was asking her to lie back against the cool, mossy stone. Well, if that's what he wanted.

"Here, perhaps this will make you more comfortable," he said, reaching around to tuck his coat under her.

Ah, it did indeed make her more comfortable. It was still heated from his body, and she melted into its embrace. Heavenly. She was engulfed in the man.

She took a great, relaxing breath, and her leaden arms fell to her sides. Then they slid right off the edge of the bench, dangling below her. Her dressing gown promptly slid down right along with them and left her in nothing more than her night rail and shift. The rail, she discovered, was all askew. Her right breast lay bare in the moonlight, pale and plump. She'd never contemplated her breasts before, but right now they were practically all she could think of. Would he like them? She sincerely hoped so. It seemed so terribly important.

"Lovely," he said, dipping to put his lips to the puckered crest.

Good. He liked what he saw. "And there's another just like it," she informed him.

"Ah, a woman of many talents."

"Just so long as you don't ask me to do sums. I could never quite master that."

He shook his head. "I promise. Nothing like that tonight."

"Good." She took in a deep breath and wiggled against the mattress of his coat. "Now, what am I to do next? Shall we go back to how you were touching me, or do we move on to something else?"

He laughed. "My dear, you do make it hard to wait."

"But I'm tired of waiting."

"I'll make it worth your while, I promise."

And she knew he would.

SO, SHE WAS A SERVANT, AFTER ALL. SHE SPOKE well and carried herself such that for a moment he'd thought her more than that. Perhaps at one time she had been. Indeed, with a few good meals and a proper wardrobe, this young temptress would rival any London courtesan.

Her skin was flawless. He allowed a few moments just to drink in the sight of her, spread out there on the bench for him. She was a buffet he was going to enjoy fully. Even his last mistress—who had come with glowing recommendations—hadn't affected him quite this strongly.

Perhaps it was the fact that this woman meant nothing. He hadn't chosen her for what people might say about them afterward or how his status among the London bucks would be improved by a reputed liaison with her. Perhaps it was because he knew instinctively she wanted him with the same unencumbered passion he felt for her—no strings, no expectations. Or perhaps it was simply the moonlight.

Whatever fueled this fierce attraction, it was all he could do to keep from plunging himself into her right now. But he would hold off. Anticipation only enhanced the moment, and he wanted her to remember him long after this little tryst was done. Indeed, he would give her good reason to remember him.

"Ladies first," he said, leaning over her.

He began with a kiss. On her lips. She seemed unprepared for that, and as before, it took a moment for her to respond fully. Perhaps her other lovers had spent less time on kisses and more time on their own pleasure. Typical.

Well, she would find that he was not typical. He had learned to take his time, to make things last. So far, it had served him well, and none of his ladies had ever voiced a complaint. Of course, none of them had ever responded to him quite like she did. It would be interesting to watch her here, to see into her eyes as she realized tonight she was getting more than just a few moments of heated coupling. He hoped she might even giggle again for him. Indeed, she promised to be a most welcome—and enjoyable—distraction to an otherwise bothersome evening.

She was making little mewing sounds as his lips left hers and began raining slow kisses on other body parts. He kissed her neck and shoulders, knowing already she would enjoy that. She did, and she responded by letting her own hands and lips explore his body. She was slow and tentative, reacting to each movement as if this were the first time. It was remarkably enticing.

Certainly, he'd had women before who'd found enjoyment

in feigning inexperience, but she was the most convincing by far. His hand found its way back to that warm, moist haven between her legs. The sounds she made smacked of honest amazement, and the quick intake of breath as his fingers dipped inside her made him almost believe she was, in fact, an innocent.

Except, of course, innocents were not generally to be found at night wandering the garden alone in a state of undress inviting advances from total strangers. No, his conscience had nothing to fear on that count. This little morsel knew what she was about, and it was her intent to be eagerly devoured tonight. He'd be doing her a favor to comply, in fact, so there was no sense in hesitating.

He stroked the hot velvet flesh. She was so receptive, so responsive; he knew he would not have to work very hard to bring her to climax. She was panting and moaning in the most arousing way already. His manhood strained against his trousers, and he knew he wouldn't last much longer, either.

She rocked against him, and he found just the right spot. He pressed his thumb against her, and she sucked in a shuddering gasp. Just a few more gentle strokes, and he could feel her muscles contracting around his fingers. Yes, she was responsive, indeed.

She cried out when the full force of the climax hit her. She arched her back and drew her long arms above her head, stretched out there on his coat and this convenient bench. It would have been nice to hear her call his name, but considering their difference in station—not to mention the fact that they hadn't exactly been properly introduced—it was not very likely. Still, he would have liked to hear it.

The waves of pleasure had full possession of her, and she was lost in them. He watched in awe of what he had accomplished. Her long eyelashes fanned porcelain cheeks, and the hint of blush rose from her breasts all the way up to color her face. Her lips were tinted as fine wine. Like this, lounging before him and completely lost in a world of pleasure and desire of his own making, she was too beautiful for words.

He could hold himself back no longer. He would have his fill of her.

Quickly, while she was still in the throes and spasms of warm ecstasy, he undid his trousers. Ah, blessed freedom! He pushed her nightgown even farther up across her belly and moved over her. He was already anticipating the feel of her surrounding him, taking him in and caressing him with her most intimate parts. He couldn't remember the last time he needed this so badly.

"All right, miss," he breathed over her. "Your waiting is over."

He nudged her legs apart with his knees then lowered himself gently. The bench was solid, and even though he'd given her his coat, he knew his weight pressing her into it would be less than comfortable. Ever so carefully he moved himself into position. He could feel heat radiating from her; feel the moisture of her body. He pressed the head of his eager cock close up against her, waiting for the welcoming moans and movements.

None came.

What? He glanced up at her face. Her eyes were still closed, her crimson lips still pursed in a satisfied smile. Her chest rose and fell in regular breaths. She was the picture of health and sated woman.

In fact, she was asleep.

Good God! She'd fallen asleep on him. Here he was throbbing with unfulfilled desire, and she was sleeping soundly. He tried to gently rouse her, but aside from a few childlike murmurings, he could get nothing from her. She was dead to the world.

Well, as he saw it, there were two options. He could finish what he'd started—Lord knew she was still ready for him, sleeping or not—or he could admit defeat. The first option was most appealing just now, but the gentleman inside him knew it was hardly fair to use her for his own purposes when she was incoherent. Damn. That left only the second option.

But what to do with her? Certainly he could not just leave her here! There was no telling what might happen to her. But he had no clue where her room was to deposit her there, either. He'd have to wake the housekeeper and alert everyone to what had transpired. He doubted she'd thank him for that.

Damn. There was but one thing he could do.

He refastened his trousers—no easy task, considering his physical state—and retrieved his shirt. The coat was sacrificed to wrap around his sleeping beauty; if someone did see them on the way inside, the very least he could do was to hide her identity. She purred like a kitten as he bundled her up, then she giggled a bit as he hoisted her into his arms.

Kicking the wine bottle out of his way, he began the arduous journey up the marble staircase and inside, toward his bedchamber. He really ought to be ashamed of himself for behaving this way under the very noses of his mother and her decorous guests, but truthfully, he didn't give a damn. This delectable armful was going upstairs with him, and with luck she would wake sometime soon.

If not, it was going to be a very long night for the viscount Dashford.

Chapter Two

❦

Evaline woke up to a gray, drizzly morning and a splitting headache that hurt all the way down to her toes. Her first thoughts were that her misery was so acute, she must be dying. When at last she cracked her eyes open to view her blurry surroundings, she discovered she was lying in the center of the most enormous bed she could ever imagine. It was quite comfortable, too, with fresh-scented linens and nothing lumpy or dubious in the mattress. If not for the headache, she might have assumed she had already died and gone to heaven.

Because of the headache, it seemed more likely she had died, but this was not heaven. Suddenly the events of last night came back to her in a deluge of images, and she realized she might have every reason to expect herself to end up somewhere other than saintly paradise.

Good God, what had she done? She'd drunk an entire bottle of wine, then allowed a strange man to ... No, she couldn't even think about that! What on earth had come over her? It had to have been a dream, but even that was shocking. She was Evaline Pinchley, prim and proper and the very picture of maidenly caution. That couldn't possibly have been her last night, writhing around on a bench with an unknown man! Sweet saints above, all these dreadful memories simply couldn't be her own!

She peeped around the room. No man in sight. Thankfully, she appeared to be quite alone. A quick look under the covers assured her she was wearing her nightclothes, although they were a bit rumpled. But at least they were there! Perhaps it had all been simply a dream, after all.

That didn't explain her presence in this bed, though. This was not the cozy, feminine room she had been assigned when she and her aunt had arrived at Hartwood yesterday. No, this was clearly someone else's room—grand and decidedly masculine. But whose? And was she even sure she was still at Hartwood? Heavens, there was no telling what had happened to her between that bottle of wine and this searing headache. Her mind raced with possibilities, each one worse than the last.

No, this was silly. She must still be at Hartwood. She simply needed to be calm and think for a moment. What was the last thing she remembered? Oh yes. Her breasts. In the moonlight. And him touching them, touching her . . . yes, she remembered that, all right. God, just thinking of it now sent waves of something tingly all through her body. That really didn't help the headache one bit, either.

She ran through it step-by-step. She had turned twenty-five and gained independence. Yes, she recalled that. She had gotten drunk. That, too, was vivid in her memory. Then she'd gone and done wild, lascivious things with a complete stranger. And she'd liked them! Oh gracious, she could only hope what memories she did have of that weren't true. Her traitorous body told her they were. Most definitely. Heavens, what was she to do about it now?

Sadly, in the cold light of day, it didn't seem there was much she could do about it. She may have come of age legally, but unless Papa's agent miraculously appeared sometime during the night, she still had no money on her person. Bother! That meant she was technically still dependent on her aunt. Drat and confound it. In her wine-induced haze last night, she hadn't been counting on that.

Oh, this was dreadful. If anyone found out what she'd done, there'd be no end to the shame. All of England would hear how she'd lived up to expectations and become a wanton woman, a hussy, no better than she ought to be.

She'd become what Papa had tried so hard to protect her from. And worst of all, she couldn't even remember it!

True, she remembered meeting the man in the garden and how he had made her feel; that much she would never forget. The way he looked at her, how his hands glided over her skin . . . his lips, his scent . . . indeed, those were things that would be forever burned in her memory. But what of the actual act? How could she not recall *that*? Was it so very awful her mind had blocked it out? She felt wretched from head to toe. Heavens, what *had* she let that man do to her?

She shifted in the bed, and the movement made her stomach churn. Oh, she wished she were dead. What had she been thinking? It must have been the wine. She'd been a fool to drink anything stronger than lemonade! Never again. Oh, but at the mere thought of drinking even warm milk, she felt she would retch on the lovely bedcovers.

Wait, sickness in the morning . . . that seemed a familiar topic. Wasn't it supposed to be some symptom of something? She struggled to ignore the throbbing in her temples and tried to recall. Yes, she was certain she'd heard of it: morning sickness. What was it she'd heard? Something terminal, perhaps? Something to do with . . . Oh, good heavens! Surely, not *that*? She couldn't possibly be! It couldn't come on so soon.

Or could it? Her education was deplorably vague on this subject. The dangers of men Evaline knew well. Her own susceptibility to twinkling eyes and a muscular frame was now completely understood. But the inner workings of her own physical being were a complete and utter mystery to her. And this specific inner working was rather significant!

Dear heavens, she was hopelessly ignorant of the most important things. Who on earth could she go to? Certainly not Aunt Bella, and even more certainly not that man whose identity was still—mortifyingly—a mystery.

Why, oh, why had she been such a fool? She should have spent last night carefully planning, not celebrating. Her birthday meant nothing, not really. She hadn't met with her agent, hadn't received any of her funds, couldn't truly embark on accomplishing the goals she'd set for herself. She'd still been literally penniless last night, still at the mercy of Aunt Bella and Lord Dashford. Now she was just as penniless, had no honor left to her, and she could conceivably be in a delicate condition!

She cringed at the very thought. *Conceivable*. Was it? Could it be possible that after one foolish, irrational night she might end up with a *child*? Heavens! What would she do with a child? A child who, if it took at all after its father, would be an exceedingly attractive little creature with particular talents that she hoped it would not put into use for a good twenty years or so. Oh, but of course she would love a child. With her whole heart she would—just as Grandmamma had done when she'd been in this same predicament. And surely the child would love her wholeheartedly, too. Yes, and wouldn't that be nice? To have family, to love someone and be loved in return . . .

Oh, but she could not think that way! How could she possibly look forward to having a child with a man whose name she did not even know? Surely she was misinterpreting this wretched pounding in her head and the lurching in her stomach. There had to be some other explanation—having a child in her situation would be, well, dreadful. What sort of mother would she make, struggling years to be moral and upright only to fall into utter ruin without so much as a hesitation? A very poor mother, indeed, who could not so much as remember the event that put her in that state!

Blast it, but she'd really made a mess of things, hadn't she? Lounging here in her nausea and self-pity wasn't likely to help matters, either. Whoever owned this bed would eventually return at some point. If she were still here, he might understandably expect an encore performance.

Or perhaps she'd already done that. Perhaps there had been many performances last night; her head certainly ached enough for that. And heavens, who was to say this one gentleman was the only one she'd encountered? Good Lord, but Dashford's infamous carousing might have allowed for several of his vile acquaintances to be present here at his estate. While he was entertaining his mother's elderly guests indoors, who knew how many leering rakes Evaline had been entertaining in the garden? By God, perhaps she was a great whore now, servicing many men all in one fell swoop!

Oh, her poor little child never would know its own father. This was dreadful! It was time to look for the chamber pot before she lost whatever was left in her stomach all over the counterpane.

Gingerly she moved to the edge of the bed and sat upright. The room was spinning, and sounds like pounding surf rang in her head. At any moment her skull would explode; she was sure of it. She looked forward to it, as a matter of fact. Then at least all this misery would be over.

Her dressing gown was nearby, draped over the back of a chair. It looked particularly ragged in the daylight. God, how could anyone have found her remotely attractive, drunk as she was and dressed in Aunt Bella's cast-off rags? No wonder the man had made himself scarce by morning. Then again, perhaps he truly was scarce. Perhaps he was not even still here at Hartwood, if indeed this was Hartwood. Hadn't the man said something about leaving soon? Oh, she hoped he'd done just that. Yes, surely he—and any possible others—would be gone rather than to stay and run the risk of facing responsibility for their actions last night. That, at least, was some comfort. She would not have to face him today.

She tried to stand, but the crashing waves of pain and nausea were too much for her. She plopped back down on the bed. Bother. Now how was she to find out where she was and get back to her own room if she couldn't even stand upright?

Then she noticed something. Beside a careless (and tempting) pile of coins on the stand beside the bed, a fine piece of vellum was propped up in easy view. In masculine script she made out two words: *Sleeping Beauty*. She forced herself to leave the coins, as they clearly weren't hers, but it seemed appropriate she investigate the note. She took up the vellum and found it folded. Her numb fingers fumbled a bit, but finally she revealed a note. It said, simply, "I've left a restorative. Tastes like hell, but it'll mend your head. Drink it all, and I pray your mistress goes easy on you today. You may trust my silence." It was signed with a very elaborate letter that she perceived was either a *B*, an *R*, or a *D*. Wonderful. She now knew at least three possible initials for some part of her lover's name.

Her lover. No, that was certainly not appropriate to this situation. Love had never entered into their association. Still, he had been kind enough to tuck her up in someone's bed, and apparently he knew she would not be feeling quite the thing this morning. Perhaps she could solidly rule out the possibility of multiple gentlemen or kidnapping last night. Thank God.

She looked around her. There, on the nightstand beside where she'd found the note, was a tall glass with something thick and murky in it. She could only assume this was the "restorative" his note referred to.

Or perhaps it was deadly poison. At this point, she hardly cared. She would try anything. Sniffing it and recoiling, she wondered if poison wasn't indeed the most accurate description for this. Well, he had gone to the trouble of leaving it; she ought to at least give it a try.

She sipped and found his note had been right. It did taste like hell. Well, it would either kill her or help her, so, grimacing as hard as she could, she downed it in one gulp.

Oh, it was vile. It burned her throat. Certainly she'd be worse off for taking it. Then slowly, the burning went away and she realized the room was not spinning quite so much. Another minute or two, and she had to admit she was feeling decidedly better. Not immensely better, but somewhat. That was at least a step in the right direction.

Thank heavens. She no longer wanted to cast up all accounts. Her stomach was slowly settling, and as she sat very still, the pounding gradually eased. Perhaps she was saved, after all. Her gentleman's putrid restorative was a miracle worker. If she ever saw him again—which she highly doubted and truly hoped not—she would have to thank him.

Well, all she had to do now was figure out where she was. Assuming she had not been carted off to some distant place, she would have to get herself back to her own room. If she had any luck at all, she would open the door to find herself in Hartwood, in the same wing where she had been yesterday. With great luck, she could get to her room without coming across anyone or having to ask directions. With extraordinary luck, it would still be early enough that Aunt Bella had not yet missed her.

Sadly, though, the last few years of her life had proven that she was not what could accurately be called a lucky person. Still, she couldn't very well stay here, and it appeared that she wasn't going to die anytime soon. Drat, that. Death would have been far preferable to walking, the way her head was.

Standing on shaky legs, she straightened her dressing gown and squinted at the mantel clock. Well, what wonders; here was a small bit of luck already. If the clock could be believed, it was indeed a full hour before Aunt Bella generally rose. Evaline might just be able to pull this off with no one the wiser.

Patting her hair and swallowing back a last wave of nausea, she headed for the door. She'd have to face her future eventually, so she might as well do it now. Besides, she was a full-grown woman today. She knew the secrets of a woman's desire, of a man's body, and of passion. She just couldn't remember most of them.

One fortunate thing she did remember, though. She decided to cling to it as she faced her future. She may have ruined herself last night, but at least it had not been at the hand of Lord Randolf Dashford.

DASHFORD FROWNED AT HIS FRIEND. BY GOD, Rastmoor was annoying when he wanted to be. Why on earth had Dashford thought it would be a good idea to invite his friend to travel with him from London? He was turning out to be less salvation from Mother's dreary guests and too-obvious matchmaking than expected.

"You know good and well why I didn't come to breakfast today," he grumbled in response to Rastmoor's inquiry. They were crossing the yard, their polished boots crunching on the walkway on their way to the stables for an early morning ride. Hopefully the damned rain would hold off long enough to let Dashford exercise off some of this pent-up frustration.

"I'm damned hungry," he continued. "But Mama's insipid little heiress would no doubt be there, batting her lashes at me and looking for any opportunity to get me in a compromising position. I'll starve before I sit at table with that in my own home."

"I tell you, she's not like the rest of them," Rastmoor persisted.

"So you've become an admirer?"

"We were briefly introduced yesterday evening, is all," his friend said with a shrug. "Still, it was enough to recognize that she's different."

"Fine. Then you marry her."

Rastmoor laughed. "Oh no. Marriage is highly overrated, and I intend to avoid it as long as I can."

"You weren't always singing that tune," Dashford said and regretted it immediately.

"Yes, well things change, don't they?" Rastmoor snapped.

"Sorry," Dashford amended. He shouldn't have brought up the painful subject. "It would appear I'm in a foul mood this morning."

"Yes, you are. Care to explain that?"

"You already know it; Mama's blasted heiress."

Rastmoor shook his head. "Oh no. I've seen you weather husband hunters before. This is old hat to you, my friend. No, today it's something else. Not pining for something—or someone—you left back in London, are you?"

"Decidedly not."

"Hmm. Then what else might be worthy of such blue devilment? I'm at a loss."

"Give it up."

"No. Tell me; who is she?"

"No one you know."

Rastmoor started laughing. "Aha, I knew it."

Dashford swore. He was not about to discuss last night's events—or lack thereof—with Anthony Bloody Rastmoor.

But his friend persisted. "What, have you got Madeline stashed away at some inn nearby? Is she not happy with that last trinket you gave her?"

"No, Madeline is not stashed away. That last trinket I gave her was the last she'll ever get from me, and as far as I know, she's gone to see the Continent with Lord Someone-or-other."

"So Madeline is no longer anything to you?"

"No."

"Pity. I had high hopes. She would have got on so well with your mother."

"Hell," Dashford said, fighting back the awful image of his mother ever encountering one of his ladybirds.

"Then again, perhaps Claudia—oh, sorry, Miss Graeley— is the right one for you after all," Rastmoor added. "She's coming, you know."

"What?"

"Oh yes. I heard your mother mention it last night when I made my obligatory appearance. Miss Graeley and that blustering father of hers are due to arrive before dinner."

Dashford grumbled some choice words under his breath. Damn, but Mother hadn't mentioned she'd invited Claudia. All he'd known about was the heiress.

"So I've got to avoid a fiancée and one who wants to be, do I?"

"I thought Claudia had already cut you loose?"

"No," Dashford said with a few more choice words. "She just postponed the hanging."

"Postpone an engagement? Can she do that?"

"Hell, yes she can! As long as her father's got my name on those damned betrothal papers, she can do whatever she wants."

Rastmoor frowned. "But you've been so blasted awful for going on two years now! She can't honestly still want to marry you, can she?"

"Apparently she hasn't found another victim."

"So, just give her a few more reasons to hate you. A few more rumors about your wild living and bankrupt state, and she's bound to throw you over."

"I don't know what more I can do to convince her I'm a bad prospect. I've been throwing away as much blunt as I dare in those blasted gaming hells. I hired that brute you found to go around posing as a cent per center out to repossess my hide. Hell, I've been tupping French whores, for heaven's sake."

"Poor man," Rastmoor said, having the nerve to laugh again. "Oh, the sacrifices you must make."

"It's no laughing matter. This bloody charade has gone on too long. I'm sick to death of it, Anthony. My own mother thinks I'm a disgrace, and I'm beginning to think she may be right."

"Is this why she brought in the heiress?"

"She thinks we're about to get thrown out on our ears and intends to save me with a rich wife. I suppose she figures if Claudia won't have me, this one will."

Rastmoor shrugged. "Maybe she will. What do they say she's worth?"

"I don't need an heiress!"

"Well, you obviously need something. Come on, Dash, what's got you so out of sorts? Who is she?"

"Give it up, Tony."

"I will not! It's deadly dull around here, and this is the only sign of something interesting. You must tell me. Is she someone local?"

"She's no one."

"But she is *some*one."

"Drop it."

"Someone who rejected you?"

"No!" *Damn*. He said that with entirely too much passion.

Rastmoor picked up on it immediately. "She didn't reject you? Then why on earth, man, are you tongue-lashing everyone who comes near you today?"

"She fell asleep, all right?" There, he'd admitted it. Let his friend roar and howl; Randolf Dashford had put a woman to sleep.

"She fell asleep?" Rastmoor repeated.

"Yes. In the middle of . . . of it. And I, being a gentleman, did not choose to wake her."

Slowly, Rastmoor's eyes grew large. Oh, he was going to have a field day with this.

"You didn't wake her?"

"No, damn it. Now come on. I thought we were going for a ride."

"But you did want her, right?"

"Yes, of course I wanted her. Why else would I bother to take a woman to my bed?"

"You took her to your bed? Here, while your mother is giving a house party full of geriatrics and both of the tender virgins you're supposed to marry?"

"I'm not marrying anyone, and I said drop it, Anthony."

Rastmoor was pensive for a few minutes as they marched across the lawn in silence. The sky was gray, and the air was so thick with moisture it might as well be raining. He was a fool to come out here alone with Rastmoor and his myriad questions.

"So, what did you do all night, then?" Rastmoor asked at last, predictably not dropping it.

Dashford didn't answer but simply glared at him. They had reached the stable now, and a groom brought out the horses and stood by to offer assistance, should the gentlemen need it. They didn't. Both were in the saddle and out of the paddock in moments.

"Hey, these knacked old saddles are a nice touch," Rastmoor said, shifting in his uncomfortable seat. "When Claudia sees them, she'll be bound to believe your pockets are truly to let. Clever, old man."

Dashford decided not to explain that the ancient saddles were a result of his mother's attempts to prevent his escape. The conniving woman hadn't known there were spare saddles around the place, apparently, when she'd decided to have the groom see to a thorough refitting of the ones she did know about. Blast, but what wouldn't she do to force him into company with her damned heiress? Tampering with a man's saddle was beyond the pale. His backside cursed her already.

"So, what did you do?" Rastmoor asked.

"What?"

"Last night, when your wench nodded off. Did you tend to matters yourself, I suppose?"

"Good God, man!"

"No, I don't suppose you did, else there would be less reason for the foul mood."

"Can we not discuss something else?"

"No. I'm trying to figure this out. The nefarious rake, Dashford, allowed a tender morsel to fall asleep before he'd finished the job. How can this be? It's unnatural!"

"Shut up, Anthony."

"So what did you do? Lie there all night and think of wizened old grandmothers with big, hairy moles?"

"What?"

"Well, it has worked for me a time or two."

"Thank you for that image, but no, I did not."

"Then what did you do?"

"I stared at her and wondered what her bloody name was, all right?"

He thought Rastmoor would lose his seat from laughing so hard. Damn, he should have known better than to tell his friend anything about it.

"You didn't even know her name?"

"It never came up."

"Apparently not. Well, so you had a disappointing night. At least she isn't someone you care about."

No, at least he had that in his favor. Still, he'd wanted her badly, and it was frustrating to have missed out. And yes, it was embarrassing to admit he hadn't been able to keep her awake.

True, she had drunk nearly a whole bottle of wine. He supposed he shouldn't allow her slumbering to reflect badly on him or his famed virility. She was a nameless servant, pie-eyed and incoherent, after all. Perhaps how he found her last night was how she passed every evening. Lovemaking probably meant nothing to her. She had likely spread her legs for dozens of others, and no doubt she'd been uninspired by most of them. He should have taken his pleasure with her right from the start and not been so concerned about hers. Then it wouldn't have mattered that she fell asleep.

But he cringed mentally even as those thoughts ran through his brain. No, he did not regret taking his time with her, watching the glow of ecstasy flush over her alabaster body. Her sighs, her surprised little gasps, the total abandon when she writhed and trembled under his ministrations—it had all been worth it. He just wished . . . Oh, damn it to hell. He didn't know what he wished.

"You *don't* care about her, right?" Rastmoor asked just a bit too pointedly.

Dashford snapped back. "I don't even know her name."

"That isn't exactly an answer to my question."

"I'm worried about her. It's my duty to be concerned for all my staff, isn't it?"

"Your staff?" Anthony questioned. "She's one of your servants, and you took her to your *bed*?"

"How foolish of me. A quick tussle against the pantry wall should have been sufficient, shouldn't it?"

Rastmoor shrugged. "Well, it might have kept her awake, at least."

"Shut up, Anthony."

"But an anonymous servant in your bed. Asleep, even! That's rich, Dashford."

"I'm so glad it amuses you."

"It does. But I'm concerned, too. If the mighty Dashford, who could have any woman in London, is reduced to tumbling servants in his own bed—servants who don't even have the decency to stay awake for the festivities, I might add—well, there's no hope for any of us."

"You're being an ass. Now, do we ride, or do I go back and face Mother's little heiress? Anything seems preferable to this."

Rastmoor gave in to more laughter. "All right, let's ride. I'll leave you and your miserable wench in peace. For now, anyway."

"Good. I need to get down to the village and find out how the bridge is faring," he said, directing their horses toward a lane that would lead them to the main road. "The river's up, and the wood's rotted. I should have fixed that thing a year ago, but I hated to let on I was so flush."

"And now you'll pay for that by being stuck here God knows how long until you can find men to build you another bridge when this one washes away."

"Hell, they'll probably want payment up front, too. Damn, we did it too well, Tony, convincing folks I'm the bad seed and have run through all my father's money."

God, he hated being thought of that way. With Claudia and an eager heiress in his home, it hardly seemed these past two years of lies and exhausting lifestyle had been worth it. But damn it, he'd see that it would be. He'd been vulnerable, had let his guard down two years ago when his father died. Claudia nearly trapped him then, but he was in control of things now. No way in hell Claudia Graeley would ever be lady of his house, and not this damn Pinchley heiress, either. He'd find a way to take care of her, too.

Mostly though, what he wanted to take care of right now was a pale and giggling servant girl whose name he still did not know. Well, he'd track her down. Hartwood wasn't so huge he couldn't learn the whereabouts of one very distinctive servant. He'd see that she was being treated well and being looked after, although probably it would be best if he did not actually see her again.

Tony was right; it was concerning. He'd never let himself care about Madeline or any of the light-skirts he'd taken on as a part of his new persona. Things would only be worse if he let himself start caring about this new chit. He'd been doing very well at not caring lately, and he was not about to start now. Not for anyone.

Chapter Three

Aunt Bella's shrill laughter was enough to trigger another sick headache in Evaline. Probably in Lady Dashford, too, from the look on the dowager's face. Evaline gingerly pushed the food around on her plate. Ugh, how on earth did she think she would be able to eat breakfast—even a late one—with the others today? The very thought of food right now turned her inside out.

"I declare, Lady Dashford," Aunt Bella was saying, speaking to their hostess yet fluttering her eyelashes for Mr. Mandry, one of their fellow guests. "Your house party is an overwhelming success. What fascinating friends you have! And everyone is so gracious, except . . . where *is* your elusive son this morning?"

Ugh. Not exactly subtle. What was Aunt Bella thinking, pointing out in front of Lady Dashford and everyone what a poor host his lordship was? If she intended to get further into the dowager's good graces, public acknowledgment of the woman's only son's many shortcomings was probably not the best way to go about it.

The few other houseguests who had gathered in the breakfast room shifted nervously in their seats. Evaline couldn't blame them. Aunt Bella's conversation was deplorable. Mr. Mandry, however, must have been somewhat affected by the eye fluttering. He actually spoke up in agreement with Aunt Bella.

"That's right, where is the young pup this morning? Don't tell me he found adequate diversion here at Hartwood to keep him up all hours so that he's still abed this late!" Mr. Mandry was the only one present who seemed to think that was funny.

Even Aunt Bella had the good grace to be embarrassed. From what Evaline had heard about Lord Dashford, it was entirely likely the man had found adequate entertainment last night. Probably brought it here from London with him.

Lady Dashford gave the uneasy sigh of a mother who'd very nearly given up. "I hope you will all forgive my son his lax manners. Apparently he has chosen to skip breakfast and go for an early ride with his friend, Lord Rastmoor."

"But it's raining," Aunt Bella noted, nodding her head toward the window where fresh raindrops streaked down the pane.

"My son never lets a few drops of water deter him from pursuing his pleasures," Lady Dashford replied, her disappointment evident. "I hope he'll have the good sense to dry off before luncheon, so he can finally attend to his . . . duties."

The woman did not say it, but clearly everyone had heard the same rumors. Their averted glances said they were well aware of the man's reputation. Lord Dashford generally put everything ahead of duty.

The air hung thick with tension until Lady Dashford wisely changed the subject. "So, Miss Pinchley, I trust you slept well?"

Oh drat, that was an even worse subject! The dowager was just being polite, yet still Evaline felt the color rising in her cheeks. The last thing she wanted right now was to discuss last night. Surely everyone would know just by looking at her what she'd done. She'd be mortified.

"Yes, ma'am," she choked out, not able to meet the dowager's eyes. "I was quite, er, comfortable."

"But I see you've barely touched your breakfast," Lady Dashford continued. "Please, if there is something you would prefer, I'm certain cook would be only too happy to provide it."

No, no more food swimming on the plate before her! The thought of it was almost more than she could bear. The unknown gentleman's thoughtful restorative had been helpful, but not *that* helpful.

"No, thank you," she said, quickly raising a piece of toasted bread as if to eat it. "This is all lovely."

"Here, then," the dowager said to the gentleman seated beside her. "Pass this marmalade down to Miss Pinchley."

Marmalade? Oh, please God, no. She couldn't possibly! That bowl of sickly sweet gooey gobs had best stay far, far from her just now. She'd have to risk being rude.

"No, truly, Lady Dashford," she objected more strenuously than marmalade ought to merit. "I really am quite fine."

Her passion must have been evident. The marmalade stopped before Mr. Patterson, the gentleman whose turn it was to pass it. Thank heavens.

"Evaline is not a big eater," Aunt Bella explained quickly and truthfully, although Evaline's usual disinterest in food was often less due to a poor appetite and more to the company in which she was forced to eat. Or the expectations that came with it.

"Though as you can see, she still maintains a very fine figure," Aunt Bella went on, as if this line of discourse could make things any better. "Men are often drawn to such things, I'm told. If Lord Dashford would ever grace us with his presence, I'm sure he would be impressed by her temperance and lack of gluttony. He could rest assured that in later years our dear Evaline would likely not embarrass him by turning to fat."

Oh, good grief. Evaline would give fortunes to be able to sink into the carpet just now. What a thing to say in front of anyone, let alone a room half-full of matronly gentlewomen all comfortably—and corpulently—in their later years. Oh, how she longed to stand up and disown Aunt Bella right now.

It was much safer, however, to shove the toast into her mouth. Her stomach rebelled, but not violently. She could weather this. Perhaps if she seemed very interested in eating, the conversation would be forced to turn elsewhere. Anywhere but on her and how she passed her night.

"Well I, for one, will be a bit miffed if his lordship does not lunch with us," Aunt Bella rambled on. "I understand he is a man with many responsibilities, but surely he could have joined us for supper last evening. I swear, I shall begin to doubt whether he exists at all!"

She laughed lightly to let everyone know she meant it in jest, but Evaline knew she did not. Not entirely. Apparently the brief appearance his lordship made last night in the drawing room was not enough for her. She would be well and truly miffed indeed if Lord Dashford did not appear soon to throw himself at Evaline's feet. Aunt Bella never liked to see her plans thwarted, even by a lord of the realm.

Apparently fate feared her, too. Just at that moment, in the hallway outside the breakfast room, male voices could be heard.

"Ah, I believe our wandering apparition is about to join us, after all," Lady Dashford said with a relieved smile.

Sure enough, the door swung open, and in stepped a rather damp and bedraggled Lord Dashford. He was the same ruddy-haired man she vaguely recalled from their brief introduction in the drawing room last evening, and just as last night, he hardly spared a glance her way. How odd. If the man were truly as desperate as Aunt Bella had been led to believe, Evaline would surely have expected him to at least make some attempt to charm her. She'd heard much about the Dashford men and their remarkable abilities to charm. Well, perhaps this Dashford was not quite as gifted as his forebearer.

Grandmamma had been well acquainted with the Dashford charm. Indeed, even in her dotage she'd still been brought to blush when Lord Dashford had been mentioned. A previous Lord Dashford, of course. Two generations ago. Often Evaline had admired the man's portrait where it hung in a place of honor in Grandmamma's house. She tried to see any hint of that man in this, his grandson, but could find none.

True, this young viscount was a fine figure, but whatever Evaline had expected to find in him was lacking. What could it be? Not simply the man's features, for they were nice enough, but something in his bearing . . . something like . . . Well, something like what she'd found in her gentleman of the garden. Yes, that had been a man who could charm! That particular gentleman had been beyond fantasy, and the young man in the breakfast room today could hardly hold a candle to him. The man in the garden had been extraordinary. Men like that didn't simply appear around every corner.

Wait a moment—panic slowly washed over Evaline. There had been two male voices out in the hallway, hadn't there? It dawned on her that the young viscount was not alone. He had a companion.

Heavens, Lady Dashford had made mention of some other gentleman, had she not? Someone her son had gone riding with. Could it be . . . oh, but Evaline's heart was pounding, and her breath caught in her throat. Surely this was jumping to conclusions. Surely her exceptional gentleman was not the other voice out there, just around the corner!

But who else could it be? Good heavens, her anonymous lover would be following Lord Dashford into this very room any moment now! Oh, she was not prepared for that. Not at all! What would she do? What would she say? Oh, everyone would recognize what had passed between them; they'd see that secret knowledge written on her face. Dash it all, but she was ruined!

The toast inside her began a churning effort to return to the table.

"Well, I see the rain did not wash you away, after all." Lady Dashford greeted her son cheerfully.

"Not quite, though we were fortunate to arrive back when we did," he replied, going to the buffet and helping himself. "It's coming down in buckets now."

"And my son?" Lady Dashford asked.

The words were jarring. *Her son?* Whatever did she mean? Wasn't *this* her son? Evaline frowned.

"He just left me," the gentleman replied, nodding toward the hallway. "Some pressing matters with his steward, I believe."

Wait a minute. This was *not* Lady Dashford's son?

"Well, I see rumors of Lord Dashford's existence are still highly unfounded," Aunt Bella said and laughed at her own presumed cleverness.

Evaline felt as if the room began to whirl, but Lady Dashford simply continued her conversation with a worn sigh. "Well, at least he is out of the rain. At least I don't have to fear he will die of catching cold."

Now her ladyship managed a smile for the group. "I believe you all met Lord Rastmoor after dinner last night," she said politely by way of presenting their newcomer. "He, at least, was kind enough to make an appearance for a few moments."

The damp gentleman at the buffet nodded toward them all. His smile for Evaline was kindly and benign. She choked back the toast.

Oh no! If this was Lord Rastmoor, who in God's name was Lord Dashford?

EVALINE RAN IT ALL THROUGH HER HEAD, BACK-ward and forward. She sat alone on her bed and struggled to make sense of things. Try as she might, there seemed only one way to put the pieces together. She had succumbed to the infamous Lord Dashford.

Oh, but this was dreadful.

Shortly after Lord Rastmoor's arrival at breakfast this morning, Evaline had excused herself and come up here to hide. Hours of introspection had resulted in unending self-chastisement but had provided her no wisdom for what to do next. It had, however, given her a monumental headache.

When luncheon time arrived, she was completely honest in claiming herself too ill to attend. Aunt Bella fumed, but it gained her nothing. In the end, a cold plate was sent up for Evaline, and she was left alone. The plate still sat on the table, hours later.

There was no way around what she'd done. She had slept—in the truly biblical sense—with Lord Dashford. She had thrown away years of moral training, two generations of struggle against this very evil, and she had become what she most feared. And still she could not even remember it! How on earth had she let this happen?

She'd listened to Grandmamma's stories, that's how. Papa had always worried there was too much of Grandmamma in her. Now she knew it was true. She should have never been subjected to those dangerous tales of the irresistible Dashford men and the almost magical power they wielded over women. Grandmamma had put this cursed fascination with them into her head years and years ago.

Although that really didn't account for the fact that she'd willingly given in to Dashford long before she'd learned he *was* a Dashford. Bother. That meant she couldn't credit Grandmamma's stories for her own disgraceful behavior. No, she'd gone and been disgraceful all on her own. Perhaps what Grandmamma had said was true; there really was something mystically irresistible about Dashford men.

Well, knowing that certainly hadn't kept her from falling under its spell, just as it hadn't helped Grandmamma all those years ago. Lord, history was repeating itself through her! Papa would have been so disappointed.

What a fool she'd been last night. Aunt Bella had likely introduced Lord Rastmoor in the drawing room, but Evaline was so preoccupied with her childish fantasies she must have mistaken his name for that of their host. Perfectly silly, of course. *Dashford* and *Rastmoor* sounded nothing alike. Well, almost nothing alike.

She flopped down onto her back and sighed. What in heaven's name was she to do? Surely she couldn't hide from Dashford forever. When he found her, he'd no doubt threaten to tell what she'd done if she didn't agree to marry him and let him run amok with Papa's money. Then all her careful planning would be in vain, and someone very dear to her would be lost forever. Surely Lord Dashford would never allow his wife to open his home to a known prostitute and her illegitimate child, even if they were family.

Turning over, she glanced again at the letter crumpled in her hand. She knew the words and the hand intimately, but still she read her young cousin's words over again, hoping for some solace. They contained none.

Dearest Evaline,

By now you've received my last letter and know the truth. It must have come as a painful shock to learn the

*address where you've been sending your kind letters
all this time is something far worse than the simple
dressmaker's shop I led you to believe. Forgive me for
deceiving you. I pray no one ever learns your
connection to such a place!*

*I know you are too kind to suggest it, so for your
own good I must insist we refrain from further contact.
Soon you'll be reaching that important birthday, and
your life will be your own. I'm happy for you and wish
you all the best.*

*For myself, my situation is changing, as I told you
it would. I am leaving Madame Eudora's this very
week. I wrote of the special arrival we anticipated, so
you will be relieved to learn the babe is here and all is
well. A darling girl. The particular gentleman I spoke
of has invited me to work for him in his household, and
I am going. I will miss Madame and all the girls here,
but this is for the best. You needn't worry.*

*I've cherished your friendship, and I pray over the
years you remember me with fondness. Grandmamma
would be so very proud of you.*

> *Your loving friend and cousin,*
> *Sophie*

It was a beautiful letter, and Evaline's heart ached to think
she might never see her dear little cousin again. And, oh, the
questions she had! Despite Sophie's words, Evaline had
never received any previous letter explaining things—just
the simple correspondence that passed between them over
the years when Evaline thought Sophie had been nothing
worse than a dressmaker's apprentice.

Truly, though, Evaline needed no further explanation. It
was obvious what Sophie referred to. The poor girl had
become so destitute she'd been forced into prostitution and
now had borne a child. An illegitimate child. A child just like
Evaline's mother.

Oh, it was tragic! If only Evaline had known, perhaps she
could have done something to spare the girl. No, what could

she have done? Aunt Bella and Uncle Troy spent Evaline's allowance faster than the bank was authorized to release it. When not parading her before potential suitors, Aunt Bella kept Evaline practically under lock and key. Indeed, there was nothing she could have done for Sophie if she had known.

But now she did know, and now she was soon to be self-sufficient. By God, she would help her poor cousin. Why else had she agreed to leave their run-down rooms in Bath and come here with Aunt Bella? Heavens, the last place she would have wanted to be was stuck in Warwickshire with the descendant of one of Grandmamma's lovers! But of course, this was the best place to be if she was to help Sophie.

Grandmamma's house was just a mere three miles away, sitting vacant all these years. It had been given to her by the previous Lord Dashford, and she'd been so proud of it—the sloping thatched roof, the vibrant garden. Evaline could only imagine what state the place was in now.

Somehow the Dashford family had seen to it that Grandmamma's true heirs had been robbed of the home. Grandmamma had only ever been a thorn in their flesh, the scandal that never went away. Evaline supposed she should be grateful they hadn't simply torn the place down once Grandmamma died. But they hadn't, and now Evaline was at last in the position to get it back.

She'd purchase it from the Dashford estate and hand it over to Sophie. The girl would be free from having to sell herself just to eat. Her child could be brought up here, in peace and quiet just as Grandmamma had done with Sophie's mother. And once again Evaline would have family—Aunt Bella and Uncle Troy didn't count.

If only word would come from her agent! Whatever could be keeping that man? He was supposed to have arrived in Lack Wooton a full day or two ahead of Evaline so he could make inquiries into the house and begin negotiating with the Dashford family. It would all be done anonymously, of course, and when it was finished, Evaline would have her trust fund, Grandmamma's house, and a sort of revenge on the Dashford family who left Grandmamma to die old and alone out there in her beloved cottage.

The part about sleeping with Lord Dashford had not exactly been in her plans. Indeed, that was obviously a misjudgment on her part. If Dashford chose to use that to manipulate her into accepting his proposal, things might get a bit awkward with her real estate negotiations. Hopefully it wouldn't come to that. She'd just have to find a way to avoid her host for the duration of her stay. No one could know anything he might accuse her of was actually true!

There was a quiet knock at her door. What? Could it be time for the maid to come get her dressed for dinner already? She was certain she wasn't ready for that. It would be just her luck that Lord Dashford would decide to finally show up. Oh, why had she not simply died this morning when every part of her body wanted to?

The knock again. Well, if she didn't let the girl in, all this knocking would just serve to rouse Aunt Bella from her afternoon nap, and then things would get prematurely ugly. Bella was not happy that Dashford had eluded them thus far. No doubt she would find some way to make it all Evaline's fault.

She hopped from the bed and refolded Sophie's letter, tucking it safely away. She straightened her hair—not too much—and gave a couple of loud coughs. If she did decide to fabricate another excuse to avoid a public meal, it would need to be convincing.

"Come in," she called out, making sure there was just the slightest break to her voice.

The door opened. "Miss Pinchley?"

Oh no. It wasn't her sweet-faced little maid after all. It was the dowager hostess, Lady Dashford herself.

"My lady!" Evaline's voice clearly had enough sudden energy that any illness she may choose to claim as an excuse from dinner would be, sadly, unbelievable.

"Goodness, my dear," the lady said with a motherly smile. "You certainly are a bundle of nerves."

"Oh, well, I just . . . I'm surprised to see you here."

"I'm sorry, but am I interrupting anything?"

It was obvious she wasn't. "No, of course not."

"I was hoping we could have a little chat," the lady went on, taking obvious note of the untouched luncheon nearby.

"Yes, certainly. Of course. I'd like that." Evaline was flustered but had just enough sense to offer the one comfortable chair in the room to her hostess.

The dowager took the seat gracefully and motioned for Evaline to sit in another, smaller chair beside her. It took a moment to grasp this, but eventually Evaline caught on and sat. For a painful few seconds she just smiled dumbly, at a loss.

Had Dashford confided in his mother? Did she know what had transpired last night? Was the lady here to convince Evaline to do the honorable thing and marry her son? Heavens, perhaps Lady Dashford had been a part of this whole sordid scheme all along, ever since Evaline had met the lady in Bath last autumn. Could it have been her goal even then to find a way to lure Evaline into Dashford's clutches all for the sake of attaching Evaline's money? And to think Evaline had rather liked the older woman!

"I do hope you are enjoying your stay here," her ladyship began.

"Of course. How could I not?" Evaline smiled as best she could. After all, what was there not to enjoy here? The weather was dismal, the guests were geriatric, everyone seemed to be scheming to steal her inheritance, and Evaline had already ruined herself by shagging their detestable host. What a wonderful time all around.

"This is not at all the way I envisioned it, you know," Lady Dashford said, shaking her head ruefully. "Such shocking behavior."

Evaline felt the blood drain from her face. Dashford must have told her! "Shocking beha—? Truly, I never meant to—"

"Oh, trust me, I can well imagine how you feel today."

Somehow she highly doubted that. "You can?"

"Indeed. I was a girl once myself, you know."

"You were? I mean, of course you were."

"I can recall the fiery hopes of youth."

"The what?"

"Indeed, my dear, I have a fairly good notion how my son made you feel last night when your head hit the pillow."

Evaline couldn't quite respond to that one. She did make a little squeaking sound, though. Her ladyship went on with a motherly smile.

"In fact, he's made me feel the same way a time or two."

Another squeaking sound. "He has?"

"Indeed. His upbringing has been my responsibility, after all."

Good God, what sort of household was this? Evaline struggled to breathe. "Lady Dashford, I'm not certain we need to discuss this, you and I."

"Oh, I don't mind, my dear. I think it's high time you and I do discuss this, in fact. You are a guest in his home, and my son should have made a finer show of tending to your needs."

What? Was the lady to critique her son's nighttime efforts?

"His manners are deplorable," Lady Dashford went on.

Evaline grimaced. What an odd understanding of manners this family held!

"They weren't really as deplorable as all that," Evaline struggled to say. From what she could recall, she'd found Dashford's manners quite, well, satisfactory.

"You are too kind," Lady Dashford went on. "But my son has behaved badly. He's insulted you and everyone here."

"He has?"

"Of course. Why, he completely avoided us all last night when everyone knew he'd returned from London. Very inelegant."

Evaline struggled to comprehend. She believed Dashford had avoided Evaline? Then just exactly what shocking and deplorable behavior was she apologizing for?

"And now today," the dowager continued. "What sort of host goes riding in the rain instead of greeting his guests? It's shameful, shocking behavior!"

Ooooh, so *that's* what she meant: his lordship's shocking behavior as an inattentive host. Gracious, what a relief! Heavens, what was she coming to for her mind to wander the way it had? Evaline put her hand to her mouth to hide the giddy grin.

"I promise you," Lady Dashford went on grandly, "I taught him better than to behave this way. It breaks my heart. Why, he did not even acknowledge your presence as a guest in his home. Reprehensible."

"Really, I'm sure his lordship had other things to tend to."

"No need to make excuses for him. He's been abominable. You must have cried your eyes out into your pillow last night, being snubbed by that insulting bore."

"No, I assure you I, er, slept just fine."

"Now, don't hold back on my account. Your aunt told me the whole story."

Oh dear. "She did? And what story would that be?"

"Well, when you didn't come to luncheon today, I simply commented on how peaked you seemed at breakfast—no, please don't be offended, my dear, but I was concerned—and she explained how upset you had been over not meeting Randolf."

"Oh, *that* story. Yes, I rather suppose that would explain it, more or less."

Lady Dashford was patting her hand again. "Of course. I remember being young and having hopes and dreams about the man I might marry. After all the glowing things I must have told you about him when we met in Bath last year, no doubt you were hoping Randolf would come to sweep you off your feet."

Evaline cringed. Lord Dashford hadn't really had to sweep her off her feet, had he? She'd already been rather swept of her own accord by the time he found her there in that garden.

"Really, I'm not at all upset, my lady," she said, eager to end the conversation. "Clearly Lord Dashford is simply not interested in marriage at this time. I can understand that. No harm done."

The dowager sighed and shook her head sadly. "Yes, I expect you would see no hope in it at this point. Pity, though. After getting to know you, I was so certain you two would fit perfectly."

Evaline cringed again. Did the poor dear have to use those words exactly? "You mean, he generally prefers the peaked type?"

Lady Dashford rolled her dewy eyes and slumped in her chair.

"Oh, I don't know what he prefers anymore," she said, her voice catching in her throat. "He's changed so since coming into his title, Miss Pinchley. He used to be concerned about looking after the estate and upholding the family name. Now I hear only of his gambling, and the horrible women . . . forgive me, my dear. I shouldn't mention such things, but it's hard for a mother to suddenly realize she doesn't even know her own child anymore."

Now there were tears welling up in the lady's eyes. Evaline didn't quite know what to do. What could she say to comfort the poor woman? Her own experiences with Lord Dashford didn't exactly point to a reformed character.

"There, there," was all she could muster. She did procure a handkerchief, though. Her ladyship took it gratefully and blew her nose in it.

"Thank you, Miss Pinchley," she said, composing herself. "Since the day we met, I knew you were just the sort of girl I wished for my Randolf. Of course, he was already engaged to Claudia at the time . . ."

That caught Evaline's attention. "What's that?"

"Oh yes, he was engaged to Miss Graeley shortly after my husband passed away. It's only been recently that things between them are not entirely certain."

"He's engaged? To be married?"

Lady Dashford frowned. "To a girl from just up in Kenilworth, Miss Claudia Graeley. They became engaged shortly after my husband passed away, but lately things have become, er, complicated. I thought months ago things had been called off, but just recently Sir Graeley made it quite clear the engagement still stands. Claudia, however, has made it clear she will not marry Randolf as long as he is . . . well, as long as his life is in such disarray."

Well, this was news to Evaline. Good news, as a matter of fact. If Dashford was already engaged, he couldn't very well be expected to marry her! Yet, then why had he gone to all the trouble of seducing her? Unless, of course, the engagement was as tenuous as Lady Dashford indicated. That might be bad.

"So you believe Miss Graeley is planning to jilt him?" she asked.

Lady Dashford sighed. "Honestly? Yes, I do. His troubles seem to be mounting rather than declining, and Claudia is not one to deal well with troubles."

Evaline nodded. Dashford was just about to lose one fiancée, so his mother had generously procured him another. Blast it, but Evaline had played right into their plot, hadn't she? She clenched her fists and struggled to stay calm.

"Forgive me, Miss Pinchley," Lady Dashford went on. "I should never have presumed to involve you in this, but when your aunt suggested you might be agreeable to meeting my son, I couldn't help myself. I arranged to bring you here."

Well, at least the woman wasn't trying to hide her schemes. It didn't do much to relieve Evaline's worries, however. Was Dashford in on it? And just how much about last night had he told his mother? Evaline could only hope for the best.

"I'm so sorry," her ladyship said. "You're upset. I see that I've allowed your hopes to be raised, only to dash them with these distressing details. Forgive me, but I had hoped for so much better. Clearly my son is bent on self-destruction, and there's nothing I can do."

The lady's remorse was convincing. Evaline wasn't sure how she was expected to respond, so she gave a thin smile and pretended she was hurt, but not overly hurt. "As they say, your ladyship, nothing ventured, nothing gained."

The dowager smiled in return. If she was disappointed that Evaline wasn't as eager to marry Dashford as a girl in her position ought to be, the lady didn't show it.

"You're too kind, my dear," she said. "Certainly you deserve better than the neglect you've received from my useless son. And I can see"—she turned her head and indicated the plate of uneaten food—"it has taken a toll on you."

Bother. Her stomach troubles and lack of appetite were getting too much attention. The last thing she wanted was for Lady Dashford to become suspicious and realize neglect wasn't exactly what she'd received from her host last night.

"Truly," she said with a casual shrug, "I'm just not a big eater."

"Odd, I never noticed that during our time together in Bath."

No, because last autumn in Bath she hadn't been recovering from a night of obviously forgettable passion with a man to whom she'd not yet been introduced!

"Don't worry, Lady Dashford." Evaline smiled as warmly as possible, considering that all this mention of food had set her stomach to lurching again. "I'm feeling much more the thing as the day has gone on. Truly, I'm sure my peakedness has simply been due to the travel fatigue."

"I hope so. I'll look for you to join us at dinner."

Oh pooh. She'd actually meant to maintain her "headache" through the dinner hour. Well, Aunt Bella probably would not have allowed that anyway. She supposed there was little way to avoid it.

"Of course. I'm already looking forward to it."

Lady Dashford seemed remarkably cheered by this and increased the hand pats. "Lovely. I still don't know where my delinquent son is or whether he'll make a dinner appearance or not, but I do hope to see your smiling face over the table tonight."

"You're too kind."

"And who knows, perhaps he will decide to present himself. Surely once he actually meets you, he will find you as charming as I have."

Evaline wasn't exactly sure "charming" was what Lord Dashford had found her, but she managed a sickly smile.

"Well, I'll not weary you further," Lady Dashford said. "Please, enjoy your afternoon's rest, and I'll look forward to seeing a hungry young woman tonight."

The dowager smiled and stood to make her exit. Evaline stood with her and followed her to the door. Once there, her ladyship paused and gave her one last, long look.

"You are certain it's merely the strain of travel that has you under the weather?"

Was that a hint of suspicion behind the lady's concern? Evaline swallowed back her worry and brightened up her smile.

"Of course. What else could it be?"

Lady Dashford eyed her just half a second too long, then shrugged. "Yes, you're right. I'm sure I worry too much. Have your girl bring in some tea to help restore you."

Evaline assured her she would and graciously received the used handkerchief that was returned to her. With another few kind pats to her hand, Lady Dashford took her leave, and soon Evaline was alone, sighing against her door.

Heavens, but the woman had been obsessed with

Evaline's eating habits. Did her hostess have some suspicion Evaline needed to know about? Surely not. This was nothing more than Evaline's guilty conscience tormenting her.

Yet the way the lady had looked at her—studied her, really—with those piercing gray eyes, she couldn't help but wonder. What had she seen in her to cause such concern? Well, of course there'd been no hiding the fact that neither breakfast nor lunch had been consumed. Last night's dinner was hardly touched either, for that matter. Of course Evaline's nerves were on end; this was a difficult time, even aside from her obvious—and enormous—blunder with Lord Dashford. But why exactly had Lady Dashford stared at her so intently? What was she looking for?

Her stomach was turning in knots again, threatening to dislodge anything that might still be in it. She wrapped her arms around herself and looked longingly at the cold plate left from earlier. Perhaps she should attempt a bite of something. Bread or the hard cheese, perhaps? No, the thought was enough to assure her food was not the answer.

Once more she recalled the horrible awakening this morning, when she felt as if the world was about to end for her. Surely this recent trouble was just a remainder of that. Last night's wine—and other things—were truly out of the ordinary for her. Of course it would take a while to recover. But how long? And what if . . . ?

Lord, the horrible thought plagued her again. She'd shoved it ruthlessly from her mind several times already today, but it kept sneaking back. What if there was more to it than a simple case of nerves or too much wine? What if her reckless activities of last night had left her with some lingering . . . consequences?

Oh, why had Mamma gone and died when she was so young, before she'd been old enough to receive motherly tutoring in such matters? Her annual visits to Grandmamma seemed so few as she looked back on them now. There had simply not been enough time to learn all she should have learned from her. Well, she had learned, but Grandmamma's lessons tended to be more fanciful and romantic than practical. At least, that's what she was beginning to realize now.

So here she was at age twenty-five, hopelessly confused about the possibility of her own condition. Could she have gone to the garden a perfectly normal individual last night and now woken up today plural? What a thought! Still, it did seem things worked that way. After all, hadn't that happened to a girl Evaline knew back in London?

It had, and the thought of it dredged up some still painful memories.

Evaline had been just seventeen, still a child really, as she looked back on it now. Papa promised her a great season that year—the introduction to society his exorbitant wealth could buy her. She'd gotten caught up in the usual silliness of dresses and balls, and one particular gentleman named Ellard Bristol.

Ah, how foolish she'd been then. Ellard Bristol was a struggling young poet from a good family. He was pale and beautiful; all the girls threatened to swoon when he entered a room. She felt so honored when he seemed to select her from the crowd.

He wrote her sonnets in April, but by summertime he was married to someone else, a girl Evaline was vaguely acquainted with and who had much better connections to recommend her than Evaline could claim. That was the end to Evaline's hopes where Ellard Bristol was concerned.

For Ellard, fatherhood came quickly. Very quickly. Indeed, his particular chit seemed to have developed her condition overnight, too. Likely well before the hasty wedding. Indeed, that was the full extent of Evaline's knowledge on the subject, and now she couldn't help but wonder whether she did indeed have something to worry about.

But how could she know? Pity she wasn't home. Her father had always said, "A good library contains all the learning of the world." He'd been a great collector of books, despite the fact that his business kept him far too busy to read. His library had been expansive. Surely there she could have found a volume to answer her burning questions. Except, of course, that Uncle Troy had sold all Papa's books to pay for more of his horses, or wine, or whores.

But wait; Lord Dashford had a huge library right here in this home, did he not? Of course he did. All proper gentlemen did, whether they made use of them or not, as she suspicioned was the case with Lord Dashford. Surely he possessed a medical treatise or a book of human ailments or something that might help her. Obviously, then, she needed to take a trip to the Dashford library.

With luck, it would be vacant, and she could read to her heart's content on the worrisome subject of making babies.

Chapter Four

What in the bloody hell could that blasted chit be doing? Dashford had wasted literally hours today worrying about her. Hell and damnation, he was a fool. The actions of an insignificant servant girl should have meant nothing to him, yet he couldn't help himself. He'd been hunting for her since late morning, to no avail.

It was as if she'd simply disappeared or not even existed to begin with. He'd stalked through the kitchen, pretended interest in the workings of the laundry, then even taken to interviewing his own staff in search of her. Bother. No one seemed to know anything about her.

Of course he'd been subtle. He hadn't wanted to draw attention to her unnecessarily, for her own good. First he'd hinted to his valet about there being an assortment of new and attractive maids among the staff here. Had the man noticed them, as well? Perhaps he knew where some of them had come from?

Well, that tactic had gained him nothing. Carothers was miffed with him today because Dashford had had the nerve to tell the man his services weren't needed this morning. Well, he'd not wanted servants running in and out of his room this morning for obvious reasons. His bed already contained one servant too many. Blast, now there was no telling how long he'd have to go with a crooked cravat before Carothers would deign to serve him properly again.

Blast it, he hadn't meant to insult the man this morning. He was only thinking of protecting his bedmate's identity when dawn rolled around and the servants began to stir. He'd ordered up that restorative for her and left word that no one was to enter his room, under penalty of death. It was childish for Carothers to take such umbrage at this. It's not as if the man's sole purpose for living was to dress his master, for pity's sake.

All that, and now he hadn't been able to locate her. Well, if the lack of information he'd gathered on her was any indicator, his precautions to protect her had been successful. There was no fresh gossip of any sort that even remotely seemed to touch on her. Unfortunately, though, that meant he still had no clue who she was.

After failing so miserably with Carothers, he'd gone on to Cook. She'd been less than helpful. All he'd learned in the kitchen was that a cat in the village had recently birthed a kitten with two tails and that Cook suffered from recurring gout. Oh, he'd learned entirely too much about gout, but nothing of some new alabaster-skinned maid on staff who might be prone to steal wine and seduce her master.

It was that way with everyone. His staff was just far too busy to be bothered with gossip about the underservants. The footmen, too, must have gone uncharacteristically blind when it came to noticing—and discussing—any promising young maid who may have come on staff here recently. Bah, what a helpful lot they turned out to be.

Short of coming right out and giving a physical description of her to every servant in his employ, he could think of no way to get better information. Obviously she had never done anything to draw attention to herself or give anyone reason to mention her at all. Perhaps she was not quite the wanton he'd thought. Perhaps last night had been something of a novelty for her. Dash it, though. That didn't help any.

He was losing his touch. What had gone wrong? What had he done last night to lose her interest so prematurely? He had a reputation to uphold, after all. True, it wasn't a reputation he was particularly proud of right now, but he'd worked hard to cultivate it over the past two years, and thus far it had served him well.

At least, it seemed to have been serving him well. The fact that Claudia was expected to show up here for this blasted house party seemed to suggest she hadn't yet abandoned all hope. Hell, he'd rather marry his drowsy doxy from last night than a shrew like Claudia Graeley!

He'd certainly never meant to get engaged to her in the first place. No, this engagement had been all Claudia's doing. He'd been too busy grieving his father to notice how she weaseled her way into his life, turning up everywhere he went and making sure everyone assumed things about them.

That's what had finally clinched the deal for her, too. She'd let her father start assuming things, and next thing Dashford knew, Sir Graeley confronted him with an ultimatum. He'd been caught so unaware he didn't know what else to do but consent to an engagement. It appeared Claudia had lied to her father about the true nature of their relationship, but being a gentleman, Dashford was left with little recourse. He didn't deny the accusations, and the noose tightened around his neck.

So, the day after he signed the papers, he marched off to London to get seriously drunk. That's when he and Rastmoor came up with the brilliant plan of making Claudia regret her actions and break off the engagement. They'd conspire to make Dashford a blight on society and an embarrassment to his breed. Well, they'd done that, all right. Lord, how they'd done it.

Apparently Dashford played his part too well. He studied his peers who'd squandered family wealth and honor. He followed their lead and made sure to be seen in the lowest of the lowly gaming hells. He paid for the acquaintance of high-fliers and women who were well-known among the ton. Too well-known.

At first he'd found himself a bit nervous on that score. How did a gentleman farmer behave in the company of women like that? Well, his father had always taught him to approach things from a scholarly, informed foundation. So he'd sat down and read a book. Yes, indeed, he'd studied that book cover to cover and had been only too happy to implement what he learned.

He hadn't learned it well enough to impress one simple

servant girl in his garden last night, though. Dash it all, what had he missed? What of his technique had been lacking? Blast, it was driving him mad. He simply had to find that girl and have another go at it to redeem himself.

"So here you are."

It was Rastmoor, probably come to critique his cravat. Bother, he wasn't up for conversation just now. "Of course here I am. This is my office; I'm the one usually working here."

Rastmoor sauntered in, eyeing him with a cocked brow. "Still on the outs with Carothers, I see."

"He's making me suffer a full twenty-four hours, I fear, so the rest of you will bloody well just have to stand looking at me as I am."

"So you'll be joining the group for dinner?"

"Mother claims her life will be meaningless if I do not."

Rastmoor chuckled at his misfortune. "Well, cockeyed cravat aside, Miss Pinchley will love you."

"Miss Pinchley can go to Hades."

"Oh, go easy on her, Dashford, she's not so bad as all that," his friend defended. "True, I only met her for a moment or two, but she's nothing like the typical mushroom heiress we might expect. No huge trains of flounces, no hats with a whole flock of birds, none of those hideous airs and affected speech. She seems a nice, sensible girl."

"Oh, well that makes her entirely more interesting then."

"Well, I daresay she won't throw herself all over you like your darling Claudia. Oh, but darling Claudia was no mushroom heiress, was she?"

"No. Nor was she ever my darling."

"That's not what she says." He said it with a sinister leer then broke into laughter again. How grand for Rastmoor that all this was so very amusing to him.

"I wish you would have just married her when she set her cap for *you*, old man," Dashford said. "Sure would have saved me a lot of trouble."

Rastmoor's smile went away. "I had other things on my mind at that time, if you'll recall."

Damn, he'd stepped in it again. Rastmoor was his friend. Dashford had no excuse for dredging up ancient history.

Hell, just because he was miserable didn't mean he had a right to drag Rastmoor down with him.

"Apologies again. I'm just so damn frustrated about—"

"Putting your servant girl to sleep last night?"

"No, I was going to say I'm frustrated about this whole bloody plot to get rid of Claudia. I'm fed up with it, Anthony. It's a terrible plan."

"No, it's a fine plan," his friend said. "We just didn't figure on it working so well."

"We were drunk. We shouldn't have been figuring on anything that night."

"True enough. Still, I say it was a grand idea. Why, think of it; you won't even be invited to Almack's this year, my friend, and that is something to celebrate!"

"I never went to Almack's anyway."

"Well, just think of the things you *have* been going to; the sorts of invitations you *have* been enjoying," Rastmoor said. "Ah, now *that* is not a terrible plan."

Dashford could only grumble under his breath. Yes, there were some aspects of this little ruse he rather enjoyed, but after last night, he wasn't so certain he was up to playing the part any longer. Damn, but he couldn't seem to get past this, could he?

He closed the ledger book he'd been pretending to study and stood. "Look, Tony, if you don't mind, I've got some things to attend to."

"Oh? You haven't by any chance located your little wench, have you?"

Blast! He hadn't especially wanted Rastmoor to know he'd been looking for her. "No, of course not. She seems to have gone, and that suits me perfectly."

"So this means you've set your sights on some other delectable bit o' muslin?"

"No, it means I've got to dress for dinner."

Rastmoor frowned. "What? So early? Well, then I suppose I'd best toddle on up to my room, too."

Dashford led the way out of the office and into the dim hallway. No, he was not at all looking forward to dinner. Perhaps Rastmoor was right and Miss Pinchley was not the horror he expected, but that was still no reason to rush in to make her acquaintance. No doubt she was already in love with his title, and any polite attention from him would mean he'd have to go to all sorts of lengths to lose her.

And then there was the added complication of Claudia. If Claudia showed up in time to see him making nice with the heiress, she'd be just the sort to get all jealous and decide she did want him for herself, after all. She'd be stuck to him like glue after that. Clearly he'd best ignore the heiress with all possible effort.

Then again, shunning the heiress might make it appear as if he only had eyes for Claudia. Good Lord, but that was not what he wanted, either. And being cool but polite toward either young lady would only insinuate that he was reforming and becoming a decent human being and gentleman again! Both females would like that, wouldn't they? Bother, but no matter how he handled himself at dinner tonight, it seemed one bloody chit or the other would force him into a wedding immediately thereafter.

Damn it, he didn't have time for all this! He needed to find his servant girl.

Rastmoor was blathering on about his hopes that the weather would clear up, and perhaps tomorrow an impromptu outing of some sort could be put together. Dashford had seen the skies and didn't think it likely. His steward agreed; more rain was on the way, and things were looking very chancy for that bridge on the main road. Not that the road itself would be easily passable if there was any more rain. No, it seemed escape from Mother's dangling brides would be difficult, both socially and logistically.

They rounded the corner into the grand entrance hall, where Dashford planned to mount the staircase up toward the first story, when they were accosted by a tooth-jarring voice. Was that some form of female laughter? God, it was awful.

"Lord, it's that damned aunt," Rastmoor said under his breath, pulling Dashford up to a stop just out of view from the staircase. "Sounds like she's got your mother captive right now and is in full sail. You might want to make yourself scarce if you don't want an early introduction."

"You mean the Pinchley aunt?"

"The same, though her name's something different, not Pinchley."

Dashford shuddered. "What could be worse than Pinchley? She sounds hideous."

"She is. Hard to believe she and her niece come from the same line."

"And I'm expected to marry into it? I think not." He patted Rastmoor's shoulder and took another step back into the dim hallway. "Keep them busy, old man, and I'll be forever in your debt."

Rastmoor sighed but nodded. "All right, I'll throw them off your track. But see that you don't leave me alone with them at dinner again tonight! I beg of you, these other guests your mother has assembled here aren't exactly a riot of good times."

"Fear not, I won't do that to you. I'll be there."

He gave his friend a gentle shove toward the staircase. His mother and her prattling companion were nearly on the bottom step and could turn this way at any moment. With luck they'd spot Rastmoor and engage him long enough to let Dashford get away.

"You owe me, Dash," Rastmoor muttered.

Yes, he did. The aunt appeared a perfect fright, her vibrant attire as loud and obnoxious as her voice. Dashford ducked around the corner and left Rastmoor to his fate. He heard the man's carefree voice as the ladies greeted him. It sounded as if they were heading in the other direction, probably toward the formal drawing room. Thank God.

Fussing with the limp cravat, Dashford wasn't quite sure he was ready to brave the staircase yet. With his luck, the Pinchley chit would be swooping down it any moment now. No, he'd best find a place to hide here on this floor.

Well, the library was handy. He poked his head in there and was happy to see it empty. Good. This would give him a chance to retrieve something: that certain book he was determined to give further detailed study.

EVALINE STUDIED THE BOOK WITH HER MOUTH gaping. She'd never seen anything like it. Good heavens!

Could human beings truly be capable of the astounding things depicted in this small leather-bound volume? She stared at the meticulously detailed engravings. It would appear some ladies were surpassingly, er, flexible.

Some gentlemen, too, apparently. My, but some of these depictions were nothing short of disturbing! She felt the heat rising in her cheeks and for literally the first time was exceedingly grateful those events of last night were so foggy in her memory. Was this at all indicative of what she'd allowed herself to engage in? Inconceivable. This must be a book of fantasy. At least, she hoped so. Especially since she was finding the depictions so terribly interesting. She must be a truly corrupt person if this was real and she found it so irresistible!

She glanced again at the title page of the book she'd accidentally come upon here in Lord Dashford's library. *My Hours With the Fairer Sex: The Informative Notations of a Particular Gentleman*, it read. *An Illustrated Compilation of the Memoirs of an English Gentleman. His Most Congenial Relations Carefully Recorded and Illuminated for Instructive Purposes.*

Instructive, indeed! As if Lord Dashford wanted for instruction on topics concerning congenial relations with the fairer sex! She herself could verify he was already rather an expert on the topic.

She scanned over the table of contents. "Chapter 1, In Which a Gentleman Discovers the Rose Most Lovely." Well, she'd seen enough of the gentleman's illustrated compilation to have a fairly good idea just exactly what was meant by "rose." She wrinkled her nose but turned to the page anyway.

Authorship of the thin volume was credited to someone named Sir Langwood Cocksure, but she wasn't entirely convinced that was an honest name. More likely, the Particular Gentleman had chosen to avoid any possible repercussions of flouting the obscenity laws by publishing under an assumed name. She couldn't entirely blame him.

Hmm, the pages of chapter 3 seemed a bit more dog-eared than the others. The contents page listed this chapter as being "In Which a Gentleman Discourses on the Rose with Many Keepers." She thought she had a fairly good notion what that might be about, as well. Sir Cocksure didn't appear to let silly things like morality and monogamy slow him down in his search for education.

She smoothed the pages. Yes, dog-eared indeed, and there were even a few haphazard marks scrawled in faded ink here and there. This chapter had definitely seen more attention from the reader, and it was easy to see why. The engravings depicted gentlemen in a variety of poses with an equal variety of ladies. The text proclaimed boldly that "the wise man will learn from each amorous encounter valuable insight into the female sensibilities and desires and will carry that with him into future liaisons until he shall gain such a vast wisdom that his proficiency will be sought after by even the most jaded of courtesan." In case his readers were not fortunate to have enough of those amorous encounters, Sir Cocksure went ahead and gave ample insights of his own. Heavens, but her face was growing warmer the further she read!

She really ought not to be looking at this, she knew. A lady barely acknowledged that conjugal displays occurred, even so far as for propagation of the species. To sit here now, tucked comfortably on Lord Dashford's floor, eagerly devouring page after page of this shocking little book, was certainly not acceptable behavior.

It was Dr. Buchan's familiar text on domestic medicine she'd come for; that's what she ought to be studying right now. And she had started reading it. She'd just begun a tentative study of his chapter on "Diseases of Women, Including Pregnancy"—Lord, just the word alone was enough to send her stomach lurching into sick waves again—when some hand-scrawled notes regarding possible remedies for a putrid throat came spilling out. Of course she'd stooped to pick them up, and that's when she'd found this other book, wedged between the wall and the low bookcase and nearly invisible to anyone who was not crawling on the floor, which she had been.

It seemed a shame to have a perfectly good book fallen useless there, so she'd taken pains to dig it out. She'd only given it a halfhearted glance out of simple curiosity—the title alone hadn't been much to pique her interest—but the first page she opened captured her attention fully. Dr. Buchan sat forgotten across her knees as she continued devouring Sir Cocksure's unusual primer.

And why shouldn't she, after all? She could hardly be called an innocent, not after last night. So why shouldn't she learn all she could on this unsuitable subject? It wasn't likely any of her female acquaintances were going to volunteer this information. And who knew? Perhaps someday she'd have another opportunity to make use of this very carnal knowledge on a more personal level.

With luck, she'd be sober for that opportunity.

IT WAS A CRYING SHAME THE GIRL HAD BEEN drunk last night. Hell, if not for that, he'd surely have finished the job and be well on his way to forgetting all about her. That must be his problem today: unfulfilled lust. That's what was making him surly and a bit irrational. Irrational, in fact, to the point that he'd begun planning how he would hide the girl in his bedroom again tonight. Provided, of course, he could find her.

A sound in the library caught his attention. He'd come into the room and was just standing in the doorway, lost in his thoughts. Now he realized he was not alone here. Someone small sneezed from behind a low shelf of old books.

Elves, perhaps? He went to the shelf and peered around it. A startled face peeped up at him. It became more startled when recognition set in.

"Dear God, it's you!" he exclaimed.

And it was. The very woman who had disrupted his thoughts all day long was seated there on the dusty floor, a book open on her lap. She was wearing a drab gown, the color of dead moss, just what one might expect to be worn by a servant. Her fawn-colored hair was not tucked under a cap but pulled up stylishly on her head. She looked prim and proper and untouchable. And with every fiber of his being he wanted to touch her.

Flustered, she slammed her book shut and sent a dust cloud into the air around her head. Another sneeze, and she struggled with her skirts as she scrambled to her feet. He chuckled at the delightful sight of one perfect ankle but reached out a hand to help her. She did not take it.

"What are you doing here?" she asked quickly, glancing around, probably for a way to escape.

"I think I should ask you the same thing. Am I interrupting your reading hour?"

"No, I just—" She noticed the clock on the mantel. "Oh no! I had no idea it was so late!"

"Don't worry. I'll see that you don't get into any trouble."

"Oh, I doubt that."

He had to chuckle at her perception. "Perhaps if you tell me where it is you're supposed to be right now? Then I could take you. There."

She didn't seem to find much humor in his double entendre. She was still glancing around the room for the quickest way to get out. Wherever it was she should have been, he was awfully glad she wasn't there just now. He tried to keep his face passive and his tone soothing, but his blood pounded. Seeing her in proper clothing only made him remember all the more vividly what she'd looked like in improper clothing. Or out of it.

"I had a few minutes to spare, so I came to get a book. Only I guess I got distracted. Now it's . . . we'd better . . . I should . . ." she stammered.

It was quite endearing to see her so flustered by his presence. Perhaps he could fluster her some more. He leaned close to see the book she clutched to herself.

"Dr. Buchan? This is what you read in your spare time?"

"No, I just—well, it was a headache. I was looking for a remedy."

He could well believe that. He'd had his fair share of Madeira over the years, and he had no doubt the girl had well exceeded hers last night. Poor thing, clearly that little restorative he'd sent up for her had not been entirely effective. He wished he had something a bit more helpful to offer. Smiling, he reached to touch a smudge of dust on her cheek.

"It's good to see you again. I trust you have no other negative effects from, er, last night?"

She blushed nearly crimson. It went well with the dull

dress and brought fire to her blue green eyes. "I'm fine, thank you."

"No, I should thank you."

He moved closer to her. Her creamy bosom was rising and falling rapidly now. Good. He was glad to know he still affected her, that her mood last night hadn't been simply owing to the moonlight or the wine. With luck, perhaps some of that mood might still remain. To find out, he slid his hand to her shoulder, barely touching the skin where her collarbone faded into soft flesh. Tongues of heat ran though him.

"You look even more lovely indoors, you know," he said finally.

"Please, we should go," she said. There was just the hint of a quaver in her voice.

He moved closer, looming a full head taller than her. She tried to scoot away, but it was a weak protest. He had her securely tucked between him and the bookshelf, and he could feel the thrills of attraction tracing between them. Already, smoky desire filled her eyes.

"Eventually," he said. "You know, I was looking for you today."

"You were?"

"I was. I've thought of little else."

"You have?"

"And I'm glad to find you here. Alone."

She hardly seemed to notice when he took Dr. Buchan from her and laid the book on the shelf. It seemed a bit lopsided—stuffed with something, perhaps—but he ignored that. There was something far more interesting than a medical digest to occupy him just now. He slid his arms around her and leaned in for a kiss.

For half a second he felt her body tense; her feet shifted as if she would break away, but she didn't. She melted into him the way he so hoped she would. His arms went tighter around her, and dinner was forgotten.

"We can't," she said, although her actions clearly disagreed.

"You don't want my attentions?"

He hoped he wouldn't regret asking that. She met his eyes. She had to feel what he did; neither of them could deny it. He found himself holding his breath anyway, praying she would give in as she had so easily last night.

But the struggle inside her was strong. She didn't pull away from him, but she didn't melt back into him, either. She knew what he was offering her, and yet she was uncertain. He could see it on her face. Had he been wrong? Was she not the free-spirited wanton he'd thought? Everything about her today spoke of propriety and caution. Had he made a terrible mistake last night? God, he hoped not.

At last she came to her decision. Her clear eyes—now a smoky green—met his.

"I do want your attention," she said.

Thank God. Those were the most beautiful words she could have uttered just now, and he could suddenly breathe again. He crushed her to him and kissed her lips, her neck, her earlobe. She tasted better than he recalled.

"Last night was not nearly enough," he breathed.

She sighed against him in acquiescence. "No, not nearly."

But he could make up for that discrepancy right now. He *would* make up for it. Perhaps even several times. And when he was done with her this time, she would not be sleeping.

She was small, and he scooped her into his arms without much effort. Indeed, the poor thing needed to eat more. Now that he'd found her again, he'd see to it she was better cared for. He'd give her everything she needed and then some. He'd chase that hurt and fear right out of her eyes once and for all.

The library was in an older part of the house. It had at one time been parts of several different rooms, so there were many nooks and corners that would provide ample privacy for what he had planned. In fact, at the far end there was a windowed alcove that would be just the thing. He carried her there and deposited her gently on the cushioned seat that filled the area. She sighed with arousal as he lay down beside her, covering her with his body, as his kisses never ceased.

It would have been perfect if she'd still been in her night rail. This gown she wore today was far too restrictive. And all those ruddy undergarments! But he knew how to deal with them. He wanted her skin; he wanted her rounded breasts. Hell, he plain wanted all of her. And he was going to take her. There would be no sleeping or frustration this time. He would take all he wanted and give her even more.

And she was willing. Whatever internal battle she'd had, clearly passion had won out in the end. She was writhing against him, drinking in his kisses, grasping at his shoulders and back as she fought to bring herself closer to him. She wanted him every bit as much as he wanted her, and that was intoxicating.

He pushed her bodice as far out of the way as he could until one dark, hardened nipple was free. He rolled it between his fingers then dipped his head to taste as she moaned. Oh, but he did love how she responded to him.

The cushions were soft, and he thanked heaven for them. When he finally came inside her tonight, it wouldn't be gentle or cautious. He would have her, and he could feel his control chipping away. It would be no quiet coupling for them now. She would take all of him, and he would give it to her. God, she was willing.

His hand found its way under her skirts. She was wet and waiting for him. He could take her right now, without any further love play, and they would both be glad for it. Still, he'd waited so long for her. There was something he wanted before he dove himself in and found his release.

She whimpered when he left off kissing her breasts. Her fingers dug into his hair as if to pull him back, but he soothed her by cupping one lovely breast in his hand and massaging there. With his other hand he moved her undergarments aside and lowered himself to trail kisses along her thigh. She tensed and writhed for that, too.

Yes, indeed, she was ripe for the taking and would let him try this. He'd not bothered to pursue it with any of his few mistresses, but this girl was different. Finally tonight he'd experiment with one of his favorite chapters from that informative little book he'd turned to when first he endeavored to play his part as sophisticated rogue. Sir Cocksure had been very specific about the joys associated with this certain interaction. As his partner moaned before him, he kissed the warm, wet place between her legs. She let out a surprised cry.

"What are you doing?" she asked, breathless.

"I want to taste you."

"There?!"

Had no one ever pleasured her like this? No, obviously not. This was a first for both of them. Well, that nearly undid him. He'd have to be quick about this before he embarrassed himself. Although, the way she was arching and churning against him as he went back to work, he didn't think this would take very long.

It was beyond wonderful. Evaline shut her eyes tight, but still the light in her soul was blinding. His lordship knew exactly what to do to her, and he was doing it, all right. Thank God she hadn't run away as had been her first instinct.

But then she'd seen the desire in his eyes. For her. She'd felt the response in herself and knew she couldn't leave. Lord, after reading a few pages of that little book and gazing at the shocking engravings, every bit of her was more than eager for his touch. Last night he'd awakened something in her, and the craving for more had only grown. She wanted this, and she wanted it with all of her being.

And now he was kissing her in the most intimate place! Never in her wildest dreams had she imagined people could do this, and never had she imagined the waves of pleasure that flooded over her because of it. She would let him do anything he wanted, and today she would remember it, by golly. What memories they'd be!

She pushed her body closer to him, spread her legs, and shifted herself to make it as easy as possible for him to continue. He had to continue; she would simply die if he didn't. Something was building, as if she was desperately struggling to reach the end of a long, dark tunnel. Or was it a high mountain he was raising her up? Wherever he was taking her, her breath came in ragged gasps, and she wanted to beg him to hurry, to get her to their final destination quickly.

She felt his tongue, pressed inside her. He was lapping against her, and a wave of passion like she'd never known crashed over her. For a moment—or an hour—she was lost to the world. Everything disappeared, everything but his fiery touch and his gentle hands. She heard herself calling out, cries for help and cries for more. She didn't care, though, since nothing existed but him and this sudden, sated warmness.

At last his ministrations tapered off, and she was left panting, clinging to his shoulders for dear life. What on earth had just happened to her? Perhaps it had not been on earth, for it felt like no earthly thing she'd ever come close to experiencing. She certainly could never explain it to another living soul.

"What have you done to me?" she asked when she could form words.

"Did you like that?"

"Immensely!" she managed, breathless. "Is it always like that?"

"With me it is," he replied. "Now, catch your breath, my lovely. There is much more."

More? Good heavens, she wasn't sure she could survive any more. What she recalled of last night had been lovely with indescribable pleasure, but this was something otherworldly! Surely he was not capable of creating anything even more dramatic within her. This must be a man far above average in the arena of physical intimacy. She was certain she would have heard of it if this sort of thing were commonplace.

She slitted her eyes open and watched as he stripped off his coat and then began to unfasten his breeches. At last she would see him, see his manhood, and then give herself freely to him. Of course she must have done so last night, but this time there was no wine to block out the memory. Knowing she'd done this before was a comfort to her. There was no fear, only desire; desire for more of those unbelievable waves and desire for more of *him*.

But it was not to be. Sudden voices in the hallway distracted him, and then he was refastening his breeches and grabbing up his coat. It took her a moment to realize what was going on. So he was not going to bring out his manhood and thrust it inside her, after all? Disappointment was a tangible taste in her mouth.

"Hurry," he said, brushing her skirts back down. "They can't find you here with me!"

Her mind was in a fog. What was he talking about? Who couldn't find her? Where were they, anyway? Wait, she had to think. Oh yes. She was in Lord Dashford's library. She'd come here to avoid him! Drat, she hadn't done that very well, had she?

But someone was in the hallway outside. She could hear voices, male and female. Someone was coming this way! And they would find her here, half-undressed, with the glow of passion in her cheeks and Lord Dashford on top of her!

"Hurry," she agreed, jumping to her feet and stuffing her breasts back into her bodice. "They can't find me here like this . . . with you!"

He smiled at her yet looked a bit pained all the same. "Don't worry. I'll tell them I was alone."

He would? She could hardly believe him. How on earth would that help him manipulate her into marriage? She had to disappear. She glanced quickly around, noticing a door just a few feet away.

"It goes into an anteroom." He answered her unasked question. "From there you can go into the music room, then out to the hallway. Go. I'll keep them in here until you've had time to get away."

She nodded. Thank God there was a way out of this, and he was just as eager for it as she was. Maybe her earlier fears had been unfounded. He could have easily kept her here to be found out, trapping her with him. Perhaps he was not after her money, after all. Perhaps he really did just want her body.

She felt the blush cover most of her and dropped her gaze from his. Oh, but that was almost too much to hope for! A man—a fine, wonderful man—cared more for what she could do to him than what he could do with her money? The very idea was making her dizzy all over again. Without knowing what else to do, she curtsied and started toward the small doorway. But he stopped her with a firm hand on her arm.

"Wait," he said. "Your name. Give me your name."

Her name? Their families were conspiring to get them married, and he did not know her name? Well, perhaps he had never heard her first name. Certainly they were well enough acquainted now that they should be on to first names.

"Evaline."

"Evaline," he repeated.

A chill ran through her. In his voice, her name sounded like a prayer. She'd never felt important or special, but just now, with his gaze on her, desire burning in his eyes, and her name on his lips, she did. And she knew she'd better leave before she began hoping someone *did* find them together like this.

She hurried out the door and pulled it shut behind her, even as the large library doors from the hallway creaked open. She heard voices but couldn't tell who it was. Her legs were weak, and her face still burned, but she didn't dare linger. She patted her hair and moved quickly to the music room then out into the empty hall. The grand staircase was nearby. She would dart up it and send word to Aunt Bella that she was overcome with a sudden headache and couldn't make dinner. Yes, that was a good plan. She would have time to collect herself before facing Lord Dashford again. Before hearing him breathe her name and wishing she still believed in fairy tales.

But she was stopped in her tracks. Aunt Bella was there, on the stairs. Evaline froze and had to put a hand on the nearest table to steady herself. Her aunt's eyes shot daggers. Oh Lord, did she know?

"I was looking for you, Evaline."

"Sorry. I got distracted. I didn't realize how late it was."

"They are waiting for you to go in to dinner."

"I'm sorry," she repeated, gathering her strength for the fight, "but I have a headache. I won't be taking dinner with the rest of the group."

Aunt Bella would have none of that. She grabbed Evaline's arm in a vise and dug in her nails. Struggling only made the pain worse.

"Oh yes you will, girl," she sneered then paused to study her appearance.

Evaline bit her tongue to keep silent, though she knew what Aunt Bella would see. Surely what had just transpired could not be so easily hidden.

"You look a sight. Damn it, Evaline, did you go off and fall asleep somewhere?"

Evaline blinked at her aunt. Asleep? Is that what the

woman thought, that the flush in her cheeks and the mess of her hair was from *sleeping*? Well, how quaint! An unwelcome laugh escaped her.

"I'll teach you to laugh at me, ungrateful sluggard," Aunt Bella spat. But her hand stayed when Evaline cringed from the expected slap. "No, it will wait until after dinner. Dashford is expected to join us tonight, and I'll not do anything to jeopardize your chances with him."

"Perhaps his lordship has had something unexpected come up, and he won't be joining us after all," she suggested, assured of the truth of it.

"He will! And you will be pleasant and amusing, and if he shows the slightest interest in you, I'll see to it that you respond. Or, I swear to you, the consequences will not be so easily forgotten as the last time you were punished."

Evaline realized it would be futile to argue. The scene that ensued would do nothing more than bring unwanted attention on herself and would surely be an embarrassment to Lord Dashford. All right, for tonight she would go to dinner and pretend to obey her aunt. She sincerely doubted Dashford would make an appearance tonight, not after what had so recently happened between them. He'd succeeded in publicly avoiding her so far, and there was no reason to doubt he could continue to do so. It seemed he was more interested in their private time together, and that was fine with her.

"All right, Aunt," she said, taking a deep breath and forcing herself to be calm. "Let us go in to dinner."

Chapter Five

Ah, at last he had a name for her. *Evaline*.

It was a good name, and perfect for her. Most servants were Emmy, or Polly, or Daisy, or some such thing. His was Evaline. An uncommon name for a most uncommon servant.

Perhaps she had not always been of that station. Everything about her said she had at one time known privilege and culture of some sort. Well, now that he had her name, he could find her again and have all his questions answered.

And finally take her fully. Damn, but he ached. The last thing he needed was to be confronted with Rastmoor and his blasted mother, yet here they were. They barged through the huge library doors even as the small door to the anteroom clicked shut behind Evaline. At least she had escaped. Once again, he'd managed to protect her. He hoped.

He stepped behind a waist-high armchair to greet them. With luck, his person would be back to normal before he would be expected to accompany them in to dinner, which was undoubtedly why they had come for him now. It was hard to get himself under control, though. He knew her name and could track her down anytime he wanted. That was a most arousing thought.

"So here you are!" his mother exclaimed, storming over toward him. "And what, in God's name, have you been doing here?"

"I came to find a book I've misplaced. You haven't by any chance seen it?"

She didn't buy that. "You had someone in here with you. Dash it, Randolf, you are in no position to continue with this life of moral decay you insist on leading!"

"Mother, really, let's not get into this just now," he said. He really was not up to trying—yet again—to convince her he had not lost the family fortune on riotous living.

His mother stared at him without expression, then her eyes scanned the room. They rested, he noticed, a half second too long on the rumpled cushions of the window seat. Damn. Did she have to be so ruddy perceptive? He'd never been able to get away with anything around her.

"We have guests," she said softly. "Decent, respectable guests who have not made us outcasts, even though you have turned out to be a disgrace to your father's name. If I find that you've been bringing your whores into this house . . . into the presence of these honest people . . ."

"Damn it, there's been no whore in here," he growled. "All right, I'll go in to bloody dinner with you, if it will make you hold your tongue."

She glared at him a moment longer, and he saw something so cold and unfamiliar in her eyes it almost made him wish he could have explained things.

"I don't even know you anymore," she said, then turned on her heel and walked away.

He and Rastmoor were left to stare after her. Damn, he'd certainly made a muddle of things. But certainly marrying her little Pinchley chit was not the solution! Somehow he'd have to convince her that things were not as he'd worked so hard to make it seem they were. And he'd never, never let her know about Evaline. The girl had been through enough already to suffer being sacked by a grumpy dowager the minute he had his back turned.

"You found her again, didn't you?" Rastmoor said quietly when they were alone.

Dashford didn't bother to answer. Well, at least the chill emanating from his mother had solved his physical problems. He could come out from behind the armchair now.

"Let's go in to dinner," Dashford said.

Rastmoor followed dutifully. Just before they reached the door, he asked, "Did you by any chance get her name this time?"

"Evaline," he answered, though it was none of Rastmoor's damn business. He just liked saying the name.

His friend frowned, but they were in the hallway following his mother, and it seemed prudent for the conversation to cease. He marched along toward the dining room and wondered if this wasn't a bit like what the French royal family had felt on their way to Madame Guillotine. What he wouldn't have given to be marching away from his mother and her stuffy guests and toward his Evaline.

AUNT BELLA DRAGGED HER INTO THE DINING room. Apparently when she'd not shown up in the drawing room, there was some concern about her. She didn't for one minute believe Aunt Bella had actually been concerned for her welfare, but she must have used that as an excuse to let everyone else be sent on into the dining room while she went off to hunt her wayward niece. Oh, if she only knew just how wayward she really was!

But the guests were genuinely concerned for her, it seemed, and commented at her flushed appearance when they did arrive. Bella took it upon herself to make excuses for Evaline, claiming she'd been tired from a busy afternoon of industry over her embroidery hoop and had accidentally fallen asleep in her room 'while studying the worn Bible that always traveled with her. The story seemed to make the others so warmhearted toward her that she decided to let them go on believing it.

Lady Dashford, however, was conspicuously missing from the group. Apparently she had been there when Bella excused herself to search for Evaline. The others seemed a bit embarrassed to explain that when Lord Dashford had not shown up with his friend, Lord Rastmoor, she stormed out to locate him and had not yet returned. Lord Rastmoor, apparently, had gone with her. Probably, one elderly gentleman suggested, to protect his lordship from getting his ears boxed.

But heavens, that must have been who was entering the library as Evaline was leaving it! Oh, how dreadful it would have been if they'd not heard the voices in time and been found there in that compromising situation. Her face—and other parts—burned at the thought of it.

She was interrupted mid-burn by the entrance of Lady Dashford. The dowager was visibly upset, though her smile tried to hide it. Her eyes fell on Evaline first thing.

"Oh, good," she said, pausing in the doorway. "We were afraid perhaps you'd been unwell."

Aunt Bella spoke up before Evaline was forced to admit just how very well she'd in fact been.

"My silly niece was up safe and sound in her room," she said loudly. "The poor thing had fallen asleep! I suppose we should have taken the time to make her more presentable"—at this, Bella frowned at her hair—"but we hated to keep any of you waiting. I hope our rush was not in vain," she went on, to Evaline's chagrin. "Will his lordship be joining us at last?"

"Yes, he will be with us momentarily," Lady Dashford said and turned back to face the hallway. "Indeed, here he comes now."

What? He was joining the group for dinner, after all? Did he not realize Evaline would be here? Oh, God. How could she face him so soon after they'd . . . well, afterward. Perhaps this would not be uncomfortable for him, but she felt her nerves unhinge at the very thought of being so near him again.

What could he be thinking? She struggled to keep herself calm, but her hands shook. The glass of lemonade she lifted to her lips in an effort to soothe the choking dryness of her throat wobbled, then slipped from her grasp. Lemonade splashed around her and nearly covered poor old Mr. Patterson, who'd been seated, unfortunately for him, at her left. What a disaster this dinner was turning out to be!

HIS MOTHER WAITED FOR THEM AT THE DOOR-way into the dining room. Damn, but he wasn't going to get out of this, was he? Oh well. What was one more heiress to him? As Rastmoor had said, he'd dodged them before. He just wished he didn't have to do it in his own home. Especially when there was something he'd so much rather be doing.

"Dash, wait," Rastmoor said quietly before they got close enough to his mother for her to hear. "I'm not sure, but I think you ought to know . . ."

He seemed hesitant to go on. "What is it now, Tony? My cravat askew? So what else is new?"

"No, it's just that this girl you've found, you say her name is—"

He hushed his friend immediately. "Damn it, keep quiet. I'll not have you discussing her!"

Rastmoor looked a bit stunned by Dashford's tone. Well, so he should. Gentlemen don't discuss such things after the fact, especially not with their mothers standing watch over them. He stomped away from his friend toward the dining room and his mother's obvious disapproval. Hell. Might as well get this over with.

There was nothing that Rastmoor could do but follow Dashford as he ungallantly brushed past his mother and strode into the dining room. Let them think him the most horrible brute; he didn't care. With luck it would only serve to turn Miss Pinchley from her quest for his title. If not, he would simply tell her after dinner how much he loathed the idea of being in any way joined to someone the likes of her.

Mother wouldn't like it, but he'd have the mushrooms packing their bags by morning. Hell, maybe he could get them all out of his house so he could be left alone to finally finish what he'd started with the fair Evaline. Servant or not, he had plans for her, and half a dalliance was nowhere near enough.

Well, first things first. Expectant eyes were on him, and he had a dinner to muddle through. There'd be time for making plans—and executing them—later on. It was time to enter the lion's den. He swept into the room.

"Forgive my negligence, but there has been unexpected business to attend—" he began grandly only to be stopped short.

A frightened pair of fiery green eyes peered up at him

from near the head of the table. Somewhere behind him, he heard Rastmoor's muttered "Oh shit."

HE WAS LOOKING AT HER. EVALINE FELT FROZEN, pinned under his sudden gaze as if they were the only two people in the room. The lemonade soaked unchecked into her gown, but she could do nothing. His eyes held her as firmly as if he had placed his hands on her. Everything she'd ever felt in his arms washed over her at once, and for a moment the room swam around her. Was she going to further mortify herself by swooning right here in front of everyone?

"Randolf," his mother was saying. "This is the lovely Miss Evaline Pinchley, who you've so noticeably not yet had the pleasure of meeting."

"Evaline," he said, but this time the sound was cold, dead. And what was coming over his eyes? An icy hardness she'd not seen before took over, and she was gazing at the startling face of a stranger.

"What an uncommon name," he added. The chill in his voice was terrifying.

"My father chose it," she said like an idiot.

"I wonder what he'd think of it now," he said and finally turned away from her to give his mother a dazzling smile.

"Well, you see I can be an obedient son after all, Mother. Now what would you prefer? Shall I simply lead you to your seat and call for the servants to bring in the first course, or shall I drop to one knee and offer for your Miss Pinchley right away?"

Now it was Aunt Bella's turn to drop something. Her jaw hung slack, and an audible gasp escaped her. Evaline was surprisingly silent. Her worst fears were realized.

Lord Dashford had never been carried away by pure animal lust for her. The heated passion she'd thought she'd felt between them had been purely one-sided. Drat this carnal weakness. Her base nature had led her into being deceived once again. Dashford never really wanted her. All along he'd held but one goal: coldhearted seduction to trap her into marriage. He was like all the others. The only value she held for him was Papa's money. There was nothing but contempt in his eyes for her now. She'd seen it enough in Aunt Bella's eyes to recognize it.

What made her stomach churn and her throat constrict was the sudden realization that she cared what he thought of her. She cared deeply. Oh God, this was worse than she could have imagined. What Grandmamma had said about the Dashford men was true! Evaline's inborn weakness still made her crave him, even knowing what he obviously thought of her. However was she going to survive a polite dinner with the man?

"It's rude to tease our guests so, Randolf," Lady Dashford said with a nervous laugh.

"Oh? I had no idea my compliance with your schemes could be construed as rudeness," Dashford said, bowing as his mother gracefully slid into her chair. Then he turned and bowed toward Evaline. "I'm sure the fair and virtuous Miss Evaline will forgive me."

Lady Dashford looked horrified, but there was clearly nothing she could do. Dashford continued, turning his attentions to Aunt Bella.

"So, you must be Miss Pinchley's aunt I've heard so much about."

Aunt Bella actually appeared to blush under his piercing eyes and dizzying smile. Evaline had no idea the woman was capable of such a thing. Clearly the Dashford dark magic worked on all females.

"We met your mother during her stay in Bath this autumn past," Aunt Bella said, her voice taking on a girlish giddiness as she batted her eyes in his direction. "She's such a dear to extend her hospitality to us."

"Yes, isn't she just?" he agreed flatly, seating himself at the head of the table. "Now that I've kept you all waiting to bless you with my wonderful presence, why don't we eat?"

The servants recognized their cue and rushed to set food before everyone. The guests fell into strained conversation, and Evaline forced herself to relax. Perhaps the worst was over. She could take a few deep breaths and get through this. No one seemed to suspect a thing. Yet.

His lordship discoursed on favorite local spots for fishing, and she was pleased to find the other guests were happy to ignore her. She concentrated on keeping her face passive and pushing the food around on her plate. She wasn't going quite as unnoticed as she'd hoped, though. When she glanced up after several moments, it was to find Dashford's cold gaze on her once more. Oh Lord. Her face went warm, and her blood pounded.

"My dear Miss Pinchley," Lady Dashford said, startling her. "You've hardly eaten a thing. I'm becoming convinced our fare here disagrees with you."

"Oh, certainly not at all!" Evaline assured her, staring down at her plate and fighting back the urge to vomit on it. "Everything is lovely here."

"Well," Lady Dashford sighed. "Almost everything. I fear my son is showing us something less than his best side."

No one quite seemed to know how to respond to that, but Lord Dashford just laughed. "Oh, don't worry, Mother," he said. "I'm sure Miss Evaline has been pleased enough with the sides of me she's seen so far. Pity I haven't had opportunity to show her more."

"Perhaps if you were to attend your guests more often, then *Miss Pinchley*"—Lady Dashford put special emphasis on the *Miss Pinchley* part to point out her son's too-familiar use of their guest's first name—"might at last have that opportunity."

Lord Dashford's smile was not kind. He let it burn with an overabundance of familiar heat and directed it fully at Evaline. She knew precisely what he meant by it, too, and damn her, but she wanted to respond! Heavens, her cheeks felt on fire. What must everyone be thinking of them?

"Miss Pinchley is welcome to my attendance whenever she desires it," Dashford said in a slow, heated tone. "I always strive to see that my guests' every need is met in full. Tell me, my dear Evaline, have you found your time here to be pleasurable thus far?"

He was toying with her. My, but the man was cold. He thought her a worthless strumpet to be used and then demeaned right here in front of everyone. Well, she had no one to blame but herself for that, she supposed. She was, however, not about to sit here and allow it.

"No, sir," she said firmly. "I have found my stay here to be nothing less than tedious, in fact."

Aunt Bella gasped and began to rapidly fan herself. Evaline forced herself not to notice.

"Tedious, ma'am?" Dashford replied, far from offended. If she had to guess, she would have said his face showed nothing more than mild amusement at her outburst. Damn him!

"Oh, Lady Dashford has been kindness indeed, but I fear her son has a few too many, er, shortcomings for my taste," she said and hoped he got her meaning. Two could play at his stupid little game of insinuation and insult.

His eyebrows rose slightly as the only sign he caught her intended slight. She took that as encouragement and went on.

"There is nothing further I desire at Hartwood than for this infernal rain to end so I may leave."

The room was deadly silent, and Lord Dashford's eyes narrowed, though they never left hers. She wondered if perhaps she might have gone too far. He looked stormier than the clouds outside. What had she done? She'd been foolish enough to insult him in front of his guests and announce her wish to leave. What was stopping him from throwing her bags out in the elements and letting her make good on that desire? Drat, but if she was going to continue speaking her mind, she was going to have to learn to do it at more convenient times.

Aunt Bella stuttered for something to say, but Lord Dashford ignored her and went right on glaring at Evaline as if they were the only two people in the room.

"But if you leave, my dear," he said casually, "how on earth can you expect to bring me up to snuff? A gentleman, after all, can hardly be expected to propose marriage to an absentee heiress. So, I suppose I'll have to get right to business, since that's so clearly what is demanded. All right, Miss Pinchley. You have your proposal. Marry me."

"Marry you? Good gracious, sir! I'd sooner drink poison. Why on earth should I wish to marry you or any other of your profligate kind?"

Now even the servants were gaping openmouthed at

them. Oh Lord, but she'd really put her foot in it now. He'd likely be only too glad to explain loudly and graphically one very good reason why she should wish to marry him. If she denied it, he'd simply throw them out on their ears, and she'd finally get that beating Aunt Bella kept threatening.

Bother. That moonlight and Madeira had been her complete undoing. She must still be under its spell, else why would she be so bold? She knew no gentleman would let anyone speak to him this way and go unchastised.

But her dismissal would have to wait. A sudden commotion in the hall just outside their door seemed to overtake everyone's attention. The butler appeared at the door and announced grandly, "The Graeleys, your lordship. Would you have them added to your dinner table, or shall they be invited to refresh themselves upstairs?"

The room was strangely silent at this news. For just a moment his lordship looked stricken, then his face was stony again. He caught Evaline's gaze and gave her an icy smile.

"Well, Miss Pinchley, this is good news," he said. "I'm sure you and Miss Graeley will find you have much in common. By all means, Williams, do have places set for them. I'm sure our guests would love more company. We are, after all, being decidedly informal tonight, aren't we?"

That last question was directed at Evaline. She pointedly scowled at him. Heaven only knew what the other guests would make of such an exchange, but she hardly cared. Judging by Dashford's expression, he was not happy to have these Graeleys here. Good. Let all his enemies appear to plague him this evening. The man deserved it.

Besides, she was remarkably curious about this Miss· Graeley. His fiancée, was she? The man was clearly not overjoyed at that prospect. What a sweetheart she must be. Oh, Evaline could hardly wait for their meeting.

A middle-aged gentleman was escorted into the room, bringing with him the most beautiful young woman Evaline could ever recall seeing. She was tall, elegantly dressed in layers of peach-colored flounces and crisp white lace. Her chestnut hair was twisted expertly in an elaborate design, and the smile she gave Dashford was nothing short of radiant. Evaline must have been staring with her mouth gaping open.

This was Dashford's fiancée? And to think Evaline flattered herself to imagine Dashford might have possibly favored her small, mousy form.

The girl was annoyingly lovely. And Dashford thought they might have much in common, did he? Evaline was willing to wager the only thing she and Claudia Graeley had in common were ears on the sides of each of their heads, and any fool could see Claudia's were much fairer than Evaline's. Why on earth would Dashford be so distressed to learn of Claudia's arrival? Most normal men would kill to have a fiancée like this.

Then again, perhaps he knew Claudia would see him for the bounder he was and break their engagement straightaway. Indeed, that would be distressing for a man in his position. But Miss Graeley seemed quite content to be here, smiling at Dashford and presiding over the dining room as if she were its mistress already. If Dashford knew he had a fiancée like this ready to walk down the aisle and rescue him from his self-induced ruination, what could he have been thinking to have wasted his time on someone like Evaline?

It made no sense. It did, however, mean one thing. As long as Dashford was engaged to be married to this brilliant diamond, Evaline was in no danger of him announcing the specifics of their, er, acquaintance. He'd never want this paragon to learn of his indiscretion. As long as Claudia was happy, Evaline was safe.

She slumped down into her chair. Indeed, she felt no little relief in this realization. On the other hand, she wouldn't have minded one bit if Claudia Graeley accidentally stepped off the edge of the earth.

Chapter Six

It required much shuffling and clatter, but Dashford had his servants bustle about to set extra chairs and tableware for the Graeleys. He wasn't happy. Damn, so the bridge had held fast, had it? It was looking pretty chancy this morning; he'd thought perhaps it would go before the Graeleys made it across. Dashford cursed the surviving structure silently. The very last thing he could stomach right now was Claudia.

It wouldn't be so very bad if she was in one of her sullen moods, but from the moment she stepped through that door, she'd made it very plain he was, once again, in her favor. Damn and blast. Why did she continue to smile at him like that? What would it take to finally be rid of the girl once and for all? Probably something illegal, and he was fairly sure even *he* wasn't ready to stoop to that. Yet.

A quick glance at Evaline gave him the idea she might not be overjoyed by Claudia's presence, as well. But of course she would resent the new guest. Claudia Graeley was Evaline's greatest rival, was she not? Poor little heiress, she'd done so much to assure herself of winning the prize, and now to be faced with the bothersome detail of a fiancée must be quite vexing. No doubt some interesting interaction was brewing between the two ladies. If Dashford didn't know his very neck to be the disputed prize, he might actually consider baiting the two of them just to see what would happen.

But he'd learned the hard way how cunning Claudia could be, and he'd certainly learned that Evaline would stop at nothing to gain his attentions. Certainly Claudia had never bothered to actually seduce him. Odd, that. Beautiful as Claudia was, he could have easily been able to resist her, while it seemed he was frail and powerless to keep his hands off Evaline.

Of course, that was easy enough to explain. He hadn't known until literally minutes ago there was indeed a good reason to keep his hands off Evaline. He'd always known the dangers of Claudia; her family had wanted the Dashford title for her since their childhood. Still, he'd thought they were friends, and he'd fallen prey to her seemingly innocuous attentions. Well, never again.

He now knew exactly where he stood with both these conniving females. He might be stuck here in their presence, but he was not at their mercy. Let them tear and claw at each other; he was not about to fall victim to either of them ever again.

"Dashy!" Claudia said brightly, floating toward him after she'd allowed a reasonable time for everyone in the room to admire her statuesque pose. "I can't tell you how lovely it is to see you again! I've missed you for ages!"

He cringed. *Dashy*. Oh, how he hated that stupid nickname she insisted on. Perhaps it had been cute when she was five years old and his mother had paid him two whole shillings to play with the little brat when the family came to visit, but it was not so adorable now. Especially now that he knew her for what she was.

He was spared from having to answer when her father came blustering over to pound him on the back. "Good to see you, Dashford. Finally decided to let London run on without you, eh?"

"For a day or two," Dashford replied.

"Please join us, Sir Graeley," his mother said, rising and motioning for them to take seats. "Here, we've had places set for you."

Dashford was only too glad to step back and let her monopolize the newcomers. The other gentlemen at the table stood and effused their joy at having more company.

Rastmoor, from his place across the table, gave a private scowl. Dashford couldn't have agreed more. He would have slunk out the door if he thought he could have gotten away with it. In fact, he was very seriously considering it, when his mother elbowed him in the ribs.

"You should introduce your guests, Randolf," she hissed behind a guileless smile.

"I suppose I should," he said with no initial intention of doing so. Her glare forced a change of heart. "Very well, then. Everyone, please allow me to introduce our neighbors and friends, Sir Victor Graeley and his most accomplished daughter, Miss Graeley."

Now it was Claudia who was glaring at him. Sir Victor, too. Bother. It appeared he would have to be completely honest with the people.

"Miss Graeley, I should add," he went on, "is my fiancée."

Claudia beamed, several of the elderly guests murmured among themselves, and Dashford glanced at Evaline—not that he'd meant to, of course—only to be surprised by her expression. What was it, exactly? Not so much shock, not even anger or jealousy. What, then, did he see on Evaline's soft face?

Perplexing as it was, he thought he read relief. What? That didn't make sense. Evaline Pinchley had come here for the express purpose of snagging his title for herself. She'd lured him and seduced him into the most compromising situations! So why the hell did she look so damn relieved to learn he had a fiancée?

"Tell us, Sir Victor," Lady Dashford said as everyone settled down to the table again. "How are the roads holding up out there?"

"Oh, they're simply dreadful!" Claudia answered in her father's place. "I thought we'd overturn at every corner. All the way from Kenilworth I was nearly rattled to death! If Papa's new barouche weren't so very well sprung, I'm sure that I would have been."

"And what of the bridge to Lack Wooton? Did you come by way of that?" Mr. Patterson asked eagerly. "We've heard it is in danger of being overcome!"

Claudia basked in the attention. "Oh, it was terrifying,

sir," she said with high drama. "I begged Papa to have his man thrash those lazy horses to get them over quickly. I can't believe we made it with our lives. Surely that bridge cannot hold out the week. I fear"—and here she gave Dashford a too-meaningful glance—"we may have to impose on our gracious host much longer than initially intended."

"I assure you, my dear," he said, "should anything happen to this bridge, I will move mountains to find you another."

She fairly glowed. "Oh, Dashy. You take such care of me."

He'd like to take and carry her right back to that bridge and chuck her off the side of it.

Conversation circulated, the topics of tumbling bridges and inclement weather giving way to far more important subjects such as the gown Claudia had chosen to wear tonight and the gown Claudia would probably wear tomorrow night. She reveled in the adoring stares of several elderly gentlemen and chatted brightly with Mr. Quinley-Pierce, who was seated happily at her other side. Her lilting laughter traveled over the room. Dashford supposed it was intended to be reminiscent of tinkling bells or fairy song. He decided it was rather more like magpies fighting over a stale crust.

He spared another look at Evaline. She sat quietly pushing her food around her plate. The persons seated near her seemed to have completely forgotten her existence as they focused worshipfully on Claudia. For one desperate second Dashford caught himself feeling sorry for her. By God, he almost spoke up to engage her in conversation! Well, that would have been the wrong thing to do. It might encourage her. Wouldn't want to do that, would he?

No, of course he wouldn't. Right now he would just be thankful for a brief respite while Claudia prattled mindlessly on with the others. He would be able to concentrate on enjoying his dinner. Cook's turtle soup was well renowned. Renowned soup or not, though, Dashford realized he'd much rather be tasting Evaline.

"WELL, THAT WAS AN INTERESTING DISPLAY AT dinner tonight," Lady Dashford said at last. She'd been very definite in her instruction to Dashford: meet with her in her private sitting room before retiring. He knew it would only prolong the agony if he ignored her summons, so he went.

"I'm always glad to keep you entertained, Mother," he said and waited for her to fly into a motherly tirade.

She had good right to it, he had to admit. He'd been a beast at dinner. First he'd started in on Evaline like that—not to say she hadn't deserved it, but it certainly hadn't shown him in a very good light—then he'd been irritable and surly toward the other guests once Claudia and her father had arrived. No, he had no excuse for his public behavior, but he was certainly not about to justify his reasoning to his mother, for God's sake.

She didn't ask for his reasons, though. She merely shrugged and examined the embroidery she'd been poking at. "I see Claudia is once again delighted to be your intended."

"Apparently."

"And we should be glad Miss Pinchley showed her true colors before you had gone to all the trouble of becoming interested in her."

What? He'd expected a lecture, but what was this?

"Miss Pinchley's true colors?"

His mother sighed. "I was quite amazed to see her like that, Randolf. From what I know of her, the girl is ever pliable and most accommodating."

Indeed, he himself had found her exactly that on more than one occasion. Yes, she had been most pliable and most accommodating. That wasn't exactly what his mother meant, though, of course.

"Miss Pinchley's outburst was not altogether unprovoked, you must admit," he said. Good God, was he defending her?

"True, you were rather harsh. I wonder why? Are you acquainted with the girl beyond what I'm aware of?"

"No. Of course not! I merely recognize Miss Pinchley for the upstart she is, and I reacted badly." He hoped he hadn't said that too quickly.

"You treated her very badly, you know. I'm surprised she didn't just fall into a fit of tears—vapors even! That would be how Claudia might react in such a situation, I'm sure."

Ugh, he had no doubt of it. It would take far less than the verbal abuse he'd given Evaline to bring Claudia to hysteria. All things considered, Evaline must be commended for her actions tonight. She'd weathered his attack, then gone on to hold herself with dignity throughout the rest of dinner and everyone's obvious preference for Claudia. Afterward, when the men rejoined the ladies in the drawing room, he'd seen immediately that Claudia was taking every opportunity to slight Evaline.

The poor girl was not allowed a word in edgewise. Claudia's very gestures and demeanor toward Evaline made it clear she saw the girl as no one worthy of a second glance. It was quite distracting, really. He had to keep forcing himself to play the doting fiancé and not rush to Evaline's aid and make up for Claudia's snubs.

"And you're certain you've never met her before today?" his mother was saying.

"Of course not. Where would a disreputable git like me ever encounter a virtuous heiress from Bath?"

"True. It surprised me her aunt was so enthusiastic about a match, knowing what people say these days about you. I suppose I had convinced myself they were exaggerating, but after that display at dinner tonight, I see I was wrong."

"I am a terrible person after all, you see?"

"It just breaks my heart to think you would put your own reckless lifestyle ahead of your duty to your family and to your father's title. You're ruthless, immoral; you've squandered the family fortune . . . What decent woman would have you now?"

"It seems Miss Graeley would," he grumbled.

"Your father must be turning over in his grave."

All right, enough was enough. "Mother, it's not so bad as all that. I've explained to you we're in no danger of coming to ruin. Our finances are quite secure."

"Don't lie to me, Rand. Sir Victor told me you finally had to sell that pair of grays you loved so much. I know you wouldn't have done that if you didn't have to."

Hell, he'd wanted Graeley to hear of that but not come running to his mother with the information. Damn. He'd sold the grays to Rastmoor with the understanding that he could buy them back when the coast was clear. Lord, how well they'd done their playacting! How was he going to convince her it was all a lie?

"And I heard you lost your mistress, too," she went on.

That, too? "Good grief, Mother!"

Casting off Madeline had certainly not been a part of his plot to prove his own poverty; he'd done that out of sheer self-defense. No woman—no matter how beddable or attractive—was worth the whining or vapidity he'd had to endure with Madeline. But how on earth had his mother heard about it? He must truly have created a greater stir than expected. Blast. There was no telling what folks were saying about him now. He'd be lucky to be allowed in a simple card game next time he visited White's.

"And to think I was so easily swayed to believe the poor girl was every bit as sweet-natured as she seemed," Mother said with a sigh.

"Who, Madeline?"

"Who's Madeline? No, I was speaking of Evaline."

"Oh, *that* poor girl." He breathed in relief. "But I thought the fact that Evaline—Miss Pinchley—is anything *but* poor is what attracted you to her in the first place."

"No, *she* attracted me to her in the first place. I stumbled across her in Bath last autumn and enjoyed her company immensely. I found her to be intelligent and artless, quite a charming young lady. But for your information," she said, "Miss Pinchley is in fact a penniless pauper. Oh, there's a large inheritance to be sure, but she can't touch a penny of it yet."

"What? That's ridiculous."

"Is it? You've seen her—what she was wearing at dinner tonight. She hardly looks the part of heiress, does she?"

Dashford was caught off guard by this. His mother might be right. Evaline had certainly not looked any heiress he'd ever seen. Indeed, he himself had readily mistaken her for a servant, hadn't he? But if she indeed had no fortune, what was Mother up to?

"Penniless, is she? Why did you bring her here for me then, Mother? Isn't this whole thing about selling my title in exchange for ready blunt?"

"Presumably it's about finding you a reason to take your responsibilities seriously, although it appears that will require more than a sweet-natured woman with a healthy fortune. Oh, yes, there is a fortune, Randolf. Miss Pinchley will be quite flush once she finds a husband; don't think I didn't verify that. That was the constraint of her father's will: the money must be held in trust until she marries."

"Seems dashed unfair of the bloke, if you ask me."

"I would assume it was an attempt to protect the funds from falling into the wrong hands. You didn't have much opportunity to converse with the aunt, I take it."

"Awful, is she?"

"Dreadful! No doubt this financial arrangement is the only reason Evaline still has any fortune left to her. I get the idea Bella Stump cares little for Evaline's person."

"What wonderful people you run with, Mother."

"Miss Pinchley is nothing like her relatives! Tonight is the first time I've heard her utter a sharp word. Then again, I only ever treated her with civility, unlike some others tonight."

"Although she wouldn't hesitate to drag some unwilling bloke into marriage if it meant she could get her hands on her money, I don't doubt. It was bloody wrong of her father to force her into that."

"Randolf, let's be frank. She isn't quite in the same category with someone like Claudia Graeley or a hundred other debutantes out there trying to find husbands. Her father probably set up her trust the way he did in hopes it would assure her finding a husband at some point."

"What? Are you saying she couldn't get a man's notice without the promise of a healthy bank account?"

"I'd say twenty thousand is more than just healthy, wouldn't you? But she's not exactly an incomparable, you must admit."

"She's a hundred times easier to look at than Claudia Graeley! And a damn sight easier to have a conversation with and . . . that is, at least she would seem that way, from how you describe her, and whatnot."

"And whatnot? Are you certain you've never met her before?"

Damn. She knew! Somehow his mother knew there was something between him and Evaline. This was not good. It would be the Claudia Graeley situation all over again, except that this time he actually *had* involved the lady in a compromising position. More than one of them, as a matter of fact.

"What difference would it make if we had met before, Mother? I'm bloody engaged to Claudia."

"Yes, I suppose you are. And we all heard Miss Pinchley declare she was not the least bit interested in marrying you."

That's right, they had. He'd nearly forgotten that. She'd been most adamant in her declaration, too, as he recalled. It must be part of her scheme, a ploy to make him let his guard down. Indeed, that had to be it. If only Claudia had tried such a thing. He'd have called her bluff and been a free man today!

His mother had drifted into silence, squinting over her embroidery so long he thought perhaps the conversation was over. Good. He was more than ready to be done with it. Finally, though, she looked up.

"I suppose Evaline's attitude toward marriage might have something to do with that man."

Blast. Now she had his attention. "*That man?* Which man would that be?"

"Bella swore it was nothing more than a childish infatuation and that it was over and done long ago. She assured me it had never gone anywhere, and that Evaline was completely over him." His mother clucked her tongue and shook her head. "Perhaps that is not entirely the case."

"Exactly which man are we talking about?"

"Some young gentry she knew years ago. Elton Barstow or Brighton or something like that."

At first it meant nothing to him. Then suddenly the name clicked. "Ellard Bristol?"

"Yes, that's it. Do you know him?"

He shrugged and made his face passive. "Oh, I've run across him in London a time or two."

Yes, run across him, paid him to help in their scheme to create the rumors of Dashford's decay, and invited him to come to this blasted house party. Thank heavens for the torrential rain that had obviously kept him away. Ellard Bristol was a self-serving weasel with an eye for easy women.

Despite Dashford's conviction that Evaline came here
with mercenary purposes, he was not at all prepared to
share her with the likes of Ellard Bristol. His head might
still be a bit confused about Miss Pinchley and her dubious
motives, but his body was perfectly confident of one thing:
he was not at all done with her. He'd be damned if she took
up with someone else until he'd finished what they started
in the moonlight last night. Well and truly finished it, for
both of them.

SLEEP HAD BEEN IMPOSSIBLE. EVALINE HAD KNOWN
before even climbing under the covers how futile the effort
was, but she really had not been prepared for the barrage of
feelings that flooded over her there in the silent darkness.
First she hated herself for letting Dashford affect her so
blatantly at dinner tonight, then she hated him for all other
the things she'd let him do to her. Then she wished he'd
suddenly appear and start doing them to her again! Oh, it was
dreadful.

So, after battling guilt and anger and a shocking amount of
lust for over an hour, she'd done the only thing she could think
of. She'd tiptoed down to the library for a book. Surely there
would be something there to take her mind off her troubles.

Now here she was, alone in the dusty library with just a
flickering taper for company, and what had she done? She'd
sneaked another glance at Sir Cocksure's book! She'd found
it right where she'd left it earlier, tucked between the pages
of the medical digest where she'd hidden it when Dashford
came in and found her.

The first page she opened to sported a detailed illustration
of a happy couple, face-to-face and skin on skin, gleefully
engaging in what Sir Cocksure insisted was a posture best
suited for the mutual benefit of both parties. Evaline had to
agree she could definitely see the benefit of that position.
She felt the blood rush to her cheeks, and a tingling warmth
flooded into her nether regions. Bother, this was not going to
help her sleep.

She tried to escape the thoughts that were plaguing her by
slamming the little book shut and stuffing it back where

she'd originally found it, between the wall and the bookcase. Then she made the mistake of turning around. Moonlight drifted through the leaded panes of the nearby window and the seat nestled there. Her eyes easily fell on the soft cushion. It still bore the impression of two impassioned bodies. It was as if she could feel him all over again: his arms around her, his hands touching her in secret places.

She stood there; her gaze finally left the cushion, and she stared out the window to the moonlit landscape beyond. She wasn't seeing it, though. Dashford filled her mind entirely. He had been wonderful, hadn't he? For the rest of her life she'd remember those moments with him. It was impossible to imagine she'd ever experience anything like that again.

"So, here you are again," he said, materializing behind her.

Her breath caught, but somehow she really wasn't shocked by his presence.

"I just came to get a book," she said quickly, not turning to see him.

He came up close. The cushion in the secluded window seat loomed large beside them, moonlight causing it to glow.

"You haven't found one," he noted.

"No. I got, er, distracted."

He didn't say anything, but he didn't move away, either. The house was so quiet she could hear him breathing. He was so close she could almost feel him. An electric thrill coursed through her. She didn't dare turn to look at him. If she did and found no desire burning in his eyes, she would be crushed.

"Evaline," he said softly. "Look at me."

She couldn't disobey and finally turned. His cold blue eyes were indiscernible. The silence dragged on, but she was frozen there, trapped in his gaze. What did he want of her? She knew what she wanted of him, drat those infernal passions she'd unintentionally inherited. Why did she have to take after Grandmamma? Why couldn't she have been naturally pure and virtuous, like her mother?

Very slowly his hand went up to touch her face. Somewhere in the back of her mind she knew she really ought to move away, but of course she didn't. She stood quietly as he gently traced his finger over her cheek, her jaw, her neck. She shuddered. It was even better than she remembered it.

"You like to be touched," he noted.

"It seems that way."

He still was only barely brushing her, but already her knees were weak, and she felt the warmth radiating off him. She forced herself to remain still, to let him work his magic. Slowly he pulled her to him, turning her back against him so his breath caressed the nape of her neck. His hands trailed across her shoulders and came around to cup her breasts.

"I will not marry you, Evaline," he said.

She had to laugh. "I wouldn't let you marry me, my lord. Besides, you have Miss Graeley for that. Personally, I think you deserve each other."

"You're too cruel."

"Not used to honest women, are you?"

His solid chest rose and fell against her as he chuckled. She felt his hot breath. His mouth was on her ear, and his hands kneaded her. Oh, but she did love this too much.

"Why do you let me touch you?" he asked.

She sighed. "Because I can't help it. I enjoy it too much."

She hated admitting it, of course, but it was truth. Something about the warmth of his hands, the fire in his eyes, and the tenderness of his kiss made her helpless. Let him think what he would, as long as he kept holding her this way.

"How should I touch you now?" he breathed at her throat.

"I don't know."

"Now, now, Miss Pinchley," he said, pushing her night rail off her shoulder and sliding his lips across the skin there. "No need to be demure on my account. We are more than passing acquaintances, you and I. What would you like me to do to you now?"

Oh, it was so hard to think straight with him breathing on her like this. Of course she had to stop him. This just couldn't go on! He would respect her wishes and allow her to escape. She could simply pull away and run out of here right now. Surely he'd not come after her.

Of course she'd *want* him to come after her.

"Make love to me," she said. Drat this pesky penchant for honesty.

He seemed to like honesty, though. She could feel his smile through his words.

"Oh, you mean like this?" he asked as he intensified his efforts with his lips and his hands.

Yes, actually, that was pretty much exactly what she meant. She nodded, since her voice didn't seem to be working right now. He pulled her gown off the other shoulder, sliding it down so that her arms were pinned to her sides and her breasts were bare to his touch. A thrill of excitement shuddered through her.

He tightened his hold, and she felt him pressing against her from behind. He was hard and ready for her. She leaned back into him, and a little groan escaped her when his hand skimmed the length of her body to rest at her thigh.

"Why?" he asked, surprising her.

Why? What did he mean, *why*? "Why what?"

"Why would you not let me marry you?"

"Because neither of us wants it, my lord," she said in an unsteady voice.

"But you do want this?"

"Oh yes!"

"So, you didn't come here to snag yourself a title?"

How could he be discussing this so calmly while his hands were doing the most amazing things to her body? Was this really all so very commonplace to him that he could carry on conversation during it? It was all she could do to keep from falling over, the waves of sensation he was creating in her were so strong.

"No," she managed. "That was my aunt's idea. She thought maybe since you, er, were having some financial difficulties, you might, uh, you might . . ."

"I might grab the first heiress who fell in my path?"

Oh, he was grabbing her, all right. In just the right places, too. "Something like that. Can we perhaps not discuss this right now? It makes it rather difficult to concen . . ."

She lost the thread of her conversation when she realized her rail was being raised up high onto her thighs. Good Lord, but his hands felt wonderful on her skin. But now what was he doing? Oh heavens! He was leaning her toward the cushioned window seat, pressing himself against her from behind. What an unusual sensation this caused.

"You were saying?" he questioned when she was quiet.

"It's difficult to concentrate when you are . . . I say, isn't this supposed to be done with me facing you? I mean, for mutual benefit?"

Now he was laughing. "Such an adventurous soul, yet so many things you've not done! I swear, Evaline, in the future, you really ought to insist on better quality in your lovers."

She started to remind him that he was not the one to berate the quality of her lovers, but her words came out somewhat strangulated, so she didn't bother. One of his hands had slid down to press in between her thighs, barely brushing her and sending searing sparks of desire through her body. It took all the control she had not to cry out as the familiar waves of passion rolled over her, drawing her toward the depths of the ecstasy only he had ever brought to her.

"Of course, you can understand my concern," he said, though his actions seemed anything but concerned. "Should anyone discover us, marriage will be all they care about."

"Then we'll just have to be careful not to be discovered," she said. "Do you wish me to move down so you can reach better and . . ."

No, he could reach just fine. So far he was only teasing her, stroking her with his fingers and leaning in so she could feel the hard bulge still concealed behind his trousers. Bother, the man was driving her to distraction!

"And should you ever feel compelled to mention this to anyone, you realize of course I should have to deny it?" he asked, still caressing her skillfully.

"Of course, and . . ."

Wait a moment. He thought she might feel compelled to mention this to someone? *This?!* Why, if he were not making her so dizzy with passion, she would be highly insulted just now. Well, she was not so dizzy as to be able to stand here—lean here, rather—without setting him straight on a few things. Taking a deep breath, she pushed herself into a more upright position and turned to face him.

"Look, you are not the most eligible bachelor on the planet, you know," she said, happy to assure him. "Every female that walks the earth does not do so with the single purpose of aiming to become your wife."

He actually looked surprised to hear this. And a bit pained, too. In fairness, though, perhaps that had more to do with his trousers than her words.

"The only reason I ever allowed myself to be brought here to this party," she explained, "was because I had plans to meet someone in the area. On business. To be honest, Hartwood is convenient for me just now." Her voice was remarkably steady. "The fact that you and I have . . . that we . . . well, you know. And I'm certain it never would have begun if not for that blasted bottle of wine! Usually I keep myself well controlled, but obviously I've slacked a bit since arriving here."

"Obviously," he agreed.

"Well, since that is the case, and since I've obviously not made any attempts to use our intimacy to extort you into matrimony, don't you think perhaps you just might be willing to trust me?"

He seemed unconvinced. "Trust hasn't always worked out so very well for me."

"Then perhaps in the future you may be prudent to insist on a better quality of persons to trust." It was clumsy, but she enjoyed throwing his words back at him.

"Evaline," he said and gave her a smile she knew was intended to melt her. "I just want to be certain we are in agreement, that we both understand what this—whatever it is we have between us—is nothing more than temporary. I don't want to be accused of raising your expectations."

"Trust me, you haven't."

He grimaced.

"I'm not here to gain a husband," she announced carefully, in case he hadn't heard anything else she'd said.

"But what of your trust fund? I know you cannot access it until you are wed."

Oh, so he knew about that, did he? Well, he obviously didn't know the details.

"My marital status no longer has any bearing on my finances," she assured him. "Papa set up the trust to go to me upon my marriage *or* upon my reaching twenty-five years of age."

"Twenty-five? And when will you reach that?" he asked, touching her face and looming disturbingly close.

"Yesterday."

"What? You can't be as old as that."

"Thank you—I suppose—but I am. As of yesterday I'm competent to gain complete control over my money, and I don't need to dredge up a husband at all. So you see? You're completely safe. We can do this all day and all night with nary a commitment or obligation."

"God, that sounds good," he said and fairly shoved her back down onto the cushion. She giggled as he crawled up to loom over her.

It was pointless to protest, because the minute she found herself gazing up into his smoldering eyes, she was dizzy again. Oh, but she was a bad, bad person, and she wanted him to do very bad, bad things to her!

He smiled at her willing response and propped himself up on one elbow, using his free hand to stroke between her thighs again. Instantly the flame inside her reignited to a full blaze. She murmured as the air was crushed out of her when he brought his lips down to kiss hers. His hardened shaft pressed into her thigh and reminded her again just exactly what it was they wanted from each other.

He pulled her closer. She arched into him and reveled in the variety of textures: his clothing, her clothing, his hands, his face—she wanted to feel all of it.

"This rain may keep up for days, and the bridge is close to failing. You'll have to stay here," he said as he kissed her hair. She knew exactly what they'd be doing during her extended stay, too.

"My aunt will be troublesome, you know." She figured she'd better warn him now. "She's a bit confused about my age, actually. She thinks she can still arrange something between us—something permanent and legal."

"I'm bigger than she is. I'll win."

Oh, but what a delightful thought: Aunt Bella in mortal combat with Lord Dashford. She couldn't dwell on it, though. He was grinding himself against her and setting her skin on fire with his hands.

"We'll just have to be discreet," she said, then sucked in a sharp breath as his head dipped to take one of her nipples between his teeth.

Then, as if on command, the sounds from the hallway started up. The taper Evaline had carried down from her room flared in the sudden draft that blew in. Down the hall it sounded as if someone was coming in through the huge front doors. Several sets of footsteps sounded out there, and it was obvious their private liaison was at an end.

"Good God!" Dashford grumbled.

He helped Evaline pull her night rail back over her body and then hauled her unceremoniously up to her feet. She really was dizzy now and furious at whoever might be interrupting them. The taper nearly blew itself out when he grabbed it up and shoved it into her hand. She realized he had one of his own; he must have put it down before she even realized he'd come into the library.

"Go," he said, pointing to the door where she had made her previous escape. "I'll find out what the hell is going on and try to get the hall cleared out so you can make it upstairs unnoticed."

She nodded and started off, only to be stopped short. He had taken her arm and pulled her back to him. Swiftly he leaned in to kiss her, and all the desire she'd been feeling was channeled into that one heartbeat. But the kiss was brief, and too soon he released her, only to meet her eyes with a gaze full of the same frustration and longing she felt.

"We *will* finish this," he said.

She nodded again, and this time he let her leave. She shut herself into the small anteroom to wait until the noise of footsteps, voices, and—was that luggage being hauled in?—everything settled down. It seemed another of Dashford's houseguests had arrived with less than impeccable timing.

Great. She wondered just what sort of beautiful and charming lady this newcomer might be. If it was another husband-hunting heiress, Evaline thought she might scream. The place was becoming lousy with them.

Chapter Seven

It was not another heiress, Dashford quickly ascertained. It was worse.

"Hey, Dash," the newest arrival called out when Dashford entered the rain-soaked entrance hall. "What about this demmed weather, eh? Nearly washed out every road between here and London!"

Ellard Bristol. Good God, how bloody wonderful. The man was barely tolerable in London where there were plenty of other distractions around. Trapped with him here in his own home—with Evaline nearby—Dashford was likely to end up damn near suicidal.

"Bristol, I thought even you would have the good sense to decline my invitation in weather like this," Dashford said, stepping out of the way as the butler and two footmen rolled back a very expensive carpet to protect it from the growing puddle surrounding Ellard and the young gentleman he'd brought in with him.

"Well, it's lucky for this fellow I didn't stay home," Bristol said, shaking out of his greatcoat and giving a hearty slap on the back to his soggy companion. "This is Carrigan. Found him some miles back with his carriage buried axle deep in mud and the horses run off, don't you know. Thought I'd better bring him along here just to get him out of the wet. Hope you don't mind, Dash."

"No, certainly," Dashford said, somewhat relieved by the disapproving glance the young man sent Bristol's way. "You're welcome to stay as long as you need, Carrigan."

"Thank you, my lord," the man replied curtly, his critical gaze shifting from Dashford to Bristol and back to Dashford. "But it's *Carrington*, and I hope to have my carriage repaired swiftly so as to be on my way and not further impose upon your generous hospitality. My lord."

Well, he certainly was a stuffy one, wasn't he? Oh well. Dashford presumed he'd be a bit out of sorts after an ordeal like that, too. At least he wasn't one of Bristol's blighted cronies, here to debauch the women and drink up all his brandy.

As to the subject of debauching women, Dashford recalled his main priority right now was getting everyone away from the staircase so Evaline could scurry back to the safety of her room.

"Come, gentlemen," he said, "shake off this rain and join me in the drawing room. I'll pour us something to drink and have the housekeeper roused to attend to rooms for you. The place is nearly full right now, but I daresay we can find room for two more."

He began to usher them from the entrance hall. The sooner that could be accomplished, the safer Evaline would be. If what his mother said was true, that there had been some tender feelings between Evaline and Bristol at one time, the last thing Dashford needed was to arrange a happy reunion in the middle of the night. Knowing Bristol, he'd be attempting that with her himself soon enough.

Hopefully Evaline would not be inclined to make it too happy.

"Got a bit of a party here, do you?" Bristol was saying as the three gentlemen left the servants to deal with the wet floors and dripping baggage. "I thought you said it was just you and Rastmoor heading out here."

"That's all I knew about," Dashford said. "My mother surprised me with a few additional friends."

"If my arrival causes you any difficulty, sir, I ask that you please simply allow me the use of a conveyance to the nearest inn and . . ." Carrington began, but Dashford cut him off.

"No, you're fine, Carrington. We've got plenty of room. Every Dashford viscount from time immemorial has felt compelled to add his own wing to this place. There are bedrooms I've never yet located."

Bristol chortled. "That's not what I hear about you, old boy!"

Great. Bristol brought every ounce of his bawdy charm with him. Dashford would simply have to see to it that Evaline was kept at a safe distance. With Bristol recently widowed and Evaline possessing a healthy libido—not to mention her bank account—it was a fair guess what the scoundrel would have on his mind as soon as he knew she was here.

"So, a house party, eh?" Bristol commented, giving Dashford a sly wink as he shut the drawing room door behind them. "Got anyone particularly interesting here, Dash?"

Damn. The man was practically salivating already.

"No one of any current interest to you, Bristol," he said. "Sorry."

But he wasn't.

DRAT. THE BREAKFAST ROOM WAS FULL WHEN Evaline stuck her head in the doorway that next morning. She'd hoped she'd waited long enough that everyone would be done. They weren't, and the smell of livers and eggs made her stomach roll over. Worse, she'd been spotted.

"Oh, Evaline!" Lady Dashford called. "We were just talking about you. Come in, come in."

With everyone staring at her and Lady Dashford smiling so engagingly, how could Evaline refuse? She couldn't. Aunt Bella was there, and the look she wore said Evaline's decision to join the group was not open to discussion. The look Miss Graeley wore said she would have preferred it if Evaline's heart was served up on the buffet table.

"Come, come, Evaline," Aunt Bella scolded. "Don't just stand there and ignore her ladyship's most kind invitation."

Very well, she'd best get this over with. Evaline took a deep breath, conjured a convincing smile, and stepped into the room.

"Good morning, everyone," she said. Claudia glared.

"We were just wondering where you were," Aunt Bella said with a pointed look at the large clock on the mantel. "I thought perhaps you intended to sleep all day."

Evaline gritted her teeth and held back some tart remark about this being the first time in recorded history Aunt Bella had roused herself before noon. Her time for speaking freely with Aunt Bella would come soon enough. She could wait.

"We were afraid you might still be feeling a bit under the weather after what happened last night when his lordship—" a well-padded matron she'd been introduced to as Mrs. Quinley-Pierce began. The woman stopped herself with a quick glance toward Claudia.

Evaline's heartbeat quickened. Mrs. Quinley-Pierce knew what happened last night with his lordship? There was no way! How could she? Evaline had been completely alone with his lordship, hadn't she? They'd been . . . Oh, but wait. Mrs. Quinley-Pierce must be referring to what happened at dinner, not what transpired later on. Yes, that was it. Just as Lady Dashford had been, this woman was worried Evaline was still wounded from Dashford's less than courteous greeting at dinner. Thank heavens.

"Well, we're all glad Miss Pinchley is feeling more the thing this morning," Lady Dashford said. "You are feeling more the thing, aren't you, dear?"

Evaline swallowed back the panic that had been rising and forced another smile. "Yes, of course, ma'am. Quite the thing, in fact."

"Good. I knew you couldn't be the type to let careless words from boorish gentlemen get to you for long," her ladyship said. "But do try to eat something, dear. Livers?"

Evaline stared at the brimming buffet table before her. The ham and eggs and sausages and breads and livers and strawberries all might just as well have been salamanders for what it did to her appetite. Lord, she was expected to eat in front of all these people? While pretending Lady Dashford's boorish son hadn't "gotten to her"? Impossible!

"Wonderful news indeed," Aunt Bella said. Her cheerful expression was not nearly as sincere as Lady Dashford's. In fact, her smile was rather more catlike. "Perhaps there is a reason for your vast improvement today, Evaline. Did his lordship have an opportunity to apologize last night?"

Evaline audibly gulped. "What?"

"Well, you did run across him last night, didn't you?"

She knew her face gave it all away. "Er . . . last night?"

Aunt Bella smiled. "Yes, after we'd all gone to bed, wasn't it? I heard sounds in the hallway, and since I knew how upset you were after that display over dinner, you can understand I became concerned. Well, when I peered out into the hall, I could distinctly recognize his lordship's voice downstairs. I thought nothing of it until you came up to your room a moment later, Evaline. Yes, my dear, I was watching. So tell me, did you manage a conversation with him last night?"

Everyone waited for the explanation, Claudia especially. Evaline would very much have liked to have one for them! She blinked back her horror and managed a smile.

"Yes, as a matter of fact."

Lady Dashford was shocked. "You did? Good heavens, I hope he was civil toward you, my dear!"

"Come, Evaline," Aunt Bella prodded. "Let's hear about it. Whatever did Lord Dashford say in the middle of the night that has you so cheerfully restored this morning?"

You could have heard a heartbeat, the room got so quiet. Dash it, but Aunt Bella was nothing short of evil. How dare she manipulate Evaline into shaming herself and admitting Dashford had compromised her! Well, she wasn't going to cooperate. She'd just have to come up with some plausible—and perfectly innocent—explanation for what went on last night.

"All right," she said, keeping her face as passive as she could. "It's not a very dramatic tale, but I suppose his lordship would not mind. I was upset last night; you all know that. I couldn't sleep. So I went to the library to find a book. On the way back to my room, I ran across Lord Dashford, and he kindly expressed his regrets for some of the things he said that may have been interpreted as unpleasant. I also apologized for my words, and we parted in agreement to forget the dinner incident entirely. I returned to my room without further event, and that's all there is to it."

Except, of course, for the part about Dashford bending her over the window seat and pressing his hot body against hers. But she wasn't going to bring that up just now.

"Was it good?" Aunt Bella asked.

Evaline gulped again. "What?"

"The book. Was it a good book?"

"Yes. That is, I mean, I didn't read much of it."

"Oh, I see," Bella nodded. "Your conversation—the one with his lordship, in the middle of the night—calmed your nerves entirely."

Evaline narrowed her eyes and met her aunt's cold gaze. The woman knew something more, didn't she? But what, and how much?

"Yes. Something like that."

The room was uncomfortably quiet. Evaline supposed she ought to say something to break the tension, but she wasn't entirely sure she could trust herself not to give Aunt Bella any more ammunition for her marital schemes. Until she learned the truth about Evaline's age, this was only going to get worse. Oh, she hoped and prayed that business agent would hurry up and contact her.

"You poor little thing, Miss Pinchley," Mrs. Quinley-Pierce said, tsking loudly. "What a jolt to your system this must all be."

"Heaven knows *I* certainly suffered a jolt to *my* system," Claudia huffed, shamelessly drawing attention to herself and looking for all the world like a preening duck in her yards of daffodil flounces. "The fact that I'm even alive to eat breakfast this morning is a miracle. Those roads yesterday evening were treacherous. I'm surprised I can so much as swallow a morsel today."

"Yes, and you've swallowed more than several morsels, I see," Lady Dashford noted. "We are all glad you survived your journey, Claudia dear, just as we are even more pleased to see that Evaline is well enough to join us this morning."

Claudia laughed lightly. "Heavens, I had no idea Miss Pinchley was so frail. So what if Dashy was somewhat cross with her? At least he apologized."

"Cross? The lad was downright rude, if you ask me," a garishly turban-wrapped Mrs. Coddleston chimed in with a nod to their hostess. "Forgive me, Margaret, but your son was ill-mannered, to say the least."

The breakfast guests dove in with zest. This was just the

conversation they'd been dying to have, apparently. Evaline brought her nearly empty plate of food and sank into the seat that had clearly been left vacant for her between Mr. Mandry and Mrs. Patterson. Oh Lord, but this was her worst nightmare.

"Indeed, it was quite out of character for him," Mrs. Quinley-Pierce agreed. "Imagine, speaking to a guest in his home that way."

"I couldn't believe my ears, the things he was saying," Mrs. Coddleston said.

"I tell you, I hardly recognized the man when he came to dinner last night. Such sharp words! Nothing at all like the young Dashford I remember," the corpulent Mr. Coddleston concurred with his wife.

"Perhaps we misheard him last night," Mr. Patterson said, adjusting his spectacles. "Dashford was always such a dutiful sort."

"He's been tending to the wrong duties of late, from what I hear," Mr. Coddleston said, chuckling.

"Well the rest of us certainly don't want to hear about that," Mrs. Patterson chided sharply.

"I worry for him," Mrs. Quinley-Pierce proclaimed. "He was downright spiteful last night, and for no good reason, I'm sure. Why, just look at Miss Pinchley—such a dear girl. What on earth could she ever have done to the man to merit his treatment? Too cruel, he was."

"But of course he's not really that sort at all," the tiny and most elderly of their group, Lady Brennan, said with a warm smile to Lady Dashford for reassurance. "We must have misunderstood."

"Miss Pinchley didn't," Mr. Patterson said, slathering cream on a sweet roll. "She gave his lordship a right fair set down for it, too."

Evaline thought it might have been nice to slide under the table about now.

"I'm sure Miss Pinchley never intended to be taken as so outspoken," Lady Brennan said with certainty, as if her opinion should settle it all for everyone. "And we all know Dashford isn't the cruel sort."

"Indeed," Mrs. Quinley-Pierce agreed, seeming to realize

at last they were being unfashionably harsh with their host. "It's likely all this rain that's put him in a foul mood."

Her husband was seated beside her, and she jabbed him in the ribs. He barely seemed to notice but dutifully nodded and mumbled something in an encouraging tone as he worked away at his second helping of ham.

"No, he's really not a bad sort," Mr. Mandry started up, filling in where Mr. Quinley-Pierce could not. "You must understand, Miss Pinchley, he's got a lot on his mind right now. That's all it is."

"That must be it," Mrs. Quinley-Pierce agreed. "Nothing wrong with him a good woman couldn't repair."

Mr. Quinley-Pierce's slight eye roll indicated he'd had his fill of wifely repairs. Evaline could well imagine.

"Poor Dashy," Claudia said, latching onto Mrs. Quinley-Pierce's theme. "I suppose I shall have my hands full. It seems there are more than a few parts of the man that need improvement."

Now Evaline rolled her eyes. Frankly, from what she'd thus far encountered, Dashford's parts were entirely fine just as they were.

Oh drat. She slopped her tea. Thinking of the viscount's various fine parts sent the blood racing to her cheeks, and her extremities were decidedly weak. Well, perhaps no one had noticed and . . . oh bother. Lady Dashford noticed. But instead of commenting on Evaline's clumsiness, she gave a motherly smile. Without hesitation, the lady graciously changed the topic.

"Speaking of improvements," she began, turning brightly to Mr. Patterson, "do tell us about that new project you've been working on, Mr. Patterson. You're consulting with the engineers enhancing our canal systems, I hear?"

Mr. Patterson practically shone like a sun. "Indeed, I am! It's quite enthralling work, really. The regent has a vision to upgrade our nation's water transport, you know, and he heard of my extensive studies on the lock systems in the North Country, so naturally he asked personally for me to assist his engineers. From an advisory position, of course."

"How fascinating," Lady Dashford said with enthusiasm. "Canals were a passion of my late husband's, you know. For a while it seemed as if Randolf would carry on with some plans he'd had, but . . . Well, do tell us about your work."

Everyone became politely interested in this discussion, and for a blessed few moments Evaline could relax, attention drawn away from her. This gave her an opportunity to push the food around on her plate. At some point, however, she knew she'd have to eat it. Mr. Patterson's dry discourse could not be counted on to hold the guests' attention for long. Sooner or later they were bound to notice Evaline's still-present breakfast and begin commenting, once again, on her poor appetite and what could possibly be causing it.

Of course it was just nerves that did this to her again today, wasn't it? That was the most likely cause. Quite common in fact, considering. Surely it was nothing more.

But what if it was something more? Oh, if only she could be certain! Well, she would simply force herself to get through this morning then find time to get back to Dr. Buchan's book. She'd only barely started in it when she'd found that other little volume. How silly of her to have become so easily distracted! She needed the information in Dr. Buchan's book far more than anything she might learn from the dubious Sir Cocksure.

Indeed, as soon as she could escape the breakfast room, it would be on to the library to continue her quest. No doubt she'd find exactly the information she'd need to let her rest easy. There was likely some rule of nature specifying that a woman must be sober and responsible for her actions—or at least recall them—for propagation to take place. Surely it didn't just happen by accident after one single, reckless encounter!

She'd known couples who were married for years before finally receiving their little bundle of joy. It couldn't be as easy as one simple lapse in judgment, could it? A full perusal of the medical book was bound to confirm that. Then she could forget all these silly concerns and move on to more pressing matters.

Such as, why on earth hadn't she heard from her agent yet? Surely, even with the bad roads, the man must have arrived in nearby Lack Wooton by now. London wasn't across the globe. The man simply *had* to turn up sometime soon.

Her thoughts were interrupted when she heard her name.

"But what do you think of it, Miss Pinchley?" It was Claudia, obviously aware Evaline had not been paying attention and determined to embarrass her now.

"Well, er, that is . . ." Evaline fell into the trap and stammered.

"Oh, I'm sorry," Claudia said sweetly. "I suppose I should have realized this conversation is beyond your understanding. The rest of us, you see, were discussing the sad state of affairs when landowners are expected to bear the burden of financing waterways that will be of no great benefit to them."

Evaline didn't overlook Mr. Patterson's deep frown. "Not all of us were discussing that, Miss Graeley," he said.

"Of course not," Claudia said, completely missing his implication. "How silly of me to think Miss Pinchley might be able to participate."

"Not at all, Miss Graeley," Evaline said with equal sweetness. "You are too kind to exclude me from your discussion. I'm sure you understand how it would pain me to publicly disagree with your one-sided and clearly uneducated opinions."

Mr. Patterson choked on his eggs. Aunt Bella glared daggers. Claudia gasped. Apparently being disagreed with was something rather new to Miss Graeley.

"But go ahead and continue your discussion, by all means," Evaline went on. "I'm terribly interested to hear how the furtherance of productive industry and the promotion of our national economy is of such little benefit to those landowners who are the very cornerstone of it."

"What do you know of it?" Claudia snapped. "Your father was nothing but a merchant!"

So Miss Graeley had been asking after her, had she? Well, she felt no shame for her father's profession, though it was obvious Claudia thought she ought to. What a shrew. Evaline would have just loved to launch into a detailed retelling of exactly how successful and respected her father was in his various endeavors, but she held her tongue. It would be pure folly to think she could win that debate. When it came to pedigrees, Claudia had the advantage. Evaline would have to go back three generations on Papa's side to procure anything even close to gentry, and the very last thing her reputation could survive was any question about her mother's connections. No, she needed to avoid that at all costs, especially here at Hartwood, where Grandmamma's name was, no doubt, well-known.

"You're correct," she capitulated. "My father earned his living through trade, and he was kind enough to share aspects of his work with me. Forgive me if I do not apologize for having an understanding of the advantages accessible transportation brings to every class in our society. I think Mr. Patterson's canals are a capital idea."

Aunt Bella buried her face in her hands and groaned. Evaline turned her attention back to her plate. So much for holding her tongue!

"Hear, hear!" Mr. Patterson said.

"Thankfully I've been able to devote myself to more lady-like pursuits," Claudia sniffed. "Accessible transportation, indeed! No wonder Dashy was forced to make a scene at dinner, Miss Pinchley. The way you conduct yourself around your betters is truly quite shocking. I should be surprised if he had *not* spoken harshly with you."

Evaline was about to say something even less ladylike when a deep voice from the doorway stopped her.

"I was not scolding Miss Pinchley last night, Claudia," Dashford said, leaning against the doorframe as if he'd been there all morning. "Did no one tell you? I was proposing marriage to her."

His sudden appearance startled everyone at the table. Cups rattled on saucers, and tense bodies jolted. How much of their conversation had he heard? How embarrassing! He'd likely think Evaline's sharp words toward Claudia were spoken out of jealousy. Well, he'd be wrong about that. Claudia was detestable enough without Evaline lowering herself to squabble over a man. Still, Evaline had to admit she enjoyed the unattractive way Claudia's mouth suddenly hung slack as Dashford's words sank in.

"Proposing to her?" she cried. "Proposing marriage? But you can't; you're already engaged to me!"

"Yes, your father was just reminding me of this,"

Dashford said with a sigh. He nodded toward the other guests and came to lay a quick kiss on his mother's cheek. "Good morning, everyone. Good morning, Mother."

Then he met Evaline's eyes, and she had to catch her breath. So far she'd only seen him by the warm glow of candles or the pale shimmer of moonlight. But now it was daytime, and even in the dull, gray light filtering through cloudy skies and rain-spattered windows, he was magnificent. His eyes burned right through to her soul, and she spilled her tea again.

"Good morning, Miss Pinchley," he said, moving toward her.

Toward her! Oh, all she could think of was how long it would be before nighttime and how silly it was to expect he might find her alone in the library again. She'd be there though, of course, just in case he came looking. She could only pray he'd come looking.

He leaned in toward her, and for one maddening moment she hoped—er, feared, rather—he would kiss her in front of everyone. He didn't, of course. Instead, he handed her his handkerchief.

"I believe this might be helpful," he said.

She blinked at him, temporarily at a loss until she recalled the tea. Oh, blast it, the man was not trying to entice her, he was trying to tidy her! Bother, but she'd gone and embarrassed herself again. No telling what everyone thought about the way she must have been ogling him. For God's sake, that business agent had better show up quickly and rescue her from all this.

Thankfully, Dashford moved away, and Evaline could breathe easier. At least, she could until Claudia's whining filled the room.

"Papa!" the girl cried. "Dashy says he proposed to Miss Pinchley!"

Evaline glanced up from wiping her tea and discovered the girl's father, looking a bit sour and more gruff than usual, entering the room.

"Pipe down, Claudia," the man said. "I've heard all about it."

"Indeed, Sir Victor intercepted me on my way to breakfast this morning," Dashford said and didn't sound altogether pleased about it. "We've been discussing the subject at great length in my office, while my stomach growled."

"If you were any sort of gentleman at all, we wouldn't have had to discuss it to begin with," Sir Victor grumbled.

"Have some food, Sir Victor," Dashford said. "I'm sure no one wants to hear any more about this."

"I do!" Claudia complained.

"Hush yourself, girl," Sir Victor growled.

The two gentlemen filled their plates in uncomfortable silence. The other guests busied themselves with their own food, eyes carefully averted. Claudia pushed her plate petulantly away, and Evaline stabbed at a strawberry so vehemently that it skittered off her plate and onto the white table cover. Drat.

"Now then," Dashford said convivially when he and Sir Victor were seated at opposite ends of the table. "What were you all discussing before we interrupted? Transportation and the economy, I believe?"

Was that Aunt Bella who let out a slight groan, or someone else? Evaline couldn't be sure. She was trying to subtly push the strawberry back onto her plate.

"Canals!" Mr. Patterson said with enthusiasm. "It seems Miss Pinchley has a fair understanding of the value of improving our inland waterways to keep up with the growing industry."

"Does she now?" Dashford said.

"Her father was a merchant," Claudia interjected, lest anyone had forgotten this distressing fact over the last two minutes.

"Mr. Patterson says many of the plans your father had to improve the waterways right here around Hartwood are still quite viable," Lady Dashford said to her son, clearly hoping to pique his interest in domestic matters.

"Mr. Patterson has been most generous in discussing the matter with me upon several occasions," Dashford said.

"As I recall, Dash," Mr. Patterson said, "you had some fine ideas of your own on the subject. Have you done any more to put in that short channel you proposed?"

"No, I'm afraid I've been unable to make any headway

there," Dashford said. He sounded as if he honestly regretted it.

"Well, if it's engineering help you need, lad, just say the word! I'll gladly advise on any design or surveying you might require," Mr. Patterson offered.

"No, I'm sorry to say the project cannot even get to that point as of yet." Dashford shook his head. "It's more of a geographical issue, I'm afraid. I need to gain access through a particular property."

"Oh? That area is not all Hartwood land?"

"No. Not exactly."

"Well, there's nothing out there but farmland and a few cottages," Mr. Patterson shrugged. "Surely no one would turn down any reasonable offer you might make. Why, it would take but a few hundred pounds to . . ."

He stopped himself. He looked down sheepishly as it seemed to dawn on him—and everyone else in the room—what he was saying. Dashford's money troubles were no secret.

"Er, well, pity about that, Dashford," Mr. Patterson muttered.

Dashford frowned. "Yes, isn't it, though?"

The room was overtaken by awkward silence again until Lady Dashford cheerfully spoke to her son.

"So tell us, Randolf, where is Lord Rastmoor this morning?"

Dashford's already stormy expression turned even darker. "He and our other guests are out riding, which is where I was hoping to be by this time."

"Other guests?" Lady Dashford asked.

"Yes, I didn't get a chance to tell you—as I have been cloistered in my office for what seems ages already today— that two more guests arrived in the night."

"Oh, how lovely. Friends of yours?" his mother asked.

"Marginally," Dashford responded with an odd and indefinable expression as he glanced at Evaline.

"And they are riding in the rain?" Claudia asked. "Honestly, I should think you'd be grateful to have missed joining them."

"Not so much," he said with conviction. "But listen. I believe I hear them returning already."

So, the guests from last night were not beautiful heiresses after all. Evaline was frustratingly relieved. Lord, how she wished she didn't care so much whom Dashford kept company with, but she couldn't seem to help herself. As the voices came closer, she watched the doorway with deep curiosity.

Three dampened gentlemen entered. The first one she recognized easily as Lord Rastmoor. His ruddy hair was wild, and his bright expression said he actually seemed to enjoy what must have been a very bracing ride. Behind him came a smaller gentleman. He was remarkably neat in comparison with Rastmoor, and his expression said his morning ride had been somewhat less enjoyable. The third gentleman had his companions easily beat with elegance and impeccable dress. His dark, smoldering eyes scanned the room with fashionable ennui and then came to rest on Evaline.

She recognized him immediately.

Good heavens, Ellard Bristol. What was he doing here? It made no sense and could not be possible, but here he was, nearly as tall as Dashford himself and still exuding that smug languor that used to be so attractive to her. The years had aged him, but aged him well. There was no doubt as to his identity, and she shuddered inside when she realized he recognized her, too.

"Well, I can't believe my eyes," he said. "Evaline."

She was taken aback by his greeting, supremely informal as it was, considering they had not seen each other in seven full years. Heavens, the mere fact that he still recalled her first name after all these years answered so many questions she'd long harbored. Ellard *did* remember her. She *had* been important to him.

But just what was she supposed to say to him now? She didn't know. She could only sit there mute, wedged between Dashford's gaze and Ellard's. It was Dashford, in fact, who broke the spell. His voice was hard when he addressed his friend.

"I see you and Miss Pinchley are acquainted."

Ellard smiled warmly, not taking his eyes from Evaline. "Indeed, very well acquainted. She was my fiancée!"

Evaline could have been knocked over by a feather. His fiancée? The man threw her over to marry someone else, and now he claimed they'd been engaged? Well, it seemed Ellard's memory of what occurred seven years ago was quite different from hers.

Evaline wasn't the only one surprised by this revelation, it appeared. Lady Dashford's eyes narrowed expressively, and she showed no qualms about questioning their new arrival. "Your fiancée, sir?" she asked. "And just who might *you* be?"

Dashford rose and cleared his throat. "Mother, everyone, allow me to introduce Mr. Bristol. Sorry he doesn't have time to stay and chat. Come, Ellard, let's you and I go somewhere else."

"What? Go where?" Ellard asked, understandably confused.

"Somewhere else," Dashford said through gritted teeth.

"But I'm famished, old man!"

Lord Rastmoor laughed. "Oh, come on, Dash. Let the man eat. What harm can he do with you standing guard?"

"Standing guard? Over what?" Ellard asked.

Rastmoor leaned in, and Evaline thought she heard him whisper something about "certain valuables" but didn't have a clue what that meant. Ellard didn't seem to either.

"I say, I didn't come here to rob anyone!"

Rastmoor just laughed some more, while Dashford glared at him. "Fine," he said eventually. "You can eat, but don't take too long. I'm sure you're in a hurry to get back on the road."

"What? But I just got here."

"London needs you back already," Dashford said firmly.

Rastmoor was very nearly beside himself. "Oh, that's rich, Dash! Honestly, it's not worth it, man. Besides, Bristol isn't going anywhere for a while."

"No, afraid not, old chap," Ellard said with his familiar lazy laugh. "None of us is. We just returned from trying to reach your local village here, Lack Something-or-other. The bridge, I hate to tell you, is out. Sorry, Dashford, but it looks like we're all stranded here."

"Damn," Dashford grumbled.

"Say, any ham left? That smells frightfully good."

Dashford's expression was thunderous. "All right, fine. Help yourself to breakfast, Bristol. But nothing else."

"Thanks, Dashford," Ellard said and converged on the buffet table. "Don't mind if I do. Come on, Carlisle, tuck in."

The middle gentleman grimaced. "It's Carrington, sir."

Evaline's ears perked up at that. Carrington? The man's name was Carrington? As in *Mr.* Carrington, Papa's business agent? My, but he was so young! And what on earth was he doing here? He'd been scheduled to stay at an inn in Lack Wooton. His arrival was supposed to be secret; her dealings with him were to be kept anonymous! Oh, everything was fouled up today.

Dashford seemed to recall his manners. "I'm sorry, everyone. This is Mr. Carrington. He arrived late last night, as well. Mr. Bristol found him along the road; his carriage had suffered some damage, so it appears he will be staying with us until he can continue on to . . . where were you headed, exactly, Carrington?"

"On business," Carrington said primly, glancing briefly at Evaline then shifting his gaze to somewhere on the wall over Claudia's head. She was too busy glaring hatefully at Evaline to so much as notice Mr. Carrington's existence.

"I was traveling on business," he continued. "Hopefully even with these setbacks, I will still be able to settle matters to everyone's satisfaction."

"Good for you. Let us hope you can do so," Dashford said absently.

Evaline chewed her lower lip. Poor Dashford. The man didn't know what he was agreeing with.

Chapter Eight

"I never thought you could do it!" Bella said with sincere amazement when the two of them were alone later in Evaline's chamber. "A quiet little dormouse all this time, and yet you did it, my dear! Spectacular. Not only is Dashford interested in your fortune, but he actually seems interested in *you*. I actually think he's a bit jealous of your friend Mr. Bristol. However did you work that out?"

Evaline had no idea how to answer this, so she could do nothing but sit on the edge of her bed and stare, mute. Aunt Bella was actually praising her for the way things had gone at breakfast? Aunt Bella was *pleased* with something?

"No matter," Bella said after Evaline's silence. "Getting Bristol to show up here like this is sheer brilliance. Can't believe I didn't think of it myself, actually. And it worked like a charm! I must say, Evaline, you never let on that you could be so devious."

"Aunt Bella, I had nothing to do with—"

"I must say, I was concerned about you sneaking off to meet him last night. Er, that was Dashford you were meeting, was it not?" Bella said, as if it suddenly dawned on her there were a whole slew of men Evaline might have been taking up with.

"Of course it was Dashford," Evaline said quickly, then stopped herself. "I mean, I ran across Dashford. No one else."

"As you say. But keep in mind that while you are running across Dashford in the night, he is still engaged to Miss Graeley. It would be a shame for you to be spreading your legs for nothing, my girl."

Evaline's mouth dropped open, but Aunt Bella went on.

"Dashford has proven he is not afraid of controversy. Legally he's bound to Miss Graeley—curse her virginal, well-connected hide—and he cannot so easily slip out of that. You, Evaline, are not so difficult to discard when he has had his games."

"Then I should think you'd be quite concerned about this turn of affairs, rather than patting me on the back," Evaline said.

"I was quite upset with you last night. I thought I would have to take matters into my own hands today and dredge up some way to paint you an ill-used martyr or some such rot. It appears, however, you have hidden talents. You've left Dashford champing at the bit and now have contrived to get Bristol to come! I must say, I am impressed."

"Aunt Bella, I didn't plan Ellard's arrival here," she insisted. "And I was not sneaking off on some planned meeting with Lord Dashford last night. We met by accident, and only briefly, just as I said."

"There was nothing brief about it, my girl. I know. I followed you to the library and watched Dashford enter a bit later. Oh yes, it's true. There are a remarkable number of darkened corners one can conceal oneself in, you know. Dashford nearly walked right into me in his rush to get to your little tryst, my dear! No, don't send yourself into a fit. I didn't stay long enough to watch. That bloody Lady Brennan was prowling about, convinced your footsteps had been marauders. That woke up Lady Dashford, and I had the devil of a time convincing them both to go back to bed. I figured letting them wander around and find you two in flagrante would only turn the viscount against us and provoke Sir Victor to call him out. Well, the man is no use to us dead, so I thought it best to leave you to your own devices. Apparently I chose wisely."

Really? All that was going on last night while she and Dashford were . . . well, in flagrante? She must make a mental note to be much, much more careful with him in the future! No, wait. Of course there could be no future. She was simply going to be strong and deny her passions. It was far too dangerous to keep giving in.

"But tell me, Evaline," Bella went on. "I really must know. How do you expect to steal him away from Miss Graeley? I mean, it's clear he's more than willing, but you know he's legally entangled. You aren't planning something, er, unsavory?"

"Unsavory?"

"There are ways, of course, to see that a person goes missing . . . permanently."

"Aunt Bella! You're not suggesting I do away with her?"

"I know; it's far too risky. But pity. Well, I suppose you'll come up with something. I'll just have to trust you. After all, you do have hidden talents."

"Not for that sort of thing," Evaline muttered. Oh, but she surely was well on her way to utter ruin. She should never have taken that Madeira. It was just as Papa warned: when you give in to one passion, you lose your defense against all of them.

"It's really such a shame that damned will your father left specifies you must marry so quickly," Bella sighed. "If I'd only known a title was your weakness, I'm sure I could have procured you an earl or even a marquis."

"We do not know any earls or marquises, Aunt Bella," Evaline reminded her. "And I wouldn't want one, even if we did."

"Oh, so it's not the title but the man, is it? Lord, girl, don't tell me you fancy yourself in love! What rubbish. Don't be a fool, Evaline. Silly sentiment was the last thing on his lordship's mind when he climbed on top of you last night, mark my words."

Evaline felt her face heating rapidly. Oh, why wouldn't Aunt Bella just shut up and leave her alone? This was no time to make matters worse by discussing love.

But Bella stayed, and her voice lost a bit of its hard edge. "All the same, things are working in our favor, so I don't suppose I ought to lecture you now. Bit late for lectures, anyway. You were Bristol's girl, weren't you? Daresay he taught you a thing or two before he got that other girl with his brat, and she dragged him to the parson."

Evaline cringed. Yes, Ellard had taught her a fair bit, but not what Aunt Bella apparently thought. All Ellard taught her was that trust and love and faithfulness were nothing more than fairy stories and daydreams. Ellard's more interesting lessons were spent on others, apparently.

"Just do be cautious, Evaline," Bella went on. "It's fine to pique one man's interest by giving attention to another, but Dashford isn't the sort to take kindly to sharing his woman. Don't let Bristol overstep his bounds, or you're likely to find yourself alone and disgraced. Without reputation, all the money in the kingdom won't fetch you a decent husband. By the time you finally come into your majority, we'll be long in the poorhouse."

"I'll keep that in mind, Aunt. Now, if you please, I'm rather tired and could use a rest before luncheon . . ."

But she didn't get to finish dismissing her aunt. There was a quiet knock at the door, and the young maid who'd been assigned to her stepped in, sheepishly bowing and nodding.

"Yes, Molly?" Evaline asked. "Is it time to start dressing for lunch already?"

"No, miss . . . my lady," the maid stammered nervously. "But I've got a note here for you."

"A note? From whom?" Evaline asked at the same time as Aunt Bella.

The maid simply held a folded paper forward and stared at her feet. "I cannot say. It was given to me by one of the footmen, and he said he was sworn to not tell."

An anonymous note? From Dashford, perhaps? Was he trying to lure her into meeting him again? Well, she would not! She could not! Not even if he was very cautious about asking her to meet him at a late hour in a perfectly secret, undiscoverable location that might be just right for passionate trysting. Not even if he would be waiting there for her with his cravat all askew and his trousers unfastened, the telltale bulge evident of his desire for her and his hands just waiting to slide across her skin and hold her . . .

Heavens, she was breathing heavily already! How dare he put such things on paper. What if it should fall into the wrong hands? She yanked the note back from Aunt Bella, whose hand it had fallen into just now.

"I believe Molly said this is for me," Evaline chided.

Aunt Bella frowned. "I was merely handing it to you."

Not likely. Evaline stepped away from the others and opened the note. Her heart beat rapidly, and she fought back the burning ache that called her to abandon her sensibilities and run to the man, no matter where he was or what he was asking of her.

However, the note was not from Dashford.

"You may go now," Evaline said. No one moved.

"You heard her," Bella said to the girl. "You may go."

"I didn't mean her," Evaline said. "I meant *you*. I would like Molly to stay and help me dress."

She could tell Aunt Bella was more than a bit perturbed. "What? Well, who's the note from, then?"

"It's a private matter," Evaline explained. "Now, if you'd please, I need to change my attire."

"Fine, then," Aunt Bella grumbled. "But don't think I can't figure out what's going on here. I have a fair idea who that's from, and let me just remind you, my little hussy, have a care. So far you've got things in hand, but it only takes one moment of carelessness, and a fire goes out of control."

"I'll keep that in mind."

"Good. Get dressed for your meeting, then, Evaline," Bella said, giving the maid a sharp glance as if to warn her of something, then glaring back at Evaline. "And do try to look respectable. What you do is hardly as important as how you present yourself, at least if a man is to consider marrying you. Don't lose sight of our goal, my dear."

Good grief. "Yes, Aunt Bella."

There was obviously more her aunt would have liked to say, but with another quick look at the maid and a longer, lustful glance at the note crumpled in Evaline's hand, Bella let herself out of the room. Finally. Evaline breathed a sigh of relief.

"You wish to change clothes, miss?" the maid asked when they were alone.

"Yes," Evaline said and went to peer out the window into the gray morning. At least it wasn't raining right now. "I'll need something for outdoors. My gray walking dress, perhaps."

The little maid hid her surprise. "All right, miss. Let's see what we can find to keep you warm out there on a wet day like this."

Evaline had to smile. It wasn't as if she had much to choose from, yet the maid very politely didn't point that out. Despite Dashford's apparent dissipation, he still managed a more than competent staff here at Hartwood. Good thing he'd be marrying Claudia soon. She'd no doubt see to it things kept running smoothly in this fine house.

"Thank you, Molly," Evaline said, then turned back to her. "And would you by any chance know the way to something called a boating grotto?"

The maid frowned. "The boating grotto? You're not planning on heading down there, are you, miss? No one's used that place in years."

Really? Not in years? Well, that was just perfect, then.

DASHFORD WAS ALONE IN HIS STUDY, DRUMMING his fingers on his desk and mentally berating himself for giving in to convention and not throwing Bristol out. Bother, the way the man had practically devoured Evaline with his eyes, it was clear keeping him away from her was not going to be an easy task. And blast it all, but the girl had actually blushed under the man's attentions!

Damn, the two of them were made for each other: immoral libertines, both of them. He ought to be thrilled that Bristol was here to take Evaline off his hands when she could so easily cause him so much scandal. Hell, wasn't this the best thing that could have happened? No, damn it, it wasn't. He'd rot in hell before he'd let Bristol anywhere near Evaline. Not until he was done with her, at least.

But he would be done with her at some point, of course. True, he couldn't quite imagine it now, but that was just his frustrated lust speaking for him. This ridiculous obsession was merely the result of unfulfillment. Once he'd found a way to get her alone long enough to sate the burning desire, she'd be just like Madeline or any other whore he'd taken on in the last two years. There was nothing truly unique about Evaline.

Indeed, she was like countless others, and from what he'd seen so far, she didn't view him as anyone special, either. Hell, he and Bristol were probably just two on a long list of men she'd welcomed into her life and into her bed. This would all be over and done with in no time. Then Dashford would only have to concentrate on ridding himself of Claudia to get his life back. Finally.

Perhaps he would even considering marrying someone of his own choosing at that point. That would certainly redeem him in his mother's eyes. And it would be nice to settle back into his life here at Hartwood with someone warm in his bed. Someone who hadn't drunk herself into a stupor, of course. Although, it was hard to imagine bringing anyone there who was not Evaline.

Damn, what was wrong with him? He'd had only a taste of Evaline, and now he couldn't get her out of his head. He'd had a taste, and he wanted more. He wanted the full meal. Well, then he was just going to have to get it.

He'd have to find her and arrange to get her alone with him. Soon. Far away from any interruptions or distractions. Now that they were all trapped here—thanks to the damned bridge he should have tended to a year ago—he was just going to find a way to make the best of it. He was going to enjoy Evaline at every possible moment.

But how? And where? The house was full to capacity. They'd been nearly found out several times already; he doubted their luck would hold much longer. Certainly the library was too public an area, and with the house brimming with curious guests, he couldn't just bring her to his bed. Indeed, they'd been remarkably lucky so far, and he knew better than to push it. But what else was there?

He needed to find a place—somewhere they could be alone that he could count on to be private. Surely in all of Hartwood he could think of someplace they might be able to . . . ah, then it hit him. Father's boating grotto! Of course. The place was out of use. The roof leaked, so no one would think to go there. It was set off from the house and gardens, down near the lake. And it was fully furnished.

By God, it was perfect! He'd take Evaline there. Indeed, he would; he'd take her, and take her and take her until finally the desperate hold she had over him was gone, and he could think straight again. Perhaps even this afternoon he could find a way to contact her and get her to agree. Of course she'd agree. She wanted him as badly as he wanted her; that much he knew for certain.

That settled in his mind, he closed his ledger books and decided he'd head down to the lake right now. There might be a few things they'd need to add to the grotto for their comfort, so he'd best go look the place over and make preparations. Everything would be just perfect for them there. This affair might be short-lived, but he'd make sure Evaline never forgot about it.

His planning session was interrupted by a knock on his study door. What now?

"Come in," he growled.

To his surprise, that icy Aunt Bella came in. Oh hell. Whatever could she want with him? Probably to set a date for his blasted marriage to her niece. The woman's ambitions were easy to guess.

"Yes?" he asked. "Can I help you?"

"Perhaps, my lord," she said—no, purred. Indeed, Bella's ambitions were blatant. "Perhaps we can help each other."

He was fairly certain anything he needed help with would not require her involvement. He didn't ask her to sit or to go on with her suggestion, but she did anyway.

"I've heard of your financial difficulties," she said bluntly. "They say you're living well into dun territory."

"So I've heard."

"And you know, of course, that Evaline will inherit her father's vast fortune as soon as she is married."

"Yes, I've heard that, too."

"Her fortune makes Miss Graeley's look like a pittance, my lord."

"Is that so?"

"And forgive me for saying, but I've detected some coolness in you where Miss Graeley is concerned. Am I safe in saying you are not exactly eager to make her your bride?"

He had to laugh. "Yes, you might be safe in saying that."

"But I have also detected your feelings are a bit, shall we say, warmer regarding Evaline. Isn't that so?" Bella said, smiling sweetly.

"You are most perceptive, Mrs. Stump," he said, although he was sure only a blind lamp stand could have missed the way he'd been watching Evaline of late. "But what are you suggesting? You know, of course, I'm a man of honor. I cannot simply detach myself from Miss Graeley."

"Pish. You are a peer, and you can do as you please; everyone knows that. No doubt Sir Victor can be persuaded to let you out of your agreement. If you are married to Evaline, after all, money would be no object. How much do you suppose Sir Victor would require?"

"It's as easy as all that?"

"It is, my lord."

He pretended to contemplate her words. "But I'm sure you heard as well as I what Miss Pinchley thinks of the idea of marrying me. How can I be sure she'll agree to your plan?"

Bella clucked her tongue. "You know that was purely for show. Don't think I'm unaware of what has transpired already, my lord. I could, after all, call you to account for it. You invited us here under false pretenses. Shame on you for leading an innocent girl to believe you had honorable intentions, then seducing her under our noses—it could cause untold difficulties if this were to become public information."

"Now I've seduced an innocent girl, have I?"

"Of course. As innocent as the driven snow, my lord. And just how will Miss Graeley take to that? It seems to me she's come very close to breaking your engagement already. Another indiscretion will not likely bring her to the altar more quickly. Indeed, you could find yourself without prospect of a wealthy fiancée. What do you suppose your creditors will do about that?"

"I see. So it appears either way I must marry your niece."

"It does appear that way, doesn't it?"

"So what is the bargain to be? How long will you give me to extricate myself from my current engagement before you start slandering Evaline?"

"Two days."

"Two days?"

This caught him off guard. Good Lord, he had no honorable intentions toward Evaline, but still he had no wish to see her so badly used by her aunt. Evaline might be a trollop head to toe, but the whole world didn't need to know about it. He'd have to find some way to get Bella Stump to keep quiet about this, for Evaline's sake.

"All right. But I may need more than two days."

"Then you may begin to hear some very unpleasant things being whispered about your future wife, my lord."

"Take care, woman. I don't like to be bullied."

"You also won't want everyone to hear just what sort of bride the great Viscount Dashford is being forced to take just to save his hide. Don't think I'm not aware of how desperate things are. Why, word is you're in pretty deep with some rather unpleasant folks. Folks who wouldn't mind taking their payment in flesh, if you know what I mean."

He knew exactly what she meant. He'd concocted those bloody rumors himself. But he'd never thought they'd be used against him this way, with Evaline as the victim of it. Damn this Bella Stump and her devious mind.

"You just keep silent about Evaline," he said through clenched teeth. "There may yet be a few things you don't know, Mrs. Stump. Let me deal with this my way. Evaline's reputation is not to be damaged. When it comes down to it, I will contact her uncle, and things will be handled in the proper fashion."

"I am her guardian, my lord, and it's up to me to decide what's best for her."

"Oh? And what of Mr. Stump? Surely we will need to wait for the roads to clear before he can be contacted to give his consent."

"He's indisposed, my lord."

"Oh. Of course." He had a fair idea what sort of "indisposed" Troy Stump was. The sort that left him with empty pockets, a throbbing head, and little concern for the niece he should be protecting. Damn them both. Poor Evaline never had a chance.

"But he would feel the same way as I," Bella said. "Evaline would make you a fine wife."

"Indeed. Then I have your word you'll do nothing to cause her insult?"

"Certainly, so long as you can find some other way to get out of your contractual obligations to Miss Graeley."

"Oh, you may trust me on that, Mrs. Stump," he said. Indeed, his morning with Sir Victor hadn't been entirely wasted. He'd found the man's weakness. He just wasn't sure he was ready to give in to his demands just yet.

"One other little thing, though," Bella said slowly.

This didn't bode well. "Oh? And what is that?"

"It's just that Evaline is very important to us. We've invested much into her future, you see."

"Invested? I thought Evaline's father left her the funds to see to her own future. How then, exactly, have you invested in her?"

"Oh, but we have! Evaline has relied on us for everything. Her money is unavailable. No one can so much as touch it until she is wed; not Evaline herself, not even her own flesh and blood relatives who have looked after her all these years."

Looked the other way was more like it. But if he'd already led her to believe he'd marry the girl, what was it Bella Stump could still want from him? Ah, most likely she needed assurance; some promise that once Evaline's bank account was opened, she and the "indisposed" Uncle Troy would not be forgotten.

"I take it you hope Evaline will be generous toward you, after all you've done for her. Is that right?"

Bella blinked innocently. "Let's just say, my lord, I recognize her husband will gain control of her money once she is legally wed. It is not my niece's generosity I worry about."

"Of course. You need reassurance then. And exactly what form will this reassurance need to take, Mrs. Stump? Is my word as a gentleman adequate?"

"But of course, my lord. And I'm sure you won't mind signing this document I've had drawn up." She pulled out a paper she'd had folded at the ready in her pocket.

Remarkably, it was indeed an official legal document. A bit dog-eared, probably from being carried around on her person for such a time as this, but very proper and official. He read it over twice before finally looking up at her.

"This grants a full half of her fortune to you!" he said in amazement.

"It promises that once you are married to her and take possession of her inheritance—which is more than adequate to pay off your debts twice over, my lord—you will immediately bestow a fair portion of it on her loving aunt and uncle who were so integral in bringing you two together."

It was half of all Evaline rightfully owned. Damn this scheming old crone! He shoved the paper back at her.

"Of course I'll never sign this."

"Then you'll never marry Evaline. She's still under age and requires our permission to wed."

He was silent for a moment, although it was difficult to contain a chuckle. So Evaline was right. Bella Stump was a bit confused about her niece's age. Plus, she was confused about his level of desperation to wed an heiress. Well, she was as foolish as she was coldhearted.

"Perhaps you wrongly estimate the urgency of my debt," he said.

"Or perhaps you do," she replied evenly. "With the type of creditors you have, that may not be healthy, my lord."

"Well, if this is the price of Evaline's hand in marriage, you may continue your hunt for a suitor. I'll not sign this, and I'll not marry Evaline!"

For half a heartbeat Bella looked shaken, but then a sly smile stole over her face. "You and Evaline are more than passing acquaintances. Don't forget: one word from me, and you'll lose Miss Graeley as well."

"Evaline and I will both call you a liar."

Bella merely shrugged. "Fine, then. Any husband is as good as the next; my brother's will never stated whom Evaline had to marry. Do you suppose I should approach Mr. Bristol, perhaps?"

"Hell no!"

Now Bella was smiling in full. Damn, why couldn't he simply keep his mouth shut?

"Why not?" she asked. "Evaline used to be quite taken with him. She still speaks very highly of him, as a matter of fact, despite the way he broke her heart. Now that he's lost his scrawny little wife birthing another of his brats, I daresay he'll be more than interested in Evaline. And half her fortune."

"I'll see to it he never signs your paper, either, Mrs. Stump."

"Oh? And just how will you do that? From what I hear, Bristol has developed expensive tastes over the years. You can't bend him to your will just by asking nicely, Dashford. It would take more blunt than you've got these days."

Well, she was right about Bristol's tastes, actually. The man was a veritable bottomless pit when it came to his monetary requirements. It had cost a fortune simply to convince Bristol all these rumors of Dashford's ruin and eminent demise were authentic. No doubt he'd easily sign away part of Evaline's fortune for a chance at half of it.

Blast, why was this getting so damned complicated? All Dashford wanted to do was get Evaline out into that boathouse and forget about such things as rumors and scheming aunts and randy Ellard Bristols. Was that so bloody much to ask for?

Apparently it was.

"But I'd much rather have her with you," Bella said. "Imagine my own dear niece a viscountess! Besides, I know that's what you really want, too. I've seen how you look at her."

"You have a lively imagination."

"Oh? Truly, I could have never imagined things to be as sordid as they are," Bella said with a sultry laugh. "Honestly, I never thought Evaline had it in her; she had me believing she was the sort to keep a man fully at arm's length until the wedding night. Obviously, though, I was wrong. Does she know how to please you, my lord? She likely learned that from Bristol; probably gave it up for him years ago. Funny thing is, I never suspected. He does seem to have fond memories of her, though, doesn't he? The way he was looking at her this morning . . ."

"I should warn you to hold your tongue."

"I wonder who else she's let bed her over the years," Bella went on. "I should have paid closer attention, I suppose. There was that young man I introduced her to at Christmastime, and several men before him . . . oh, I'm sorry. Does it pain you to realize how many have gone before you?"

No, but it pained him to keep from shaking the woman senseless and demanding she keep a civil tongue when speaking of her niece. Damn, if he were any sort of gentleman at all, he *would* marry Evaline, just to keep her away from her god-awful family. He almost said something about it right then and there, until he remembered what Bella did not know: Evaline was of age. She could never be forced to wed any of Bella's bought-and-paid-for suitors. He drew in a deep breath and tamped down his rage.

"I think you should leave my office now, Mrs. Stump."

"I will," Bella said. "As soon as you sign this document. Then we can go find Evaline and give her the good news."

"You're wasting your time. I'll never sign that thing."

"No signature, no Evaline. No Evaline, no inheritance. No inheritance, and you get a visit from a certain unsavory type with but one eye! Oh yes, I've heard about him, prowling around your London home, making terrible threats against you."

Now he did chuckle. Yes, hiring that particular gentleman had been a stroke of genius. Really, he was Mr. Tucker, a newly returned soldier whom Rastmoor took on to work in his London house. The man had such a hard look about him, it wasn't much of a stretch to believe him a desperate thug with criminal intent.

He'd made a couple of appearances at Dashford's London address and claimed to "have it in for 'is lordship." Set Dashford's butler into a state of apoplexy, he did, which was quite understandable, given the man's raw scars and gravel voice. Yes, they'd certainly gotten their money's worth out of Mr. Tucker's playacting. He seemed to enjoy himself with it, too. Promised to be on hand anytime they needed an encore performance.

"So, you know about that?" he asked, struggling to keep his voice low and ominous. With luck, Claudia knew about it, too. That ought to help scare her off.

"Yes. And we all know how you've squandered the family fortune on whores and filthy gaming hells."

"And horses, don't forget the horses, Mrs. Stump."

"I've heard all of it. Your life has become an orgy of wine and waste, and you're going to pay a high price for it if you don't sign this paper."

"No wonder you're so eager to marry your darling niece to a paragon like me."

She waved the paper at him again like a weapon. "You'll sign this if you know what's good for you . . . and for Evaline!"

Damn, but the woman's desperation was showing. Mr. Stump must have the family pretty deep in the hole for her to rail at him this way. Just what would happen to Evaline once Bella realized she'd lost her hold over her? Until the roads were clear and Evaline could escape, he'd best keep a close watch over her. Indeed, very, *very* close.

"Two days, Mrs. Stump," he said, deciding to let the woman cling to her hopes. "Give me two days to think. You ask a great deal, but as you've pointed out, my situation is rather bleak. I will endeavor to rid myself of Miss Gracley, and then I will consider your offer."

She didn't like it, but she capitulated. "All right. Two days. I'll bide my time, Dashford, but you know you cannot win. If you know what's good for you, you *will* sign this document—or I'll ruin you."

He *did* know what was good for him. He just wished he could think of a way to get some more of it without ending up married.

Chapter Nine

❧

"Thank you, Molly," Evaline said, smoothing her gown and taking a quick glance in the mirror. "Are you certain the gray dress wouldn't be more fitting for the weather?"

"The gray dress would fit in a little too well, if you ask me," Molly said, then blushed. "Sorry. I don't mean to be disrespectful, but it's a shame such a pretty young woman like you has to go around in these."

Evaline had to agree. Indeed, her clothes were terrible. Usually she didn't mind, since the last thing she wanted was to encourage any of Aunt Bella's suggested beaux by looking the least bit presentable. Not that it ever seemed to matter to them. No, the men Aunt Bella introduced her to couldn't have cared less what she wore and how she looked. They had all only ever cared about Papa's money.

But that was in the past. Things were different now. Everything was different—she was different, and she would have truly loved to be wearing different clothing. But, alas, she was trapped here with the same old clothes she'd been wearing for years. Uncle Troy's credit was worthless, so fabric and seamstresses were a luxury they hadn't enjoyed for a while. Molly had sensibly talked her out of the gray and into a somewhat less threadbare morning gown. The fabric would be adequate for walking, so long as it didn't rain again, and at least this gown was in a cheerier color than the others Evaline had worn the last couple of days. Instead of gray, or a dead, earthen brown, this one was decidedly beige.

Aunt Bella always told people it was Evaline's choice to stay in half mourning for the seven years since her father's death. Apparently she thought it enhanced her image of a sad, grieving heiress, desperate for some man to come and sweep her off her feet. Well, until very recently Evaline had been convinced such a man couldn't exist. She'd been proven wrong, though, and now she truly wished there was something other than gray and beige in her wardrobe.

"Well, when you've come into that fortune, you'll have a whole wardrobe of dresses to choose from, won't you?" Molly said, obviously understanding Evaline's sighs. "And so pretty you'll look! I'll bet that's the first thing his lordship does for you: dress you in silk and the finest continental fashion. They say he does like a woman who looks her best."

Heavens, what was this? "But Lord Dashford and I aren't . . . that is, I'm not his kept woman!"

Molly laughed and plunked Evaline down in the chair at the dressing table to start combing her hair. "No, of course not, miss! I was talking about when you're married to him."

"Oh, when I'm . . . what, married to him? No, I'm not marrying him!"

"Well, if it's not you, it's that horrible Miss Graeley," Molly said. "Forgive me for saying so, miss, but she's no good for him. Tricked him into offering for her in the first place, she did."

"What?" Evaline couldn't help but ask. "How?" Not that she was really interested, of course.

"Oh, he was in a bad way after his father died, miss," Molly explained, combing Evaline's honey-colored hair into long strands, then sweeping them up into miraculous curls that would be doomed the minute she went out into the damp. "Miss Graeley came around, acting his friend and making sure she was included in everything he did. Comforting him, she said. Well, one day I heard word the two of them had been caught alone together, in a compromising position, no less. Next thing I know, the engagement's announced, and his lordship runs off to London."

"Oh." So Dashford had been in a compromising position with Claudia, too. Well, Evaline supposed she should have expected that. Claudia was as beautiful as she was annoying. Dashford wasn't the type to ignore any woman who made herself available, and clearly, Claudia had. She should be glad Claudia was there first, or perhaps she would be the one forced into an engagement right now.

"You don't need to go to extra effort," Evaline said as Molly worked over her hair. "I'm merely going out for a walk, after all. Just to stretch my legs."

"Nonsense. You want to look your best, don't you? Might run into his lordship." Molly winked.

She'd made it obvious she thought the note Evaline received had come from Dashford. Evaline hadn't corrected her. Well, she couldn't very well tell her she was secretly meeting with her business agent and plotting an effort to get her hands on Dashford property that, by rights, should have come to her when her grandmother the courtesan passed away, could she? No, that aspect of their dealings needed to be kept strictly confidential.

"Ah, you look lovely, miss," Molly said. "Now, let me just weave a bit of ribbon in here and there, and you'll be done."

Evaline had to admit that she did look nice. She also had to admit that she did wish she might run across Dashford. Would he notice the improved hairstyle?

"I heard tell," Molly said, her voice dropping conspiratorially, "from one of the girls who's come in service to Mrs. Quinley-Pierce that Miss Graeley was seen at several balls in London during the Christmas holidays. They say she encouraged attention from several prominent gentlemen, not at all behaving like a young woman engaged to be married."

"Really?" Evaline said. Drat, she shouldn't encourage this sort of gossip, but again, she couldn't help herself.

"And his lordship never once made an appearance at any of the same parties she attended," Molly said. "His valet told the cook who told the housekeeper he was busy after other pursuits, if you know what that means. And it's common knowledge Miss Graeley disapproves of his lordship's lifestyle, so I say it's just a matter of time before she throws him over."

Evaline supposed this was told to encourage her, but it didn't. What did she care whether Dashford married or not? Except that she had heard he might be in grave danger if he did not. Aunt Bella told her wild stories of creditors hiring thugs to threaten his lordship. Could they be true? So far, Dashford himself had never denied these rumors, and clearly Lady Dashford was quite full of concern. If Dashford did not marry Claudia—or someone with a fortune—and soon, he'd be in a world of trouble.

"What will he do if Claudia breaks the engagement?" Evaline couldn't help but ask. "Are things as desperate as they say?"

The maid's voice dropped another notch lower. "Worse, I fear. Deanie, the parlor maid, says John Coachman told her he heard just awful things when last he drove his lordship to town. Things about how he hasn't paid his creditors for a while. And one day a horrible, big brute of a man with only one eye showed up at the door of the London house, claiming he was owed a huge sum, and if he didn't get paid soon, then bad things would happen."

"Bad things?"

"Oh, miss, the worst kind of bad things! If his lordship has crossed the wrong people there with his wild ways and silver tongue, we can be sure he'll pay dearly. With life and limb, even. And there's no heir to his estate, so no telling what's going to happen to us all. It's got the whole house full of worry, I must say."

"But what of valuables, things he could sell? The estate here looks absolutely intact."

Molly shrugged. "I don't know, but they say things are desperate. Why, he even had to give up his fancy French mistress."

"Mistress? He's got a mistress?"

Molly sucked in her breath. "Oh, er, I mean he did. He used to, though they say he can't afford any of them anymore, not the Frenchie or the ballerinas or any of them."

Evaline cringed. Ballerinas? No, she was not going to ask about this. She didn't care what Lord Dashford did with ballerinas or mademoiselles or fishwives, for that matter. It meant nothing to her.

"A lot of mistresses?" Oh bother. Why couldn't she just keep her mouth shut?

Molly didn't seem to mind the question, though. Her eyes got bright with secrets, and her voice dropped even lower. "So they say, though he's never brought any of them here. Keeps them all in London, high in style, you see. At least, he used to."

Well, if Dashford had to give up his mistresses, she supposed that ought to be proof enough things were bad. So bad his very life was at stake? She hated to think it.

Molly blushed. "You can see, miss, why we are all hoping things move in the right direction between you and his lordship. It would be so good to see everyone around here happy again."

"I'm sure it would." She didn't know what else to say. She hated to think of beautiful Hartwood auctioned down to an empty shell, and poor Lady Dashford's face bore worry lines that had not been there when first they met in Bath last year. Maybe Claudia wasn't the nicest sort, but something must be done to make sure she married Dashford before it was too late. Evaline vowed to do all in her power to smooth things between the two of them for the rest of her stay here.

"There, miss. You're as pretty as a picture," Molly said, stepping back to admire Evaline from another angle. "If you should happen to run across his lordship while you're out walking today, I promise he'll be too busy staring at you to so much as notice the sun's come out at last."

Drat it all, Evaline knew she should not, but she hoped Molly was right.

DASHFORD FROWNED AT THE SUNSHINE. DAMN, but the weather had broken. If this kept up, the roads would dry, and Evaline would find a way across that blasted river. Well, of course it wasn't as if he wished her to stay. No, that would mean no end of troubles—for both of them. Claudia would continue to dig in her heels if she felt there were a rival, Bristol would make an absolute ass of himself, and that banshee of an aunt would find some way to destroy every shred of reputation Evaline had managed to hang onto. He really ought to welcome the sun and do all in his power to help Evaline escape it all.

And he would. Just as soon as he'd gotten the woman alone and made love to her until they both begged for mercy. Then he'd have her out of his system, and no doubt he'd be glad to let her go. But not a moment sooner.

He made his way through the rose garden and onto the pathway that wound through a grove of trees toward the lake. It was a quiet path and out of view from the house. The boating grotto sat several hundred yards farther still, out of the way and completely alone. It was perfect for what he had planned.

His boots rang a dull thud as he crossed the old wooden bridge that led across a swollen stream that was generally nothing more than a trickle. The grotto was just up around the next bend, still out of view. The trees were thick, and the underbrush was left to grow in its natural state here along the bank of the lake. The light around had a green hue, and he could smell the damp earth. It made him think of all the damp, earthy things he was going to do to Evaline when he got her alone out here.

But he wasn't alone. All of a sudden he was aware of the rustle of footsteps nearby. The rustle of clothing, too—women's skirts, actually. His senses pricked to alert, and he pushed aside the heavily budded branch of a young willow. Evaline? Had she anticipated his plans? A female form moved toward him from up ahead.

It was Claudia. Damn, what in God's name was she doing out here? She saw him and smiled.

"Dashy! Why, how clever of you to find me out here!"

"What are you doing here, Claudia?" he said, not quite able to find it in himself to be charming.

"Here?" she asked quickly. "Oh, I'm just enjoying the dry weather for a change. Isn't it delightful to see the sun again?"

"We're in the woods. You can't see the sun from here."

"I've always loved nature, Dashy, you know that," she said, overly bright. "But come, I'm tired of the damp. You can walk me back up to the house now."

Well, he supposed he'd have to. There was no way he was about to be found alone with Claudia out here, or worse yet, let her follow him the rest of the way to the grotto! Good God, then he'd never get out of this damned engagement. He held out his arm for her.

"Come along, then," he said. "Let's get you back inside."

Claudia slipped her arm through his and glanced around. Damn, the baggage was probably hoping someone might come along to see them this way. Just one more nail in his matrimonial coffin. Thankfully, though, they were alone.

"You always were too kind to me, Dashy," she said, her whiny voice somewhat higher in pitch and volume than usual. "No one has ever treated me as well as you do."

Obviously everyone else was far more intelligent than he was, then.

Hellfire, how was he going to get rid of her? His jaw ached from clenching it. But Claudia didn't seem to notice and merely walked slowly along with him, smiling as if her life was perfect. She giggled, in fact.

"Oh, Dashy! You are quite impossible," she said, though for the life of him he couldn't see how he'd given her any reason to think that.

He was going to comment on this, but she let out another ripple of laughter, loud and echoing through the misty grove. What was this about? He glanced at her, quickly assessing her pale skin and the slightly wild gleam in her eye. Something went tight in the pit of his stomach. More was going on inside Claudia's little brain than he knew, and that could only be bad for him.

"I've come to a decision, Dashy," she said, her voice so loud now it would easily be called shrill. "I'm going to forgive you for your lapses in judgment, and I'm going to ask Papa to arrange for us to be married right away. Within the month, as a matter of fact."

He stopped walking and just stared. "Within the month?"

Another one of those disturbing giggles and she clung to his arm. "Wait, Dashy! Please, you're so impetuous! Surely you can wait a few more weeks."

Now his mouth dropped open. Good God, he was not marrying Claudia in a few weeks! Hell, that's what had Sir Victor all stirred up and irritated. He'd tried to push the wedding, but Dashford had managed to hold him off, claiming it was clear that Claudia had not entirely made up her mind if she was certain she still wanted to marry him. Now, it seemed, she had. Blast it all; this was enough to ruin a man's day.

"Come, Dashy, let's go tell your mother the good news," Claudia said, fairly dragging him along the path.

It was as if his life passed before his eyes. All the appalling, deceitful, immoral—though often quite entertaining—things he'd done these past two years were for naught. Claudia had at last made up her mind, and now he would have to marry her or live with the consequences. Unless, of course, Sir Victor chose to call him out over this and shoot him dead on a field of honor. In that case, he would unfortunately *not* be living with the consequences. All things considered, though, he supposed that would still be preferable to being married to Claudia.

They approached the rose garden, and he realized Claudia's footsteps had increased their pace, but her conversation had stopped. She had a strange, wooden expression on her face, and as they stepped into the sunshine, her hand dropped from his arm.

"Shall we speak with your mother together, or do you wish to tell her the happy news alone?" she asked, though the word "happy" sounded odd coming from a face that appeared so absolutely not.

"I think perhaps I should speak with your father first. There are, no doubt, some matters we will need to straighten out," he said, embarrassed that he didn't have the courage to mention that one of the "matters" to be straightened out was the fact he would not be marrying her.

She nodded but didn't look at him. "All right. You speak to Father, and then we'll proceed. But be sure to inform him that I wish to be married without delay. I have adequate wardrobe with me, and surely in three weeks' time we'll find some way to row across to the chapel or something."

What? Oh hell. If Claudia was prepared to be married without even ordering a new gown, it was obvious her mind was set. Damn damn damn. This was going to be problematic, for certain.

Without so much as a glance at him, Claudia led the way

into the house. Dashford could merely stand back and hold the door for her as she swept by. As a condemned man might give his cell one last look before being led to the gallows, he turned and surveyed the rose garden. Surprisingly, a movement off to the side caught his eye.

Evaline. There she was, strolling leisurely through the flowers, wisps of honey gold hair escaping her wilted bonnet and glistening in the sun. Was it a new hairstyle? Since that first morning, she'd been wearing it so tight to her head as to be obscured by a bonnet. And the gown she wore was not the usual brown or gray he'd come to expect but something that might at one time have been a pale yellow. God, she looked good to him.

But she hadn't seen him. She was lost in her own thoughts, apparently. He wondered if he occupied any of them. Not likely. Her leisurely pace picked up, and now he realized she wasn't merely meandering the garden but was headed in a definite direction. She was headed toward the path he and Claudia had so recently come from. Without a moment's hesitation, she left the rose garden and headed into the trees, following the path that would take her to the grotto.

Lord, but he'd like to go with her.

"My father's likely reading his papers," Claudia called to him from just inside the house.

Dashford dragged his mind away from Evaline long enough to comprehend her words. Damn, he still had Claudia to deal with. Rejecting the urge to slam the door in her face and run after Evaline, he stepped inside, as was expected. Blast all those years of training in civilized behavior.

"I think I'll retire to my room for a bit," Claudia said. "You may speak with Father now, and we'll all discuss this together later."

Her words were formal; her voice was cold. It was as if now that the matter had at last been settled, she and he were complete strangers. So, she thought she'd won, and now his torture would begin? Well, he was not about to let it be that simple.

"Fine," he said, and she appeared oblivious to the coolness in his own voice. "I'll speak with your father."

"Good. I'll be resting in my room," she said and turned on her heel. "Let's just get this over with."

Get this over with? What on earth was that supposed to mean? It was her blasted idea. Why was she so suddenly unmoved by her prospects? Lord, he never would understand women.

He bowed slightly out of habit, but she was already walking away with her back to him. So, just like that, she'd made up her mind, and now she wasn't even going to gloat or so much as smile about it? Unreal. Well, at least he didn't have to fear breaking the girl's heart when he threw her over. Obviously her heart was not a part of this transaction. Hell, Sir Victor was likely to be more upset than she, if this was any indication of her emotions.

Well, that was just fine with him. Sir Victor could whine and wail and make all manner of threats for all he cared. No sense precipitating such actions right away, though. There would be plenty of time for selecting seconds and choosing weapons. Right now, Claudia had left him alone, and Evaline was on her way to the boating grotto. Sir Victor could wait. Dashford had something better to do.

SO THIS WAS THE BOATING GROTTO, WAS IT? Evaline ordered her nerves to calm as she stood outside the door. Well, not a bad place for a private meeting. Fortunately, the rain had gone. It was still chilly, though. Or was that simply her nerves? Indeed, this was a big step for her. Mr. Carrington held her future in his hands. Hopefully he had some much-needed money in them, too.

Holding herself with as much confidence as possible, she slowly pushed the door open. The little grotto was small and built into the side of a hill where the landscape was allowed to grow thick and wild. The air indoors was musty and damp. Clearly the place was long out of use, just as Molly had said. Good. She wouldn't have to worry about their meeting being discovered.

Inside the grotto was a large open space. The door opened

through a little niche in the side, where the structure was built right into the side of the hill. The whole front of the building was lined with windows, so green-tinted light filtered in and made the interior nearly as bright as the forest outside. Evaline's eyes had to do very little adjusting before she could notice the lone gentleman in the room: Mr. Carrington. He was standing at the far end, staring out the window, and hadn't noticed her. She cleared her throat.

He looked up, blinking a bit, and seemed truly surprised to see her. Hadn't he sent her the note? Yes, in half a second the blank expression on his face was replaced by the coolness she'd seen earlier. Indeed, Mr. Carrington was all business.

"Miss Pinchley," he said, moving toward her.

"Nice to meet you, Mr. Carrington," she replied awkwardly. "Thank you for offering to meet with me."

He looked around and pointed to a nearby table with chairs pulled up to it. Apparently the boating grotto had once been a place for al fresco dining and general relaxation. Aside from this small round table and its accompanying seats, the room held several other chairs and even a settee or two. Pity it was no longer in use; such a lovely view of the lake it provided, and it would, no doubt, be most comfortably cool even on the warmest of summer days. Evaline went to the round table he indicated and brushed away the dust.

"Sorry," he said. "Apparently this little building is not currently in use by the family."

"Well, I don't mind a bit of dust," she said, slipping her bonnet off and using the dilapidated thing to chase away a spider.

She seated herself gingerly on a creaking chair. It was obvious Mr. Carrington was uncomfortable in his surroundings, but she couldn't let herself worry about it. Right now they had business to tend to.

He grabbed up a leather case that sat against one of the chairs, and carefully he laid it upon the table. He took the chair opposite her and sat, opening the case slowly. Odd, were his hands shaking a bit as he worked the clasps? Well, likely that was due to the damp and the cold air. Everything else about him seemed perfectly collected.

He was much younger than she would have imagined, though. He was perhaps only a year or two older than she, in fact. That was surprising. Then again, it could be this was another generation of Carringtons than the one who her father had worked with. This must be Papa's agent's son, or something. That made sense. As long as he had what she needed and would carry out her plans, she didn't care how many generations junior he was.

As she watched, Mr. Carrington laid out several papers in front of her. Most particularly, he laid out a pile of bank-notes. Actual currency! Good heavens, there must be a hundred pounds there. Was this hers? Hallelujah! She had to put her hands to her mouth to keep from breaking into girlish giggles.

"I wasn't certain how much you would require for your immediate expenses," he said. "But I thought it better to err on the side of caution. One never likes to travel with so much cash—you being a young lady on your own, and all—so I decided this amount would have to suffice."

She had no idea what amount of cash would or would not suffice for a young lady on her own, but she didn't really care. All she knew was that the pile of bills on the table now looked like a king's ransom to her.

"Thank you, Mr. Carrington. This looks quite satisfactory."

"Fine. Perhaps you'd like to put it someplace safe?"

He waited. At first she just stared at him. Someplace safe? Wasn't that what he was supposed to be doing? Oh, but this was her money! He expected her to take it.

But she was afraid to touch it. She'd dreamed of this for so long, and now that the day was finally here, she hadn't the slightest idea what to do. What did one do with such a sizable fortune? Well, he obviously expected her to do something with it. She took it into her hands.

Ah, it felt heavenly. She touched it gingerly, thumbed through it, and let the bills blow a tiny breeze into her face. She smelled it. God, she'd waited for this a long time. If Carrington hadn't been staring at her with a rather dazed expression, she would have rubbed the pile against her lips, just because she could.

But he was staring and he was dazed and he was waiting for her to put it someplace safe. But where on earth was that? She hadn't any reticule or purse with her, and this gown was not equipped with pockets. Well, there was just one other place. Indeed, she'd see to it the money was safe there. She turned her back on Carrington and tucked the bills safely into her bodice. Yes, she would see to it they would be untouched there. Even if Dashford came around. Darn it.

She turned back to Carrington. He still had that dazed look. Whatever was wrong with the man? Was he sweating now? The poor thing. Perhaps he'd taken a chill in all that rain.

"Are you ill?" she asked.

He seemed to snap out of it. "What? Er, no, thank you. I'm fine. Now, if you'd just look at these papers here, they will line out some of the ways your father instructed us to invest his money . . . your money, that is. How much are you aware of your father's finances, Miss Pinchley?"

She glanced at the papers he pushed toward her. She had to admit most of the figures there were meaningless to her; it had been so long since she'd had opportunity to look at such things. Papa had done much to educate her with figures and sums, yet he'd always claimed his efforts a failure. She seemed to grasp the greater concepts of supply and demand and general commerce, but the mathematics of accounting were lost on her.

Then again, she'd never had reason to care about such things. Now that Papa was gone and this was hers, she would simply have to relearn. Given time, she had no doubt this would all become clear.

"Thank you, Mr. Carrington," she said, hoping he wouldn't recognize her confusion. "Papa shared quite liberally with me his knowledge of finances." She carefully didn't mention her lack of appreciation for what had been shared.

"Then, no doubt, you'd like to discuss these with me?" he asked, referring to the incomprehensible pages laid out before them.

"Of course, yes," she said, knowing this was the right answer. "I'll definitely want to discuss it all . . . after I've had time to go over these in detail. If that is all right with you."

"Yes, that's quite all right," he answered quickly.

"Wonderful. And would you be so kind as to have them sent quietly up to my room for me? I fear I have nothing to carry them in at the moment." And the place she might inconspicuously tuck them was currently in use.

"Of course, Miss Pinchley," he said quite confidently. "I will see to that as soon as is convenient."

What an efficient agent. And how pleasant that he treated her as an intelligent human and not some silly female who couldn't be bothered with such things as her own finances. Perhaps, despite his stuffy demeanor and nervous behavior, she and Mr. Carrington would work well together. She certainly hoped so. It was a bit daunting to think of entering into this new phase of her life without someone she could trust.

"Now this document gives some of the essentials regarding that certain real estate transfer you had inquired about," he said, choosing one paper in particular.

His glance darted around the room in a too-obvious effort to make sure they were still alone here. As if someone might be lurking around a corner out here! Well, she'd warned him to be secretive about the purchase of Grandmamma's property. She supposed he was just trying to follow instructions.

"Good. I was hoping we could discuss that," she said, trying to make heads or tails of the document.

The price listed there was what had been initially disclosed, and everything seemed to be in order. Lord Dashford, it appeared, was more than eager to sell without delay. Good. Just one thing she needed to be certain of.

"Lord Dashford will certainly profit from this transaction, won't he?" Evaline said and felt a sort of pride at being able to help the man.

Mr. Carrington frowned. "A bit, I suppose. Do you feel the price is still too high?"

"I don't know. Do you? I'd rather not waste time with lengthy negotiations," she said and realized that she really didn't mind paying more than she ought if it would be of benefit to Dashford.

"It is priced higher than one might expect, given the state of the property."

"You've been there? Is it so very ruined?" She couldn't bear to think of Grandmamma's lovely home crumbling from neglect.

"Are you so very certain this is the property you want, Miss Pinchley?" he asked. "There are many others in the shire that could be had for considerably less."

"No, I want this one," she said defiantly. "Please continue with the deal as soon as is possible. It's very important to me."

"I'll do what I can, Miss Pinchley. And as requested, I'll see to keeping your name out of it."

"Thank you, Mr. Carrington. And I appreciate your efforts since you've arrived here to keep our relationship undisclosed."

"Of course. I understood that to be of high priority."

"It is. I can't stress enough how important it is that no one learns of it, especially my aunt. I hate to require you to keep such secrets, but I do hope you'll humor me."

"Of course, Miss Pinchley. I understand."

"Excellent. Now, what will be our next step? With the roads swamped and the bridge out, is there any way we can continue our transaction?"

He nodded. "I believe so. I've learned her ladyship retains a solicitor who lives nearby. It turns out he is just this side of the river."

"Her ladyship retains a solicitor?"

"Of course. It is, after all, her property."

"*Her* property? I thought it was a part of the Dashford estate."

He shook his head. "No, this is separate. There are some abnormalities to the deed, and I don't quite understand it, but when the previous resident died, there was a stipulation the property be granted not to the blood heirs but to Lady Dashford."

This was news to Evaline. Why on earth would the old viscount have done that? All those years Grandmamma had talked about the property as if she owned it in fee simple. It was her hope that someday her younger daughter and little Sophie would inherit. Did the ancient Lord Dashford deceive Grandmamma while she spent her life in scandalized exile for her love for him? Oh, but what an insult to the woman's faithfulness!

All this time since Grandmamma's death, she'd thought the son of Grandmamma's Dashford had manipulated the property back into his estate. When she met Lady Dashford in Bath last year, it nearly killed her not to ask about it and find out exactly how Grandmamma's final days had been spent. Now to find out that all along Grandmamma's lover had deceived her about his grand gift—well, it was just unfair. Damn these Dashford men and their irresistible charm!

"Miss Pinchley?" the agent was asking. "Is there something troubling you?"

"No, it's just that I was unaware Lady Dashford was the current owner. I'd been told the property was not part of any entailment and that the previous Lord Dashford deeded it as a gift."

"Yes, that was in the original deed, I believe."

"Original deed?" There was more than one?

"Yes. Some years ago another was drawn up, transferring ownership, I believe."

"I was under the impression an older woman remained the owner until her death?" Evaline questioned. Oh, but this was confusing! What on earth had happened here during those years after Mamma's death when Papa no longer allowed her to visit? Poor, poor Grandmamma.

"I'm sorry, Miss Pinchley. I do not have a copy of the deed to look at, and I'm not familiar with it enough to give you the specifics. Perhaps this is not the property you are interested in, after all. Shall I ask the solicitor if there are other properties around that . . ."

"No! No, please, Mr. Carrington. If you would be so kind as to find out the particulars on this deed and how it affected the previous resident, I would be so very grateful. The property at the direction I gave you is, indeed, the property I want."

"All right, then. I'll see to meeting with the agent as early as later today, if I can manage it."

Relief flooded her. "Thank you, Mr. Carrington."

"Indeed. Lord Dashford has graciously given all his guests free use of his stable, so I will have no difficulty procuring a mount to ride out. It seems saddles are a bit hard to come by for some reason, but I shall manage. So long as the weather holds like this, I should have no difficulty."

"I appreciate it," she said. "The sooner this is accomplished, the better for everyone. Especially for that other matter I wrote you concerning. You haven't by any chance heard anything of that, have you?"

He took too long in answering. She knew what that must mean.

"No, I'm sorry," he said at last. "The man I hired has had no luck finding your cousin. He did, however, investigate that residence you asked about."

"He did?"

"It was, er, it was a rather infamous house of ill repute, I'm sorry to say."

Evaline sighed. So it was true. For the past four years little Sophie had been living in a brothel. Not that Evaline had ever truly doubted her cousin's letter, but she'd hoped that perhaps it had not been as bad as it sounded. By the look on Mr. Carrington's face, she knew it was. And now there was no telling how low the poor girl had sunk. If only Evaline had any clue what man Sophie had been going to work for!

She didn't, though. If Sophie had ever mentioned the man in a letter, Evaline had not gotten that letter. Nor any letter explaining about the baby and its possible father. Oh, if there was anything she could have done for the girl! Well, she was doing all she could now. Sophie had to be somewhere out there. Evaline wouldn't rest until she was found.

"If you don't mind, Miss Pinchley," Mr. Carrington said, checking his watch and reminding her they ought to get back to the house before anyone noticed their absence, "I just need your signature here to acknowledge you are in receipt of the two hundred pounds I brought you."

"Two hundred!" Her hands flew protectively to her bodice.

"It should all be there. Do you wish to count it?"

"No, I trust you, Mr. Carrington." She forced her hands back into her lap. Good heavens, two hundred pounds shoved unceremoniously into her bosom! She'd best sign the man's paper and get herself safely up to her room and find somewhere to stash this fortune. She read over the receipt and signed it for him.

"Here you are," she said, calming herself and sliding the paper toward him. "Is there anything else?"

"No, not in particular, it's just that . . ." He wouldn't meet her eyes and shifted uncomfortably in his seat.

"What is it, Mr. Carrington?"

"It's just that . . . I know you've made your intentions clear, but I would be remiss if I failed to advise you."

"Advise me of what?"

"Well, er, I feel it would be a waste of your resources to purchase this property just now, Miss Pinchley."

"What?" True, she hadn't explained everything about her cousin's dire circumstances or the reason for her interest in this particular, unimpressive little home, but surely he understood she was determined to make this purchase.

"Don't worry, Mr. Carrington," she said with appreciation. "I understand your concern, but I assure you even in its neglected state, I am quite determined to purchase this property."

"Really, Miss Pinchley, it's no business of mine why you should wish to purchase that dilapidated cottage, but are you not aware this property is intended to be given to Lord Dashford's bride upon his marriage? It is specifically written up in the deed this way."

No, she hadn't heard this, either. "You mean, even though Lady Dashford is now the owner, she doesn't have a clear title to it?"

"She does, although there was an understanding when the deed passed to her that it would someday be passed on to her future daughter-in-law when, of course, she might have one. Quite irregular."

"So despite all our efforts, she really cannot sell?" she asked.

"Certainly she can sell," Mr. Carrington said. "I just wonder why you wish her to sell it to you now when she already plans to give it to you when you wed her son."

"When I wed her son? Oh, Mr. Carrington, you're mistaken. Lord Dashford is engaged to marry Miss Graeley!"

Carrington sat up stiffly. "I assure you, Miss Graeley will not be marrying his lordship."

"What?"

"Trust me when I say Claudia Graeley will never be Lady Dashford."

"Oh? But how can you be sure? Miss Graeley seems so . . ."

"Miss Graeley is a spoiled child. Take my word for it; certain insurmountable obstacles have arisen, and that marriage will never take place."

He seemed so confident in his pronouncement. Well, Evaline had to admit she was inclined to believe him. Claudia *was* a spoiled child. Perhaps Carrington was right, and Dashford would not end up shackled to her. The thought made her unaccountably relieved, although, perhaps, it should not. Losing Claudia would leave Dashford with some very unsavory creditors and no source of fresh funding.

Then again, she was about to purchase Grandmamma's home for a very healthy sum, and Lady Dashford would no doubt use that money to defray her son's debt. Indeed, she'd have to convince Carrington not to negotiate too strenuously for a fair price.

"So you see, Miss Pinchley," he was saying, "Dashford will be free to marry you. If you wait just a bit, Lady Dashford will be giving you the property as a wedding present, free of charge. It would be a waste to purchase it for yourself now."

"And you'd lose a hefty commission. Fear not, Mr. Carrington, I'll not be marrying Dashford," Evaline assured him quickly. "I'll spend my money and gain ownership this way, if you don't mind."

This seemed hard for him to grasp. "Really? You aren't intent on marrying his lordship?"

"No, I am not."

"Well, no matter. It makes no difference. I simply thought it fair to tell you where things stood."

"And I thank you, but please do proceed with the transaction as planned. If, as you say, insurmountable obstacles have removed Miss Graeley from the picture, I have a feeling it will be a good long time before Dashford gets around to procuring the dowager a daughter-in-law."

Likely that was too true. Left to his own devices, Dashford would no doubt continue his dissipated bachelor lifestyle for years. At least, as long as he was able before the consequences caught up with him. Poor man, he was only prolonging the inevitable if he failed to snag his wealthy bride. Grandmamma's house was not so valuable as to save him from himself for long, unfortunately.

"Very well, Miss Pinchley," Carrington said, gathering his documents. "I will proceed as planned. As you don't want our acquaintance to be public knowledge, do you have any suggestion how we should arrange to meet for further discourse?"

She chewed her lip. Indeed, with everyone trapped here, it would pose a bit of a difficulty to continue clandestine meetings like this. "I don't know. I fear I hadn't quite worked that matter out when I set to planning things. Perhaps you should send a note, as you did today, and tell me when you have need to meet. This location seems ideal for such things."

"Indeed," he said, a bit doubtful. "Then that is what we shall do. I'll endeavor to meet with her ladyship's solicitor to arrange the sale then notify you as things have progressed. I'm afraid I cannot give you a fair estimate of when that might be, however."

"That's fine. I trust you will do your best."

He was fussing with the case, straightening papers, and far too involved to make eye contact with her. "Yes, of course."

The light in the grotto had lost a bit of its brightness, and Evaline glanced out the window. The lake rippled serenely outside, but the sky reflected in it was once again filling with clouds. They were in for yet more rain, it appeared.

"I think we'd best get back to the house," she said. "The rain's coming back."

"Hmm? Oh yes. Which direction did you come from?"

"By way of the rose garden. Is there another?"

"Yes, the path continues on then wraps back up around the other side of the house," Carrington replied. "I'll go that direction. We are less likely to be seen together."

"You'd best hurry, then, so you don't get wet," Evaline

encouraged, rising and going to peer out the door. "I'll wait until you are out of sight before I start out."

He was silent, shutting up his case and adjusting his coat. "Thank you for your time, Miss Pinchley," he said, moving to take her hand in a most businesslike manner. "I'll contact you when we can meet again."

She gave him a warm smile. "I shall be looking forward to it, Mr. Carrington."

Graciously he gave her hand a polite buss and then turned with his case and stepped out onto the path. His feet crunched softly in the damp earth, and he started off. His direction would take him past the front of the grotto and then around the corner, following the path up the hill and into the woods. He was out of sight quickly.

Good. She had no desire to linger out here alone with the spiders. She could dash back up the path now before the rain arrived. She patted her bodice and shifted things into a more comfortable position there. Then she smiled. Two hundred pounds! By God, things were looking up for her.

Oh, but she'd forgotten her bonnet. She stepped back into the little grotto and found it lying on the table, right where she'd left it. But now the light in the room dimmed, and she whirled around quickly to realize something—no, some-one—blocked the doorway. Surprised, she found herself looking up into Dashford's stormy eyes.

Chapter Ten

It *was* a new hairstyle. Dashford studied her. Indeed, the chit had forsaken the tight chignon she'd worn yesterday and at breakfast, and now her hair was pulled elegantly up into alluring loose curls. It was a perfect style for her small face, and she'd obviously gone to great lengths to improve her looks.

For damn Carrington, apparently.

Good God, Dashford had wanted to kill the man when he'd appeared in the grotto doorway beside Evaline. The way Evaline smiled at him, all innocent and grateful, and the way he took up her hand and kissed it. He said he would contact her about meeting again, and she claimed to be looking forward to it. Bah, it was disgusting.

Dashford saw Evaline's satisfied smile when the man sauntered away. And if that weren't enough, she had begun straightening her clothing, readjusting her bodice and patting herself here and there, and he knew. Evaline and Carrington had been out here for a blasted tryst, and Dashford's blood was boiling.

"Miss Pinchley," he said, managing to sound somewhat civil. "How unexpected to find you out here."

"Yes," she said, flustered, wringing her bonnet in her hands. "I came out for a walk to get some fresh air."

"Fresh air seems to agree with you," he said, letting his eyes roam over her and picturing all the decadent things she'd been letting Carrington do to her.

Blast, he should have stormed in here the moment he knew where Evaline was headed. He could have stopped them, but instead he'd taken his time and been cautious. Hell, he hated caution.

"Then again," he went on, taking two steps toward her, and she had the good sense to back away, "we both know a few other things that seem to agree with you, too. Perhaps that is what brings such a charming glow to your cheeks this morning?"

She seemed at a loss for words. Good. Talking wasn't really what Dashford had on his mind right now, anyway. She took another step back and put her hands up to her chest as if to protect herself.

"Modest are you now, my dear?" he said. "Since when have you adopted that characteristic? Does Carrington like it that way, you acting all missish and prim?"

Indeed, she was doing an excellent job of portraying the frightened innocent just now. He could almost believe she was terrified, except that he knew better. He'd felt her respond to his passion and knew hers ran every bit as deep and fiery as his. Choose pale and reticent Carrington over him, would she? In five minutes he could prove to her who was the better man.

"I wasn't with Mr. Carrington," she said, though her voice quavered.

His temper flared, and he ruthlessly tossed a chair that had inconveniently ended up between them. She jumped.

"Don't lie to me," he said, still advancing. "I saw you with him not half a minute ago."

"Yes, he was here, but I wasn't *with* him," she protested. "Not like you suggest!"

"Oh? Then how were you *with* him?"

"We were having a conversation. Not every man is quite the rutting animal you are, my lord," she said, her voice gaining a bit of its strength back.

He took another step toward her, but her back was against the wall. She couldn't move away. He smiled.

"Any living man who found himself out here alone with you would be, my pretty little vixen."

He leaned in toward her, one hand resting on the cold

brick wall beside her face and the other reaching slowly to tease the faded silk bow at her neckline. He watched her chest rise and fall with her accelerated breathing. He felt the gasp escape her when his finger slipped off the bow and brushed her skin. He recognized the fire burning in her eyes when he raised his own to meet them.

"Mr. Carrington and I are not this well acquainted, I assure you," she said softly.

"You mean he's not done this to you?" he asked, tracing the edge of her bodice, dragging his fingers slowly over her skin.

"No, he has not."

"How about this?" he asked, letting his fingers slide under the fabric and come perilously close to brushing the hardened nipple that puckered against her gown.

"Of course not."

"Or this?" he questioned, leaning over her to kiss the throbbing point at her neck where her blood flowed and pounded to the same cadence of his own pulse.

Her arms slipped up and enwrapped him. She sighed into his ear. "No, not this either."

"Good," he said, taking a break from kissing her to take her jaw in his hands and study her clear green eyes. "Until we are through, I have no intentions of sharing you. Is that clear?"

She just blinked up at him, and he didn't bother waiting for an answer. He took her lips with his and made sure she understood whose she was. For now.

EVALINE BREATHED DASHFORD. IT WAS AS IF HIS arms, his face, his lips were all she needed to live. How silly she'd been to think she could avoid this. She was helpless to stop it. Her ruin was complete, it seemed. Her course was dictated by her passions, and her passions were ruled by this man.

Oh, but what a lovely tyranny it was. What he did to her body! And when he claimed he had no intentions of sharing her . . . well, that undid her immediately. The very thought of belonging solely to this man—being the focus of his attentions and the ministration of his expert hands—it was enough to make her giddy.

But she wasn't giddy. She was perfectly aware of everything she did, every way her body responded to his. Determined not lose this moment, she ran her fingers through his thick hair to pull him closer, to kiss him harder. His lips pressed against hers, and her tongue danced over his. He groaned.

His arms went around her, pulling her away from the cold brick wall and more tightly against him. She felt his manhood grow taut against her. Icy heat burned through her, and she slid one hand down between them. She brushed against his trousers.

He groaned again, but this time his arms around her tightened like a vise. He hoisted her up and physically moved her two steps over to a dusty buffet table against the wall. None too gently, he set her there on her backside, his arms loosening just slightly and his kisses becoming more demanding. She grasped the fabric of his coat and pulled herself closer to him.

Her skirt slid dangerously up her burning thighs, and he pressed himself between her legs. She felt him hot against her, right where she wanted him. She was at exactly the right angle to take him in now, and she would. God, how she wanted him! Her legs wrapped around, and she reached to unfasten his trousers.

But he was reaching, too. This time she was the one to groan as he slid one hand down between them to stroke her moist flesh. She couldn't deny the sensations and could only lean into him, fighting back the waves of ecstasy that threatened to overtake her.

She was breathing in loud, ragged gasps, and there was not one ounce of modesty in her current position. But she didn't care. She found the fastenings on his trousers and could feel him there, separated from her only by these damn clothes. Her determined fumbling was hampered by her own reactions to his persistent touch, but finally she found success. The trousers were loosened, and she slipped her hand inside.

God, he felt enormous! She could have never imagined the heat. Lord, how smooth the skin was but how solid underneath. He shifted, and she felt him slide against her.

That simple motion produced a fresh wave of throbbing heat within her.

Amazing. So this is what she had forgotten the other night? It was impossible to imagine how. He gave a low growl and pressed himself against her hand. She wasn't entirely sure what to do next, but it seemed logical to take a good hold of the thing.

"God, I want you so bad," he murmured against her neck and sounded almost pained. "I think I'll die if someone comes in here and interrupts us again."

"Perhaps we'd better try to hurry then," she said.

By heavens, she knew she couldn't go on like this much longer. Likely she'd topple right off the buffet table if some form of release didn't come soon. She was rapidly losing all sense of time and place, lost in sensation as his hand caressed her and hers caressed him. It startled her when he spoke again.

"Stop," he said. "I'm going to embarrass myself."

"What?"

He gently pushed her hand aside and was finishing the job she'd started loosening the trouser fasteners. Oh my, but he was bringing the item out for display! She bit her lip and got up the courage to glance downward.

Oh my. Oh good gracious. There it was.

"It's beautiful," she said with far too much awe to be respectable.

He laughed. "You have a way with words, Miss Pinchley. Among other things. Now, come here."

He slid her toward him. Her breath caught in her throat. So she was finally going to have her moment to remember! Lord, but why was she so darn nervous? Perhaps because it had been dark the first time they'd done this, and she hadn't actually seen, er, *it*. Heavens, how on earth was it going to . . . But she lost track of coherent thought when he touched her again.

It was so warm! Indeed, this new implement was much warmer than his hands had been, stroking against her there. She pressed into him, wrapping her legs around to bring him closer. Still, he did not press back.

Instead, he merely teased her, rubbing slowly against her most sensitive part. It was the most delightful torture. But what did he want her to do? She still couldn't remember this, what they'd obviously done already. She would, however, have to start screaming in about a minute or two if something didn't happen. Whatever was building inside her was too strong. She buried her face against him and sank her teeth into the rough fabric of his coat.

He pressed lightly on her. The wonderful waves of emotion increased. He stroked her gently, but still she knew he had not entered. What was he waiting for? Couldn't he see she was falling apart around him? He pressed again, a bit more forceful now. She arched herself against him and felt the passions well up to overflowing. Just one more moment and he would be there, filling her and giving her everything she needed from him. She could barely breathe. Her lungs heaved in little gasps of air, and she did all she could to pull him into her.

But he had stopped. His hands went suddenly to her shoulders, and he held her away from himself. She blinked up at him for explanation.

"Someone's coming," he said, then amended with a smile. "Someone *else* is coming, I mean."

"WHAT THE HELL ARE YOU OUT HERE BELLOWING in the woods for?" Dashford asked, stepping out of the grotto and leaving a dazed and disappointed Evaline inside to put herself back together as best she could.

Rastmoor was twenty feet away, tossing stones into the lake, belting out some ridiculous tune they'd learned in school. And not from the prudish choirmaster, either.

"Oh, there you are, old man," he said, looking up. "Had no idea you were around."

"Like hell you didn't," Dashford growled. "I've got half a mind to pitch you into the lake and wait for the bubbles to stop."

"Tut tut. You really ought to be thanking me, you know. Saving you from yourself, and all that."

"I'm not in a very thankful mood right now, as you might guess."

"No, I suppose not. Entertaining in there, were you?"

"This is none of your business, Anthony."

"And it ought to be none of yours!" Rastmoor exclaimed,

tossing his last stone with particular force and stomping up the bank.

"I'll be the one to decide that for myself," Dashford said, positioning himself clearly between Rastmoor and the grotto.

"She's trouble for you, Dash. I don't know what, but she's up to something," Rastmoor said with assurance. "Carrington sent her a note this morning. Did you know that?"

No, he didn't. Damn. So she'd lied to him after all. She *had* been with Carrington. Damn the pretentious little bastard to hell.

"I guess you didn't. I've met Carrington, Dash," Rastmoor went on, having to stand there on the sloping bank with one knee bent because Dashford refused to step out of the way. "I met him in London over the winter, at a couple of those parties you refused to attend because Claudia was sure to be there. He's some sort of financial man, I gathered. They say he's being groomed to take over his father's firm. Now, I just wonder what reason a man like that might have to send private missives to a demure little heiress."

"Shut up, Anthony," Dashford said, grabbing his friend by the arm and yanking him up to stand on solid ground.

He took a quick glance back at the grotto and realized the interior was quite easily visible through the windows. Evaline wasn't in sight now but, damn, Anthony must have had a perfect view of what had been going on inside. Hell, he ought to grind his fist into Rastmoor's face right now. He dragged his friend up the path off to the side, out of view and earshot of the woman beyond the windows. Rastmoor didn't seem to take exception to the rough treatment. Probably a guilty conscience; he knew he deserved it.

"You're playing a dangerous game, Dash," his friend said. "You're liable to get burned. I tell you, that girl isn't what she seems. She's hiding something."

"Everyone has their secrets," Dashford said, although he had to admit not everyone had quite as many as Evaline seemed to have.

"Look, I can understand you want her. She's easy enough on the eyes, and I take it she's easy on everything else, too. But what do you really know about her? Where is this famous fortune of hers, if she's running around dressed in rags? I say her uncle's already taken it, Dash, and she and that aunt are trying to get it back at your expense."

"You're wrong, Rastmoor," Dashford said, his voice hard as steel and his conviction surprising even himself. "Evaline has had plenty of opportunity for that, and she's not taken it. Besides, as far as they know, I'm no better off than the uncle. Evaline still has no idea of my true situation."

"Oh? You don't think perhaps Carrington might have told her?"

This gave Dashford pause. "Told her what? How the hell would Carrington know anything about my finances?"

Rastmoor shrugged. "Who knows? It's what he does. I daresay every banker, agent, and solicitor in London knows the truth about your situation. You haven't exactly been leaving your creditors to go hungry, you know. Somebody's bound to see your legitimate bills are getting paid and take note."

Dashford had to frown. Yes, this was true. He never dreamed this charade would have to be carried on so long, and he certainly never expected to have to deceive everyone. All he wanted was just enough rumor and insinuation to reach Claudia that she might leave off her insane notion to marry him.

Now his own lack of foresight could prove to be his undoing. If Carrington did indeed know the truth about Dashford's healthy accounts and fiscal responsibility, it was logical to assume he might mention it to someone. Perhaps, in fact, he had.

"Claudia insists we are to be wed before the end of the month," Dashford said.

"What? Suddenly she believes you worthy of her high standards?"

"Carrington must have told her the truth. Damn him! I'll kill him twice!"

Rastmoor didn't seem to care much about murder, but he wrinkled his brow. "Now why on earth would he do that? Doesn't seem to be anything in that to benefit him, does there? If he's in league with your Pinchley chit, the last thing I'd expect is to see him ruin her chance to snag a title. Unless, of course, he wants her for himself."

"Son of a—"

"Too bad about Claudia, though," Rastmoor went on. "What are you going to do to get rid of her now?"

Dashford fumed. Carrington wanted Evaline; that much was obvious. Mild-mannered Mr. Carrington was a sneaking bastard who weaseled his way into Dashford's home with malicious intent. Hell, that bogus story about Bristol finding him on the road was far too convenient, wasn't it? Evaline and Bristol had a history, for crying out loud. What were the chances she and Bristol and Carrington all converged here by simple coincidence? Not very high, he had to admit. Likely the three of them were plotting something together. Damn! A man with half a brain could see it. Rastmoor was right; something *was* going on here.

Well, Dashford liked to think he did have half a brain. Indeed, his eyes were wide open now, and he was not about to let Evaline lead him about by the nose—or any other body part that seemed especially susceptible to being led around by her. He'd find out what the chit was up to, and he'd use it to his advantage.

Carrington wanted her for himself, did he? Well, he'd be welcome to her once Dashford was done. First, though, he'd let Miss Pinchley help him with a little problem. Well, two problems, actually. To start with, he needed to get rid of Claudia, and a torrid, public affair with Evaline might just do that trick. For that other little problem? Well, a torrid affair with Evaline would undoubtedly fix that, too. By God, he simply had to finish what he'd started with her.

He glanced back up at the grotto. She must be hiding in the shadows there, plotting her strategy and thinking Dashford was comfortably unaware. Well, she had a few things to learn, and he was looking forward to teaching her.

"You're not going back in there, are you?" Rastmoor asked. "Your mother's sending out the troops to hunt you down, Dash. That's why I came out here to find you. She's got some notion to move all the furniture out of the dining room and hold an indoor picnic there for luncheon."

"What?"

"Oh yes. I think the natives are getting restless, all this rain and whatnot."

"But an indoor picnic?"

"And she expects you to help. Now."

Dashford sighed. "Oh, very well. I suppose I'll get no peace until she finds me and I end up trucking chairs on my back."

"That's the spirit."

"Come on, then," Dashford said. "Let's leave Miss Pinchley to her schemes. No doubt we'll cross paths again."

"Make sure that's all you cross, old man, or you're likely to wind up with another fiancée you don't want."

"No, I don't think that's likely to happen, Anthony," Dashford said. It was true, of course, but he wasn't sure if that was because he was so certain Evaline wouldn't end up pressing for a match or if it was because he feared there would never come a time when he didn't want her. He hoped it was the former.

THE RAIN WAS POUNDING STEADILY ON THE windows. Indeed, Evaline had barely made it back indoors before it started up. Why on earth had Dashford stood so long chatting with his friend Lord Rastmoor out in front of the grotto when he knew she was in there, panting and flushed from what they'd been doing? Blast, she couldn't think of it even now without getting a bit warm.

Finally the men had gone, and she'd been able to steal quietly back to the house. As far as she knew, no one suspected. Heavens, what a mess she was making for herself. What a fool she was! Well, no longer.

The first thing she'd done on her return to the house—after heading to her room to pack away her money, tidy herself, and splash cold water on her face as well as a certain unmentionable other part—was head for the library. Fortunately, it was unoccupied, and she was able to give her attention to Dr. Buchan's *Domestic Medicine*. She found a quiet chair in a far recess and curled up there to read. If anyone came in, she decided to flip the pages rapidly to chapter 34, where she might be found to be reading about simple aches and pains. Who wouldn't, after all, have aches and pains on a day like today?

Really, of course, she was poring over chapter 48 again.

And what she was finding disturbed her. It seemed, oddly enough, that this whole procreation thing could indeed happen with but little input on her part. Indeed, for all the information Dr. Buchan offered on the subject, it seemed she was to believe true ladies indeed had no input in it at all. Well, she'd already been forced to acknowledge her own lack of ladylike behavior where things of this nature were concerned. She took after Grandmamma most thoroughly in this area, sad to say.

Dash it all, but why wasn't this blooming book more specific? So far, all she knew for certain was that gastric troubles, disruption of appetite, and various other uncomfortable malaises were quite common to those afflicted with blessed expectations. Not encouraging information, to say the least.

Her stomach rumbled as if to voice its own opinion. She certainly did have something to worry about. There was nothing in this book to absolve her! What on earth would she do if her fears were confirmed? Heavens, it was frightening to say the least.

Frightening also were the voices from the doorway. Drat! Someone was coming. She quickly flipped to the other chapter. Bother, wrong one. This was chapter 11, "Common Evacuations of the Stool." Ah, there! She found her page on headache. Much better.

But the high-backed chair she'd chosen sat with its back very nearly to the door. It was clear as Lord Rastmoor and Mr. Carrington entered the library they had not noticed her. They were in the midst of a rather heated discussion, it appeared, and Evaline felt it awkward to announce her presence. Timidly, she sank down deeper into the chair cushion.

"If you insist on this discussion, let us at least have a modicum of privacy," Mr. Carrington was saying as they entered. He sounded none too pleased.

"I don't know why. It's bound to be common knowledge before long," Rastmoor said with obvious contempt.

"What is that supposed to mean?" Carrington practically growled.

"I'm figuring things out, Carrington. I can't believe I didn't see it right at first. She's getting a bit desperate, isn't she?"

"Keep a civil tongue, sir! You may be a peer of the realm, but you've no right to speak ill of her."

"How fortunate she has such a champion. Her little bastard will no doubt appreciate that someday."

Her little bastard?! Evaline drew in a sharp breath. Good heavens, where they talking about her? But who else could it be? Drat drat drat . . . Lord Rastmoor suspected already. Oh, this was dreadful! He'd certainly tell Dashford—and perhaps everyone else. What was she to do?

"You'll keep your dirty suspicions to yourself, Rastmoor," Carrington said. "This has nothing to do with you."

"Dashford is my friend," Rastmoor said. "Don't think I'll stand by and let him get dragged into a forced marriage. I swear to you, Carrington—"

"I'm sure marrying Dashford is not her intent."

"That's not how it seems to me."

"Just give me a chance!" Now Carrington was practically begging. "I haven't yet explained things to her."

"Explained things? What is there to explain? Seems to me the damage has already been done."

"There are other factors."

"Oh? What more could there possibly—"

"She is penniless."

"What did you say?"

Yes, what did he say? Evaline held her breath. *Penniless?*

"I am familiar with her father's accounts," Mr. Carrington said, his voice heavy and slow. "His investments have not done well. Indeed, they've done badly. Very badly. The funds she's been counting on? Well, they're gone. I haven't told her yet. I haven't had the heart."

The men were silent. Evaline was silent. The clock on the mantel ticked. Good heavens, could this be true? She was penniless, and Carrington hadn't told her? Indeed, she knew he'd seemed nervous and a bit preoccupied earlier, yet she'd simply counted that to a generally nervous disposition. Apparently, though, it was more than that.

"Penniless, you say?" Rastmoor asked.

"Very nearly. There is a bit, but nothing like she has been led to expect," Carrington said and sighed. "So you see, my lord, there is always more to the story."

"What will she do?" Rastmoor asked.

"It's none of your concern. I'll deal with the matter. I'm certain that once all has been explained she will—"

His voice broke off quickly. Evaline strained to hear more, but all she detected was a set of footsteps from the hall. Rats. Now she would probably not be privy to Carrington's suggested solution.

"We'll continue this later, Carrington," Rastmoor said.

Their footsteps shuffled toward the door, and soon Evaline heard Lord Rastmoor give a cheerful greeting to Lady Dashford. Their voices came from the hallway.

"Ah, just who I was looking for!" her ladyship said brightly. "We've very nearly gotten all the furniture moved for our indoor picnic. Now come and convince my son that you are quite taken with the thought of eating on cushions, reclining on the dining room floor."

"On the floor, ma'am?" Carrington said, doubtful.

"Oh yes! Isn't it just the most marvelous notion? I can hardly wait. Just listen to what we have planned."

Her ladyship's chatter rippled through the distance as she clearly led the gentlemen away. Soon all was silent in the library again, and Evaline could breathe at last. She certainly couldn't think straight, though. What had just happened?

She was penniless. The funds Carrington had given her were likely the whole of her inheritance. Could she live the rest of her life on two hundred pounds? Not likely. And it was worse.

Rastmoor had guessed her condition. Heavens, if people were recognizing it this easily, then clearly she was doomed. It didn't matter that her memories of how she got this way were still a bit murky or that she had no idea how Rastmoor and Carrington knew anything about it; the truth was she carried Lord Dashford's child!

For a moment or two she just stared into space. *Lord Dashford's child.* This was dreadful. This was awful. What was worse, for the life of her she couldn't keep from smiling like a simpleton. *Lord Dashford's child!*

Chapter Eleven

The chilly gray skies outside gave a lazy feel to the atmosphere inside. A fire burned in the grate, sending out warmth with its crackling glow, even though it was the middle of the day. The floor was scattered with blankets and pillows. Evaline looked perfectly fetching there, her gown and coiffure recently tidied and the cushions surrounding her so terribly inviting.

Except that also surrounding her was Ellard Bristol. The only thing good about that was the fact that he looked every bit as frustrated as Dashford felt, neither of them able to do more than stare at Evaline and make small talk with the crowd of guests all gathered here for Mother's indoor picnic. Indeed, it was clear that Bristol would have very much liked everyone gone to Hades so he could have Evaline to himself. Good. Let the man suffer. He could have her enough when Dashford was done.

"Dashy, I'm cold," Claudia simpered, resting an elbow on the silk pillows piled beside her and very clearly offering Dashford a too revealing view of her scooped bodice.

"Then put some clothes on," he suggested.

Claudia pouted. Damnation, she was more cloying and petulant than usual today. How could she expect any man to be attracted to that? Even that damned Carrington prig seemed particularly annoyed by her this afternoon. Well, he didn't have to suffer her leaning against him and demanding his attention all through lunch, did he? No, that was Dashford's privilege alone.

"What a lovely idea this is," Lady Brennan said, to the agreement of several others. "I daresay I've never been to a more enjoyable picnic."

"Neither have I," Bristol chimed. "Although, I suspect for myself it may have something to do with the company."

He batted those damn long eyelashes and gave Evaline such a heated, overly familiar smile. Dashford nearly stalked over there and planted him one. He managed to hold himself back, however, due only to the fact that Evaline didn't seem impressed. Of course, why should she? She had every gentleman in the room wrapped securely around her finger. The older ones doted on her, Carrington followed her with his eyes, Bristol was nearly salivating, and even Rastmoor had his gaze locked on her. Oh, she must be loving the attention.

She hardly seemed aware of it, though. It must be an act. How could she not know how enticing she appeared as her lips puckered around the strawberry she toyed with, and how her rounded bosoms were pleasantly enhanced when she leaned forward to place the strawberry stem back onto her plate? God, if Bristol didn't put his eyes back into his head, Dashford was going to do it for him forcibly.

"Dashy," Claudia said in her most annoying whine. "Please pass me the cream."

Not wishing to be subjected to more whining, Dashford practically dove for the cream. Hell, he'd pass her anything she liked, just so long as it kept her quiet. Unfortunately, though, he hadn't stopped to realize how she might possibly mistake his eagerness to please.

"Oh, look at that," she said loud enough for everyone to hear. "Dashy, you're too sweet. I barely had to raise my little finger and how quickly you leapt to my service. If only more gentleman were like you. What a fine husband you'll be."

"So long as you don't mind the bloke proposing to other ladies every now and then, Miss Graeley," Mr. Carrington said, unexpectedly casting himself into their conversation from his position two blankets over.

Dashford chuckled. Indeed, poor Carrington must have heard about Dashford's now infamous proposal at dinner last night. So the pup was holding a grudge, was he? Let him. Dashford was quite content with that.

At Carrington's surprising mention of Dashford's actions last night, a few guests chuckled. Evaline, however, frowned at Mr. Carrington. It appeared she most certainly did not appreciate him making light of what had been a very uncomfortable dinner conversation. Good. Perhaps she'd be less inclined to tryst with the self-important little twit for the near future.

In an obvious—and quite successful—bid to change the subject, Evaline turned a kindly smile on Dashford's mother. Indeed, the girl could appear so very tender and innocent when she chose to.

"I declare, Lady Dashford," Evaline said brightly, "these strawberries are the best I've had in years. They're grown here at Hartwood, are they not?"

"They are," his mother replied with pride. "They are an old cultivation here. In fact, the Hartwood hothouse is well-known for supplying the most exquisite strawberries in season as well as out. My late husband's father was an accomplished horticulturalist and had quite a penchant for them."

"Well," Dashford added, giving his mother a wink. "The strawberries themselves were not exactly my grandfather's penchant, now were they?"

Lady Dashford blushed. "Now, Randolf, it hardly matters to our guests how much your ancestor did or did not love strawberries."

Mr. Mandry chuckled. "Oh, we all know the stories about the former viscount and his strawberries. Those famed Dashford strawberries!"

Indeed, Dashford had no doubt most of the guests—longtime family friends—knew the old stories of the former viscount and his strawberries, and all that was associated with them. Several older guests were smiling visibly, and a suppressed chuckle or two was heard here and there. Oh, everyone knew the stories, all right. Well, almost everyone, anyway. Claudia was clueless.

"I don't know the stories, Dashy," Claudia pouted. "You never told me your strawberry stories. To think your strawberries are famous, and you've never mentioned it to me! Oh, you simply must tell us the story."

Rastmoor, reclining near enough to the large tray of cold meat to repeatedly help himself, laughingly agreed. "Yes, do, Dashy. You know, I thought I'd been subjected to your bragging on everything here at blessed Hartwood, but apparently I was wrong. Go ahead; regale us with your strawberry tale."

Bother. Rastmoor knew the strawberry tale just fine and knew it was not a fit story for such a gathering as this. Then again, perhaps this was just the sort of gathering where Dashford ought to enlighten his darling fiancée about the true nature of his ancestor. She wouldn't like it one bit, would she? Indeed, Grandpapa and the strawberries was just the perfect story to entertain Claudia.

"You wish to hear the strawberry tale, my dear? Very well," he began. "My grandfather was indeed an accomplished horticulturalist. His strawberries especially were most, er, tempting."

"Good heavens!" his mother interrupted. "You aren't seriously going to discuss this!"

"But Mother"—Dashford sighed—"Miss Graeley has a point. She's never heard this story. If she is going to be expected to marry into our family, she might as well hear the worst of it."

"But in front of everyone? Randolf, really . . ."

"It's all right, Mother. Your friends already know the story, and they still respect you."

"They are not engaged to be married to me," his mother grumbled.

Claudia's eyes had grown large. "Dashy, what on earth kind of story is this? Are these scandalous strawberries?"

"None of us needs to hear the blooming strawberry story," Sir Victor announced. "I'm sure Claudia has no desire to hear any more about it."

"But I do, Papa!" she said, defiantly. "Go on, Dashy. Tell your story."

"With pride," Dashford acquiesced. "The story begins

when my grandfather married. He selected his bride more out of duty than preference, I suppose, and it turns out the woman was a shrew."

"Randolf, that's a horrible thing to say," his mother quickly chided.

"Although it's true," Dashford fearlessly asserted. "I have rather limited memories of her, but all accounts agree; she was a shrew. Grandpapa could find rest only by escaping to his gardens. In fact, he built our extensive hothouses as a retreat from her, I believe. At last her nagging and simpering became so dreadful the poor man was reduced to developing political inclinations, taking his seat in Parliament and removing himself for months at a time to London."

"Wise man," Mr. Quinley-Pierce muttered. His wife jabbed him with her fan.

Dashford went on. "Grandpapa was a sober man and tended well to his finances—very much unlike his grandson, you might be saying—but in one area he and I are kindred souls. While in London, Grandpapa found himself quite able-bodied with the ladies."

Lady Brennan squeaked, and Mrs. Coddleston giggled. The aging dears even seemed to be blushing. Could it be they had firsthand knowledge of his dearly departed ancestor? Dashford had known these old biddies for all his life. Had they been Grandpapa's acquaintances in London all those years ago? An unsettling thought. He decided he'd best get back to the story.

"One lady in particular caught his attention. Or should I say"—he paused to heighten the drama—"she was not quite a lady."

"Randolf, really now!" his mother chided.

Evaline appeared to agree. "Surely you do not need to share this with us, Lord Dashford."

How odd. Even with her high instep, Claudia was hanging on his every word, yet Evaline, with her decidedly less conservative views of things, was nearly ashen at this point of the story already. Whatever was that about? Did she think to impress by suddenly claiming tender sensibilities? Well, he certainly knew better than that.

"The lady was a courtesan," Dashford announced. "The

incomparable Becky Gwin, infamous at court for her many charms and her many close friends. Why, the king himself had looked her way a time or two."

"The king? Truthfully?" Evaline questioned.

Ah, so she couldn't hide her interest, after all. Indeed, he might just find he was killing two birds with one stone by continuing this story. Claudia would take such offense as to despise him, and Evaline's blood would race hot and unsated in her veins. He intended to take full advantage of both results.

"It's quite true, Miss Pinchley. Grandpapa was often heard to brag what it had cost him to steal his Mrs. Gwin away from those who outranked him. But steal her he did, and she never regretted it. Their liaison was a lengthy one, in fact."

"Those fancy women do like the lengthy ones," Rastmoor said with a randy sneer. "Come, Dash. What has this to do with strawberries?"

"Don't interrupt," Dashford said. "I'll continue. So taken with Mrs. Gwin was he that when the time came for him to return here to Hartwood, he couldn't bear to part from her. So he didn't. My father was an adolescent away at school by that time, and my grandmother was content alone—at least as content as the old bat reportedly could have been—so Grandpapa left Hartwood in the care of his steward and simply remained in London. Two years, in fact, he stayed with Mrs. Gwin."

"I say, she must have been a pretty piece of work, the old gal," Rastmoor interrupted. "But where do the strawberries come in?"

"Have faith, my friend," Dashford assured him. "All will be revealed. The story took a turn when my grandmother became quite ill. Grandpapa realized he could no longer avoid returning. He had duties and responsibilities here, and I'm sure his gardens were quite overgrown. He decided to come back and begged his mistress to accompany him. She refused, of course, knowing that was hardly the way proper people conducted polite affairs."

"Naturally," Rastmoor said, laughing. "We must be very proper about these things. Pity I never met the old man."

"He was a lively one, that's certain," Dashford said. "But he finally found a way to lure his ladybird here."

"Strawberries," Evaline said.

"Strawberries," he repeated and hoped she was not reading more into the story than was there. Dashford was hardly interested in following his ancestor's example. Grandfather's situation had been unusual. He and his lover had given their hearts to one another, and there was never any doubt his mistress was true to him. Evaline—it was obvious—was nothing like Becky Gwin.

"Strawberries?" Claudia asked, dubious.

"Mrs. Gwin had a great love for them, and Grandpapa promised if she came here to live, he would keep her in strawberries for the rest of her life."

"That's how strawberries play into this?" Rastmoor gaped. "He paid his light-skirts in strawberries?"

"You have no sense of the romantic, do you?" Dashford asked his friend, shaking his head. "Why, I'm sure my female listeners find this all very endearing."

"I find it deplorable," Claudia said, as predicted. "Did your grandfather honestly believe he could bring this woman here to darken the doors of Hartwood?"

"No, he realized she would never agree to that, not with his hateful wife lying here in her sickbed and his teenage son sometimes in residence. So he offered to bring her to the area and set her up in her own home."

"Not a bad arrangement. Did he succeed?" Rastmoor asked.

"Of course," Dashford said, grinning. "He was a Dashford. That woman never had a chance of resisting him. She came to live nearby, not three miles from here. He bought her a lovely cottage of her own in the little village of Findutton-on-Avon. They christened it Loveland, of all things, and she lived out her days there, happy as a clam. Why, I myself even took her Hartwood strawberries a time or two."

"What?! Never say you and she . . . that is . . ." Evaline exclaimed, then faltered.

Claudia gasped, and Lady Dashford choked a bit, but Dashford just laughed. Evaline truly was far more enthralled by this story than he'd expected.

"What are you suggesting, Miss Pinchley?" he asked her.

"That I took my grandfather's place in more than just title? I'm flattered, but you give me too much credit. I was a mere lad when Grandpapa hung up his spoon. Sorry to disappoint, but Mrs. Gwin was nothing more than a kindly old matron to me. She baked the finest tarts, so I took her strawberries."

"You called upon a woman like that?" Claudia asked, astonished. "She was allowed to stay in that house even after your grandfather was gone?"

Oh, Claudia was livid, and by God, Dashford was enjoying her fury. The fact that he'd befriended a social outcast like Mrs. Gwin would tarnish him in her eyes worse than all his other transgressions combined. At last he'd found the key to getting rid of the woman. He should have brought up the sordid tale of Grandfather's grand passion ages ago.

"Of course she was allowed to stay," he said simply. "It was her house, deeded quite legally."

Now Claudia turned her incredulous expression on his mother. "Good heavens, she's not still there, is she? You can't possibly still be living near the woman who . . . well, such a person as that!"

"No, sadly, she died four years ago after a brief illness," Lady Dashford said without the contempt Claudia so clearly expected. "She had no family to speak of, so we buried her in our family plot."

"What?!" Claudia nearly shrieked.

Evaline had much the same reaction, surprising Dashford.

"I say, Evaline, are you quite all right?" he had to ask.

She blinked rapidly, and her face colored under his gaze. What in the world was this all about? Why pretend his story so greatly affected her? He didn't get the chance to ask. Claudia's clawlike grip on his arm called his attention back to her.

"Of course she's quite all right. Even *she* can't believe you'd be so vulgar as to pay polite house calls on a fallen woman," Claudia said. "Honestly, Dashy, what was your father thinking not to oust that woman immediately?"

"There was nothing wrong with my father's thought processes, Claudia," he said, glaring at her. Ah, her disgust for him was evident. It was the perfect, perfect opportunity for her to denounce him once and for all. At last he'd be free.

Unfortunately, his mother must have realized the same thing.

"Forgive my son," she rushed to say, her words clipped and hurried. "He's known this sordid family history so long, he forgets how shocking it must sound to others."

"Shocking indeed!" Claudia agreed with vigor. "Dashy, I'm appalled at how easily you condone your grandfather's disgraceful actions."

"Did I say I condone them, my dear?" he asked.

"It's evident, the way you speak of it. Have you no thought to how scandalized your grandmother must have been by such a thing?"

"My grandmother was a sour woman who went around scandalized by every action others made and felt remorse for none of her own."

Claudia pursed her lips in frustration. "Even so, the man should have kept his wanderings confined to London like decent men do. Bringing that woman here—so near to Hartwood—is beyond the pale. I will never allow such behavior, I assure you."

"I promise you, Claudia," he said, his teeth grinding, "if there is a woman I wish to have, I'll damn well bring her right into Hartwood for whatever shocking and scandalous purposes I choose."

And he would, too. Hell, he'd done it already, hadn't he? His thoughts and his glance went to Evaline. She must have known it. Her own eyes were fastened on her lap, and her cheeks colored nicely. He'd wanted her, and he'd taken her into his home and his bed while he'd still thought her a mere servant. Yes, he supposed he did condone Grandpapa's disgraceful actions—to a point. He might not be planning to promise Evaline a lifetime of strawberries, but by God, he'd like to give her a few more hours of sweetness.

"You're positively barbaric!" Claudia fumed, crossing her pale arms across her chest and turning her face defiantly away from Dashford. "I will not be married to a brute who would shame me by bringing his light-skirts into my home. I won't!"

"Fine with me," Dashford growled.

Could this be his long-awaited salvation? In front of God and everyone, Claudia was about to break off their engagement! He was almost afraid to breathe.

His mother, however, was vigilant as ever. "Good news, everyone," she called with a too-bright smile. "I've prepared some games for us today! Yes, how about a game to keep us all entertained?"

Everyone naturally agreed that a game would be just the thing on a dreary day like this. Damn them all. He was more inclined toward a good stiff brandy right now, but it would have been useless to mention it. Mother had already launched into her game preparations, and the guests were at least feigning enthusiasm for her. Dashford could do nothing but fold his arms and pout, very much as Claudia was doing.

The game appeared to have few rules. His mother handed out small bits of paper to each gentleman with the instruction he was to write his name on it and then deposit it into a hat. Dashford had little choice but to obey. When the task was complete, his mother passed the hat from blanket to blanket and invited all the ladies, one by one, to draw a name. Each lady was to call out the name on her paper, and that gentleman would be her new partner for this game.

Dashford ground his teeth. The way things had been going lately, it would be just his luck Claudia drew his name, and he'd be stuck with her on this blanket for the duration of Mother's tedious game. He prayed to a benevolent God to strike him dead before that might happen.

God, it seemed, had other plans.

THE HAT WAS PASSED AT LAST TO EVALINE. SO FAR, Dashford's name had not been drawn. What were the chances she might avoid it?

Gingerly, as if even the man's signature was dangerous for her, she reached into the hat, and her fingers fumbled around the few papers that were still left there. She selected one and was almost relieved that it did not burn her skin. With luck, her new partner would be Mr. Patterson or Mr. Carrington or anyone but Dashford. She'd even manage to survive a few more uncomfortable minutes sitting here beside Ellard rather than trade him in for Dashford. And that was saying a lot. Ellard Bristol was an ass.

She withdrew a paper, unfolded it slowly, and grimaced.

Her heart pounded as she gradually raised her eyes, slowly looking up and meeting Dashford's glance. He obviously recognized her expression, and his lips curled into a dark smile.

"Does your paper have a rather dramatically executed D?" he asked when she remained silent.

She nodded. He smiled more broadly, and her heart pounded all the more. Oh dear. She was expected to be his partner in a game on a blanket? This was really, truly not a good idea. She could think of nothing to say, so she mutely passed the hat along.

Claudia happily announced her new partner was her own father and blatantly turned her back on Dashford. Lady Dashford fluttered about with contagious excitement, giving instruction and encouraging the gentlemen to reposition themselves and start the game. Dashford was still smiling when he came to join Evaline on her blanket. She tried not to watch as his trousers hugged his various body parts when he sank down to sit beside her. She didn't succeed very well. Their interrupted time in the grotto was all too vivid in her mind.

She couldn't think straight. But how on earth was she to get through this with some sense of decorum when all her senses were filled with Dashford? He breathed her air, his suggestive eyes raked her body, his warm shoulder brushed against her as he lounged there, as comfortable on the floor as if they'd been at a proper dining table. She wished they were at a proper dining table. It was too easy to think of other things they could be doing spread out here on these darned pillows instead of playing Lady Dashford's game and helping him redeem himself in Claudia's eyes.

"Now," Lady Dashford was explaining, "gentlemen, you must each ask three questions of your partner. When time is up, you gentlemen will all switch to the next blanket for a new partner. Remember, gentlemen, take care to ask only the three questions you most would like an answer to."

Dashford leaned in toward Evaline. "Is she serious?"

Heavens, but his voice made her think of things she had no business thinking. "Perhaps she doesn't know you very well."

"Oh, she knows me. I just can't believe she'd give me carte blanche like this."

"She probably expected you to be sitting with Claudia."

"Then she should have been more careful passing out that hat, shouldn't she?" he said. "Now, which three questions would I most like you to answer? Hmm."

He was studying her, his eyes roaming her as if he owned her. Sadly, she was responding as if he did. God, how on earth would she get through this? She had to control herself. No one could guess what they'd done.

"You know, there is a time limit to this game," she said, keeping her voice light.

"So you'd like me to get down to business, would you, Miss Pinchley?"

Yes, please! No, wait. That was not the sort of business he needed to be about. He needed to behave like a gentleman and convince Claudia he was decent husband material. He needed to smile that smile and make such heated insinuations not to her, but to Claudia. Lord, she hated Claudia.

"All right, first question, then," he said and leaned yet closer to her. Her pulse quickened, and she made the mistake of glancing up at him. His eyes sparkled. "Would you like me to kiss you right now?"

Oh bother. He wasn't going to make this easy for her, was he?

"I didn't say I was going to do it," he said when she didn't respond. "I merely asked if you would like it."

"I won't answer that. You're wasting questions," she replied sharply, refusing to look at him again.

"You don't need to answer," he said, his breath drifting over her and warming her neck. "I know the answer."

She rolled her eyes and pretended to be unaffected. "Then why on earth ask?"

"It's part of the game, isn't it? I'm supposed to be asking questions."

"Well, then you ought to get to it, don't you think? Next question, please, and do be sensible this time."

"All right," he said. "Second question: would you like me to kiss you where I kissed you yesterday?"

She frowned. "In the library?"

He laughed. "No, I did not mean geographically, Miss Pinchley."

His heated expression told her all too plainly what he had meant. Her body told her she would most definitely like to reply in the affirmative. She wouldn't, of course.

"Please, we're supposed to be playing a polite game here, my lord," she said, hoping she sounded prim as a headmistress. Those dratted tingling sensations, however, were bombarding her in regions no headmistress would ever admit to having.

"I thought you and I were playing a different sort of game," he responded.

"Well, we're not. We're done. See? Your mother is calling for everyone to change partners again."

"But I haven't asked my final question," he protested.

"It appears you'll have to save it. Gentlemen are supposed to move one blanket to the right and interview their next partner," she said.

He frowned as Mr. Carrington began making his way from Mrs. Patterson's blanket toward Evaline's. From the look on his face, Mrs. Patterson had not been an inspiring conversationalist.

"Very well," Dashford said, his voice dropping to nearly a growl. "I will save my question, Evaline, but be prepared to answer when the time is right."

"Indeed, my lord," she said, wishing he would not call her by name like that. What were people to think? Heavens, what was she herself to think?

Dashford stood when Mr. Carrington arrived. The viscount skewered him with a dispassionate glare, and Mr. Carrington skewered right back with a glare no less dispassionate. If Evaline hadn't known better, she could have assumed them to be old rivals. Finally, Dashford turned in a huff and moved on. Mr. Carrington dropped gracelessly into the spot the viscount vacated.

His brooding expression did not lighten when Evaline greeted him. Apparently, she decided, the burden of keeping her true financial situation secret from her was becoming too much for him to bear. Bother. Would he bring up this sensitive topic right here and now?

No, it appeared not. In fact, it appeared he had no desire
to discuss any topic at all. His attention was instead trained
elsewhere. Evaline followed his gaze, and her eyes lit on
Dashford, settling in once again beside Claudia. Neither
party seemed too pleased with this arrangement. Evaline
knew she most certainly was not but reminded herself that
for Dashford's sake, this was exactly as it should be. He
needed to be with Claudia and make amends for the many
ways he'd offended her of late. It was obvious to everyone
she was close to jilting him.

But perhaps her attitude toward Dashford was not as
hopeless as it first appeared. In fact, Claudia actually smiled
at him now; all trace of whining and petulance was gone.
Maybe Sir Victor had reminded her of all she'd be giving up,
were she to cast off a viscount. Perhaps there was hope for a
happy ending yet.

But Evaline's own happy ending was somewhat in
jeopardy, wasn't it? She forced her mind back to her own
troubles. Mr. Carrington was settling in beside her, the
tension radiating off him so that she felt her own body start
to seize up and her mind fill with heavy dread. Likely he was
building up to give her the bad news.

"So, Mr. Carrington," she said, hoping a casual tone
would help the poor man relax a bit. "What three questions
do you have for me today?"

He seemed momentarily taken aback by her query, but
quickly his faculties were restored. "What? Oh, forgive me,
Miss Pinchley. I fear I've been a bit distracted."

"I see that. Anything that might pertain to my particular
business?"

He sighed. "I'm afraid so. Surely we should not discuss
this here, though."

Actually, perhaps they should. It would certainly ensure
she did not allow herself to give in to petty emotion and
make a scene by blubbering all over herself. She already
knew it was bad; she might as well have the details.

"Please, Mr. Carrington. I have a clue all is not well, so
let's not pretend further. I promise I will not give in to
vapors or embarrass us."

She'd save all that for later, when she was alone and

being put out of Dashford's home to make room for his new bride. Yes, there'd likely be plenty of time for embarrassing herself.

"Oh? Have you already an inkling of what I've discovered?"

She smiled. "As I count, Mr. Carrington, that would constitute your third question. Are you certain you have no better questions you wish me to answer just now? Remember, we are still playing Lady Dashford's delightful little game."

"Bother the game. All right, Miss Pinchley. Here is my information. Other buyers have surfaced for the property you instructed me to purchase on your behalf."

She'd been wrong. She'd had no inkling of this. "Other buyers?"

"Very motivated buyers, in fact. Two of them. They also are choosing to remain anonymous, and now that the rain has started up again in force, I am not in a position to visit the solicitor to negotiate the transaction for you. I fear your offer will go by the wayside, and one of the others will succeed."

She frowned. This certainly was not what she expected him to tell her. Could it be true? But who on earth was trying to purchase Grandmamma's house? It had sat vacant for four years with no activity. What was the sudden interest now?

Or perhaps there was no sudden interest. Perhaps Mr. Carrington was merely telling her this rather than to admit he could not purchase the property for her because she had no funds. Oh, the poor dear was so very concerned about her that he must be resorting to fabrications and half-truths.

But why would he do this? Could she be fortunate enough that perhaps he held some hope her situation would turn around in the near future? He knew how overjoyed she had been to finally be achieving the freedom she had so desperately longed for all these years. He would, no doubt, have done all he could to save her. Maybe there were still some small investments that might prove valuable, given time.

"Mr. Carrington, please be honest with me. Why should interest in that house suddenly appear from out of the blue? What is your real news?"

He seemed honestly perplexed. "Real news, Miss Pinchley? But I assure you this is the news. Two unexpected buyers have turned up, and as long as we are stranded here, my hands appear to be tied. I only wish I had known about the special circumstances before I made your initial offer, though of course I understand your reluctance to disclose such a thing."

"Special circumstances?" She frowned. It had not been her intent to give him details of the situation nor her connection to Grandmamma. Could it be that he recognized Grandmamma's identity from Dashford's story? Heavens, she had not bargained on that.

"I wish you would have told me. Such a thing makes that property highly valuable, you know."

"It does?"

"Naturally. You can't imagine you're the only one who might be interested in the treasure, Miss Pinchley."

For a long moment she just stared at him. "Treasure? What treasure do you mean?"

"Come now. Of course you know of it. Why else would you have retained me to negotiate this purchase of such an out-of-the-way property if you had not somehow become aware of the Loveland treasure? That is the name of the house, is it not? Really, Miss Pinchley, you should have trusted me. I could have made your offer more attractive, and perhaps your success would be much less in doubt at this time."

"Loveland treasure? But surely you cannot think there is such a thing!"

She nearly laughed. Indeed, she'd heard of this Loveland treasure. Grandmamma had used those words frequently, and truth be told, there had been a treasure—of sorts. It was certainly not the kind of treasure Mr. Carrington seemed to believe, however! Oh my, had these other buyers heard of it and assumed a great store of wealth was included somewhere in the Loveland property? It was really quite humorous.

Except, of course, for the fact that this error might very nearly keep her from ever attaining her dream. With her finances depleted, now more than ever she would need to find a way to possess Loveland at an affordable price. Scores of misguided fortune hunters tripping over themselves with inflated bids to purchase the place would only stand in her way. And, oh! What would happen to the place if any of them did get ahold of it? This was dreadful.

"It hardly matters what I believe, Miss Pinchley," Mr. Carrington went on. "The fact remains that others have become aware of this so-called treasure, and they will no doubt see to it that their offers are higher than yours. No doubt the current owner will wish to gain the highest price, and as long as I am stranded here by the unfortunate weather, there is little hope of negotiating your success. You should have told me."

"But there is no treasure!" she said and had to catch herself from letting her voice rise noticeably. "Truly, Mr. Carrington. My goal is to purchase Loveland, and I am well aware that economy is of the essence just now. Is there no way we can achieve this? Can you not inform the owner and these other buyers that tales of any treasure are nothing more than myth?"

"And who would believe that, especially coming from one who has already expressed an interest in the property? I'm sorry, Miss Pinchley. Is it impossible for you to reconcile that Loveland is out of your reach?"

"That is another question, Mr. Carrington," she said, carefully hiding her pain. "But look. Lady Dashford is calling for the gentlemen to move on again. Allow me time to digest your information, and we will discuss it later."

He nodded. "Of course. And truly, I'm sorry I was not able to assist you further, Miss Pinchley."

He was every bit the polite gentleman, and his demeanor was all she could ask for in a professional, but something in Mr. Carrington's eyes didn't quite match up with his words. Indeed, there was a sadness and a remorse behind them, but Evaline could not be sure either of those emotions had anything to do with his inability to secure Grandmamma's house for her. Womanly instinct said Mr. Carrington was hiding something more.

"I'll find you later, Mr. Carrington," she said.

Chapter Twelve

He was facing Claudia again. Damn it. He'd been forced by polite behavior and the constraints of this bloody game to present himself at her blanket once more. This time Sir Victor was there as well.

"Just can't keep away, can you Dashford?" the older man said with a knowing smile.

"No, apparently not," Dashford had to agree.

Graeley got to his feet but turned back long enough to give his daughter a cryptic look. Dashford was afraid he had at least a vague clue what it meant. He suspected the man was admonishing Claudia to mind her manners and do nothing to alienate her fiancé. It would be just Dashford's luck that she was the obedient type. Damn it again.

Instead of moving on to the next blanket, Sir Victor excused himself and left the picnic altogether. Now, why didn't Dashford just think of that? Hell, he could have been long gone instead of trapped with a suddenly tolerant Claudia.

The change in her attitude was dramatic. True, she was still cool toward him, but gone was any indication she might have desired murder rather than marriage. Hell, this is not what he had hoped for. Sir Victor must have convinced her to keep a civil tongue or risk losing all she might gain by snagging a peer.

Although what she might think that gain would be at this point, Dashford couldn't guess. How could she for one minute think she might be happy in a union with Dashford, after all he'd done to destroy anything good in his life these past two years? Apparently his actual title carried far more weight than he'd expected. But what more could be done to make her despise him? He was nearly exhausted from trying over these last two years.

Surely, though, if he'd brought her so close to discarding him once, he could do it again. If he could but find that one little detail, that final straw to break this camel's back, he'd be loose of her. But what could it possibly be?

And then he caught her scowling, staring with a burning envy at the couple on the next blanket. Evaline and Carrington. Jealousy glowed in her eyes. Hmm, he certainly had noticed how irate Claudia became at the possibility of one day being confronted by her husband's mistress. She must recognize his interest in Evaline. Well, now. This was exactly the opportunity he'd been waiting for. He'd see just how much this burr rankled.

"Our friend Mr. Carrington seems rather taken with Miss Pinchley, does he not?"

"I wouldn't know," Claudia said with an uninterested sniff.

"I suppose it's only natural. Miss Pinchley is quite attractive."

"If you believe so."

"She has that certain something a man is powerless to ignore. For myself, I have found her a most pleasant distraction."

"Gentlemen are easily distracted, my lord."

"And Miss Pinchley—in my experience, at least—is quite easily pleasant."

He was all too happy to allow his thoughts to appear in his expression as his eyes lingered on Evaline. She sat entirely too close to Carrington for propriety, but in this instance Dashford would allow it. Claudia, it seemed, would not.

"I find Miss Pinchley's behavior strongly lacking in virtue."

"Surely you are too harsh," Dashford argued. "If you were

to ask me—or Mr. Bristol or apparently Mr. Carrington—I daresay we could list a handful of virtues Miss Pinchley possesses in ample quantities."

"Gentlemen are poor judges of virtue, I fear. At least where women of a certain type are concerned."

"Oh? You believe Miss Pinchley to be of a certain type?"

"Everyone is of a certain type. I just happen to believe her type is vastly different than mine."

"Of course it is. Evaline—Miss Pinchley, that is—is an heiress of independent means. She does not need to mind her reputation so much as a gentlewoman headed for marriage, such as yourself. Fortunately for gentlemen—which, you may note, I am—Miss Pinchley is in the position where her dealings can be more, shall we say, casual. I will certainly enjoy getting to know her better."

"It seems you would have to stand in line behind Mr. Carrington," Claudia hissed as Evaline and Mr. Carrington dipped their heads toward one another in intimate conversation.

Dashford couldn't say he was any happier about it than Claudia appeared, but for now he'd allow Carrington to keep breathing—just long enough for Claudia to be convinced there was nothing noble or honorable in Dashford's intentions toward Evaline. Then he'd knock Carrington's block off.

"They do look cozy, don't they?" he had to admit. "But I daresay Miss Pinchley will recognize a better offer when she hears one."

"I thought you already made her an offer?"

"I did—of a sort," he said, his voice low. "But I'm a gentleman, so pray don't ask me to reveal whether or not she accepted."

Claudia was steamed. "You men! You're all a pack of worthless curs barking after but one thing alone. Any woman who gives it to you deserves what she gets."

He sat back and waited for the explosion. Finally it was all going to pay off. By the looks of things, Claudia was ready to make bold statements about where he might spend eternity. Clearly she would be happy to never see him again; all he needed was to hear her speak the words. With all these witnesses, he would be free for good. Then he could see about castrating Carrington. And Bristol, too, for good measure.

Yet once again his watchful mother must have detected the coming storm. She called for partners to be switched again. Damn and blast! Her timing couldn't have been worse. Claudia seemed to take control of herself right away, regaining composure and remaining his fiancée. Whatever condemnation she'd been about to make was trapped behind locked lips and a well-schooled expression. She would not even look at him, staring into the distance instead.

"What a shame," he said. "Our time is up, and I haven't even gotten around to my three questions."

"I'm sure you'll survive the loss."

The other couples began shifting around, and it was not a moment too soon when Carrington finally disengaged himself from his intimate discourse with Evaline. Dashford watched them. Both parties did not seem eager to leave their conversation. Evaline, in fact, appeared quite distressed. Dashford heard quite clearly her parting words to Carrington, "I'll find you later, Mr. Carrington."

So, she told Dashford the game between them was over, but she promised to meet Carrington later? Like hell she would. This game they'd been playing since that first night in the garden was far from over, despite what Evaline may have decided. Dashford still had plans for her, and they did not include finding Carrington later. Indeed, Evaline would be finding a man later, but Dashford would see hell freeze over before he'd let it be anyone but himself.

Freeze over it just might. The icy cold that emanated from Claudia when Carrington approached was enough to give them all frostbite. No doubt she would have preferred a partner who did not bring with him the reminder of her fiancé's interest in another female, but the hateful glare she pinned on Carrington was going a bit far.

Carrington obviously noticed. He shifted on his scrawny legs and didn't bother to sit. "Forgive me, my lord, Miss Graeley," he began. "But I'm afraid I really must excuse myself from this delightful game."

Oh, the man was a fool. Could he not see that Claudia

would not appreciate this and would only view it as a personal insult? Of course he couldn't. His mind was still back with Evaline, no doubt, and he didn't wait for permission before bowing slightly and removing himself from the dining room.

Claudia was seething.

"Don't worry, my dear," Dashford assured her. "I'm sure Mother has other games the group can play that don't require Carrington's sparkling presence. If we're lucky, perhaps it will be a game where gentlemen are allowed two partners at a time."

Claudia turned her chilly gaze on him. "There is not a game in this world I wish to play with any of your kind today, sir."

At that, she tucked up her skirts and scrambled to her feet. Without another word, she left the room. Well, now. This did have merit. He wasn't exactly unengaged, yet, but a storming and furious Claudia was progress.

He met Evaline's eyes. She looked away quickly, and soon they were all occupied in his mother's flustered instructions of some new game they could play that didn't require an even number of couples. It sounded dreadfully dull, but Dashford resigned himself. As long as Evaline had it in her mind to find Carrington later, he was determined to keep a close watch over her.

After all, Rastmoor and Bristol were still about, and a sideways glance at each of them confirmed that they, too, were keeping a close eye on Evaline. Well, let them. Evaline would need protectors once he was done with her. If such a thing could happen.

THE GAMES SEEMED TO DRAG ON FOR AGES BEFore finally their hostess decided her guests had suffered enough entertainment. Evaline was never so relieved to come to the end of a picnic. Dashford's eyes hadn't left her throughout the entire afternoon, and she was literally exhausted from being under his scrutiny so long. What on earth did the man want from her?

Well, she thought perhaps she knew the answer to that.

Drat her immoral urges, but she wanted the same thing from him. She wasn't giving in to him again, though. She'd dabbled with that folly more than enough already. For his sake as well as hers, it simply had to be over. As soon as the picnic began breaking up, Evaline claimed a headache and retired to her room. Unfortunately, Aunt Bella followed.

"He's smitten with you, girl," Bella said when they were alone, heading up the hall toward Evaline's room. "It's just a matter of time before that Graeley chit is done for good, then you'll have him all for yourself. He knows what's best, I'll say."

"Please, Aunt, I really am quite worn out. If you don't mind . . ."

"All right, I'll leave you. I daresay you've earned some rest. Keep it up, my dear, and your father's money will be ours in no time."

Ha! How nice it would have been to inform Bella she was too late, that all her scheming had been in vain. Papa's money was gone, and Bella would never, ever get her grimy hands on it. For that, at least, Evaline was glad to be a pauper.

For everything else, however, it didn't seem like such a blessing. How would she live? How could she ever save Sophie? And, heavens, what if her fears were realized and she was to find herself with another mouth to feed come nine months? Yes, Papa's money would be sorely missed at that point.

Bella left her alone, and Evaline took advantage of the quiet. She sat in her room and contemplated her options, nothing really coming to mind that might be of any great help. Unless, of course, Mr. Carrington did indeed have some hopes for her finances.

She needed to speak with him. He alone knew exactly where she stood. Was she as destitute as she feared, or were there some residual funds that could possibly promise a return? Just exactly how bad was it? Yes, Carrington was the one with the answers.

When she was sure the coast was clear and Dashford and Aunt Bella were at last done breathing down her neck, she decided to creep out of her room. The house was still, most of the guests appearing to have retired for an afternoon's rest.

All the better for her. She would find Mr. Carrington and discuss things in detail.

She'd learn exactly how much money it would take to purchase Grandmamma's house. Surely it couldn't be that exorbitant. The house was old and had been vacant and unkept these four years. That rumored treasure couldn't possibly be so believable as to drive the price up drastically, could it? Mr. Carrington simply had to know of some way they could work around this setback. There was too much at stake.

She made her way down to the drawing room, but it was empty. Well, at least she hadn't run into Dashford. Hesitantly she poked her head into the other few rooms in that section of the house, but they, too, were unoccupied. So just where could Mr. Carrington be? Perhaps he had gone to his room. Should she send in a note asking him to meet her?

Looking around a bit more, she found the housekeeper in the hall.

"I beg your pardon, Mrs. Kendall," she asked, "but how would I go about getting word to Mr. Carrington that . . ."

"Mr. Carrington? Oh, he left word for you, miss."

This caught Evaline off guard. "What?"

"I heard him tell Williams that if the young lady was to come looking for him, she was to be sent round to the music room, miss. He must be waiting for you there."

Oh, so he knew she'd be interested in speaking with him and had already arranged it with the butler. How very competent of him to be prepared for her summons. Good. She'd meet with him and know where things stood.

"Thank you, Mrs. Kendall," she said and left the woman.

Evaline hurried toward the music room through deserted halls. Perhaps she'd been too hasty in her disdain for Lady Dashford's indoor picnic. Apparently all that getting up and down from blankets had been quite taxing for the older guests, or perhaps they were simply hiding for fear her ladyship would force them into more games. Either way, they'd retired, and Evaline would have privacy with Mr. Carrington.

She put her hand to the music room door but surprisingly it did not slide open for her. Could this door be locked?

Perhaps Carrington did that so they could be uninterrupted. She ought to knock to let him know she'd arrived. Then again, what if not everyone was resting? If there were anyone in nearby rooms, they would surely hear a knock. Evaline would have to go through all the trouble of concocting some reasonable story for why she should be meeting Mr. Carrington alone like this—most uncomfortable. He should have thought of that.

Fortunately, she knew the other way into this room: through the library. She'd just hurry around that way and be assured of better privacy. Her feet padded silently on the highly polished floors, and her stomach rumbled. Bother. What could it be now? Was she simply hungry—at last—or was this more of her special troubles? It was most annoying.

She wished she dared take Dr. Buchan's book up to her room for a more thorough study. It seemed she was constantly being interrupted down here. But she didn't dare; the book was huge and surely would draw attention to her. If only it were smaller, more like the volume by Sir Cocksure.

She paused a moment. And what of Sir Cocksure's book? It dealt in the most frank manner with delicate issues. Could it be the man had some chapter or mention somewhere in his primer regarding her specific worries? It would make sense that a book giving instruction on all manner of conjugal recreation might also give some information on what could possibly come of all that recreating. Hmm, it was an interesting thought, indeed. She moved around to the side of the bookshelf where she'd hidden the book.

Of course, this was not the time to stop and peruse it, but the volume was tiny. She could easily tuck it in her shawl and carry it to her room for later. Yes, that's just what she'd do. She'd read it tonight when she was alone and there was no chance for interruption. Perhaps it might answer some of her questions.

At least, she told herself that was the only reason for absconding with the naughty little book. She balled it up tightly in her shawl and tucked it carefully under her arm. Best get into the music room before Mr. Carrington feared she was not coming.

She made her way into the little anteroom—a place,

perhaps, for musicians to ready themselves before a formal musicale. It appeared the room was used very rarely, and dust covered every surface. Oddly, the door that led to the music room was not closed up tightly. Clearly someone had come through here since last time she'd made a hasty retreat through it. Perhaps Carrington had anticipated her use of this door.

Approaching, she would have pushed it the rest of the way open, but suddenly she realized Mr. Carrington was not alone. There were voices inside the music room, and Evaline instinctively stepped back out of view, lest anyone notice her through the cracked door. Drat, but she'd done more hiding since her arrival at Hartwood than she'd ever done as a curious child. This was getting to be normal behavior for her!

She waited a moment to be sure she had not been seen and was surprised to realize that none of the voices drifting out from the music room belonged to Mr. Carrington. Was he even in there? As she listened, it became obvious that he was not. The only two voices she heard were those of Lord Rastmoor and Claudia Graeley.

"Unlock the door," Claudia was saying.

"You'd rather someone wanders in?" Rastmoor asked.

"I don't have time for this. Let me go."

"Then just answer my question," Rastmoor said, his voice almost a growl. "What are you doing in here, Claudia?"

"I came in here to be alone. In case you haven't noticed, things are not going especially well for me lately, Anthony. I just found out this morning the man I intend to marry was busy asking some little twit to marry him at dinner last night!"

Evaline narrowed her eyes. *Little twit*, eh? Well, this little twit could think of a few choice names for Claudia, too. She strained her ears to hear every word.

"Dashford was funning," Lord Rastmoor said. "I'm quite sure he never intended to marry her."

"Of course not," Claudia sniped. "He's already engaged to me. But he is rather taken with her. You don't suppose he fancies himself in love with her, do you?"

"What do you care about that?"

"I don't," Claudia said and clucked her tongue. "Well, she'll not break her heart over him, that's for certain. I saw how cozy she was with Mr. Carrington."

Rastmoor gave a knowing laugh. "Yes, odd isn't it, that a little nobody like Carrington could catch the eye of an heiress? Then again, perhaps he has hidden qualities."

"Oh, button it, Anthony. What do you want with me, anyway? I need to be alone."

"Do you? That's something new."

"Leave me so I can go back to my thoughts."

"You have thoughts, Claudia? I would have never guessed. So tell me, what sort of thoughts are they? Trying to plot a way to convince Dashford to go through with the wedding? Surely you're not fool enough to believe he truly wants to marry you, Claudia."

"Just because your own engagement didn't go the way you wanted, Anthony Rastmoor, is no reason to try to ruin mine. Don't think I don't know how you've been the one to sour Dashford against me. He loved me; he did. *You're* the one who took him to sordid places where he met horrible people and . . . and *those* kinds of women."

"Oh, I did that to him, did I?"

"Because you're still bitter that some nobody girl threw you over for your cousin, then had the good sense to die with his child."

There was silence. Even without seeing Lord Rastmoor's face, Evaline knew Miss Graeley had gone too far.

"That was uncalled for, Claudia," he said finally, his voice remarkably calm. "And to think, I was prepared to recommend you over Miss Pinchley."

"I don't need you to recommend me!" she snapped, but her voice had a tremble to it. "I *will* marry Dashford. You'll see. He'll come to his senses once he realizes just what sort of person this Miss Pinchley is. I've been learning things about her; Mr. Bristol has been remarkably free with his conversation."

"Is that what you were doing, cloistered with Bristol in that back hallway for fifteen minutes today? Carrying on a conversation about Miss Pinchley?"

Claudia had been cloistered alone for fifteen minutes with Ellard? Well, there was a lot going on in this house Evaline was not aware of! Perhaps she'd do well to spend less time being distracted by Dashford and more time keeping track of everything else.

"Mr. Bristol had some very interesting things to say about her," Claudia said. "They were quite close, you know."

"*Every* woman who spends fifteen minutes with Bristol ends up quite close to him. You wouldn't want Dashford to hear rumors about the two of you now."

Obviously Claudia didn't miss Rastmoor's subtle threat. When she spoke, her voice was tight and clipped.

"Say what you like about me. Randolf Dashford made a legally binding promise to me, and I'm going to see that he keeps it. I will be Lady Dashford, and this little shopkeeper's daughter will get what she deserves: an invitation back to the gutter."

"Have a care, Claudia," Rastmoor said grimly.

"You just stay out of it, Anthony," she warned. "I know what I'm doing."

"I don't doubt that for a minute," Lord Rastmoor said. "But don't forget, so does Dashford. He's not the gullible sot you seem to believe."

"Oh? I think that little strumpet he can't seem to keep his eyes off is proof enough that he is. Good day, Lord Rastmoor."

With that, Evaline heard the sound of Claudia's footsteps moving toward the other door and a lock being opened. Soon Claudia's feet were stomping away down the hall. The room was silent.

Why, that scheming, slandering, hard-hearted hussy! Call her a twit, would she? Lure Dashford into a clearly unhappy union, would she? Evaline had half a mind to go after her and set her straight on a few things. But that would only make matters worse, so she stayed put.

Besides, Rastmoor was still there. She was sure of it. Claudia's footfalls had gone off alone. She waited, listening intently for the welcome sounds of Rastmoor's exiting tread.

But he didn't exit. The seconds ticked by—minutes, perhaps—and still there was no sound from the other side of the partially opened door. She shuffled her feet. The book in the shawl felt heavy under her arm. She tightened her hold on it. Then she sneezed.

Drat. The book slid out of its hiding place and banged to the floor. She dove down to retrieve it, bundling it hastily back into the shawl. By the time she was rising back to her feet, she realized she was not alone. Lord Rastmoor had discovered her.

He stood there in the now fully opened doorway, glaring at her.

"So, you've taken up eavesdropping, have you, Miss Pinchley?"

She jumped back, clutching the tightly wrapped Sir Cocksure as if her life depended on it. Likely it did. She would simply die if the man found her with something like this in her possession!

"I was . . . er, looking for the library," she said quickly.

"Of course. It's right back there," Rastmoor said, then smiled as his eyes ran over her body. "Where you came from."

"Yes, of course. I thought perhaps this might be a shortcut back to the stairs."

"No, they would be the other direction."

"Oh silly me. I always was dreadful at directions."

"Perhaps your talents lie in other areas," he said, and an unpleasant smile began to form on his lips. "I must say, our friend Dashford does know talent when he finds it."

She felt her cheeks flame. Heavens, what had Dashford told this man about them? If Rastmoor had any suspicions at all about the shameful things she'd done with Dashford, perhaps he would expect her to behave that way with him!

"What's the matter, Miss Pinchley?" he questioned, stepping into the anteroom and looming over her. "You don't seem happy to find me here. Perhaps it was not me you'd expected to meet?"

"I was expecting no one," she said, her voice breaking and sounding small and fearful. "I was simply passing by."

Lord Rastmoor's brows knit together. "Is this true? You were not waiting for someone? You're all alone in here?"

Oh wonderful. No telling what he might attempt now! When would she ever learn to hold her peace? He stepped closer to her and had the nerve to raise his hand to touch her face. She took a surprised step back but found herself up against a row of chairs. Oh heavens, he had her trapped!

"Or perhaps," he said slowly, studying her features with his eyes and his fingertips, "you're simply waiting for a better offer."

She couldn't speak. He must know the truth. He must know she was a fallen woman, that she had allowed herself to give in to forbidden passions. Perhaps Dashford had bragged of it. That's what men did about their meaningless conquests, wasn't it? Now Rastmoor viewed her as nothing more than an available plaything.

She'd been such a fool to think she could keep what went on between her and Dashford a secret! Of course there was no such thing in society. Before long, everyone would know what she had become, and Dashford would be done with her. She had no funds, she could not rescue Sophie, and she would end up alone.

"You know Dashford has nothing but a title and a pretty face," Rastmoor was saying as his hands caressed her shoulders. "I, however, could put you up nicely. Tell me, Miss Pinchley, what is it you're looking for in your men? Connections with the cream of society? Travel to exotic places? What can I offer to steal you away from Dashford?"

"Nothing! There is absolutely nothing you could . . ." And there she stopped herself. Not because Rastmoor interrupted or let his touch become anything but gentle, but simply because her own words sank in.

Oh God, they were true, weren't they? Suddenly she understood why she'd let herself do the horrible things she'd done. What she'd said to Rastmoor was true. There was nothing Rastmoor—or any man—could do or offer to steal her away from Dashford. Nothing on earth.

Funny it hadn't dawned on her before this. All those times when Dashford touched her and the passion roared to life in an instant, she rather assumed that was a commonplace reaction, that it could happen with any halfway decent and attractive gentleman. Now she knew otherwise. Standing here, staring into Rastmoor's steely blue eyes and ruggedly handsome face, she realized she was unmoved. In fact, she was so cold toward him she was practically numb where his fingers touched her.

She wanted nothing more than to swat his hand away and run to Dashford. Oh God, this was dreadful. She was indeed a fallen woman, but her fall had been of the worst kind. She'd not only given her body and soul to the passion she'd found with Dashford, but she'd given her heart as well. She loved him!

"What the hell are you doing?"

Evaline choked in a startled breath. It was Dashford. He filled the doorway between them and the music room. His face was a thundercloud. Evaline shrank back, but her molester simply turned to meet his friend's deadly gaze.

How could Lord Rastmoor not seem the least bit concerned, having been found in this compromising position? Dashford's expression was nothing short of terrifying. If it wasn't for the fact that her legs were paralyzed with fear, Evaline would have run from them both as fast and as far as she could.

"Miss Pinchley and I were discussing offers," Rastmoor said smoothly. "You made her one, I believe?"

"I did, although it looks to me as if you might have forgotten about it," Dashford replied with ice in his voice.

"Miss Pinchley rejected it, if you recall."

"Oh? And you're prepared to make her a better offer?" Dashford asked.

Rastmoor kept his eyes fixed on Dashford. "Perhaps I ought to. It might be interesting to see which one she'd choose."

She shivered. What were they doing, posturing over her as if she were livestock? How foolish she'd been to let herself become involved in this muck. Both men thought her nothing more than chattel: a thing to be bartered for and won.

Is this what Grandmamma had been before that earlier Dashford had captured her heart? Is this the future Evaline had in store, forced to sell herself to the highest bidder? What an idiot she'd turned out to be. She should have settled for a modest marriage when she'd had the chance long before letting herself get dragged here to lose herself to Dashford.

"I don't want any offers," she said, shoving Rastmoor away with all her might and stepping away from the men. She couldn't quite avoid Dashford's fiery eyes, though. "I just want this dratted rain to stop so I can leave this place and pretend I never met you!"

He remained perfectly still, glaring back at her. Energy radiated off him so strongly she was afraid of what he might do. Mostly she was afraid of how easily she might give in to him again.

But she was saved. A voice called out, a door banged in the hallway, and running footsteps approached. A footman appeared in the music room behind Dashford.

"My lord," he called out, breathless.

Dashford turned, perfectly composed. "Yes?"

"It's flooding, sir. Where the bridge went down it dammed up the river. Now there's flooding, and several tenant families are stranded."

"Which tenants?" Dashford asked.

The footman looked a bit flustered. "I don't know, sir. There's a man here. He brought the news. We didn't know where to find you, but if you come with me, I'm sure he could explain."

Instantly Dashford's face took on an unreadable expression. "All right," he said. "Have my horse saddled and brought around to the front." He glanced back at Evaline then over at Rastmoor. "On second thought, make that two horses."

The footman nodded, and when no further instructions came, he took off into the hallway. Dashford turned his focus back to Evaline.

"You have your wish, Miss Pinchley. Go pack your bags. I'm sure we can find some alternate route to get you back to Bath. Or anywhere else you'd like to go."

She felt her heart drop. She was to leave. Being dismissed. Well, it's what she wanted, of course. It's what she'd asked for. But it wasn't in truth what she wanted, she hated to admit.

"I'll see to it John Coachman gets you safely where you need to go."

She nodded timidly, and he turned on his heel to leave. Over his shoulder he called back to Rastmoor, "Anthony, you're riding out with me. These tenants might need an extra hand."

With that, Rastmoor gave Evaline one last triumphant glance as he trotted up to Dashford's side. Well. Apparently

Dashford's anger at Rastmoor when he found them together hadn't been all that strong. She'd thought for a moment or two that it had been, that she'd seen a rage of jealousy in his eyes. Clearly she'd been wrong.

Damn, but these tears were certainly going to make packing more difficult.

THE RAIN WAS STEADY NOW, AND DASHFORD WAS soaked to the skin. He didn't much care, though. He'd found Evaline in the arms of his best friend. Why should a few drops of rain bother him?

Anthony was riding along beside him, equally wet. Well, a good dousing served him right. A good drowning would be even better. What sort of friend seduced one's lover? Hell. Dashford wished he was as cold on the inside as he was on the outside. Perhaps then the betrayal wouldn't hurt so badly.

"I'm sorry, you know," Rastmoor said after a long silence.

The others of their soggy little rescue party had ridden on ahead. Dashford and Rastmoor were left alone, their horses plodding along gingerly over the rutted and sticky road.

"Like hell you are," he replied, though Rastmoor really didn't deserve any response. The only reason he brought him along was so he didn't have to worry what Rastmoor and Evaline might get up to in his absence.

"Come now, Dash," Rastmoor said. "You can't possibly tell me you care that much for her!"

Dashford glared at him. "It's none of your damn business how much I care for her. You know she belongs to me."

"She doesn't belong to you. You know what sort of woman she is. Damn it, Dash. She was in your bed the first moment you met her, before you were even introduced, for God's sake!"

Now he was steamed. So Rastmoor had figured it out, had he? Yes, of course he had. The man wasn't a half-wit, and Dashford himself had inadvertently let slip the truth, hadn't he? He recalled now. He'd mentioned her name to him while he still believed her to be a mere servant. His friend had no doubt put the two together. Damn.

"If you ever so much as breathe a word of that to anyone,

I swear, Anthony, I'll forget I'm a gentleman or that we've been friends for two decades."

"Are we still friends?"

"Were you seducing Evaline?"

"No."

"Sure as hell looked like you were."

"I just wanted to see if she'd take up the bait."

"What the hell does that mean? She's not a cod, you know."

"She's an opportunist, Dash. A very pretty, innocent-looking opportunist. I merely wondered how quickly she'd dive into another opportunity. And I'd like to point out, she didn't exactly start screaming for help."

"I'd like to think that's because she didn't feel she needed to."

"Or didn't want to," Rastmoor mumbled. "Face it, Dash. She's a tasty little diversion, but you're better off without her."

"She arrived in my house with her reputation intact. I'll not be responsible for changing that."

"And just how far will these noble intentions of yours go? Everyone heard you offer for her, poorly done though it was. If you do manage to get rid of Claudia, what's to keep this Pinchley chit from squirming herself into Claudia's place? All she needs to do is cry that you've misused her, and you'll be stuck in another engagement. At least Claudia's got a decent pedigree for proper wife material."

"You're hardly one to lecture about proper wife material."

"And you'd do well to learn from my example," Rastmoor grumbled, sending them into more silence for a minute or two.

Dashford's horse slipped in the mud. He swore. The horse righted himself and got back into step with Rastmoor's. Dashford sighed.

"I told her to leave, didn't I?"

"Did you mean it?"

Dashford grimaced. Of course he'd meant it at the time, but now he wasn't so certain. It was far too dangerous to expect anyone to travel these roads in this weather. He had visions of Evaline stranded, the carriage overturned, and all manner of dreadful things befalling her. No, he'd been too hasty to dismiss her. Of course he couldn't send her off now, like this.

"You *are* sending her away, right?" Rastmoor said.

Dashford didn't bother to answer.

"Damn it, Dash! She's not your responsibility. While you're letting her warm your bed, she's plotting to get your title. And don't flatter yourself that you're the first to tarnish her reputation. She's a tart. A self-serving little mercenary. And how do we even know she's who she says she is? She doesn't look like any heiress I've ever seen. Lord, this might all be some elaborate hoax, pure rot!"

Blast it all. Who knew more about deceiving, fortune-hunting females than Rastmoor? The man had a point. What did Dashford really know about Evaline and her true origins? Nothing. She may have pulled the wool over his mother's eyes from the start. Hell, this whole thing could be a grand plot. How did he know Bristol and that damned Carrington weren't even in on it with her? He didn't. He didn't know anything.

"You still want her, don't you?" Rastmoor said after another uncomfortable silence.

Dashford kept him waiting. It was none of Rastmoor's damn business if he wanted to throw his life away on some lying trollop from God knew where. Anthony Rastmoor was the last one to berate him for that.

"You'd probably marry her if it came down to it, wouldn't you?"

Dashford thought long and hard about that one. In the end, he knew the answer. It was the same answer Rastmoor gave three years ago before his own heart was torn from his soul and trampled in the dust.

"Yes. I would."

"Holy shit." Rastmoor shook his head. "Aren't we a sorry pair?"

Yes, they were.

"Come on. Let's go catch up to our group," Dashford said, determined to turn his mind to more productive endeavors. "The worst of the flooding is upstream, at the Millers' farm. Word is the whole lot of them have taken refuge on the roof of their barn. My men are collecting skiffs, and we'll try to secure a line over to the barn so the family can be floated safely across."

"Children?"

"Eight, I believe."

"Hell. Well, this ought to keep us busy for a while."

Dashford nodded. Yes, a good long while. He only hoped it would be enough to take his mind from Evaline and the worrisome thoughts that plagued him. Facing a wall of raging floodwaters was not nearly as terrifying as what he feared might be lurking in his own heart. Best not to examine it too closely.

Chapter Thirteen

It was late, but Evaline couldn't seem to close her eyes. The minute she did, Dashford's face haunted her and she felt his hands on her body, making her long for him with a fervor she could have never thought possible. It was much safer to stay awake, pacing the room.

The house was silent, save for the rain still beating a constant cadence against the windowpanes. Was he still out there? They had heard nothing of him all afternoon and night. Lady Dashford had been somewhat concerned when he did not appear for dinner, and as the group adjourned to the drawing room for the usual evening's entertainment of cards and conversation, she seemed to become increasingly distracted. The rain had not let up, and it was easy to assume the flooding was not getting better. There was no telling what hazards were out there.

Evaline tried to convince herself she didn't care in the least what happened to his lordship. Lying to everyone else when they offered reassurances that he'd return safe and sound any moment had been simple enough. Lying to herself was a bit more difficult. Even Claudia had given up her spiteful glares and begun to show signs of worries. Evaline supposed she should be glad for the respite, but really this only served to remind her there had, at least at one time, been something tender between Dashford and Miss Graeley. She wished it had been Claudia out there suffering in the cold rain, instead.

Ellard must have recognized the tension in the room, and he was even more charming than usual. He was careful not to pay any more attention to Evaline than any of the other ladies, but she was grateful for his presence. He served as a reminder of a happier time in her life, and a part of her desperately wanted to believe it could be captured again. Yet try as she might, she would never be able to dredge up those old feelings she was sure she'd once had for him.

No, it seemed her sentiments were all for Dashford, and the fact that he was possibly in mortal danger and she could do nothing about it had not helped to make her think any less fondly of him. She struggled to make small talk as long as she could, then finally bade good night to Ellard and everyone else and headed up to her room.

But being alone didn't help take her mind from Dashford. The only book on hand was Sir Cocksure's, and that certainly didn't help. She could find no reference to any instruction on her topic of concern, and the more pages she turned, the more she missed Dashford.

Finally she threw the book across the room. Oddly, it fell open to the front page, and she noticed an inscription there she'd not seen before. Desperate for distraction, she took the book up again to read.

On the page someone had inked an elaborate design. It wasn't etched or engraved there, it was hand drawn and somewhat faded from time. The design was a twining vine, twisted and tied together to form two hearts. Little flowers had been drawn in to give the design a feminine, romantic feel. Certainly, it looked out of place on this book, to say the least!

But there were words there, as well. They were hand-written in the same ink and said cryptically, "The man bears the key while the woman holds the treasure." Well, perhaps that was not so cryptic. She had a pretty good notion what sort of key it might refer to. How odd, though, that such a loving inscription would be included here. Surely this was not the sort of book one might give or receive as a gift.

Then again, she could think of nothing more wonderful than for two persons in love to share together all the passions and pleasures described between Sir Cocksure's pages. Perhaps this had indeed been a gift at one point from one lover to another. The thought seemed unbearably sweet. What a treasure, indeed, for lucky was the woman who had a devoted lover to share all these things with her.

She sighed. It was a treasure she'd gotten barely a glimpse of but could never possess. She shoved the book under her mattress, where she wouldn't have to look at it and be reminded of everything she'd be missing for the rest of her life. She loved Dashford; she couldn't deny it. Now he'd ordered her to leave. Likely he expected her to be gone by the time he returned. If he returned.

Oh heavens, she didn't want to think about it. What if something had happened to him out there tonight, and he was lost? It was too dreadful to contemplate. If word should come that he'd been overcome, swept away, or that some other tragic mishap befell him, what on earth would she do?

She would do nothing. She would pack up and leave and have to keep her grief entirely private. She was nothing to Randolf Dashford. He was done with her, and he wanted her gone. Heavens, even if he did return safe and sound from this rescue mission of his, chances were she'd still never see him again. He would simply go to his bed tonight then summon his coachman to cart her off first thing in the morning.

And that would be that. She'd already packed, she had those funds from Mr. Carrington, and she would make no scene or dramatic exit. No, that would be for Aunt Bella to do once she realized what had happened. Indeed, Dashford would have his hands full, once Bella Stump realized she'd lost her one hope of ever getting any of Papa's money.

Certainly sleep would be impossible tonight. Desperate to clear her mind, she paced the floor, alternating between worrying for Dashford, berating herself for being such a fool, and struggling to form some plan for her life. Where would she go? How would she live?

Grandmamma's home was not to be hers, not just yet, at least. She did not even know where to begin hunting for Sophie. So where would she go? Back to Bath? No, Bath was home for Aunt Bella and Uncle Troy, not Evaline. She had no home. Home would always be here, at Hartwood, since this was where she'd be leaving her heart.

Oh, but what a pitiful sap she was, sniffling and crying into her night rail. If only she could at least know Dashford was safe, then she could gather her wits and find some semblance of peace. But rain still pounded the window, and she knew he could not be safe, not out in this.

Then there it was, a sound in the hall. Footsteps? Could it be? She'd been listening for them all night; half a dozen times she'd thought for sure it was him, returning safely. Twice she'd so much as rushed to press her ear against the door, only to find the hallway outside silent and still. Her mind was playing tricks. Was this time any different?

She stood there, all her energy focused on listening. Yes, this time it was real. She did hear footsteps. And something more. Voices! Once again she pressed her ear to the door. It was Dashford. Oh, blessed God, he was all right.

"Thank you, Carothers," he was saying to his valet. "Yes, we are fine. All the tenants have been seen to. Three homes are lost and some livestock, unfortunately, but everyone is accounted for."

She breathed a prayer of silent thanks. He was here; he was safe.

"Lord Rastmoor has a nasty cut, though," Dashford went on. "Would you be so kind as to tend to it for him?"

"Certainly, sir. Right away," the valet said.

She heard Rastmoor utter something in dispute, but his voice was tired and held little conviction. Dashford, too, sounded worn. She did note, however, that Dashford appeared on good terms with Rastmoor again. Apparently a little thing like infidelity was not enough to destroy their friendship. She supposed she'd flattered herself to think Dashford might have remained angry for her sake. How silly that she'd let herself be disappointed.

The men were talking again, but she couldn't make out the words until they came closer to her door.

"No, don't worry. I'll be fine on my own," Dashford said, presumably to his valet. "Go set Rastmoor aright, then get yourself to bed."

The valet agreed, and Evaline could make out footsteps heading up the hall. Then there was the sound of doors opening and closing. First Rastmoor's, then Dashford's. At least he was safe. But oh, how she wished she could see him one last time!

But he had gone on to bed. Alone. That's what she should do, too. Tomorrow would, no doubt, be a busy day for her.

She tiptoed back to her bed and wondered how on earth she would be able to sleep. She sat on the edge of the huge bed and almost laughed when she realized her mind was racing to think up an excuse to find her way to his room. Good heavens, wouldn't that be the height of stupidity? As if he'd welcome her with open arms after what he thought he saw in the music room, how he'd ordered her to pack up and leave his home. She'd only end up heartbroken and humiliated.

So she sat there, feet dangling off the bed, praying for the strength to get through what was bound to be a long, long night.

She heard the distant sound but thought nothing of it. Footsteps, again. Probably the valet this time, going for bandages or something like that. Still, she had to wonder that the footsteps were so quiet. If not for a slight creak in a floorboard here and there, she'd not have detected them at all.

And was she imagining it, or did they stop outside her door?

Her breath caught in her throat. Dashford. These were his cautious footfalls outside her door. He was here.

She didn't pause one second to contemplate the logic of her actions. She leapt from the bed and ran to undo the latch. The door swung open.

He was indeed there, dripping head to toe and weary to the bone, as bedraggled as a starved cat. One look at him, and the heartfelt words came spilling out.

"You look horrible!"

SHE LOOKED WONDERFUL. SHE LOOKED WARM AND soft and welcoming. Obviously she didn't feel quite the same about him, but at this point he couldn't have cared less. She was there; he hadn't even needed to knock. His tired brain was just clear enough to believe that could only mean she'd

been waiting up, worrying over him. The fact that it could
just as easily have meant she'd been entertaining one of her
many admirers was pleasantly ignored as it passed through
his consciousness. Right now he only wanted to believe what
he wanted to believe.

And he wanted to believe he'd never found her with
Rastmoor or heard about her with Bristol or seen her with
Carrington. He wanted to believe she was all his. It was easy
to believe, too. She practically threw herself into his arms.

"You're alive!" she said.

She felt better than any hot bath could have. He wrapped
her to him and just held her there. He was rather glad to be
alive just now, too.

But too quickly she pulled away and looked around the
hall. Apparently she was content they'd been unseen, so she
took his hand and pulled him through her doorway.

"Hurry, come in," she said.

He didn't hesitate to obey. She quietly shut the door
behind him then jabbed her fists into her sides and glared.

"What on earth were you thinking, letting yourself get
drenched to the bone and staying out there all night like
this?" she began, and for a minute he wondered if he hadn't
somehow mistaken her for his mother.

But her nightgown was dampened now from coming in
contact with him, and he could see her clearly defined curves
and perked nipples through it. No, this wasn't his mother,
that was for certain. He stared shamelessly.

"What are you . . ." Her voice broke off when she noticed
the staring. Quickly, she crossed her arms in front of her and
took a step back. "You had everyone here very worried about
you."

"You were worried for me?"

"Yes, well, that is, everyone was. Your mother could
hardly make it through dinner, wondering if you were all
right. We didn't know if maybe you'd been drowned or
something."

"Not quite."

"Apparently. Here, you should dry off."

She hurried over to a dressing table where fresh linens
were laid out. She grabbed up some towels and came

scurrying to unload them carelessly into his arms, then rushed over to build up the fire in the grate. It was a chilly night, and the servants had dutifully seen to the guests' comforts, he was glad to note, so it took little effort on Evaline's part before a much warmer fire was glowing there.

"You must be frozen," she said.

He was, but watching her bending over that grate there, her gown transparent before the light of the fire, was warming him up quite nicely.

"I'll agree, it's not altogether balmy out there," he said, pulling his wet shirt off over his head.

He'd left his coat back in his room but now realized he should have let Carothers remove his boots before tromping over here to Evaline. He doubted she was the type to welcome his boots in her bed, and he'd decided several hours ago that Evaline's bed was where he was damn well going to end up tonight. Tart or trollop or whatever she was, he needed her tonight. Thank God he hadn't remembered to send word to ready a carriage to remove her from Hartwood.

She turned from the fire to speak but stopped, her mouth hanging open, when she found him shirtless. Ah, but that was rather a nice expression to elicit from a lady, he had to admit.

"What are you doing?" she stammered.

"You can't expect me to spend the night in these wet clothes, Miss Pinchley. Then I will catch my death of cold."

"Yes, of course," she said, but she didn't sound entirely convinced.

A charming blush stole over her cheeks, and she prudishly averted her eyes. Was this all part of her game, to tease and toy with him until she had him so thoroughly wrapped around her little finger he could do nothing but live out his life to serve her? Damn it, but the woman was a witch. This dance between wanton and innocent was getting to him.

"Help me with my boots?" he asked. "I seem to have lost my valet for the night."

"Help with your boots?"

"Help removing them," he clarified for her. "You can't

very well expect me to get into bed still wearing them, can you?"

She was positively darling when she at last looked up to meet his eyes. Her green eyes were huge, and she blinked once, then twice. Had she only just now realized what it meant, him coming to her in the middle of the night and her inviting him in? It appeared so. She blushed again.

"But you've got to be exhausted! And you're wet."

"I'll dry quickly once I get the rest of these clothes off."

She blushed harder. He decided to see just how deep that blush could go.

"Then it'll be your turn to get wet," he added.

Indeed, another shade darker. He liked that. How she could still pull it off, he had no idea, but he liked it. He also didn't feel like waiting any longer to get her back in his arms. She'd managed to back slightly away from him, but one stride brought him to her. He caught her in his arms again.

"You haven't been keeping anyone here in my place, have you?" he asked.

"No, of course not!" she said. She smelled fresh and clean. He believed her.

"Good. I'm in no mood to share you."

"But it isn't . . . we can't . . ." She fumbled for words, struggling weakly against him.

"What is it, Evaline?" he said, holding her tight and tipping her face up to him. "You don't want me to make love to you?"

He could tell she really wanted to say no. He felt it there, almost on her lips, running through her thoughts. Damn, he didn't want to hear it, but he forced himself to let her be, to give her own answer in her own time. If he was to finally have her tonight, he wanted it to be without the silly games and her false pretenses of innocence. He wanted her to admit she wanted him the way a woman wants a man.

"I'll help you with your boots," she said after a deep, ragged breath.

To hell with his boots. He recognized a yes when he heard one, and he saw it in her eyes. She wanted him.

He crushed her against him and brought his lips to hers.

God, but she was sweet. And so damn warm. Hot, even. His body went from chills to fever. The good kind of fever. He ran his hand down her back, enjoying the womanly contours where her delightful little bottom protruded and her taut muscles resisted the gentle pressure of his touch. He could spend hours just roaming over her wonderful body.

And tonight he would.

"Lock the door, Evaline," he said.

"I did."

He could have broken into song at that phrase. Perhaps for once they would get to finish this the way God intended, with both of them naked, sweating, and wrapped around each other, panting for air. True, God might not have planned on the exact circumstances of this relationship, but then again, perhaps he had. He did work in mysterious ways, and who was Dashford to argue with the Almighty?

HER KNEES WENT WEAK. HE'D COME BACK, AND he didn't hate her. She could feel it in the way he touched her, the way his lips lingered over hers and trailed burning kisses across her throat and around her neck. He'd forgiven her for what he'd assumed she'd been doing with Rastmoor. At least, that's what it felt like.

She decided not to think any deeper than these immediate physical responses. He wanted her and she wanted him and that was all she needed to know right now. She'd spent too many hours worried for his very life; she wasn't about to start contemplating the future now. This was all that mattered, his hands on her body and her body in his arms.

She wondered how long she could stand here, thrilled by his touch and rapidly falling into senseless ecstasy. Her muscles were useless. The only thing that kept her upright was his strong, solid body. She clung to him for support, and his kisses paused long enough for him to laugh under his breath.

"You still with me here?"

She nodded, since that was about all she could do. One of his hands had slid around behind her and was rubbing that tender place between her legs. He wasn't honestly going to expect conversation now, was he?

"Let's get you out of this bothersome nightgown," he said, moving his hands and putting just enough air between them that she dared to draw in a deep breath.

Somehow he'd already undone the little ribbons that tied her night rail, and it only took him moments to slide it over her shoulders. It crumpled to the floor, leaving her cold and vulnerable in nothing more than her shift. But that, too, would have to go, she sensed. He seemed in no great hurry, though, and made some sort of game of sliding the fabric slowly up toward her waist, letting his hands linger at her thighs and abdomen before finally pulling it up higher.

She raised her arms to wriggle out of it, but he had some other idea. Somehow he took advantage of her position and, with a quick twist, her head and arms were wrapped within the garment. She was trapped! There was a moment of breathless panic, then she felt his hands at her breasts.

Oh, if she thought her legs had been weak before, she nearly pooled right onto the floor now. In the warm glow of one taper and the cracking fire, she could see him through the thin muslin of her shift; he was bending to bring his lips down onto her breast. Ah, the anticipation itself was mind-numbing. When at last he took her into his mouth, she actually cried out. His arm was around her, holding her up.

And then he wasn't holding her up. He was leaning her back, carrying her to the bed. Thank heavens; she couldn't have stood any longer. She sank into the soft mattress, and her body tingled at the feel of the linens around her.

Now there was the added pleasure of his body next to hers. By God, the man had silky hairs all over his body! She moaned at the feel of his chest against hers, his rugged hands kneading her, scorching her where they touched. She wanted to touch him back, to run her hands over his solid shoulders and the strong sinews of his arms. Drat, being all bundled up in her shift was holding her back. She struggled against it.

He had the nerve to laugh at her, then added fuel to her fire by sliding his hand across her stomach and down to the burning juncture at her legs. She was desperate to get her arms free, to pull him to her and find some release for this wave of emotion and raw passion that was building inside her. She knew what she needed; he'd brought it to her before. Tonight she would finally have all of him, and she was damn well going to remember it, too.

"I can't see," she muttered.

"You don't trust me?" he said, toying again with her nipple but still keeping a grip on the shift.

"I want to see you," she said.

"I can see you just fine."

Damn him, he was stroking gently between her legs, and his tongue lapped out to trace cool, wet circles around her nipples. She was nearly beside herself with desire, and the man had her trussed up like some sort of game bird. Any moment now he'd have her screaming with pleasure, and she couldn't so much as run her fingers through his hair.

He was moving over her, caressing her with his body as well as his hands. His fingers dipped precariously close to her heated core, but always he kept her just barely on the edge of that great chasm of ecstasy. He never let her slide over and give in to the overwhelming flames. She praised him and cursed him all at the same time.

She moved her legs, parting them for him and sliding her feet up to enwrap him. Then she jolted in surprise.

"You're cold!" she said, sliding her feet away from the offending boots.

Damn, he still had his clothes on!

He moved off her, laughing again. Oh, so he thought this was funny, did he? Bringing her to this wondrous place of physical pleasure only to disrupt the event with his wet, muddy boots? She was definitely going to have to make him pay for that.

"All right," he said, pulling the shift the rest of the way over her head and freeing her arms. "Help me out of them."

She sighed and reached for the garment to put it back on, but he withheld it. More laughter.

"What? I'm supposed to get down there and pull off your boots *naked*?"

"You've not done that before?" He actually seemed to think this odd.

"Certainly not!"

"Then I guess I'll just leave my boots on."

That would mean his trousers would remain on, which

would mean she'd not have an unobstructed view of his person. No, that was unacceptable. She'd been dreaming of this—literally—since the day she'd met him. Nothing was going to hinder her experience tonight, even if it meant she'd be crawling around naked.

"Fine. But if I must parade around in the altogether, so will you," she said.

He just laughed some more. She climbed over him and stood there, stark naked, holding out her hand for him to put his boot in it. He did.

He leaned back on the bed, and she began to pull. Lord, but this was embarrassing. How she must look, leaning over him in this position! She glanced up to see if he was going to start ridiculing her.

Ridicule seemed very far from his mind. What she saw on his face was most startling. His eyes were glazed over, his jaw had gone slack, and he stared at her as if he'd never seen a female before. At first she was horribly self-conscious, but slowly, as she pulled at that cold, damp boot, she realized how erotic this situation was. And just as he'd held her helpless in that darned shift a moment ago, he was every bit as helpless now, gazing at her body, transfixed by his own desire.

Well, there was something wonderfully powerful in that. She tugged at the boot, and it finally gave way, her body twitching in response. She watched him carefully, and his eyes never left her. In fact, his eyes grew decidedly larger when she felt her breasts jiggle at the movement of removing the boot.

He liked that, did he? She jiggled again, just for good measure. He swallowed. She twisted her body, bending dramatically to put his boot down beside the bed. He licked his lips. She straightened slowly, moving over to the other boot. His breath caught in his throat. She jiggled.

"Dear God, Evaline!" he said with a moan. "Are you trying to kill me? Just get on with it."

"Oh, I am, my lord," she said sweetly. "These boots are just so very heavy."

She tugged at it, making sure there was more jiggling. He flopped back onto the bed with a groan. His eyes stayed open, though. He could see her perfectly well.

So she rubbed her thigh against his boot. "It's just so hard. I can't seem to get it off."

He growled. So she turned her back to him and straddled his leg, yanking at the boot and making sure he had a good view of everything. He did, and he certainly wasn't laughing now. Heavens, she was behaving very badly, but she just couldn't seem to help herself. Knowing she had such power over him was addictive. She wanted more.

So did he. With a low roar he rose, grabbed her from behind, and pulled her back onto his lap. He kissed her ferociously, and she could feel his hardened manhood at her thigh, pressed between her skin and his rough trousers. Indeed, she had power she'd never known.

His boot thunked to the floor. She must have loosened it enough that he'd been able to kick it off. Or perhaps he'd never needed her help to begin with. Hmm, maybe she hadn't made him as helpless as she'd thought. Oh well. Whether she was using him or he was using her, it didn't seem to matter so much just now.

He laid her back against the mattress again, and she reached for the fastenings on his trousers. This had gone on just about as long as it could, in her opinion. She shoved his clothing out of the way.

He rolled away and off the bed. She would have been upset if not for the glorious view this provided her. His trousers slid past his narrow hips and down toward the floor. There he was, fully bare and fully man. She took in the unbelievable sight. Who would have ever thought a man could be so beautiful?

And huge. Good God Almighty, that thing stood ramrod straight and was as big as a Yule log. Had she truly already done this with him? And survived? She was glad to know it, for if she hadn't, she'd go running from the room in terror. She might anyway.

"Now, what game shall we play next?" he said, gazing down at her.

She couldn't for the life of her think of anything to say. Or take her eyes off his magnificent manhood.

"Ah, that one," he said and simply stood there, positioning himself before her for maximum visual exposure.

She couldn't help herself; she stared. The colors, the shape, the implied texture—everything about it was fascinating. What would it feel like inside her? She so wished she could remember.

Should she touch it? He didn't seem to mind the limited exploration she'd done in the boating grotto, but perhaps he'd merely humored her. Drat, but no one had ever told her the etiquette of these things. Surely he wouldn't mind if she wished to investigate it a bit more, would he? He seemed so very proud of it.

Well, nothing ventured, nothing gained. She thought to give it a try. She reached out and ran one finger along its velvety smooth side.

He groaned.

She glanced up quickly, hoping she hadn't made a dreadful faux pas. But he was smiling, and his eyes had that glazed look again. The blue of his irises had gone all smoky and dark. Yes, it seemed that touching it was a good thing. So she touched it again; this time, she used two fingers.

He groaned again.

All right, how about if she used her whole hand and just gripped the darn thing? She tried that. He groaned and moved against her. Holy Rock of Gibraltar, was it actually pulsating? No, perhaps that was only her imagination. She felt a sort of pulsating energy within her, urging her on to further experimentation. She wrapped her fingers around him and slid her hand slowly, from base to tip and then back down again.

He was hot and felt like silk, yet solid as a paving stone underneath. Surely when pressed against her, the pleasure it would bring would be great. She wanted that badly. Still gliding her hand up and down over him, she moved her eyes up to meet his. He was watching intently.

"Does it meet with your satisfaction?" he asked.

She nodded and took the opportunity to slide back up onto the bed, making room for him to join her. He did, lying alongside her so that their skin was touching and he had easy access to her body. She warred within herself, a battle between fear of what was to come and the inferno of desire that simply had to be quenched.

He touched her gently, his fingertips gliding along her side, her arms, and finally to her breasts. He let the desire build, touching her in intimate places but not quite the most intimate. He seemed to know that the longer he waited before moving her to full completion, the more she enjoyed each little sensation. She took advantage of the slower pace to let her hands ride over his body, as well.

She loved how different his was from her own body: his solid thighs, his tiny nipples, his broad and unyielding shoulders. Every inch of him was new and exciting for her. She leaned in to taste him, to kiss those tiny nipples and feel the graze of curling hair against her cheeks. It made her want him more.

Now he took control of her kisses, bringing her chin up so he could claim her lips with his own. It wasn't a gentle, seeking kiss. It was hard and possessive. She opened up to him and pulled herself closer.

He kissed her deeply, not just with his mouth but with his soul. She knew this deep within herself and responded with every fiber of her being, giving whatever he asked. It was not a conscious act now; they were both functioning fully on instinct.

With determined grace, he moved over her. She was engulfed in him, buried between his kiss and the soft bedding. Easily her arms clung to him, her legs wrapping around him to bring him closer. He was there, she felt him; he was pressing himself into her.

But he was so large! Why on earth couldn't she remember this? She wanted him, she knew she did, but something inside her was still resisting. What had happened two days ago, when she'd gone to his bed so blissfully at peace? Surely if it had been an unpleasant experience she would have recalled, or at least her body wouldn't be so eager to join him again.

And she was eager! She thought she might die without him at this point. So what was the conflict? Why couldn't she just stop fretting and let this happen?

He must have been aware of her difficulties. Without words, he was comforting her with gentle kisses at her neck. He managed to slide one hand in between them and found her rubied nipple. He rolled it gently between finger and thumb.

He was taking care of her, moving slowly so that she felt his member hard against her, stroking the most tender places. Oh, she wanted him. She needed him inside her.

Crushing her fears beneath the weight of her desire, she arched herself against him. Her legs tightened around his thighs. He groaned over her and plunged inside.

Her body froze at the unfamiliar sensation. The waves of passion she'd been waiting for seemed to suddenly dry up. In fact, she was vaguely aware of an odd discomfort. Could it be something was wrong? He went so still above her. She pinched her eyes tightly.

"Evaline," he breathed her name.

It was the sound of need, the sound of desire. It was a sound meant only for her. His body shifted, and he moved inside her. A heated flame took life, and suddenly the discomfort and awkwardness was gone. Dashford was filling her, and she pulled him tightly to her.

Ah, this was what she'd needed all her life.

It was as if there'd been a void in her being, a gaping wound in her spirit that was suddenly healed. At once her whole life was reduced to just this single moment. She felt complete.

She felt damn good, too.

He was moving inside her. Slowly at first he pulled back then sheathed himself in her again. Sparks rose through her body, tingling in every part of her. He pulled back then dove deep inside once more. Oh God, she was soaring up that mountain again. Higher and higher, with every move he made, the wave was building within her.

"My lord," she said when she was sure she couldn't take one more second of this.

But then she was falling over the edge. The great mountain was miles below her, and she was tumbling in a wave of hot emotion. Her body shook with the fury of it, and she felt him driving hard into her again and again.

Then he was with her. He shuddered, and she felt the pulsating beat of his climax inside her. She held him tight, never wanting it to end.

Finally he was spent. He fell against her, shifting just

enough to one side so she could still breathe. But she didn't care about breathing. She didn't care about anything but being here, her body tangled with his and the heat from their lovemaking radiating through the room. They lay that way for minutes—or hours—pressed against each other and sharing one heartbeat.

"Randolf," he said finally.

It startled her. "What?"

"My name is Randolf."

"What? Yes, I know your name."

"You called me by my title."

"What?"

"Just now. In the heat of passion, you called my by my title, not my name."

"I'm sorry. I guess I just wasn't sure if we were on a first name basis yet."

He turned her head to force her to look at him. She realized she didn't want to. Now that the passion was ebbing, she discovered reality was creeping back over her. Reality that he was someone she'd only just met and still barely knew. And most likely, she'd soon be leaving him.

"Evaline," he said, drawing her back into the fantasy. "We've always been on a first name basis."

"Yes, I suppose we have." He was right, of course. She'd given her body to him freely long before they even knew each other's names.

"So next time, when you feel compelled to call out while we're in the middle of making love, let us use first names, shall we?"

She nodded.

"*My* first name, to be specific," he added.

She nodded again and laid her head against him. So, this is what she had forgotten two days ago. How on earth had she managed to forget something like this? Damn that Madeira. She'd never touch the stuff again.

She would, however, touch Dashford anytime he'd let her. He was letting her now. She slid her hand between them to find that wonderful item that had brought her such joy. So, just how useful was this thing? Now that she knew what to do with it, she was eager for another venture.

Oh, but Dashford must be tired. He'd been out in the rain all day, slogging through floods and rescuing tenants and doing who knew what else. She supposed she ought to think of his well-being.

Indeed, he certainly had put plenty of effort into their union tonight. The man was amazing. Yes, she'd think of his needs for a while and let him sleep. Perhaps at some point he'd stir, and she could interest him again, but for now she'd be content just to lie there beside him and pretend things weren't the way they were.

Chapter Fourteen

Thin pink rays were just creeping in through the window. The sun was rising, but Dashford had been up for a good hour already. Literally. Lying here, watching Evaline sleep so peacefully, was driving him crazy with lust. But he'd been afraid to touch her.

He'd thought she was only playing, acting a part last night when they'd made love. The way she'd looked at him, touched him so reverently, and then hesitated when they'd come to the actual act. He assumed it was a part of the game for her, like succumbing to him in the garden, or telling stories to his mother. He'd taken her like a madman and thought that's what she wanted.

And then she'd hesitated. Her body had frozen up despite the passion he knew they were both feeling. That's when he realized something was amiss. Or, more appropriately, a maiden.

Somehow, he still had no clue how it could be, but he was convinced she'd been a maiden. A virgin. Untouched. The thought had plagued him all night.

Sure, gentlemen always claimed they could tell the difference, that no woman could ever fool them. Dashford never believed it. Then again, he'd never been with a virgin before. He still wasn't sure how he could be so certain.

It just didn't make sense. Why would a woman purposely

mislead a man to think she was more experienced than she was? Of course, if she'd been presenting herself as an expensive courtesan, perhaps experience might be something she'd lie about, but why Evaline? Was this part of some greater plot and he, foolishly, had fallen into it?

But what sort of plot could she possibly have? He'd already offered to marry her. True, it had been a very impolite offer, but there had been witnesses, and if she wanted to use it against him, she could have. But she hadn't. She'd made it very plain she was not interested. But what did she want?

Hell, he'd probably do anything she asked. She must realize that by now. So why the lies? Why the deception? And why was he still so damned hot for her?

Because he was an idiot, that's why. An idiot who fancied himself sophisticated where women were concerned, but he wasn't. He was just a rustic fool who fell for a pair of green eyes and a sad story.

She stirred, and slowly those green eyes opened. When she found him sitting there on the side of the bed, she smiled. Well, damn. That did him in. He'd believe whatever rot she tried to tell him this morning.

"I was afraid you'd leave," she said. Her voice was warm and breathy in the morning.

"I wasn't sure if you were done with me," he replied.

"I don't know. Am I?"

She pushed herself up to sit, clutching the covers over her. He reached out and pulled them down. She let him but shuddered in the chilly air.

God, she was beautiful. The dreadful gowns she was always dressed in did nothing for her small but perfect body. He was clearly going to have to get her some better clothes.

"I'm afraid you're the one to answer that question, my dear," he said. "And I have one other one, too."

"All right," she said with a smile.

"What do you want from me?"

Her smile faded to a look of confusion. "What?"

"Is it your intent to marry me?"

"What? Of course not. You are to marry Miss Graeley."

"No, I assure you, I am not to marry Miss Graeley."

She looked positively horrified. "What? But you must!"

He still could not imagine what this game was. Anger welled up, and he moved toward her. She pulled the blankets up to protect herself.

"What do you want from me, Evaline? And don't lie. I know you're old friends with Bristol, I've seen how you whisper with Carrington, and don't even remind me how I found you with Rastmoor yesterday. Why the games last night? Why try to convince me you're a skittish little virgin?"

"I seemed skittish?"

"Don't deny it. Oh, you were a hellion at first, but when it came down to it, you remembered to put on your act, feigning discomfort, awkward and hesitant. You acted like a virgin. Clearly you wished me to think you one. I want to know why."

"I'm sorry if my performance was not up to your high standards, my lord, but you of all people know I was no virgin last night."

"Your actions seemed to be trying to convince me otherwise."

"I did the best I knew how," she said, sounding a bit peeved at his conversation. "Apparently I do better when I'm drunk. In the future, should I ever find a man willing to waste his time on someone so incompetent as me, I'll have to make sure—for his sake—I'm good and sotted."

"Don't you dare!" he said. "By God, I'm not insulting you, Evaline. Not yet, anyway. Right now I'm just trying to understand. Are you planning to trap me into marrying you?"

"For the last time, no! Why must you keep harping on that?"

"Because oftentimes when a maiden is ravished in the night, she expects to be wed in the morning."

"Ravished in the night? Good heavens, is that what you did to me?"

"I made love to you in good faith that it was what you wanted."

"Well, of course it was what I wanted."

"Why? Respectable young maidens don't generally go about throwing themselves at currently engaged ne'er-do-wells. So tell me the truth. Were you or weren't you a virgin last night?"

"Certainly you should know the answer to that."

"I don't know what to believe about you. Just answer my question."

"Of course I wasn't. You know I wasn't. There was that other night."

Damn. She'd given him his answer, and still his brain struggled to believe it. "Just one other night? Only once? No wonder, then."

"No wonder about what?"

"Whoever your first lover was, he didn't do a very thorough job."

"He was you, for heaven's sake!"

"Me? But I never—"

"Well, there's certainly been no one else. That night when I met you in the garden, that was the first time."

"What? You think I . . . Damn it, didn't you notice a difference between what we did this time and what we've done previously?"

How unbelievably humiliating. He'd made love to this woman with every ounce of his heart and strength, and she still equated it to some of their botched attempts? That was cold.

She had the blankets wrapped tightly around her and was rocking back and forth slightly. "I don't remember what we've done previously!"

"Don't remember?" Shit. This just got worse and worse. "You don't remember in the library when I took you to the window seat, or when I tossed your skirts up and went down to—"

"Stop! Of course I remember that. It's just that first night I don't recall."

Thank heavens. If he was going to have to radically improve his skills just so she could at least remember her moments with him, he was in for a long and arduous lifetime. That first brief encounter in the garden was one he could easily live up to.

"You mean, in the garden," he said.

"No, I remember the garden," she replied. "It's what happened after that I can't quite recall."

Now he was confused again. "After that? What do you mean? Nothing happened after that."

"Yes it did! I woke up in your bed!"

Good God, was she talking about what he thought she was talking about? All this time she thought he'd taken advantage of her that first night? No wonder she'd been so willing to give in to him all along; she thought she already had! Thank heavens; there had been no other man on any other night. Just him. He felt like laughing.

"Evaline," he said softly. "Nothing more happened that night. You were drunk, and you were sleeping. I couldn't take advantage of a lady that way."

"You thought I was a servant—and an easy one at that!"

"I did. You looked the part, that's for certain, and we are definitely getting you new clothes at the earliest possible moment, but I never touched you after those few minutes in the garden."

"You didn't?"

"I wanted to—I'll fully admit to that—but I didn't."

"So, you mean . . . I wasn't a fallen woman? All this time and we never . . . ?"

"Well, we have now, rest assured."

She cringed at the memory. He didn't much care for that response. What was she upset about now? It wasn't as if he'd lied to her. She was the one who'd lied to him, but he was willing to overlook that. As far as he was concerned, she could go right on being a fallen woman all day long. Just so she understood he was the only one she was allowed to fall with.

"I just can't believe it," she said with an emotion that sounded remarkably like regret. "We didn't . . . so if I'd have just left yesterday like I planned, then I'd still be a . . . oh, this is awful!"

Yes, that was certainly regret. Damn, he'd given her reason to regret their night!

"Awful? You can't mean that. It was wonderful. We're perfect together! Hell, I even said I'd marry you, didn't I?"

He reached for her to let her know he was, indeed, suddenly serious about this whole marriage business, but she pulled away and jumped out of bed too quickly for him. She grabbed her shift where it lay on one side of the room and marched stiffly over to collect her nightgown from where it lay on the other.

"If you would be so kind as to turn your head, please," she said primly, "I'd like to put my clothes back on."

What? She was standing there naked after treating him to a night of passion like none he'd ever known, and now she was going all shy on him? This was incredible.

He started to protest, but she gave him a look that confirmed she'd been a mother abbess in some past life. Oh, damn it to hell. It would appear his morning was starting out much like his evening at the flood had been. Cold and frustrating.

"Fine," he said, covering his eyes.

He heard the sounds of her clothes being pulled on, and it grated. As close as they'd been, he ought at least to be allowed to watch. And then be allowed to pull them off again so they could get back to business.

Why was she so upset? What difference did it make when they'd finally gotten around to consummating their relationship? The important thing was that they had, and it had been great, and they really ought to be doing it again. Right now.

Apparently Evaline didn't see it that way. "Now put your clothes on, and you should go back to your room before anyone is up," she directed.

"It's early," he assured her. "We've got plenty of time."

"No. We don't." She seemed very certain of that. "If anyone should see you leaving here, we'd be expected to marry for sure."

"But we *are* getting married. Didn't you hear me?"

"No. We're not. You're not thinking clearly today. You're engaged to marry Claudia."

"I'm pretty sure I've been unfaithful to her."

"Put your clothes on," she said, scooping up his still-damp trousers and tossing them at his head. Luckily it wasn't a boot. She hit him square on.

"Fine," he acquiesced. "I can respect your need for discretion. I'll go."

He pulled the trousers on and tossed his shirt over his arm. No sense pulling the boots on; they'd only add to the noise and he'd run a greater risk of alerting others to his hasty departure. He had to agree, they'd best keep this part of their relationship secret until after the wedding. And, despite what she kept saying, there was going to be a wedding.

It was all perfectly clear to him now. He wanted Evaline, and she belonged to him. Rastmoor wouldn't like it, Claudia wouldn't like it, maybe Evaline herself wouldn't like it at first, but he was going to marry her.

He got to the door and turned back to her. She stood there, huddled in her ragged nightgown, holding herself like a lost child. Damn. Where had it gone wrong? And just how was he going to fix it?

"You know we're not done with this. A lot still needs to be settled between us," he said.

"I know." She nodded.

"You'll meet me later?"

"Yes, yes. We can discuss it later. Now go before the whole household wakes up."

All right, he'd go. But first, he gave one glance at the traveling bags neatly packed and piled in the corner. Damn. He'd almost forgotten about that.

"And you're not to go anywhere. I will be heading out to check on the flooding, but I expect you to still be in this house when I return."

She didn't reply, and he took that to be a bad sign.

"I mean it, Evaline. Don't go anywhere."

Now she broke his heart. Tears glistened in the corner of her eyes when she replied, "I don't have anywhere else to go."

She said it with such forlorn finality that he took a step toward her. But she backed away, as if he'd been about to punish her rather than offer comfort. Her stiffened body and icy glare convinced him comfort would not be welcome just now. Apparently she was done with him this morning. He hoped it was only this morning and not in general. She was the most complicated female he'd ever run across.

It certainly was going to be interesting trying to figure her out for the rest of his life.

"Go," she said again.

He did as she commanded, unlocking the door and pulling it silently open. The hall was still dim, and no one was around. It seemed no one else was awake. Evaline could relax. No one would know what they'd finally done.

And then everything happened at once. The floorboard beneath his foot creaked, the door on his right opened, and the door just ahead on the left opened, too. Through the door on the right crept Claudia Graeley. Through the door on the left peered a face. Lady Brennan's face, if he was correct in this dim lighting.

Lady Brennan screeched. Another door opened. This door was more important than the other two doors. It was his mother's door. At the far end of the hall one last door came open. This was, he realized as he quickly assessed the situation, the most important door of all. It belonged to Sir Victor Graeley himself.

For half a second everyone stood there gaping at each other. Dashford noticed Claudia's rumpled sleeping clothes, recalled his appalling lack of clothes, and had a brief premonition where this was going. Claudia must have had one, as well. She leapt into action, stepping to his side, looping an arm around Dashford's elbow and proudly exclaiming, "Papa, you found us!"

She turned a triumphant smile on Dashford. "Well, my dearest, it seems we've been found out—again. I guess you'll just *have* to marry me this time."

One door slammed shut. It was Evaline's.

Evaline slammed her door and stood there, panting. She was not getting involved in this. It was the way things should be.

God, how she wished that weren't so. Had he been serious about wanting to marry her? No, certainly that was just a sense of guilt he felt once he finally realized she wasn't the harlot he'd apparently thought her all along. She'd given him plenty of reason to, of course. Oh, why had she been such a fool to let herself end up drunk that night? But even then, if she'd have just not let herself give in, she would have been saved. But all was truly lost now, and the best she could hope for was that Dashford, at least, made the right choice.

And that meant marrying Claudia. He should have married her in the first place, since he did offer for her. He would marry Claudia, and the Graeley money would save his estate and reputation. She should be truly happy for him. Too bad she hadn't been very good lately at doing what she should.

She'd disobey Dashford, too. He told her to stay here until he came back from visiting his flooded tenants, but of course she would not. She'd find some way to leave, to be gone before she ever had to see those beautiful eyes again. She'd walk if she had to. From what Dashford had looked like last night when he'd come to her bed, though, she was afraid she'd more likely have to swim.

Drat, but this weather was really getting to be bothersome. No doubt it was simply all the moisture in the air that made it seem as if her eyes were welling up. Surely she wasn't going to break down into foolish tears. She had no one to blame but herself for this predicament, and crumbling into a pile of female weeping would help nothing.

It certainly would feel nice right about now, though.

THE OFFICE WAS COLD AND GLOOMY, AND DASH-ford did nothing to make it any more comfortable. His little chat here this morning with Sir Victor was not intended to be pleasant. If the damn Graeley was chilled, so be it. At least the man was fully dressed in warm clothes. Dashford had nothing to put on but the wet things he'd been caught carrying from Evaline's room.

"I've got you dead to rights this time, Dashford," Sir Victor was saying. "This time there's no dawdling around. You're going to marry the girl before the end of the month."

"Don't be too sure of that."

"Not trying to weasel out of it, are you? After we all found you together so early this morning? Don't think I'm not aware what was going on. You've ruined her, and now you're going to do the right thing—what you should have done two years ago when I found you with her then."

"You never found me with her," Dashford growled. "You saw what you wanted to see, or maybe what Claudia wanted you to see. But I've never ruined your daughter, and I won't be marrying her."

"I say you will!"

"And I say I'll meet you on a field of honor with weapons of your choice, if that's how it must be. I'd hate to kill you, though. I'd rather find some more civilized manner of settling things between us."

"And just what manner would that be?"

"Name your price, Graeley."

The older man gave a blustering laugh. "Don't be ridiculous. Everyone knows you're not worth your weight in dirt."

"Then why are you so eager to get Claudia married off to me?"

"She'll be a viscountess."

"And I'm saying that will never happen. So what do you want instead? You might be surprised."

Sir Victor was getting angry. "You have nothing I want, Dashford. You're a drunken, whoring, worthless disappointment to everyone who knows you."

"And this is what you want for your precious, innocent Claudia?"

"Hah! You know for yourself how innocent she is. She'll take you for her husband and be glad of it. No doubt after the wedding you'll head off to London and won't likely inflict your abominable self on her more than once or twice a year. She'll live quite peacefully here with her nice title and that little bit of cottage she'll get as a wedding gift."

The cottage? That dilapidated shack where Mrs. Gwin used to live? Was that what Graeley was talking about? Of course Dashford knew some odd arrangement had been worked out after Mrs. Gwin's death that the cottage was to go to his mother and be held as a wedding gift when Dashford married, but why on earth did Graeley care? The property would be best served if the house were razed and that canal Dashford had always planned on was put through. Hell, that's why he'd been secretly trying to buy it from his own mother.

Still, Sir Victor had specifically mentioned the house and Claudia's expected possession of it. Good grief, could this be the crux of all the trouble? Could it really be so simple as that?

"What have you heard about that cottage?" Dashford asked after a pause.

"Nothing." Graeley's answer was too quick.

"You want it, don't you?"

Sir Victor didn't reply, but the greedy gleam in his eyes gave all the information Dashford needed. The bastard must have heard the rumors. He wanted Mrs. Gwin's house.

"Sir Victor, this might just be your lucky day," Dashford said, smiling.

"You can't bargain with something you don't own, Dashford," Graeley warned.

"What? I don't own my own estate?" Dashford answered. "But of course I do."

"I thought there had been some odd arrangement, that your mother would own it."

Damn. The man had already checked into things, it appeared. Well, Dashford wasn't above a bit of deception if it meant getting Claudia off his neck.

"Why on earth would she own it? No, it came back to the estate once Mrs. Gwin died. So, do we have a bargain? Loveland for that betrothal with my signature on it?"

"The land and the house *and* all its contents? Intact?"

"As a child bride on her wedding day."

Graeley contemplated this for a moment. Dashford felt a growing warmth in his insides. He knew already what the man's answer would be. The treasure lust was written all over his face.

"All right. You may have your freedom—when I hold the deed to that property."

"No. I want my freedom now. You have the betrothal agreement on your person, don't you?"

"And I'm not about to trust you with it until I get my deed."

"How about vowels."

"What?"

"I give you my signed IOU granting you full title to Loveland and all it contains; you give me my freedom."

He thought for a moment. "It would be legally binding?"

"It would."

"Consider it done."

Sir Victor pulled out the familiar betrothal. Dashford recognized it right away; the man had brandished in front of

him often enough. He practically ripped it from the older
man's fingers, but Graeley would have none of that until
Dashford passed over a piece of paper of his own. Well, that
was easily done.

He carefully wrote out his note, promising to give full
title over to Sir Victor Graeley, releasing all claim to
anything in, on, or above the property known as Loveland.
With a flourish, he signed and dusted it. There, Graeley
should be content.

The man took a hell of a long time to study the note, but
finally he handed over his document. "Here. My Claudia's a
sight better off without you."

Dashford took the document, checked it over, and was
content to realize this was, indeed, the original with his
signature. Oh, what a fool he'd been to ever sign such a
thing. Well, those days were behind him.

He bunched up the page and held it to the candle. When it
was blazing nicely, he tossed it into the grate. Thank God, it
was consumed fully in a matter of seconds.

"I believe we're both happy now," he said, giving Sir
Victor a smile.

"You'd better not make me regret this."

"It was your bargain, Graeley. If you live to regret, it's no
fault of mine."

Sir Victor clutched his promissory note and grumbled his
way out of the office. By God, it felt as if a great weight had
been lifted. Dashford could have danced all the way back up
to his room to change. True, he had to go back out into the
elements and examine the damage from yesterday's flooding,
but he'd be doing it as a free man. He was no longer
entangled with Claudia Graeley.

All he had to do now was figure out how to get himself all
tangled up again with Evaline.

Chapter Fifteen

Evaline had made the mistake of trying to dress herself. Disastrous. Finally Molly showed up and took over the task of doing up the back of her drab gown, but it seemed forever before Evaline was finally able to hurry downstairs to find out what on earth had happened with Dashford and Claudia. And find out, she did.

"Oh, there she is," Mr. Mandry announced when Evaline entered the breakfast room. A sudden hush came over the five or six persons sitting at the table—one of them being Claudia herself. Oh Lord, Evaline had been the topic of everyone's conversation, hadn't she? She should have expected as much. Somehow Claudia would want to rub this in, jealous as she was.

"Good morning, dear," Lady Dashford said far too kindly.

"Good morning," Evaline replied, glancing around.

Aunt Bella was not among the group yet, but Claudia made up for it. She practically oozed a tangible smugness. Evaline found it difficult not to rush over and strangle the scheming wench. Instead, she politely took the seat her ladyship offered for her.

"I hope I'm not interrupting anything," Evaline said, realizing all eyes were still on her and no one had gone back to conversation, likely because they had nothing else to converse about.

"No, certainly not, dear," Lady Dashford said. "We're glad you could join us this morning."

"Absolutely," Mr. Mandry agreed, almost boisterous. "You're always a welcome presence here."

Everyone else muttered something that sounded vaguely positive, yet no one would meet her eyes. Lady Dashford was decidedly fidgety. Evaline had a very bad feeling about this. What on earth had transpired? Why should Dashford's long-standing engagement to Claudia suddenly be expected to impact her? What exactly did these people think had been going on?

Finally Evaline could take no more. "I beg your pardon," she said to Lady Dashford. "But has something occurred that I should be aware of?"

"No, no!" the lady replied cheerfully. "Everything is fine. Randolf returned very late last night from saving his tenants, and today all is well."

"Lovely. I know we were all quite concerned for his welfare last evening."

"Yes, we were. This is good news, isn't it?" Lady Dashford said, her voice catching.

If this was such good news, though, why on earth should her ladyship suddenly burst into tears? Evaline blinked, but Lady Dashford quickly controlled herself. There had been a tear, though. Evaline was sure of it.

"I'm sorry. I just recalled a matter I simply must discuss with the housekeeper," Lady Dashford said, rising quickly. "Please, enjoy your breakfast, everyone."

And then she left. Well, that certainly was unusual for their hostess. What could have her so discomposed today? Surely Dashford's shocking behavior was nothing more than they already expected of him. Unless, of course, she knew the truth, that he'd actually not been with Claudia but with Evaline.

Yes, that would certainly be enough to send the woman rushing from the room upon Evaline's entrance. Heavens, what if everyone knew? She glanced around but found none of the condemnation or tsk-tsking she might have expected. Indeed, even Claudia was too wrapped up in her own smugness to glare pointedly at Evaline.

But poor Lady Dashford. Her son had put her through no end of grief and scandal—and now Evaline had played a part in it. Lady Dashford must know the truth to be as upset as she was. She would certainly feel betrayed, believing Evaline to be an entirely different sort of female than she turned out to be. Evaline really should have had the good grace not to show herself at the poor lady's table this morning.

Lady Dashford had only ever received Evaline with kindness when Aunt Bella so rudely thrust their acquaintance upon her in Bath those months ago. No doubt many thought it quite shocking that such a grand lady would see fit to befriend the unfashionable daughter of a common merchant. Indeed, Evaline was quite shocked by it at first herself, but she'd enjoyed Lady Dashford's company and was pleased to develop a friendship there. It pained her to see the poor woman so devastated now—and to know it was her fault.

"Excuse me," Evaline said when she could sit no longer. She rose to leave. "I just recalled a pressing matter with the housekeeper, as well."

Claudia clucked her tongue. "That housekeeper seems like a very difficult servant." Then she glanced up at Evaline and smiled. "I should certainly think of replacing her if I were lady of the house. But of course, I will be, won't I?"

Evaline didn't bother responding. Nothing she said could have wiped that smirk off Claudia's face. So, with a quick nod to the others, Evaline hurried from the room. She found Lady Dashford in the hall, handkerchief in hand and tears barely at bay.

"My lady?" Evaline asked, coming up quietly and wishing she knew what to do.

But the dowager did her best to hide the tears and regain her usual composure. "Ah, Miss Pinchley. What can I do for you?"

"I came here to ask you that same question. It's obvious you're terribly upset. Is it because of what happened in the hallway early this morning?"

Lady Dashford's eyes grew wide, and she held the handkerchief to her lips. Her voice was very low. "You know about that?"

Did she know about that? Could it be possible the lady

truly didn't know of Evaline's involvement? "I, er, yes. I
know about that."

Lady Dashford nodded, then drew in a long breath and
took Evaline's arm. "Come. Please sit and talk with me a
moment."

Evaline nodded. Perhaps talking would be best. At the
very least, Lady Dashford deserved an apology for Evaline's
behavior as a guest in her home.

She followed her ladyship up the stairs and into the
elegant sitting room that was Lady Dashford's private space.
Indeed, it was an excellent place for a most personal
discussion. Evaline's stomach was already in knots.

"So you saw Randolf in the hallway early this morning?"
the viscountess began once Evaline was seated comfortably
beside her.

"Er, I did."

"And you know he was with . . . Miss Graeley?"

Was she testing her, or did she honestly not know? "I saw
Claudia there beside him," Evaline said cautiously.

"Well, my dear, her father saw it, too."

"Yes. How convenient for Claudia."

"Her father always manages to be present at just the right
moment."

"Indeed?"

Lady Dashford nodded, nervously toying with her
handkerchief. "Did Randolf not tell you how he came to be
engaged to Miss Graeley in the first place?"

Evaline frowned. "No, why should he?"

"Trickery. The chit tricked him. I don't know exactly
how, and thankfully Dashford is still gentleman enough not
to bandy her behavior about in polite conversation, but
somehow she lured him into a compromising situation, and
her father miraculously showed up to find them there."

"Compromising situation?" Dashford seemed to excel in
those.

"I'm sorry, it must be difficult for you to hear this. I know
you care for him."

Her first impulse was to swiftly deny that she felt any
tender emotions for the man, but she couldn't. Partly because
she didn't want to hurt the dowager further by insulting her

son, but also because it was impossible to deny what she knew was on her face. She did care for him. Far too much, it would appear.

Lady Dashford produced another handkerchief. "Here, my dear. Dry your eyes."

But this was ridiculous! She certainly could not be crying. "I'm fine, really," she protested when Lady Dashford slid a gentle arm around her shoulders.

"He may be an infuriating rascal, but he certainly is a lovable one," she said of her son.

Evaline couldn't disagree.

"I don't know what's happened to him, Evaline," the lady went on. "All his life, his greatest joy was simply to be here, working beside his father, managing things on the estate." Evaline watched a bittersweet smile ease onto her lips, her eyes misted over with memories.

"They had such plans for this place," she went on. "Randolf was going to modernize all the farms, bring in new breeds of cattle, and he wanted to study agricultural techniques from all around the country. He never had the time for the wild lifestyles some of his friends chose; no, he was devoted to his responsibilities here."

Evaline frowned. That certainly didn't sound like the Dashford she'd met. Then again, how well could she truly know the man after but a few days, and considering the unconventional start to their relationship?

"Then his father died," Lady Dashford said sadly. "I didn't notice the change in him immediately, but once he and Claudia became engaged, something was different in him. He lost interest in being here. He went to stay in London. Then reports started coming back to us of things he'd become involved in . . . things I could scarcely believe. Oh, Evaline, if you knew him two years ago, surely you would barely recognize him today! It's like he's become a different person. He's doing things he never would have condoned two years ago."

Evaline could well relate to that. She was doing things she never would have condoned two days ago. Yes, people did change, and not always for the better.

"I'm sorry," she said. "Perhaps it's just the grief from

losing his father that's made him behave so differently."

"Perhaps. But lately . . . these last days with you here . . . I was hoping I'd detected a change in him. He'd become interested in the estate again. I heard him discussing with his friend, Lord Rastmoor, how he was looking forward to coming back and tackling some project or other. I thought perhaps he was becoming himself again, and that just maybe he could find happiness with . . . but that's folly, I know. Empty wishing. What's done is done, and he must wed Claudia."

"You don't wish for him to marry her?"

Lady Dashford shook her head sadly. "I wished for him to make a love match."

Love match. The words rang in Evaline's heart. Yes, she'd always wanted one of those, too. How sad that when she'd finally found someone to love, there was no match to go with it.

"I'm so sorry, Evaline," Lady Dashford said. "I see this is making you uncomfortable. Forgive me."

"No, it's all right," she said, bringing her errant thoughts in check and taking control of the one persistent tear that hung in the corner of her eye. "I'm sure every parent wants happiness for their child. Surely he and Miss Graeley will suit well—eventually."

Lady Dashford merely shook her head doubtfully. "I don't see how. They've never been well-suited for marriage. Claudia craves society and public approval, while Randolf . . . oh, I don't know what he wants anymore. I thought perhaps when he met you . . . but it's too late for that."

"You knew he was to marry Claudia. That's how it should be."

"Perhaps," Lady Dashford confessed. "But I don't have to like it. And you don't either, I can see that."

Evaline kept her mouth closed for that one.

Lady Dashford laughed. "Nor does he, unfortunately. I've seen how he looks at you, Evaline. You could make him happy. I'm sure of it. If only he hadn't been such a fool to give in to Claudia last night! She was happy enough to throw him over for his wild ways until she realized he might have found another. I know she seduced him out of spite. Oh, how could I have raised the boy to be such a fool!"

"It might not exactly have been entirely his fault," Evaline said, her conscience pricking. "It could simply have been coincidence that he was found in the hallway at the same time Claudia was there. It might not have been her room at all he was coming out of. I mean, theoretically, of course."

Lady Dashford frowned. "And just whose room would he have been in, then?"

Thankfully Evaline was spared having to answer. A knock came at her ladyship's door. It was Aunt Bella. For the first time in her life Evaline was actually glad to see the woman when she rudely poked her head inside.

"Oh, here you are, Evaline," she said.

Lady Dashford was noticeably amazed at her guest's behavior. "Are you in need of something, Mrs. Stump?"

"I hear congratulations are in order, my lady," Bella said quickly, inviting herself inside and flashing a too-bright smile. "I went to the breakfast room and found Miss Graeley bragging that she intends to be married by the end of the month. How excited you must be, considering that just yesterday it appeared she and Lord Dashford quite detested one another."

"Yes, I can hardly contain myself," Lady Dashford replied.

"So it is true? They were discovered early this morning in the very act?"

"I'm sure I have no idea what you mean!" Lady Dashford gasped.

"But the marriage is certain? She isn't going to throw him over after all?"

Evaline cringed. Aunt Bella's manners were so lacking as to make what Evaline had been doing last night with Dashford seem the height of propriety.

"The wedding will occur before the end of May," Lady Dashford announced. Perhaps she was relieved, after all, that her initial hopes for Dashford and Evaline had not played out. Surely having Bella Stump as an in-law would be far worse than any unpleasantness Claudia might bring to the union.

"Well, then, I'll wish them happy," Aunt Bella said. "But—

and I'm dreadfully sorry to involve you in this—but I'm afraid there is some trouble."

"Trouble?" Lady Dashford asked.

"For poor Evaline, I'm afraid," Aunt Bella cooed, meeting Evaline's eyes with a doleful, sorrowful gaze. "I'm afraid the truth is known, my dear. Your reputation is ruined."

Evaline swallowed hard. She felt Lady Dashford's questioning eyes on her, but she could not meet them. So, this was to be Bella's revenge for having lost Dashford. She would trumpet Evaline's shame, scandalizing Dashford and giving his dear mother even more reason to grieve.

"It's true," Bella went on. "Sir Victor is even now on his way to the breakfast room to inform the others. Evaline has been carrying on an illicit relationship right here in this home."

Lady Dashford's questioning eyes grew larger, and Evaline tried to protest, to stop Aunt Bella from giving out the details. It was in vain. The woman continued.

"Even after all this time, she's still in love with Ellard Bristol."

DASHFORD SAT THERE ATOP HIS HORSE, HIS GREAT-coat damp in the dewy air, and gazed down the soggy slope to the swollen river below. Half the village was underwater. The buildings were covered in debris. A bloated cow floated by. It smelled rank. Damn, but his life was a mess.

At least there was no more rain yet today. The skies still threatened, and the air was thick, but he was sure the water levels were slightly lower than last night. Didn't make much difference now, though. The cold, wet torrent had destroyed any hope of planting in much of his farmland this year. It would take half the season just to dry out.

Damn. If only he'd been here, perhaps things would be different. If he'd been here on his estate this spring instead of off playing the philanderer in London, perhaps he wouldn't have let the bridge go without reinforcing it. He'd likely have noticed the condition of the levees and had them fortified. If he'd been half a man and not run from his troubles and hidden behind lies and deception for the better part of two years, perhaps his tenants wouldn't be facing starvation now.

Not that they would starve. He'd see to that. As far as he was concerned, this flood was hung squarely at his door. He'd shirked his duties, and this was the result. Damn, but it was a hard lesson to learn. Too bad he'd waited until Evaline slammed the door on him before he learned it.

"No wonder she hates me," he said aloud, though he hadn't meant to.

Rastmoor glanced up at him. "What was that?"

"Nothing."

"Damn it, Dash. This flood isn't your fault."

"No, but I should have been better prepared for it."

Rastmoor just shook his head. He'd been saying the same things since they'd first left the house an hour ago. Dashford wasn't buying it.

And to think, just an hour ago he'd been so hopeful. Claudia was out of his future, and he'd held hope he might yet convince Evaline to stay in it. But so much preventable destruction around him had eaten away at his optimism. He'd made a muck of everything.

"You can't prepare for something like this," Anthony went on. "That's why they call it a disaster."

"I let myself get distracted. I got so caught up in my playacting that I forgot it wasn't really me."

"Don't be maudlin. You did what every red-blooded male in your position would have done. You enjoyed life."

"A little too much, don't you think?"

"If you want my honest opinion, yes, I do. But not over the past months. You waited until this week to go one step too far."

"What's that supposed to mean?"

"Last night, for instance. You should have just gone to bed. Your bed. Alone."

Dashford started to deny what he'd done but remembered he'd been caught with Claudia this morning, and Rastmoor was probably just referring to that. Damn, but he was going to have to stick to that story or risk implicating Evaline.

"And don't think I'm talking about Claudia," Rastmoor corrected.

"Shit." Rastmoor knew about Evaline.

"Yes, shit. And you were going to be all noble about it and fall into Claudia's trap rather than admit to dallying with that little . . ."

"Watch what you're about to say, Rastmoor," he growled. "I don't know what you've got against her, but she's not what you keep insinuating."

"Yes, I suppose I have no idea what she is. I was not the one in her bed last night."

"No, you weren't. No one else was. Ever."

Rastmoor just rolled his eyes. "Good God, did you fall for that routine, too?"

"Damn it, I'm not some green lad with no clue. I was there, Anthony. I know what I'm talking about. I've been mistaken about her since the beginning. Now I've ruined her just like I've ruined everything else."

"You're pathetic, you know it? I think you like feeling sorry for yourself. You know what you should do? Go on and marry the girl. Marry her, and then you'll have plenty of time to feel all the self-pity in the world when she takes up again with Ellard Bristol or any other man who strikes her fancy."

"She's not like that!"

"They're *all* like that. Your pristine little Pinchley will squeeze every drop of blood from your beating heart before she's done with you, Dash. She'll wrap you around her little finger. She'll make you dream dreams you never knew you had, and she'll turn every other female on the planet nearly invisible to you because you'll spend your life looking for her face—hers alone—in every crowd."

Dashford was going to interrupt, but Rastmoor went on.

"Food will taste like dirt in your mouth, and you'll drown yourself in wine every blasted night just in the vain hope you'll be able to bed some easy wench and forget for a few precious minutes how dark and miserable you are. But you won't be able to, because it's not *her*. Then, when you least expect it, she'll rip every last shred of hope from you and die. Just to spite you, she'll die, so you know there's never any chance she'll come back to you. And you'll realize you died, too.

"That's what they're like, Dash. That's what she'll do to you."

A long silence passed between them before Dashford replied, "And you say I'm maudlin?"

Rastmoor didn't answer. Dashford didn't expect him to, really. What more was there to say? His friend spoke from experience. Dashford could trust that without Evaline, his soul would be as grim and bitter as his friend's.

The difference was Rastmoor's love had been truly lost. She had left him for another then died. It seemed his soul would never recover. But Evaline was still alive. For Dashford, there was still hope.

"I've got to make it right," he said.

Apparently Rastmoor understood. "How?"

Well, that was a good question. How was he going to do that? The flooded farms were the least of his worries. The rain would eventually stop. The water would dry up, the people would come back, and the fields could be cleared. Homes would be stripped and new walls put up, new furniture installed. Eventually things would be the way they should be again, and life would go on. Indeed, his life would go on. He was damn well going to see that Evaline was a part of it.

"I have to apologize to her and explain everything. I'll apologize over and over again until she finally forgives me," Dashford said. "And then I'll beg her to marry me."

Rastmoor just shook his head and gave a slow, quiet chuckle. "You do that. And good luck to you."

"Come on, then," Dashford said. "Let's head back and see how things stand."

"Think I'd rather take my chances with the flood." Rastmoor sighed but turned his horse in stride with Dashford. Yes, despite what the man thought of Evaline, Anthony Rastmoor was a good friend. Too bad things hadn't worked out for him.

They were wading their horses through a knee-deep puddle on the way to the road when a voice called. A party of locals from the nearest town were out surveying the damage. They waved from the next hill over. Dashford recognized most of them and waved back, deciding to make sure all was well before moving on.

"Ho there," he called, guiding his horse up the slippery

hillside toward them. "How are things up your way, in Findutton?"

"Not good," a man he knew as Stephens replied, "but not as bad as things here. Lack Wooton seems to have gotten the worst of it."

Dashford made the requisite introductions, and soon they were all sharing their stories of what each town had been through last night. It did indeed sound as though the areas closer around Hartwood had taken a much harder blow than Findutton. Dashford tried not to credit this to his own failures.

"Loveland got hit pretty hard, too," Stephens said.

Mrs. Gwin's cottage? Dashford frowned. Now, this was a bit ironic. "Really? Sorry to hear that."

"That's in your family again, isn't it?" a young man whose father was the local baronet asked. "Though I heard it might be up for sale."

"Not anymore," Dashford said. "So, how bad is it?"

"Well, the place is pretty old, and it's been neglected a long time," Stephens said.

Another stab of guilt flashed through Dashford.

"If you take the road north for a while, there's some high ground where you can double back and get down to it," the other man suggested. "Might want to give it a look, see what you think."

"Yes, I'll do that. Thank you."

They made small talk for a while, catching up on who was homeless and who wasn't, then the men continued on their way. Dashford sat for a moment. Did he really want to go look at yet another reminder of his irresponsibility? Well, he was already out here, and the horses were already wet. Might as well get this over with.

"Care to ride with me to Loveland?"

Rastmoor shrugged. "The old courtesan's house? Doesn't your mother own it now?"

"As a matter of fact, yes," Dashford said, but he couldn't keep back a smile. "You might not want to mention that to Graeley anytime soon, however."

"How's that?"

"I'm afraid I may have allowed him to think I was in a position to grant him ownership of the property."

"What?"

"It's a long story. Needless to say, if I can't get my mother to graciously give Loveland over to Sir Victor, I could be in some hot water. But I got that damned betrothal paper destroyed, so it's well worth it."

Rastmoor laughed when Dashford filled him in on the specifics. It was, he had to admit, slightly amusing. He would, however, make sure he kept his word and saw to it Graeley got what he bargained for. It wasn't Dashford's intent to stiff the poor man.

"Odd sort of arrangement, don't you think?" Rastmoor said, puzzled. "How exactly did your mother come to be in possession of that property? I thought you said your grandfather gave it to his old ladylove outright. Did he have some specification that would prevent anyone else from inheriting?"

"No, actually, it was Mrs. Gwin's family who requested this arrangement."

"What? I thought you said she had no family."

"I said she had no family to speak of. The family was opposed to any association with her, but she had family. That's the part of the story I left out yesterday."

"Well, for God's sake, don't leave it out now, man."

"Mrs. Gwin had two daughters."

"By God, there are illegitimate Dashfords running amok in Warwickshire?"

"Not that I'm aware of," Dashford said with a chuckle. "Mrs. Gwin's elder daughter was around well before Grandpapa met the old lady, so she was never any relation. Mary, I think her name was. I never saw her and didn't even know about her until a few years ago. Mrs. Gwin had her off at some school somewhere. From what I know, she only came to visit once a year, and that was always kept secret."

"Secret?"

"For the girl's sake, I guess. It must have paid off, too. Mary Gwin married well and lived in London. Mrs. Gwin was always going on about how excited she'd be when Mary and "the babe" would come to visit—that's what she called her granddaughter. They kept the granddaughter a big secret around here, too. I gather Mary married into a respectable family, and they had great expectations for the child, provided she wasn't tarnished by any hint of her ancestry. Such a shame, if you ask me. Mrs. Gwin was a capital girl, even if she had earned her keep."

"I'm sure your Mrs. Gwin understood it was for the best."

"Yes, but she missed the granddaughter, though."

"Wonder what became of her? You don't think we've run across her in some ballroom somewhere, eh? Wouldn't that be a lark? You might have been dancing with Mrs. Gwin's secret descendant and never known it. Or worse! Maybe the chit took after her grandmother and let you do more than just dance with her."

"You have a warped mind."

"It does boggle a bit. But what of the other daughter? Surely there's a story there, too."

"Of course. That daughter was a product of Grandfather's involvement. She would be my Aunt Anna, I suppose. It's all rather murky, of course. These aren't the sorts of things one explains to a child, which I was when Anna went off to get married. They traveled a lot, Anna and her husband, so their daughter came to live with Mrs. Gwin. I met her several times, though I was away at school for most of those years."

"So Mrs. Gwin had another granddaughter, and you've got a cousin."

He nodded. "A quiet little thing named Sophie. I do remember her being around. She can't be more than seventeen or eighteen now, in fact. When Mrs. Gwin died, Sophie went to live with her mother, or so I gather. I don't know after that. They've never tried to contact me, so I'm assuming all is well."

"Dash, you do have an interesting family tree."

"It's because we Dashford men have such big, er, limbs."

Rastmoor laughed. The mood was lighter now, and Dashford was relieved. He needed to keep his mind on solving his problems, not cowering under them. There was hope. His lands could be saved, and Evaline might yet come to feel at least some of what he felt for her. He would keep on believing that—forever if he had to.

They followed the high land and found the way clear to the north, just as the other men had told them. It was just three miles to Loveland, but with the ground so soft and the roads unusable, they were forced to travel overland in a roundabout path. He hoped Rastmoor wasn't in any hurry to get back for luncheon.

They came over a small rise, and there it was: Loveland. It had all the charm of a country cottage but was larger by far than many. Clearly his grandfather's mistress had not been the first inhabitant, but the home had been much improved by Dashford money.

The gardens surrounding the home, he'd been told, were Mrs. Gwin's pride and joy. He was quite sure now his grandfather's propensity for growing things must have played a part in it, too. It was such an oddly serene picture, the thought of his grandfather tending garden here with his beloved courtesan.

Dashford was taken back to childhood days spent visiting the old lady. He could vividly recall sitting in her garden, munching on those infamous strawberry tarts, and breathing the fresh air of her thriving garden. Honey cakes, too, he recalled. Even now, with most of the garden sadly overgrown and underwater, he could still smell warm honey cakes and lavender.

Such a shame he'd let the place fall to ruin like this. As they approached, he could see a line on the house where the water had risen. In fact, a door on the side of it, near the kitchen, he believed, stood open. Water must have come rushing by so fast during the night it burst the hinges. Damn, but the house had been flooded inside, a good two feet deep, from what he could tell. A muddy stream still ran beside the front stoop, churning up what was left of Mrs. Gwin's beautiful plantings.

"Looks pretty bad," Anthony said.

"It does. Come on. I want to see inside."

"Are you sure?"

"Yes."

No telling what had been lost in this flood. Most of Mrs. Gwin's furnishings were still here, many of them having their origins at Hartwood. Grandfather spared nothing to see to his ladylove's comfort. Bric-a-brac still sat on shelves; paintings still hung on walls. That lovely old portrait of Mrs. Gwin in her prime likely still clung to its spot over the mantel in the cozy drawing room. It would be a pity to see it ruined.

And the wine cellar! Damn, Dashford hadn't taken the time to clear it out, and he'd long heard Grandfather stocked the place as if it were his first home. What else had he neglected? The library, for one. It had been full of interesting things. Hell, he'd found Sir Cocksure's little treatise in Mrs. Gwin's library, as a matter of fact. Likely a gift from her protector. Ah, Grandfather must have been quite a man right up until his smiling demise.

It was a shame to let this old home and any other treasures it might still harbor go to ruin. He hopped off his horse and fastened the reins to a tree, high enough up the slope that the animal would be safe from the waters. Anthony did the same. They'd have to trudge through a good stream of muck before reaching the house, but Dashford couldn't help himself. He'd always felt the pull of something special here.

"Come on. The wine cellar was stocked before the war. Let's hope the water didn't destroy everything," he said.

"What? You left French wine here to float away in a flood? Well, that's just plain criminal, Dash."

He found himself having to jog to keep up with Rastmoor now. Indeed, he had the feeling something worthwhile was yet to be found in the cellar. He could use some of that just about now.

Chapter Sixteen

Evaline took a deep breath and followed Aunt Bella into the hallway. Lady Dashford was right behind her. Bother, what was Aunt Bella up to, now?

"Oh Evaline, I'm so sorry. I just don't know what to do," Bella began.

"You can start by being honest!"

Bella glanced sideways at her, her concern fading just long enough for Evaline to detect the sly smile lurking there. "Really? Is that what you'd like, for me to be honest with our gracious hostess here?"

"What on earth are you talking about?" Lady Dashford demanded. "What is being said about Evaline in the breakfast room?"

"Sir Victor, my lady, has found out that Evaline and Mr. Bristol were once lovers," Bella said dolefully.

"Lovers?" Lady Dashford questioned. "He said he was your fiancé."

"He was being kind. There was never a formal arrangement, was there, Evaline?" Aunt Bella asked, knowing the answer already.

"No, there was not," Evaline said, her pace quickening. "Mr. Bristol and I were acquainted some years ago, but . . ."

"You hoped he would marry you," Bella said. "You were heartbroken when he abandoned you."

"Is this true?" Lady Dashford asked.

"Yes . . . but, that is, he led me to believe he was sincere, but . . ."

"She was young, naive," Aunt Bella said with more compassion in her voice than Evaline had ever heard. "You must understand, my lady, she never meant to ruin herself like that."

"I never did!" Evaline protested.

Bella glared at her, pausing as they reached the staircase. "Please, Evaline, don't make it worse for yourself. Youthful indiscretion can be overlooked, but falsehoods now are just insulting."

Oh, blast the woman! How dare she do this. "I would expect my loving aunt to come to my defense."

Bella smiled. "And of course I am, my dear. That's where we're headed right now, to defend you, despite the fact that Sir Victor claims to have heard his information firsthand from Mr. Bristol himself."

"From Ellard himself?"

Aunt Bella moaned. "First names, after all these years!"

"Aunt Bella, really now," Evaline scolded. "Forgive her, Lady Dashford. She's beside herself. I assure you; Sir Victor is mistaken."

"But you have no idea the full extent of his claims, my dear," Bella said.

"What?" Evaline asked, pausing on the landing. "There's more?"

"How much more?" Lady Dashford asked.

"He claims you've been carrying on with another man, too."

"Another?" Evaline and Lady Dashford asked at the same time.

"Indeed!" Aunt Bella replied and suddenly looked shy. It was not attractive. "I hate to even mention it, but . . ."

"Out with it, Aunt Bella," Evaline demanded.

Bella began marching down the stairs again. "He says you've been engaging in sordid activities with Lord Dashford."

"What?!" Lady Dashford gasped.

"He's heard it from a reliable source!" Bella proclaimed.

Evaline was fairly certain she knew who that reliable

source was; a pox on her scheming little hide.

"With Randolf? Evaline, is this true?" Lady Dashford asked.

"Come, Evaline, please tell us it isn't so!" Aunt Bella pretended concern.

She was half tempted to confess. She'd been nearly about to tell Lady Dashford the truth upstairs just minutes ago. How easy it would be to simply admit it. Perhaps if Claudia heard, it would even make her angry enough to jilt the man for good. Heavens, Evaline would certainly much rather be thought of as ruined by Dashford than by Bristol! But no, she could not do it to Dashford. He needed to marry Claudia for the money.

Aunt Bella took advantage of Evaline's hesitation.

"Oh, Evaline, it *is* true! Merciful heaven, between Bristol and Dashford, you've been with the two worst rakes in England! Er, no offense, my lady."

"It isn't like that!" She tried to deny, but even she didn't find herself believable. She *had* been with at least one of the worst rakes in England, so what really was there to deny? "I was never involved that way with Mr. Bristol. Why, Ellard and I have barely spoken since he's arrived here. How could anyone believe there's ever been anything between us?"

"Poor, poor thing. Do you still care for him, then?" Aunt Bella said, turning and gently patting her shoulder when they reached the base of the stairs. "Likely that's what drove her to fall under your son's seduction, Lady Dashford."

"Please, it isn't like that!"

"Never say he forced you!" Aunt Bella cried.

"He forced you?!" Lady Dashford squeaked. She grasped Evaline's other hand. "Oh, I'm so sorry my dear! And here you are, a guest in his home."

"No, of course not, I . . ."

"Fear not, my lady," Aunt Bella said. "All is not lost. True, there may not be a shred of proof to declare poor Evaline's innocence, but still we can behave with dignity."

Lady Dashford's wide eyes went from Aunt Bella to Evaline and back again. Clearly she'd been taken in by it. "But what can we do? My reprobate son cannot marry two disgraced ladies, and Claudia did have prior claim. Heavens, you don't suppose he left you *enceinte*, my dear? Could that be why you've been so peckish?"

"I doubt Dashford's had enough time for that," Aunt Bella said. "More likely it was Bristol. No telling when Evaline was back in contact with him. I fear my trust has been too lenient with the girl."

Evaline stamped her foot. "By God, Aunt Bella, you stop this right now! I'm not with child by Ellard Bristol!"

Thankfully, she realized any fears she may have had about that the last few days were entirely unfounded. Oh wait. After last night she might truly have something to worry about, after all. Lord, what a mess.

So this was Aunt Bella's revenge, was it? Utter ruin and humiliation was to be her fate. Funny, but Evaline had never really thought Bella capable of this much. Well, that just showed how gullible she'd truly been.

"None of this is true," Evaline repeated uselessly. They had reached the breakfast room and were standing just outside the door. Evaline could only imagine what everyone inside must be thinking of her by now. Indeed, Bella had surely allowed Graeley ample time to slander her fully.

"Come, Evaline," Aunt Bella said. "Don't go in there. Come with me so you can calm down before facing everyone."

"I'm fine. I don't need to calm down," Evaline said, although she realized her hands were fisted so tightly her fingernails bit into her skin.

"That's right," Lady Dashford said, although it appeared she couldn't bear to so much as look at Evaline. "Go with your aunt, dear. I'll go in and see what damage has been done. True or not, Graeley has no right to be bandying about the reputation of one of my guests."

"Thank you, my lady," Aunt Bella agreed. "Come, Evaline."

Evaline started to protest, but it was no use. Lady Dashford turned away from her, and Aunt Bella had a death grip on her arm. So this is how it all ended, was it? Dashford would do the honorable thing and marry Claudia, and his estate would be saved. Evaline would be out on the street, her reputation shredded and her heart in pieces. Yes, that seemed to be about right, given the way her life had gone these last seven years.

Lady Dashford opened the door and stepped into the breakfast room. Like magic, the voices inside stopped. But the door was closed quickly, and Evaline hadn't seen who was still in there. Everyone, most likely, and they probably all believed terrible things about her right now. Things associated with Ellard Bristol. Ick. If they had to know the truth about her illicit activities, couldn't they at least know she'd had more taste than to throw herself away on the likes of Ellard Bristol?

What tragic irony. All those years Evaline's parents had tried to protect her from Grandmamma's shame, and now *this* is how she'd fallen. She'd lost her heart and soul to a man who was fated for another, and now her reputation was destroyed by her own aunt. Well, she supposed it was meant to be. She couldn't change who she was. She was Becky Gwin's granddaughter, after all. She supposed she should have known all along how it would end up for her. The same way it ended up for poor Sophie.

"Come, you can rest in here," Aunt Bella said, sounding caring and maternal enough to turn Evaline's stomach.

She should have let that be her warning, but her mind was too jumbled to think straight. She followed Bella past the breakfast room and through a small door. They found a small sitting room, made even smaller by the fact that Ellard Bristol was there. He smiled when he saw them.

"Ah, here you are," he said, as if he'd been patiently waiting. He came to her and took her hands in some oddly compassionate greeting.

"I've just explained to her that Sir Victor knows all," Bella said.

"My poor darling." Ellard sighed, shaking his head sadly.

Darling? Was he speaking to *her*? She supposed he was, because he was staring right at her as he continued. "I'm so sorry things have gone this way for you. I know you would have loved to become the next Lady Dashford."

"Really, Mr. Bristol, I never had any such notion!" She tried to step away, but Aunt Bella came up close beside her.

"Well, that dream can never be," Bella declared. "It's unfortunate, but Lady Dashford believes the worst, though I tried and tried to convince her it all happened years ago."

Ellard stroked his fingers over Evaline's hands. "Yes, well, some things are just too powerful to remain in the past."

"Besides," Bella remarked, "Dashford will be marrying Miss Graeley. He met with her father already, and it's obvious they will wed. After all, the man defiled the girl."

"Poor Evaline," Ellard said. "You must be heartbroken."

Evaline was too confused to be heartbroken just now. What was happening? She felt desperately trapped, a helpless victim of some cruel manipulation, but she still couldn't quite understand. What did Aunt Bella hope to gain by this? Evaline knew her well enough to know the woman did nothing that had no promise of benefit to her.

But of course! Bella realized Dashford was really to wed Claudia. She'd been holding out hope all along that the engagement would fizzle, and Evaline could stand a chance, but as of that hallway scene this morning, her hope must have been dashed. So, it was only natural for Bella to try to secure Evaline's marriage to someone else, someone lacking noble principle, someone who'd already squandered whatever small fortune he'd had and who'd be willing to agree to Bella's terms in exchange for a wealthy bride. Someone exactly like Ellard Bristol.

Good God, she'd fallen headfirst into their trap.

"Perhaps I'll just pop over into the next room and see if her ladyship has had any success in rescuing poor Evaline's reputation," Aunt Bella said.

Evaline nearly felt her jaw drop open when her aunt actually indicated she would leave the room.

"I'll go with you," Evaline said, trying to break away from Ellard. He held her hands.

"No, you'll only upset yourself, my dear," he said.

Aunt Bella agreed wholeheartedly. "I'll just be a moment. Don't worry, Evaline. I'll see that you're well cared for. Just wait here and allow Mr. Bristol to comfort you. I know how deeply you once cared for each other."

And with that, Aunt Bella slipped out of the small room,

pulling the door securely shut behind her. Well, of course she did. All the better for Ellard to seduce Evaline with his smooth words and his charming smile. Too bad Aunt Bella underestimated a few things. Ellard's ability to charm anybody, for one.

"Ellard," Evaline began, catching him off guard and pulling her hands away. "I don't know what my aunt has promised you, but I assure you that—"

"Evaline, at last!" he said, pulling her back to him. "Our prayers are finally answered."

"What prayers?"

It was extremely awkward. Ellard had an uncomfortable grip on her shoulders and was being entirely too familiar with her. In a minute she was going to have to be very sharp with him.

"I know you still want me, Evaline," he said, looming very close to her now. "I could feel it the first moment our eyes locked over breakfast. You never forgot about me and all those tender things we shared."

"Ellard, we never shared tender things," she said. "You courted me at my father's house and asked me to share tender things with you, but I'm sure you'll recall I refused."

"You were young and too afraid. But you wanted me, just as I wanted you."

"No, you wanted any female you could get. You couldn't get me, so you took up with another."

"I wanted to marry you, Evaline. You know I did. I told you we would marry."

She could have laughed. To think seven years ago she'd let this man break her heart! Unbelievable. What a gullible child she'd been.

"You never asked me to marry you, Ellard, and you never spoke to my father. You mentioned that perhaps we might marry, were I to give in to your, er, requests. I never did."

"But you wanted to," he said.

Drat. He had known the truth. Yes, even as an innocent seventeen-year-old she had wanted to give in. He'd known it then, and she couldn't deny it now. She'd always been too like her grandmother.

"But I never did," she said.

His smile turned cold. "Never? Well, perhaps not with me, Evaline. But I can't believe it is never. Your blood runs too hot for that. You've not avoided your passions this long. So tell me, who has been fortunate enough to win the attentions of Miss Evaline Pinchley? One gentleman in particular? Or have you followed in your grandmother's footsteps and taken enjoyment with several?"

She couldn't believe her ears. Not only was he accusing her of moral weakness, but he knew about Grandmamma! How had he learned? She had to find out.

"What do you know of my grandmother?" she asked, shoving him away.

But the room was small. There was no place to go. He advanced on her, coming between her and the door she had entered through. What could she do? There was one ornate settee against the far wall—she was determined to keep clear of that, what with Ellard practically salivating on her already—and the delicate chairs in each cluttered corner seemed to offer little hope of protection. She took a step back and found herself up against the paneled wall behind her.

"Isn't it ironic? Your grandmother and my grandfather were once well acquainted."

She decided to pretend as long as she could. "Really? What a small world. I don't recall Grandmamma ever mentioning acquaintances named Bristol."

"It wasn't that grandfather. It was my maternal grandfather, Hevrington."

"Hevrington? The earl?"

Everyone knew Bristol had a grandfather who was an earl. He'd certainly bragged about it often enough. But surely he couldn't be implying that Grandmamma and the earl had been . . . that . . . well, just what was he implying?

"Yes, the earl," he said. "Am I to believe your grandmother never informed you of your heritage?"

"My heritage? What does that have . . ."

And then she went silent. Her eyes got large. Was he saying what she thought he was saying? Good God, Ellard's grandfather was *her* grandfather?

He laughed at her. "I see this is news to you! Well, how intriguing. All this time I thought for certain you'd known.

So, you mean to say you had no idea we were cousins—you on the wrong side of the blanket, of course—yet you honestly thought I'd consider marrying you? You, a simpering little chit with a bastard mother and a filthy merchant for a father?"

Her breath caught in her throat. It was all too much to take in, and his words stung. God, what a fool she'd been. He'd never truly considered marrying her! He'd not been above trying to seduce her, but she'd never meant anything more than that to him. Despite all of Mamma's careful efforts, the truth had been known all along. Evaline never had a chance.

And to think she'd harbored hope that Dashford might see her as more than she was. Well, she'd truly been delusional, hadn't she? Most likely he'd known who she was all along, too. How could he not, being on close terms with Grandmamma. He must have recognized her name the moment he heard it. No wonder he'd assumed so much; he was just like Ellard.

No, she corrected herself. He wasn't like Ellard, not at all. Ellard Bristol had failed at getting Evaline into his bed. Dashford had succeeded brilliantly. Damn. She'd become exactly what her family had struggled against for years.

"Oh, come now, Evaline," Ellard said, backing her closer into the wall. "It's not so bad. You see, I've hit rather a low spot in my life. My simple wife—rest her soul, of course—misled me about her fiscal viability. Sadly, I learned too late that once her dowry was gone, her family had nothing more to contribute. I married with great expectations only to find myself with pockets to let."

"I'm weeping for you," Evaline said dryly.

He was so close she could feel his sticky breath on her face. He smelled of whiskey already. Lovely. Just what she needed; a drunken Ellard at ten o'clock in the morning. She tried to push him away, but he grasped her hands and pinned them beside her, holding them tight as he pressed his whole weight against her.

"Don't weep too hard, my dear. You forget; you hold the key to my salvation."

"I suppose Aunt Bella convinced you I'd be thrilled to marry you and share Papa's money."

"Of course you will, especially seeing that you have little choice. Your name is ruined, Dashford is betrothed to another, and I hold a rather large note that your dear Uncle Troy had better make good on, or you and your whole family will be out on the street."

"My uncle's had gambling debts for years, and somehow he's managed to survive. I doubt marrying you is necessary to prevent their starvation."

"Don't be so sure of it. I've planned this for a while, my dear. I suppose I should have gone to your auntie a bit earlier, since she very nearly ruined everything by getting you married to Dashford, but I got lucky when the randy viscount couldn't keep his pants up and got caught with Miss Graeley." He laughed, the stale whiskey nearly choking her. "I still don't know how that worked out so well, but it did, and I'm not complaining. Dashford's stuck with the consequences, and now you're stuck with me."

"I am not!" she said, struggling against him.

Her elbows thunked against the wall in an effort to pull her hands free. The wall sounded hollow behind her. To her horror Ellard bent down and tried to kiss her, but she turned her head. Her fingers scraped against the paneling, desperately searching for something she might grab onto for leverage or to use against him. No way she was going to stand here and let him take what she'd never been willing to give him.

But wait, what was that? Her fingers grazed across something metallic. A latch! By God, this wasn't a wall, it was a door. And based on where this room was, it must open into the breakfast room. Where everyone was gathered! Thank heavens, if she could just make enough noise someone would surely hear her and investigate.

Ellard, however, was determined to keep her silent. He was practically engulfing her, keeping her arms firmly at her sides and holding her still. He kept trying to kiss her, too, but all he ever caught was the side of her face. It was horrible nonetheless, so she doubled her efforts.

He was under the influence and she was desperate, so in

the end, Evaline won out. She thrashed into him, busting his lip with her head and pounding at the door behind her with her foot. She clawed at the latch. Ellard swore, but he was too late. The door swung open into the room behind them.

Unfortunately, Ellard hadn't foreseen this and wasn't prepared for it. Evaline staggered backward, his weight throwing her off balance. They tumbled into the breakfast room, Ellard landing squarely on top and knocking the wind out of her. She struggled under him, her skirts tangled and disarrayed. Ellard obscured most of her vision, but out of the corner of her eye she could see Aunt Bella. The woman smirked.

"Well, I do believe we have another engagement to announce!" she proclaimed.

"Like hell we do," Evaline said, and her knee made contact with Ellard's groin. At least, she thought it did. There didn't seem to be much there to contact.

He groaned, rolling off her and rocking on his side. With one hand he cradled his most recent injury; with the other he touched his lip, cursing when he found she'd bloodied it. Good. He'd deserved all of that for a long time.

Evaline scurried to stand and put herself back together as much as she could. The breakfast room was indeed full, with both Graeleys, Lady Dashford, Aunt Bella, Mr. Carrington, and three or four other guests staring dumbfounded at the spectacle before them. It was, without a doubt, the most embarrassing moment of her life. Well, except of course for waking up naked with Dashford this morning and realizing it was, after all, the first time.

Lord, this just was not a good day for her.

"Aunt Bella," she said when she could catch her breath. "I'll thank you never to speak to me again. I've had my fill of your lies and your schemes, and you can assume my generosity toward you is at an end. I'll be leaving Hartwood as soon as is humanly possible, and you may not expect to be traveling with me."

"But my dear," Aunt Bella said, desperate to salvage her plan. "You'll be leaving in disgrace! Why, everyone here just saw you in a most compromising situation with Mr. Bristol."

"I'd like everyone here to notice I bloodied the gentleman's face!" Evaline said, glaring at the onlookers.

"Now, if you'll excuse me, I believe I'll go lock myself in my room."

She fluffed her skirts, and Mr. Mandry nearly tripped over his own feet to get out of her way as she sailed toward the door. But Aunt Bella wasn't so easily dissuaded.

"Evaline, please, you need me. An underage lady simply cannot run off into the world unaccompanied!"

It would have been nice just to go on and ignore her aunt's pleas, but Evaline realized she'd best tend to this as she would any other unpleasant business matter. She turned and sighed.

"Aunt Bella, I'm not underage. I'm completely of age now, and if you'd ever been the least bit interested in me or my life, perhaps you might have realized my birthday is sixteen May, not sixteen September."

She paused a moment to watch the horror wash over Aunt Bella's ashen face. It was not nearly as satisfying as she'd always dreamed, dashing the woman's last hope this way. Well, she supposed revenge was never really so sweet as one wished. Oh well, Aunt Bella needed to be told, and now she had been. There was little else to do.

"Mr. Carrington," she said, turning politely to him. "I'm rather done with this. If you would be so kind, please inform my aunt of the details of my competence. She's a bit confused on a few of the particulars."

"Yes, of course, Miss Pinchley," he said with a business-like nod.

Now Evaline glanced around the room again. "If you would all excuse me. Ravishment, lies, and betrayal always leave me with such a headache."

And then she left. It felt wonderful to walk away from Ellard and Aunt Bella like that, but at the same time she was empty. Along with all her troubles, she was walking away from everything she'd ever known. Once Hartwood was behind her, she'd have nothing but a very vast, unknown future ahead. And she'd be truly alone. What did one do when one had nowhere to go and no one to turn to? Well, she supposed she'd learn. She'd find Sophie, and they'd learn together.

She started up the stairs but decided against rushing up to

her room right away. First, she ought to take advantage of this break in the rain and find someone to request a carriage be readied to cart her to the nearest posting house. The quicker she could leave this place, the better.

It was an odd feeling, having her whole life in front of her without a clue what she planned to do with it. She'd have to be careful and not think too much about it for a while. There simply wasn't time to devote a month or so to lying in bed and grieving all that had been lost these last few days.

So where would she find a footman right now? Usually there were two posted in the entry hall, just outside the drawing room, poised to give aid or receive any callers, but today that post was empty. How odd. Perhaps they had stepped outside.

She opened the large front door just as she heard voices coming from the hallway that led to the breakfast room. Drat. Probably Aunt Bella coming to beg and plead or create some other unpleasant drama. Quietly, Evaline stepped outside and pulled the door shut behind her. Just in case anyone followed, she hurried down the broad stone steps that made up the grand front entrance and ducked around the nearest shrubbery. It was then she noticed the footmen.

Ah, so that's why there weren't any of them to be found inside. Four or five were gathered in the yard, along with what appeared to be a gardener and a groom or two. How odd. The assortment of men were standing around a figure on horseback. Actually, there were two horses but only one rider. That didn't seem entirely noteworthy until she recognized the rider.

Lord Rastmoor. And Dashford had gone out riding with him at least an hour ago, Lady Dashford had said. So where was his lordship now? And what was all the excitement about? Rastmoor was waving his arms as two more servants rushed up to the group. Something about the scene alarmed her. Rastmoor was here, and Dashford was not? That wasn't right. Evaline suddenly had a very bad feeling about this. She forgot decorum and rushed down into the yard.

"Miss Pinchley," Rastmoor said when he saw her.

"Where's his lordship?" she asked, breathless. "Is this his horse? Why is he not on it?"

"There's been an accident," Rastmoor replied, and her heart sank.

"An accident?" Something happened to Dashford? It couldn't be. She just couldn't take anything more today. "No! What happened?"

"Please, Miss Pinchley, step aside. We'll handle it."

Well, she was not prepared to let anyone else handle anything for her right now. "Tell me what happened! What did you do to him?"

Rastmoor studied her for a long moment. Bother. The man was untrustworthy and suspicious. If something terrible had happened to Dashford, she wouldn't be surprised if it was Rastmoor's doing.

"Tell me!" she ordered.

"I didn't do anything to him," he snarled finally and slid off his horse. Still snarling, he tossed the reins to one of the men. He took Evaline by the arm and walked her from the group, barking out orders over his shoulder.

"You know the way there," he called to the men. "Gather ropes, and a ladder if you can haul it. Probably a lantern or two. And likely a pallet to carry him back."

"My God, a pallet?" she gasped. "What happened to him?"

The men scurried off to collect the things Rastmoor called for. The groom holding the horses shuffled nervously. Rastmoor ignored him and turned his glaring attention on Evaline.

"He couldn't get his damn mind off you, that's what happened," Rastmoor said. "He thinks this whole flood is his blooming fault, and he's determined that if he makes everything better, you might decide he's good enough for you."

"What?"

"No, it doesn't make any sense to me either, but that's the way of it. He's soft in the head where you're concerned, and I swear, if you do anything more to hurt him, I'll personally rearrange your priorities."

"But I never . . . where is he? Is he all right?"

"He's trapped in the flooded cellar of that damned old house his grandfather kept as a love nest."

She could scarcely believe her ears. "He's at Loveland?"

"You know the place?"

"Er, well, yes. I've been there. How on earth did he get trapped? What cellar is he in, the old one or the new one?"

"What?"

"There are two cellars. Please, it's very important, which one is he in?"

Rastmoor shrugged. "I don't know. Look, the stairway gave in and he's trapped in debris. There's likely water all around him. The fool was too busy going on and on about how he's determined to marry you, and he didn't take time to examine the rotted old steps and they crumbled beneath him."

Evaline's breath caught in her throat. "He fell? Is he . . . wait, he can't marry me. What about Claudia?"

"Apparently that's no problem. I suppose our clever Dashford assumes he'll survive Graeley's bullet on a field of honor."

"Sir Victor will call him out? Oh, but that's insane!"

"As I may have mentioned, since your arrival here, the man hasn't been exactly functioning with the full use of his faculties. Now, if you'll excuse me, Miss Pinchley, I need to go save my stupid friend."

This was wonderful! Dashford really did love her! No, wait. This was awful. He was trapped in Grandmamma's flooded cellar! She grabbed Rastmoor's arm with a vengeance. "Wait. There's another way down there."

"What, to the cottage?"

"No, into the cellar."

He turned back to her. "Into the cellar? How?"

"If it's the old cellar, which it sounds like, there are two secret entrances. I'll show you."

"No, you'll tell me."

"I can't just tell you. The place was used for smuggling, years and years ago. The entrances are secret. You have to know where to look for them."

"So tell me where to look for them."

"There's no time! Come on." Now she was dragging him back to the horses. "Put me on his horse, and I'll show you."

She was trying to pull herself up into the saddle, and the

groom standing at the horse's head gave Rastmoor a questioning glance.

"All right, fine. Put her up there," he said.

The man obeyed, and Evaline let him toss her up into the saddle. Lord, but she'd never ridden astride before. It took a minute to get her legs situated just right and her skirt pulled over them as much as possible. The fabric ripped loudly, but she didn't care. If Dashford was trapped down in a flooded cellar, she needed to get to him.

"Wait," Rastmoor said, holding her horse as she tried to spur it into motion. "The stirrups."

Dutifully, a second groom appeared and tugged at the stirrups, adjusting them to Evaline's shorter legs. She had to admit, staying on this blasted animal would be much easier with stirrups than without, so she made herself sit patiently and wait.

"All right," Rastmoor said when she was finally secure. He swung up onto his horse and called back to the men, "See what you can do to get everyone else ready. We'll meet them there!"

And they were off. Evaline could only pray they'd get there in time.

Chapter Seventeen

Evaline clung unceremoniously to the saddle, the mane, or anything else she could get a grip on. Heavens, it had been a long time since she'd ridden, and Dashford's enormous thoroughbred was a far cry from the sedate mare and sidesaddle she'd known as a young girl. Last night's activities didn't serve to make things more comfortable for her, either. But for Dashford, she could do this.

Rastmoor was silent as they went along. The roads were still a miserable mess, so she was glad they didn't follow them very long. Instead, Rastmoor found a path that took them along high ground and across country.

"So, how is it you know so much about this house?" Rastmoor asked, causing her to jump.

"What?"

"Extra cellars? Secret entrances? How do you know all this?"

"I, well . . . I've been there."

"To a deserted old love nest? You're a bit young to be Grandfather Dashford's light-skirts."

She didn't bother with a response for that. The last thing she would do was admit to Rastmoor just how tainted her bloodlines were. He'd be only too happy to carry that tale straight to Dashford. Perhaps the blue-blooded Claudia might look a bit better to him then.

Rastmoor didn't badger her for more information, and soon

they were in sight of the old home. It looked pitiful, as if no one had cared for it in years. Well, given its history, that was probably the case. Who wanted to live in the house of a demirep?

"This way," Rastmoor said, tying his horse to a tree and helping her down from hers.

Her legs were weak. Bother. How on earth could she help Dashford if she could barely stand up? The thought of him trapped down there, perhaps buried under decayed wood and rising water, was enough to send a surge of renewed energy through her. She held herself straight and headed for the muddy mess that was Grandmamma's former garden.

Sure enough, Rastmoor led her around back to the old room where Grandmamma had kept her gardening supplies. The stairs to the old cellar were in there. Except that they weren't. Just as Rastmoor had said, the doorframe was twisted and collapsed; only a gaping black hole leading down into the cellar remained.

Evaline ran to the hole and called down into it. "Randolf! Are you all right?"

To her joy his voice came back, loud and clear. "God damn it, Evaline! What are you doing here? Get back, it's too dangerous!"

It was the most beautiful thing he'd ever said to her. He was alive! Strong and healthy, by the sound of it. She could have cried from happiness. If only she could see him down there, just catch a glimpse to know that he was well.

"There's a lantern," she said. "Hanging here."

She could barely see it, hanging on a nail just out of reach. Grandmamma always kept it there, but usually the cellar steps were intact, and one could simply take up the lantern on their way down. Well, it wasn't completely out of reach. Evaline could just touch it with her fingertips. If she reached out a bit more, she could get it.

But things were more tenuous than she'd bargained for. She leaned a bit too much on the broken wood of the doorframe at the same time as the edge of the flooring splintered away. One minute she was standing there reaching for a lantern, the next minute she felt the boards cracking and her legs slipping out from under her. She heard Dashford's terrible shout, and Rastmoor swore.

In an instant she was in darkness, and her body ached in various places where she was banged and scraped by boards from above and who knew what all from below. Ankle-deep water splashed over her in a chilly surge. Ugh, this was not what she'd intended.

"Evaline!" Dashford said, suddenly there beside her.

"Thank heavens," she said, untangling herself from the pile of broken wood she was sitting in. "I thought you were drowned! Rastmoor said you'd been trapped under debris down here, and all I could picture was water rushing in and you being buried."

He shushed her and pulled her into his arms. She clung to him for dear life. His hands were feeling feverishly over her body, and at first she thought he was as glad to see her as she was to see him, but then she realized he seemed to be looking for something.

"Whatever are you doing?" she asked.

"I'm checking you over for injuries, you little twit," he replied. "Are you hurt? Is anything broken?"

"No, I'm fine. Really, just a few bruises."

"Good. Then I'm going to strangle you! What were you thinking, coming out here like this?"

"I was thinking you needed rescuing!"

"Oh, and you're going to do that with a broken leg?"

"I don't have a broken leg. Heavens, one would think you'd be a bit more grateful for being rescued."

"I haven't been rescued yet. Rastmoor!" he called up to the opening. "What the hell were you doing, bringing her here?"

"She said she knew how to get you out of there," Rastmoor's voice called back. His face did not appear in the opening, and he sounded oddly distant.

"Damn it, I know how to get out of here. Throw us down a rope or something."

"Sorry, Dash. Haven't got one."

"What? You came back here without a rope?"

"I brought Miss Pinchley instead."

"How thoughtful, but I can't very well use her to get us out of here."

"Yes, you can," Evaline chimed in. "There are secret passageways!"

"What? Good grief," Dashford grumbled. "Rastmoor, get over here. Reach down, and I'll pass Evaline up to you. She can't stay down in this place; she'll take a chill."

"I don't dare, Dash," Rastmoor called back. "The whole floor's about to go. If I take one step closer, I'm likely to bring this entire room down on top of you. I'm going outside to wait for the others. They'll be along any minute now with your ropes and ladders and whatnot, but I'm afraid we'll have a lot of shoring up to do out here before we can get to you. We'll get you both out of there, don't doubt that, but it might take a while. I'd say if Miss Pinchley's right and there's another way out of there, you ought to try that."

"Damn," Dashford said under his breath.

Evaline shuddered. The light filtering in through the misshapen doorway above brightened just enough of the cellar that she could see the outlines of rotten beams stretching over their heads. Too many years of damp and insects and neglect had taken their toll. Rastmoor was right; the whole room above wouldn't need much encouragement to make its way into the cellar.

"You know another way out of here?" Dashford asked.

She nodded, her eyes accustomed enough to the darkness now that she could read the worry on his face. There was mud, too, so she reached out to brush that off. He grasped her hand and just held it there, their eyes locking. Lord, what would she have done if he'd been hurt . . . or worse? She'd been wrong to think her life could go on without him.

"I'll get you out of here, Randolf," she said.

He laughed. Apparently he thought the idea of being rescued by a mere female was humorous. She would have told him just what she thought about his gallant sense of humor, but he pulled her closer to him just then and took her lips with his in a deep, steaming kiss. The warmth of his body flooded hers, and she decided to save her reprimand for another time. Kisses were much better.

She gave in to him easily, giving his tongue freedom to explore and reveling in the thrills of pleasure he was so good at producing. It seemed ages since she'd been in his arms, and she was in no hurry to leave them now. She dug her fingers into his thick, damp hair and shut out the chill and the mildew and the sounds of dripping water. Anywhere she could be with Dashford was where she wanted to be right now.

"Hey, I don't mean to pester, but there aren't a lot of escape sounds coming from down there," Rastmoor's voice suddenly interrupted. "What are you two doing?"

"Damn him," Dashford grumbled, glaring up at the empty opening. "All right, Anthony. We're working on it."

He turned back to focus on Evaline, but sadly their tender moment was done. Well, with luck, they'd be out of here in no time and could get back to more important endeavors.

"There's a tunnel at the back of the cellar," she said.

It was dark back there, and the stone floor was slippery under the inches of water, but Evaline led Dashford to the far wall. Several crates were piled there, but she was positive the door Grandmamma had shown her years ago was nearby. Unfortunately, she would have to feel around on the filthy, slimy, spider-covered wall to find it. Well, nothing to do but get through it. Dashford joined her, and she was happy to let him take over.

"There should be a door; not very tall, but wide enough for crates and things to be hauled in and out," she explained.

"Found it," he announced.

Thank God. She couldn't bear much more of this groping around in the dark. Heaven only knew what hideous creatures she was disturbing.

"Is it locked?" she asked when Dashford's first attempt at yanking it open failed.

"I don't think so," he said. "But the hinges are rusted. I'll have to find something to pound on them a bit."

Drat. More groping. She found a stone that had come dislodged from the wall.

"Will this do?"

"Should do nicely," he said and whacked the stone at a hinge.

The sound echoed, and little bits of things trickled down from above onto Evaline's hair. She shuddered. Too much more of this pounding, and the whole place might just come down.

"What was that?" Rastmoor called from outside. "You all right down there?"

"Fine," Dashford called back. "There's a door, but the hinges are rusted."

"Hit it with something!" Rastmoor replied.

Dashford just growled and yanked again at the door. Surprisingly, the hinges heaved and groaned, but the door swung open a few inches. With a bit more tugging and yanking, he had it wide enough to enter through. The only trouble was it was pitch-black inside.

"Where does this go?" he asked.

"Underground," she answered. "Straight back from the house. There's a little stand of trees near the river and a mound of earth. There's another door buried in that mound."

"Buried?"

"Well, I told you it's a secret passage. They couldn't very well just leave a door sitting out in plain sight, could they?"

"It would have been rather more convenient that way."

"Not for the smugglers."

"Smugglers?"

"Yes, isn't it exciting? Grandmamma said years ago this house was used to smuggle all manner of goods and persons during Cromwell's rule."

He frowned at her, and she realized she'd spoken without thinking. "Grandmamma?"

Oh God. "I . . . she once visited here and told me of, er, about what she heard."

But he smiled. She could see the light in his eyes. "Your grandmother was Mrs. Gwin."

"Uh, no she wasn't."

"Yes, she was. That's why you know so much about this house. You were that little girl who used to come and visit once a year."

"No, I wasn't."

"Of course you were! I always wondered about that mystery granddaughter."

"No, it's not me."

"You favor her; I can see it now."

She could feel his eyes roaming over her, studying her in the dim light. Heavens, she hadn't felt this uncovered when she woke in his arms today!

"No, you're mistaken. It's not me. I'm not related to her; I don't even know who you're talking about," she babbled. Lord, but it felt just wretched to lie to him, to deny any connection to someone she once loved so dearly. But what if he were to find out the truth? She'd promised her mother on her deathbed she'd never tell a soul, never ruin herself by admitting to being Becky Gwin's granddaughter.

But it was no use. She was already ruined, wasn't she? And she was the daughter of a courtesan's child. She might as well tell the truth; he was bound to find out sooner or later.

"It's all right, Evaline," he said softly. "If you say she's not your grandmother, then she's not your grandmother."

She shook her head. "No, it's not all right. I'm not ashamed of her. Yes, she was my grandmother. And she was a wonderful woman, despite what you've probably heard about her."

"She was a dear woman. And quite a good cook, too. Did she ever make you those strawberry tarts?"

She remembered them vividly. "And honey cakes. But was your family truly on good terms with her?"

"Quite good. My mother brought me to visit often enough as a child."

Evaline struggled to comprehend that. His mother brought him to visit the woman who had been his grandfather's mistress? How odd. She would have expected the family felt shame and bitterness toward her for all the scandal she must have brought on them.

"Was your family not angry with her?" She had to ask.

"Why? Any harm had been done long, long ago. I think my father was just glad to know his father had managed to find happiness. My grandfather loved her," he answered.

It was amazing. All this time she'd had visions of her poor, aging grandmother wasting away here alone, despised by everyone she met. How many years had Evaline borne the guilt of not being here, not finding a way to escape her father's rules and then Aunt Bella's captivity to be with her grandmother through her last days? Now, to think she'd been befriended—by the Dashford family, no less—was nearly inconceivable.

"So she was not alone? She had friends?"

"Of course she did. You never knew that?"

No, she never did. All her life her visits to Grandmamma had been very secretive; her parents insisted on that. She never saw anyone at Grandmamma's house but the few servants she employed. All along, Evaline just assumed that's the way life was for her grandmother: lonely and isolated.

"I thought," she said, and realized her voice was too thick to continue. She drew a slow breath and could finally go on. "I thought your family hated her, that everyone thought she was a . . . well, what she was."

He must have known she needed it, because he wrapped his arms around her just tight enough to be comforting. "No, Evaline. It wasn't like that for her. Maybe when she was younger, but not when I knew her. All I knew was a kindly old grandmother who loved her garden, had regular visitors, and rambled incessantly about a granddaughter somewhere who was likely to grow up into an incomparable beauty. I see now she was right."

Well, she had to laugh at that. Mostly because she knew she was anything but incomparably beautiful—especially now with muck in her skirts and spiders in her hair—but also because she was so happy to know Grandmamma had had friends. Yes, and also because she was snuggled up tightly against Dashford's chest.

"It's gotten awfully quiet down there again," Rastmoor called from above. "How's it going with that door?"

"He got it open!" Evaline called out. Dashford uttered a few choice obscenities on his friend's behalf. Apparently he was getting rather irritated by the constant interruptions.

"Brilliant," Rastmoor said, oblivious. "So, where does it go? Is there a passage, or something?"

"A tunnel. It goes out toward the river," Evaline said.

"And can you make your way through it?"

"It's too bloody dark," Dashford said, giving Evaline one last squeeze and stepping back to focus again on the task at hand. "We'll need a torch or a lantern."

"There's a lantern where that stairway used to be," Rastmoor suggested innocently.

"I know there's a bloody lantern up there!" Dashford

snapped. "What do you think I was trying to get when I tumbled down here in the first place?"

"Ironic, that," Rastmoor chuckled. "Seems it was Miss Pinchley's goal, too."

"Rot in hell, Anthony," Dashford grumbled. "Now go find us something we can actually use."

"Well, we could use that if he could get it," Evaline offered. "And there always used to be a tinderbox on a little shelf up there, just beside the back window."

Rastmoor must have followed her instructions because they heard some cautious footsteps above and then his cheerful voice. "Well, the floor seems to be holding, so far, but . . . hey, here it is. Still dry, too."

"Well, I suppose if all else fails, we can at least catch ourselves on fire," Dashford said. "Now find us something to use for light. Everything down here is hopelessly wet."

Rastmoor muttered a response, and there were more tentative footsteps. Finally a form darkened the opening above, and a long stick came into view, reaching from somewhere in the room above toward the lantern still hanging on its hook high above the pile of kindling that had previously been a stairway.

"If I stand back here, I think I can reach it," Rastmoor called. "Then I'll hand it down to you. Better stand back, just in case, though."

They did, and Evaline was glad for it. Another piece of framework came crashing down, sending up a spray of dust and cold water. She cowered behind Dashford, but the collapse was minimal. Rastmoor only paused a moment in his efforts, then went back to trying to snag the lantern with the long stick he'd collected.

Amazingly, he did it. "I've got it!" he called down, the lantern slipping off its hook and hanging at the end of the stick.

"Careful," Dashford said, stepping forward to intercept it.

Ever so slowly Rastmoor's footsteps inched closer to the opening above, and the stick with the lantern lowered toward them. At last Dashford's hands made contact, and the lantern was actually in his possession. Rastmoor withdrew the stick, and another little trickle of debris fell from above.

"Now toss me the box," Dashford called.

"All right, but I don't dare come any closer to the doorway. I'll have to throw it blind. Think you can catch?"

"Throw it."

Evaline cringed at the thought of the box sailing through the opening only to fall into the water below. Or worse, to hit Dashford's head and knock him unconscious. She prayed that this one little thing could work out positively for them today.

It did. The box came through the opening and Dashford positioned himself just right to catch it. She clapped her hands as if he'd won a tournament.

"Thank you, my dear," he said. "But let's see if this old thing can still light a lantern before we break out the champagne, shall we?"

It took several tries and several eager demands for reports from Rastmoor, but eventually the lantern was glowing. It was the most beautiful thing Evaline had seen. She could have kissed Dashford. Actually, that wasn't such a bad idea. She leaned into him as he worked over the lantern and kissed his face.

He smiled at her. "Oh, so you like it when I make fire?"

He pulled her closer with his free arm and gave her a bit more than the peck on the cheek she'd granted him. Life seemed hopeful again.

"Are you still there? Did you start down the tunnel yet?" Rastmoor called.

"No, damn your eyes," Dashford called back, but he moved toward the gaping darkness and held up the lantern. Evaline followed.

The tunnel was still awfully dark, but now they could at least see into it. The ceiling was low, but the sides were wide. Cobwebs crisscrossed the way, but otherwise it was unobstructed. The water level in the tunnel seemed actually lower than here in the cellar. That was a good sign.

"It looks clear!" she said.

"It's clear?" Rastmoor asked.

"Yes, it looks secure, too," Dashford added. "We can't see very far into it, but the air feels all right. Stuffy and stale, but breathable."

He stooped inside to feel the walls and hold the lantern out for further inspections. Coming back out into the cellar, he stretched his back and eyed Evaline. She could tell by his expression that she looked much worse in the warm glow of the lantern than she had in the dim light they'd been used to.

"Will you be all right in there?" he asked. "It's rather close quarters and not the most elegant atmosphere."

"If it gets us out of this cellar, I'll be fine," she said with far more courage than she felt.

"All right," he said. "Give Rastmoor some good directions to find this door at the other end, and we'll have him go start digging."

She did, and Rastmoor set off to find the little mound where Evaline had been told—and hoped it had been right— there was a door. There was still no sign of the men from Hartwood, and Evaline wondered at that. Surely she and Rastmoor hadn't made such good time as to be this far ahead of them. Surely they'd be here soon. They'd just have to hope Rastmoor could locate them and get help with that door.

In the meanwhile, though, she and Dashford would investigate this tunnel. She gladly let him lead the way, and they slowly edged into the darkness. Ugh, she would never complain about the glare or heat from direct sunlight again.

Dashford brushed cobwebs and creatures aside, and Evaline followed closely behind. They had to walk with their backs uncomfortably hunched over, but she supposed that was better than remaining in the cellar room to have the building collapse on their heads. After a few minutes, though, she wasn't entirely sure that wouldn't have been better. Something small with prickly little toes scurried across her foot.

She screamed.

"What is it?" Dashford said, whirling quickly around.

"Nothing. Just a mouse, I think. Sorry."

He took her hand. "It's all right. If you need to, we can turn back and wait for the men to find a safer way out of here."

"No, let's keep going. I just need to breathe fresh air."

And it was true. She realized as they made another few

feet advancement that the air was getting decidedly more stale. She was just about to comment on this when Dashford spoke.

"It's blocked."

"What?" she asked.

He moved aside so she could peer around him. The light flickered against the slick stone walls and then fell on a thick construction of mud and rocks. Water pooled at the base, eddies swirling as two small streams came through the wall of rocks about halfway up.

"The river's on the other side," he said.

Good Lord, he was right. Someone must have blocked this tunnel up in years gone by to prevent flooding. Judging by the level where the little streams filtered through, just on the other side of this makeshift dam the water was at least three—perhaps four—feet deep. Or more. She shuddered.

"It doesn't look very secure," she said. "What if the water breaks through?"

Dashford studied it for a moment then sighed. "I think we'd better head back to the cellar."

She nodded. At least they'd been able to stand up in there. And breathe.

"Come on," she said, taking the lantern and going ahead of him this time. The cobwebs were already cleared, so there was no need to hide behind him like a child. She ducked her head just a bit more to avoid any residual spiders and headed back the way they'd just come.

"Say, this is much better," he said after a few steps.

"No spiders?"

"That, and a much better view."

She stopped and twisted to glare at him. "Our lives are in peril, and you wish to gawk at my backside?"

"Indeed. I wish I could do a lot more than that, in fact," he said.

Good heavens, how on earth could he think of such things down here, trapped and disgusting as they were? She stepped aside to let him squeeze past her.

"You go first, then," she said, and handed over the lantern. "Perhaps I'll enjoy the view for a while."

He laughed again and moved forward to take his proper

place. "All right. But don't think I'll let you off that easily. Once this is over and you're safe and sound, I have plans for you and your backside. Front side, too."

She was warming at the mere thought. "Then perhaps we ought to hurry, because I just remembered something."

"Oh? What is that?"

"There's another way out of the cellar."

Chapter Eighteen

❧

They were back in the relatively roomier and slightly less musty cellar. Dashford rolled his shoulders as he got used to standing upright again. Damn. He was right back where he'd started over an hour ago. He called up toward the opening, wondering if Rastmoor or any of the others were about.

No reply.

"Perhaps Lord Rastmoor is still working at the other end of the tunnel?" Evaline asked.

God, but she looked wonderful. She was covered in dirt and wet head to toe. Her tattered gown clung to her in all the right places, and her honey-colored hair was dark and disheveled. Still, she'd not complained or whined even once. And he wanted her badly.

It was ridiculous—he knew that—but if he dared, he'd try seducing her right here and now. Something about being trapped here alone with her and uncertain when they'd be rescued was driving him wild. That, and her wet and nearly invisible clothes.

"What is it?" she said, noticing him staring.

"You'd better get us out of here quickly. I'm having a hard time keeping my thoughts from wandering."

She frowned. "Why? Did you hit your head or something?"

"No. I want to make love to you, Evaline."

"What? Here?"

"No, not here. That's why I want us to get out of here. Show me this other passage you said you knew about."

She seemed flustered and kept her distance from him. Well, he couldn't blame her. He must seem like a crazy person, dirty and damp and raging with lust. If he didn't want to ruin his chances at any future bliss, he'd best control himself now. He needed to be a gentleman and see to rescuing her, not ravishing her.

She skirted around the collapsed stairway and went to the far side of the cellar. He followed, bringing the light. She looked around hesitantly, then suddenly pointed.

"There."

It was another door, much narrower than the last and built so flush into the wall it was well camouflaged. He hadn't noticed it when he'd made his initial searches of the cellar while he'd been trapped here waiting for Rastmoor to return. He hadn't found the other door, either, so obviously his powers of observation were not all they should be. He hoped Evaline didn't notice. God, but he wanted her to see him as much more than he truly was.

He'd been an idiot to get himself trapped down here in the first place. Rastmoor had been sensible, said they ought to go slow. He recognized that the house was suffering from disuse and neglect. Dashford had been unwilling to admit how bad it was. Well, now he couldn't deny it. Things at Loveland were bad, and it was his fault.

Evaline must hate him for it. This, after all, had been a home for her. It had been her grandmother's home. She wasn't going to appreciate him for letting it decay this way. Just one more monumental thing he'd have to make up for.

"It pushes in, I believe," she said, leaning her slight weight against the door.

He came to help her. The door didn't move.

"Unless it's locked," she added. "There is a lock on the inside."

He stepped back and took his mind from his many shortcomings and Evaline's heaving breasts. One thing at a time, old man. Right now he'd best contemplate the door.

"Where does this tunnel go? Under the house?"

"It's not a tunnel. It's a narrow passageway with stairs up into the house."

"Into the house? Why didn't we try this one to begin with?"

She looked nervously at her feet. "I forgot about it. I'm sorry, but I was just so distracted, what with you and the flood and Ellard . . ."

"Ellard?" Now that was a name he hadn't wanted to hear ever again. "What's Bristol got to do with this?"

"Nothing! It's only, I had rather an unpleasant experience with him just before I left to come out here."

He didn't like the sound of that, either. "What kind of unpleasant experience?"

"It doesn't matter. Here, perhaps if we push against this door . . ."

"It does matter! What did he do to you?"

She wasn't meeting his eyes. "It isn't important. I got away."

"You got away? Good God, what was the bastard trying to do to you, Evaline?"

"He thought if he compromised me, I'd marry him, all right?"

All right, indeed! Now Dashford wanted to get out of this putrid cellar so he could go commit murder. How dare that spineless son of a bitch try anything like that with Evaline! Hell, if he could get his hands on the soulless ass right now he'd . . .

He kicked the door. Wood and mud splintered around them, and it flung open.

"Well done!" Evaline exclaimed.

"That will be Bristol's face if I ever lay eyes on it again," he said.

"I got away from him, all right?" she declared. "And I don't care that he was pawing all over me right there in front of everyone. Your mother can think of me what she likes, but I'll not marry Ellard Bristol just so people will be nice to me."

"You're damn right you won't."

"And if you end up marrying Claudia so her father doesn't have to shoot you, that's fine."

"What's that?"

"I'll make my own life on my own. My grandmother never married, and she was just fine."

"Er, that's very bold of you, but I assure you there is no hope of me marrying Claudia. I intend to marry you."

"Not if it means Sir Victor gets to use you for target practice!"

"He's not going to shoot me. I met with the man this morning, and we came to an amicable settlement. He gets what he wants, and I don't get Claudia."

"What? You already settled it? What did it cost you?"

He paused. When he'd met with Sir Victor this morning, the cost had seemed very nominal. But he'd learned a few things since then. Unfortunately, now he realized it had been far more costly than he'd realized. What would Evaline say when she discovered Loveland had been the price of his freedom? Would it still be worth it to her?

"Never mind. Let's concentrate on getting you home and into dry clothes. We can discuss everything then."

She shuddered from the chill, and he realized he really did need to worry about getting her out of here. He had no intention of delaying his wedding plans while Evaline recovered from some horrible disease she caught from the wet and the cold. He'd see to her safety first; all these other details could be dealt with later.

"I'll go first," he said, holding out the lantern and stepping through the door.

He found himself in a narrow passage. The walls were mud and rock, held secure by wooden planking. The passage made a sharp right turn, and then he could see a long set of stairs ahead. Good. Provided these were in better condition than the rotted wood of the cellar steps, they'd be up inside Mrs. Gwin's home in no time.

"Steps," he said to Evaline. The passage was so narrow he doubted she could see beyond him, even though she crowded up tight against him. "I'll check them first. You wait here."

She nodded, and he went on ahead. She looked a little forlorn there, huddled back in the growing darkness, but she managed a thin smile. Yes, he'd get her out of here and get her home to a warm fire and dry clothes. Then he'd strip her out of them and teach her a few more things he learned from Mr. Cocksure.

He put one tentative foot on the bottom step. The wood creaked.

"Oh, be careful!" Evaline cried. "I was just a child when Grandmamma showed me this passage, and even then it seemed treacherous."

"It'll hold. It's not rotten like the others. Where does this lead?"

"Up to the kitchens. There's a door there, but now that I think about it, it seems Grandmamma may have covered it up or something. But it's all right. The staircase goes on. All the way up to the first floor. It opens into her bedroom."

The bedroom? Well, that sounded promising. God, but he wanted to get the woman home.

"Come on."

She stepped forward and took his hand. Carefully, they made their way up the cramped staircase. He watched each step carefully, and they made it up to the landing without any incident. Just as Evaline said, there was a door there. He found the latch and tried it.

The door swung outward, but only an inch or two. Light streamed in, and he leaned to peer through. It was indeed a kitchen, but the door was blocked. A large bin had been constructed there, still containing a mixture of wood and coal to be used in the stoves. Bother. It was too heavy to move by pushing at it.

"We can go upstairs," Evaline suggested. "That door should still be free."

"All right." What were a few more steps when they'd come so far already? He pulled the kitchen door closed.

A puff of air swirled around them, catching the dust of several generations and mingling with the musty staleness. Evaline sneezed and lost her footing.

All Dashford knew was that one moment she was pressed against him on the snug landing, and the next minute she was falling backward, her hands flailing in the air for something to grab onto. God, she'd tumble down and break her neck! He lunged and grabbed her arm, pulling her back up against him.

Unfortunately, this upset the lantern and knocked it from his hand. It crashed onto the steps below them, bouncing down the full flight of stairs, glass breaking and the light being extinguished about halfway down. They were in darkness now, but at least Evaline was safe. She clung to him, her breathing hard and irregular.

"Are you all right?" he asked.

"Yes, I'm fine," she said. "Thank you."

Indeed, she sounded well. Perhaps it was his breathing that was hard and irregular. He knew his heart pounded in his chest as if he'd just run a marathon.

"Don't scare me that way," he said.

The darkness was complete, but he found her face with his hand. He needed to reassure himself. Yes, she was fine. He stroked her cheek.

He felt her warm breath when she sighed. It was enough encouragement to give in to a kiss. He knew he should wait, but she felt so good in his arms. He'd spare a moment for a few stolen kisses here, then get back to rescuing her.

But a few kisses weren't enough. He wanted to hold her, to touch her. He knew she wanted it, too. She pressed herself against him and explored his mouth with a passion to match his own. Rescuing could wait.

He ran his hands over her. Her body was cool, cold even. He'd have to get her out of these wet clothes. Now seemed as good a time as any. He worked at the laces at the back of her gown. She arched against him and giggled when he pulled her bodice aside to free those wonderful, full breasts and tight, hardened nipples. At least all this cold air was good for something.

He bent and found a nipple with his mouth. She moaned for him, sliding her hands behind his coat and tugging at his shirt to release it from his trousers. He toyed with her nipple and managed to finish off those laces. Her gown slipped down to fall somewhere at their feet. She had her hands up under his shirt, roaming over his chest as he started on the strings of her shift. Damn, but he really was going to have her naked here, wasn't he?

It didn't seem to matter to her. She went from crawling under his shirt to working the fastenings at his trousers. He groaned at the sensations this was causing him. Her fumbling movements and desperate unfastening was the most arousing thing he could imagine right now. Except, of course, for wishing that damn lantern hadn't crashed into pieces and was still shining some light on what was sure to have been the very erotic image of Evaline's now fully stripped body writhing against him on this stair landing.

But he had a lively imagination and didn't need to see her. He knew every inch of her body by now, and he ached to have her again. He paused from appreciating the delicate curve at the small of her back long enough to shrug out of his coat and undo the last of his trouser fastenings. He knew she'd find him hard and ready for action there.

She did. She felt over him carefully, stroking the length of him with a velvet touch that sent him right to the edge. Then she slid her small fingers around him, grasping tightly and pulling him closer. He throbbed.

"Can we do this here, this way?" she asked, her voice a dusky whisper against his chest.

"We can."

By God, they most certainly could. Wrapping his arms around her, he leaned her back against the kitchen door. He made sure her weight rested on his arms so the rough wood didn't scratch. Carefully, he lifted her slightly until her feet were off the floor. She made a surprised little gasp.

"Are you all right?" he asked.

"Yes, but, what are you . . ."

And then she understood. He leaned into her, his manhood brushing against her just above her moistened cleft. She shifted, pushing against him to slide up farther and fold her arms around his shoulders. Now she was right where he wanted her. He pressed gently.

"Wrap your legs around me," he said.

She did, opening herself up to him. Ah, but she was so warm there. He let himself just revel in her warmth, gently teasing her with the head of his solid cock and listening to her breathing. It didn't take long for both of them to be beyond teasing.

He pressed for more, and she gave it. Her body responded easily, arching into him and pulling him inside. He groaned, fighting the urge to come already. She held him, embracing him with her arms and her body. He rocked against her.

This was what he wanted to do with his life: make love to Evaline every chance he could get. His ears strained for the sounds she made, sounds of passion and pleasure and forever. He concentrated on being easy and tending to her comfort in this tenuous, provocative position, but her fingernails rasped his shoulders, and her hot breath urged him on until he couldn't think of anything but burying himself deeper and deeper inside her. He ground himself in, over and over, until the waves rose too high to ignore, and his cries were mingling with hers, echoing in the dark stairwell.

She called out his name, and he poured himself into her. She held him there, desperate in the dark and unwilling to let go. He found her lips and kissed her.

"I love you, Evaline," he said.

For a long time they just held each other there, propped up against the rough wooden door and waiting for the world to stop spinning around them. He kissed her lips, her face, her ears, her neck, anything he could reach. And she kissed him back. There was no doubt in his mind that everything he felt for her was equally returned.

Reality of the cold, damp air from the cellar below and the strangeness of their situation was only just starting to sink in when he realized there were noises on the other side of the door. It took but a second to remember where he was and what was going on.

"Dash? Damn it, where are you?"

It was Rastmoor. He was in the kitchen. Oh shit! How long had he been there?

"We're here," Dashford called back, shifting hastily to slide Evaline to the floor. No telling where her clothing was; they'd have to fumble around for it in the dark. Thank heavens for that heavy woodbin at the door; else Rastmoor might have opened it at the most inopportune moment!

"Found them!" Evaline whispered, and he felt the brush of damp fabric.

"There is another door upstairs?" he asked quietly in return. "Can you find your way and get dressed? I'll distract Rastmoor down here."

"Yes, all right," she replied.

He could tell she wasn't in any great hurry to rush naked up into the dark unknown, but that would be preferable to being discovered in their current situation. She reached out for him in the darkness and pulled him to her for one last kiss. She must have been standing on the first step up, because he barely had to tip his head.

"I love you, too," she said finally.

Then she turned, and he felt her moving away, up the darkened steps. God, it felt good to hear her say those words. What a sap he was becoming, but she could talk of love and tender feelings all day, and he wouldn't grow tired of it. As long as he could thump her like that while she was talking. He thought she just might let him, too. She was perfect.

He readjusted his trousers and stalled for time with Rastmoor.

"Hold on, Anthony. There's a fair-sized woodbin blocking the door."

"I see it," Rastmoor called back, nearer now.

Dashford shoved the door open, and the tiny slit of light was actually a godsend. It let him notice he'd done his trousers wrong. Well, a quick fix, and with luck Anthony would be none the wiser.

"Evaline says the steps here go on up to the first floor. We'll try that," he said.

Rastmoor gave a few good pushes on the woodbin, but it stayed put. "Good idea. This thing's too big; I can't budge it. I'll run upstairs and meet you. Where do you suppose those steps come out?"

"No, stay here," Dashford said a bit too quickly. If anyone was going to walk in on Evaline while she was dressing, it damn well was not going to be Rastmoor. Or anyone else not named Dashford, for that matter. He listened to her footsteps on the creaking treads, farther away and slowing.

"Why? Everything all right in there?" Rastmoor asked.

"Yes. What of the others? Did you find the group you said was on the way from Hartwood?"

"I did. I found them as I was heading down to the river. Smart people, your staff. Thought to bring everything in a skiff, just in case you or Miss Pinchley needed carrying back.

You're not going to need to be carried back, are you?"

"No, we're fine."

"Yes, I'm sure you are. However have you amused yourselves this whole time, trapped here all alone while everyone else was out trying to dig through the mud for a door that ended up being underwater?"

"Stow it, Anthony."

Rastmoor was laughing. "All right. So how far did you get in that tunnel? Walking through it, I mean."

"I don't know," Dashford replied, glad for a change of topic and deciding to ignore any double entendre Rastmoor may have intended. "A few hundred feet, perhaps. But it's blocked, and water was seeping through at a steady pace."

"Figures. We found the little mound she mentioned, but it was surrounded on all sides by floodwater. We dug as best we could for the door, but it's clear that passage is swamped. I was worried you might get caught up in it down there."

"No, we made it back into the cellar, and Evaline recalled this little staircase."

"How very clever of her. And where, pray tell, is our Miss Pinchley? Upstairs getting dressed again while you stand here and keep me occupied?"

Damn. Dashford was simply going to have to get thicker friends. "Ass. Why don't you just go back outside and tell my people everything's fine, and we'll be along soon. They are out there somewhere, I presume?"

"They are, with picks and shovels and ropes in hand."

"Fortunately, we have no need for those, as you can see."

"Yes, I can. But perhaps you and Miss Pinchley can find some alternate uses for them?" Rastmoor suggested. "You two seem remarkably inventive." The damn fool was laughing again.

"Go to hell, Anthony. And go outside. We'll join you shortly."

"Incidentally, Dash, there's a portrait in the, well I guess it's the drawing room. That wouldn't by any chance be the infamous Mrs. Gwin, would it?"

"It would."

"Funny. I thought she looked a bit . . . familiar."

God, Dashford clenched his eyes shut, and a perfect

recollection of that very portrait flashed in his mind. Indeed, why didn't he notice the similarities right away? Evaline did take after her grandmother.

"Now is not the time, Anthony," he said and hoped his friend could hear the seriousness in his voice. If Evaline was not prepared for the world to know her relationship to Mrs. Gwin, Rastmoor was just going to have to keep his damn mouth shut on any suspicions he might have come up with. "Wait for us outside."

"Well, that's going to look rather suspicious, Dash, if I go out there without you two. People might wonder what you and Miss Pinchley are up to, and you know how rumors spread. Why, folks will have you married to her in three weeks' time."

"I *will* be married to her in three weeks' time, you dunderhead. Now get out of here."

Light spilled into the little stairwell from up above. Dashford glanced up and could see Evaline's now-clothed form silhouetted in a narrow door at the top of the steps.

"I've got it!" she cried. "I'm in Grandmamma's bedroom!"

"What was that?" Rastmoor questioned, stomping closer to lean over the woodbin and peer into the thin crack at the door.

"We've got the upstairs exit open now, so rest assured we'll be just fine. Go away."

"I'll meet you upstairs then," Rastmoor said and disappeared.

Dashford heard him clomp out of the kitchen and presumably off to find the main staircase.

"Damn," Dashford grumbled. He took the small steps before him two at a time, ignoring their aged complaints, and arrived at the top landing and stepped into Mrs. Gwin's bedroom.

Evaline was there, her torn, wet clothes hanging on her body as she stood in the middle of the room. He came up behind her and began working at the closures of her sagging gown. It would not do to let Rastmoor find her like this.

She angled her head and smiled at him. "I refuse to acknowledge the expertise you seem to show for manipulating the fastenings of women's apparel."

"As long as you acknowledge the expertise I show in other areas, my dear," he said and kissed her neck.

She gave a contented sigh but he knew her attentions were not fully on him. Being here in her grandmother's private room after all these years was clearly having an effect on her. He felt her body go still as her eyes slowly scanned the furnishings.

A huge bed dominated the room. The velvet curtains were a faded blue that must have once been quite cheery, and the wallpaper was still a delicate pink tint with tiny roses lined up on it. White covers lay over everything, but a huge window let in enough light to keep the room feeling almost fresh and inviting. Hanging across from the bed was a large portrait of a man.

Dashford recognized it immediately; there was one very similar at Hartwood. The portrait was his grandfather. It was a likeness of him done years ago, with raven-dark hair curled up in an elaborate, old-fashioned style and the ornate clothing of an era more than fifty years past. The former Lord Dashford was a magnificent man; one could not simply notice the portrait and quickly glance away. In fact, the portrait held Evaline's eyes, too.

"You favor him," she said quietly.

"My father always spoke highly of him, despite how my grandmother must have felt regarding . . . well, his living arrangements."

"His sleeping arrangements, you mean," Evaline corrected.

"That, too."

"I don't blame her. No woman would want to share her husband that way."

He slipped his arm around her waist and gave a squeeze. "I promise you won't ever have to."

She didn't seem quite as enthusiastic about that as he'd hoped. Could it be she didn't believe him? Well, he could rather understand that, unfortunately. He hadn't given her the best impression of himself as a man of honor, exactly.

"Really, Evaline. I know you've heard all the stories about the gaming and the women . . ."

"And the debts and the thugs out to kill you?"

"All of that, but the truth is . . ."

"Shh. I know you'd give it all up if you could, I really do," she said with a sigh. *Another sigh?* Why was he suddenly worried about what she was preparing to say next? "But there's something you should know. About me. The money's not . . ."

Here she stopped. At first he thought perhaps she was overcome with emotion from all they'd been through, but now he realized her smooth brow was furrowed and her eyes focused on something behind him. He turned and was facing Grandfather's portrait again.

"What is it?" he asked.

"Look, in the painting," she said, leaving his side to walk closer to it. "What is your grandfather holding?"

He joined her in studying the work. What was it Grandfather was holding? A key, it appeared. Odd the man should hold a key. Most portraitists depicted their subjects holding items to represent their rank or affluence or religious devotion. But Grandpapa held a key. What for? Dashford wondered.

"It goes with the box," Evaline said and pointed to another item in the painting.

It was indeed a box, metal by the looks of it. It sat on a table beside his grandfather, unobtrusive but with a strangely familiar design etched onto it. Where had he seen that design? He couldn't recall, but the key in Grandpapa's hand was molded with the same twining design. Clearly Evaline was right. They went together.

"So it does," he agreed. "What do you suppose that's all about?"

She drew in a quick breath and suddenly her lips started moving as she silently recited something.

"What is that?" he asked.

"*The man bears the key while the woman holds the treasure,*" she replied.

That seemed familiar, too. Where on earth was it . . . oh hell. Now he remembered them both, the words and the design.

"Sir Cocksure!" he exclaimed. "By God, you've read Sir Cocksure!"

She blushed. "I'm sorry. I found it in your library."

"Well, that might certainly explain how a woman of your, shall we say, inexperience was remarkably well educated. My, my, but you are a gem, Evaline!"

"But what does it mean?" she asked, turning back to study the portrait. "*The man bears the key while the woman holds the treasure*. What treasure?"

"The treasure is only a myth," he said.

"I know. But how odd that the design in that book would match the painting."

"I found the book here, you know. When I was going through some of your grandmother's things after she passed."

"You found that book here? It was my grandmother's book?"

He laughed. "Apparently so. Perhaps that inscription was in my grandfather's hand."

"Then no wonder the design is the same. It's in the book, it's on the box, and on the key he's holding."

"*The man bears the key*," Dashford recited again.

Evaline's eyes sparkled when she smiled up at him. "Perhaps it's a clue. Maybe there really is a treasure! Quick, look behind the painting. There could be some secret hiding place."

Dashford didn't need her to ask twice. He grasped the heavy frame in both hands and gently lifted the portrait away from the wall. It was more than a little disappointing when the wall behind the painting showed no signs of anything secret, merely the fact that the silk on the wall had obviously once been far more vivid in color. Dashford turned to carefully place the painting on the floor.

Something thunked.

Evaline stooped to investigate. Lo and behold, she stood up again holding a key. The same key that was in Grandfather's hand. She smiled.

"*The man bears the key while the woman holds the treasure*," she repeated.

The key had been hidden behind the frame. That could only mean, of course, that the treasure was downstairs with the portrait of Mrs. Gwin. Good grief, so there really was a Loveland treasure? All this time, he'd never even thought to look for it. He'd thought it simply a myth, something Mrs. Gwin smiled about and likely considered to be nothing more than the happiness she'd found here. Indeed, he'd always assumed *that* was the Loveland treasure: abstract ideas about love and sacrifice and commitment and all that rot. Could it be there truly was something more tangible?

And he had just gone and promised it to Graeley. Damnation. Well, nothing had been signed in blood yet. If this treasure was real, it belonged to Evaline. Mrs. Gwin was her grandmother, and everything here by rights should have gone to her. Dashford would just have to find some other way to pawn off Claudia.

"Come on," he said, taking Evaline's hand.

They turned to head downstairs. The doorway was blocked, however. It was Rastmoor. How long had he been there? He cleared his throat.

"Come along, you two. There'll be time enough for moon-eyed sweet talk later on. Right now you both look like hell, and there is a houseful of worried people back at Hartwood who think Dashford is about to stick his spoon in the wall."

"Sorry, old chum. Something to tend to first. Care to accompany us to the drawing room for a little treasure hunting?"

Evaline frowned. Yes, he supposed he should have consulted her first before involving a third party. If this treasure was as grand as it was reported to be, she might prefer to keep its discovery quiet. Well, Rastmoor could be trusted.

"Treasure, eh? That Loveland treasure rubbish? You don't think you're onto something, do you?" Rastmoor asked.

"Why don't we find out?"

They followed Rastmoor out into the hallway and down the stairs. Evaline was unusually quiet, and he could feel her excitement in the air. It must be quite an odd feeling for her, coming back to this house after so long, learning that something her grandmother obviously held dear was still waiting here. He prayed she wouldn't be disappointed by what they found.

They came into the drawing room, and Mrs. Gwin's portrait was hanging just where it had always been.

"Indeed, Grandfather was a man of excellent taste," Dashford commented. The similarities between Evaline and her grandmother were striking, now that he had the two of them together. If he'd seen the painting more recently, he would have known instantly when he first laid eyes on Evaline that there was a connection.

"Forgive me for saying, but you look an awful lot like Grandfather Dashford's courtesan, Miss Pinchley," Rastmoor said. "That wouldn't by any chance explain how you happen to know of secret passageways in the cellar here, would it?"

"Stow it, Anthony," Dashford warned.

But Evaline smiled, gazing with fondness up at the painting. "She was my grandmother."

"What? Oh, this is too rich," Rastmoor said with a low chuckle. "What are the chances of that coming about, eh, Dash? So you did run across the granddaughter, after all."

"Help me with this," Dashford said, glad to interrupt his friend's musing. This was probably all a bit much for Evaline. No doubt she could do without Rastmoor's attempt at ironic humor just now.

The men took the painting from the wall. At first glance there seemed to be nothing more than wood paneling behind it, but once Mrs. Gwin was propped securely against a nearby table and Dashford could run his hands over the wall, he found what they were looking for. The paneling was uneven.

"I think there's a door here," he said.

"Damn, this treasure might be something after all!" Rastmoor exclaimed. "Get to it man; the suspense is killing me."

Not to mention the fact that at any moment his servants might come in here, worried about their delay. He pressed firmly against what appeared to be the movable panel and was rewarded instantly. It swung open to reveal a small compartment.

"Is it there?" Evaline asked, breathless.

"I believe something is in here," Dashford said.

He reached his hand inside.

Chapter Nineteen

Evaline could scarcely remember to breathe. Could it be true, the Loveland treasure was real, and Dashford had just found it? She stood on tiptoe to watch as he brought something out from the little niche he'd discovered behind Grandmamma's portrait. To think it had been here all this time, and no one had ever looked there.

"Is it the box? Do you need the key?" she said, offering it to him.

His face was unreadable. "It's the box, all right, but the lock's broken."

"What?" Evaline gasped. Broken? But that could only mean . . .

"Someone's already found it," Rastmoor said.

Evaline shot a glance his way. He was leaning forward to watch as Dashford brought the box down to the table beside them. Was Lord Rastmoor right? Had someone already been here before them? The house had been vacant so long, and surely there were many around who'd heard of the treasure. It only made sense someone might have come in and taken it. Hiding treasure behind a portrait wasn't exactly unheard of. It would likely be the first place anyone might look.

Drat. Grandmamma and her beau may have been great lovers, but it appeared they were none too clever when it came to hiding treasure. Too bad Sir Cocksure didn't have a chapter on that in his little primer.

The threesome gathered around as Dashford pried the rusted lid open on the little box. The two-heart design etched onto it was still perfectly recognizable. Evaline prayed there might still be something inside.

There was. A small leather pouch—the strings appeared to be torn on it—and a pile of dirt. Or was that rust? Evaline leaned closer to see.

Dashford inspected the bag, shaking it out only to find more of those dirt-like granules inside. He held some in his hand and studied them. Was this all that was left of the famous Loveland treasure? Evaline's heart sank.

"By God, it's gone," Rastmoor said.

But then Dashford started laughing. "No, I'm afraid it's not. It may have been discovered, but the would-be thieves left it behind."

"They did?" Evaline asked, reaching for a pinch of the small particles lying in the box. "Can you be sure? This is only . . . wait a moment. These are seeds!"

"Strawberry seeds," Dashford clarified.

Indeed they were. Someone had left half a cupful of strawberry seeds in Grandmamma's treasure box. Heavens, but of course. This was the treasure! Whoever had found it didn't recognize it for what it was; the thing most cherished by Mrs. Gwin and her devoted lover.

Oh, but it was a cruel joke. For a moment there Evaline had thought perhaps she was saved, that she might have something of value to offer Dashford to rescue him from his troubles. She could have cried from disappointment.

"Evaline?" he said. "I'm sorry. I know you must have been hoping for something else, something you could keep to remember her by."

She shook her head and wouldn't look up at him. He didn't need to see the tears that persisted in gathering. "I was hoping for something we could sell," she admitted.

However was she going to explain to him that he'd rejected a wealthy Claudia only to take on a miserable commoner with an empty bank account? Not that she was prepared to give him back to Claudia after all this, of course.

Evaline might be disappointed and upset, but she wasn't stupid.

Two muddy men tromping into the drawing room interrupted any sweet words of comfort Dashford might have been about to speak. The men wore Dashford's livery and carried various tools in their hands. Apparently the rescue party had arrived.

"My lord! It's good to see you're well," one of the men said.

"Thank you, Jakes," Dashford replied, quickly pouring the strawberry seeds into their pouch and closing it back up in the metal box. "Sorry to keep everyone waiting. As you can see, Miss Pinchley and I have been rescued, and I'm afraid we put you all through this trouble for nothing."

"The folks will be that glad to see you still breathing, m'lord," the other man said. "Believe me, we was all a-fright, worried for you."

"Well, then, we'd best be on our way back then, don't you think, Miss Pinchley?" Dashford said, offering her his arm. "I'm sure you are most eager to get into dry clothing. Plus," he added with a frown, "I have some business to attend with our friend Mr. Bristol. And don't try to talk me out of it, Evaline."

She took his arm. "I won't."

Rastmoor laughed. "This is why you're my friend, Dash. Never a dull moment with you."

"Let's go, then," Dashford said, leading Evaline from the stuffy room.

They emerged to the cheers of their would-be saviors who waited in the soggy midday gloom in front of Grandmamma's moldy cottage. Indeed, it would take more than strawberry seeds to make this place livable and valuable again. Even if Evaline did manage to scrounge up the money to buy it, this would be no place to bring Sophie and an infant. She would like to have Grandmamma's portrait, though.

If only there had been more than strawberry seeds in that precious box.

THEY WERE NEARING HARTWOOD. MANY OF THE rescuers had arrived at Loveland via the river and were going home the same way. Rastmoor graciously offered to stay behind to organize the rest of the group, reloading the various ropes and equipment they'd brought in expectation of a dramatic endeavor. Dashford explained how concerned he was for Evaline in her wet attire, so it was hailed as heroic when he pulled her up onto his horse with him and set off for home.

She was propped securely on his lap now, and he was getting some very nice ideas brought on by the delightful sensation of her warm bottom pressed against him. She huddled against him, and he thought this whole day's adventure was worth it just for this. He let the horse set its own leisurely pace.

"My lord . . ." Evaline began softly.

"Randolf," he corrected her.

"Randolf," she began again. "I'm afraid you're going to be very disappointed."

"At what?" He couldn't for the life of him think of a single disappointing thing, except that when they arrived home, they'd likely be swarmed by his mother and other well-wishers, and it would be hours before he'd have Evaline alone to himself again. Indeed, that was a most disappointing thought.

"My money. I know you're counting on it, but really—"

"Shh, let's don't talk about money now. Rest assured, your inheritance is safe from me, Evaline. I promise not everything you've heard about me is quite true. Here, look, Hartwood is just over that next rise," he said and nodded toward the landscape ahead of them. "The lake is beyond those trees."

She lifted her head and looked around, frowning. "I had no idea Hartwood and Loveland were so very close to one another. When I rode there with Rastmoor, it seemed to take hours."

"That's because you were distraught with worry for me, my dear," he said and kissed her cheek. "Really though, they are quite close. Grandpapa was not a patient man. When he felt the urge to pay Mrs. Gwin a call, I don't suppose he fancied a long and strenuous ride. On horseback or carriage, that is."

Evaline blushed. He was glad her mind ran rather toward the gutter, latching onto other possible definitions for *ride*, just as he'd intended. Hmm, a thought came to mind. Perhaps she would be as eager to explore it as he was.

"The boating grotto is just around that bend," he said, pointing.

She nodded, her cheeks still beautifully flushed.

"We could stop there, if you like," he suggested carefully. "For a rest, or simply to gather our thoughts before facing everyone or . . ."

"Or?"

He let his wicked smile finish the sentence for him. He could tell she was fighting a smile of her own. Indeed, the woman was a treasure.

"All right then," he said, turning his horse.

She giggled. They entered the woods and followed a little-used path along the lake. The roof of the grotto was barely visible as they started down the overgrown hillside, trees concealing them from anyone who might happen to be looking this way from across the lake. The house was farther yet, completely out of view.

Dashford pulled up his mount and slid Evaline gently to the ground. He hopped down behind her and secured the horse to a tree. Evaline stayed close, so it was easy to pull her into his arms and hold her a moment.

"These might be our last moments alone for a while," he said as he gathered her close for a kiss. Really, he supposed he ought to wait until they were inside and had the benefit of a comfortable settee or chaise longue, but she was too tempting, pressed against him like this. She gave in to his passion and melted against him.

"I hope you don't have plans to do much of anything besides this once we're finally good and married," he said when he forced himself to loosen his hold on her and pause for air.

"What else is there?" she replied, her voice strained and halting.

He loved it when she sounded like that. He knew what it would lead to. "Come on."

Time to get her inside the grotto. Just as he led the way past the horse and toward the door in the side of the hill, voices caught their ears. They froze in their tracks. Evaline stared up at him.

"Is it always like this with you? People purposely interrupting at every turn?" she whispered.

He shook his head and shrugged. Yes, it did seem to go that way, didn't it? He strained to listen. The voices, he realized, were his mother and Sir Victor.

"I tell you, he's a scoundrel!" Sir Victor was saying in a none-too-pleasant tone.

"And I tell you he's trapped in a cellar!" his mother replied quickly. "Why would Lord Rastmoor lie about that? Really, Sir Victor, you'd be far nearer to having him for a son-in-law if you'd stop this foolish investigation and come back to the house. We must find out what more can be done to save him!"

"It's a lie. A distraction!" the gentleman went on.

"Why on earth would anyone lie about my son falling into a cellar?" Lady Dashford insisted.

Their voices were getting closer. Obviously they were coming from the house and would soon be at the grotto. If they continued on the path past the recessed building, they'd run smack into Dashford and Evaline. He pulled her quickly behind the shelter of a young evergreen. With luck their horse was far enough up the hill and around the corner to remain unseen.

"He's got plenty of reason to lie," Graeley announced. "He got me to let him burn the betrothal paper! Ah, you didn't know that, did you? Well, he did. Tricked me into it. So you see? Now he can lure my innocent daughter out here and seduce her again without paying the price!"

The dowager just clucked her tongue. "Why on earth would he do *that* with your daughter when he just managed to be rid of her?"

"Because he's a randy, hotheaded son of a—"

"Hold your tongue, or I might just feel compelled to remind you that Claudia is a selfish, simpering—"

"Wait," Sir Victor interrupted. "Listen. Do you hear? Sounds inside the grotto. Voices. Aha; just as I suspected! Still going to defend him, are you? Have a look and see, my lady. Your crude, libidinous son in action!"

Graeley yanked open the grotto door. For half a second everything was dead silent. Then, out of the blue, a woman's shriek cut through the sylvan air. Dashford knew it wasn't his mother; her more familiar shriek came next. Without pause, Dashford left Evaline and darted around to join them. Evaline's footsteps came close behind.

They found Sir Victor and Lady Dashford standing just inside the grotto; the door was thrown open wide. Dashford ran up behind them and had no trouble seeing over their heads. The sounds of rapidly moving bodies and the rustle of furniture and fabric drew his eye to the rear of the room, toward the very settee that figured so prominently in his recent fantasies.

There, stumbling to an upright position and clutching various articles of clothing—not all of them masculine—was a very pink, very naked Mr. Carrington. On the settee, thrashing about to pull herself under the dust cloth that had previously been used to cover the furniture, was a recumbent—and equally naked—Claudia. It had obviously been her shriek that split the silence.

But good God, what on earth had been going on? Dashford could scarce believe his eyes. Could it be? The ever demure Miss Claudia Graeley and the always decorous Mr. Carrington had been pumping the pudding out here like wild things? Well, this was a shock to the system!

Evaline poked her head between Dashford's arm and the doorframe. A strangulated giggle escaped her. Dashford couldn't have agreed more.

"Holy saints above!" Sir Victor shouted.

"Papa!" Claudia cried. "It's not what it seems!"

"I don't know what else it could be," Lady Dashford said plainly.

"I can explain," Claudia squeaked.

"No, I will explain," Mr. Carrington said in a voice far steadier and bolder than Dashford could have possibly imagined from him.

Still holding Claudia's underthings to cover his, er, underthings, he stepped forward and cleared his throat. "Your daughter, Sir Victor, is engaged to marry me."

Sir Victor just shifted his gaze back and forth between the offending parties.

"It's true, Papa," Claudia said, lifting her pointed little

chin into the air and somehow managing to still appear regal and superior, even considering her position. "I'm going to marry him, and you have to let me. I'm pregnant!"

The room went silent. Lady Dashford was the first to speak. "My son has nothing to do with that!"

"Of course he doesn't," Carrington growled. "I'll run him through if he attempts to claim it! Miss Graeley is mine, Dashford. You'll do well to remember that."

His mother and Graeley were surprised to find Dashford and Evaline behind them. It all seemed a bit too much for poor Sir Victor. His complexion couldn't decide between going pale with horror or crimson with rage. The result was a rather blotchy appearance that did not look well at all.

"I'll remember that, Carrington," Dashford said. "No need for weapons."

It was not as if he had to fear that Carrington was concealing even so much as a paring knife on his person, but the way things were going just now, Dashford felt it might be prudent to play along. Claudia's indiscretion and Carrington's claim was a godsend. Best not do anything to spoil it.

"Claudia, I can't believe you would do this to me," Sir Victor grumbled.

"It wasn't exactly you she was doing it to, sir," Dashford kindly pointed out.

No one cared.

"I told you I wanted to marry him, Papa," Claudia whined. "But you made me think he'd been untrue and was courting another! I treated the poor darling just awfully because of the lies you told me, Papa. It's a wonder he saw fit to forgive me."

"Well, he'd better forgive you," Sir Victor blustered. "If he's got you in a family way, you can bet I'll truss the weasel up and haul you both down to the parson right now!"

"No need for trussing, sir," Carrington said. "I'll gladly speak my vows on any day of your choosing. I would, however, request that I be allowed a few moments to retrieve my clothing first."

"Fine," Graeley said, folding his arms firmly across his chest as if he intended to stand guard and watch. "But you made your bed, the both of you. For shame, Claudia, choosing this middle-class sapling when you could have had a peer! Don't expect I'll be footing your bills!"

"We don't, sir," Carrington said quite definitively. "I will see to all of Claudia's needs most effectively from here on out."

"Seems you've been doing just that," Dashford said and chuckled to himself. Evaline jabbed him with an elbow, but he knew she appreciated the levity.

"Laugh if you will, Dashford," Sir Victor grumbled. "You and your overreaching heiress, there. You're a disgrace to the Dashford name, ruining yourself in wild living only to taint your family with the blood of a common merchant just to keep the duns at bay. I hope you run through her filthy merchant money quickly, and then where will you be?"

"We'll be just fine," Dashford said calmly. "I've no intention of running through Miss Pinchley's money."

He gave her a reassuring smile, but all her giggles were gone now. She actually looked quite concerned, as a matter of fact. By God, did she truly believe Sir Victor's words? Could she think after all this that Dashford was still after her for her funds?

"Evaline, really," he said softly. "Your great, infamous fortune is quite safe from me."

But she shook her head. Hellfire, were those tears welling up in her eyes?

"No, it isn't," she said and looked so tragic he almost couldn't bear to hear what she might say. Was she refusing to marry him? Good God, had he messed things up so badly as all that?

"I'm so sorry," she went on, not meeting his eyes, "but it's gone. I have two hundred pounds to my name and no idea if there is any more. I'm truly sorry, my lord, but I'm not going to be any help to you."

This didn't make sense. "What?"

Now she turned her gaze on the still-pink and still-naked Carrington. "It's all right, Mr. Carrington," she said, and for the life of him Dashford couldn't quite figure how Mr. Carrington played into this. "I overheard you and Lord Rastmoor talking. You were mentioning how Papa's investments all went bad and how my fortune is gone now."

Mr. Carrington looked confused. "But Miss Pinchley, I don't recall ever—"

"In the library, Mr. Carrington. You didn't know I was there, but you and Lord Rastmoor were discussing my finances as well as that other, more private matter, and . . ."

Here she paused, and her eyes grew large. Dashford watched closely as something important seemed to dawn on her. Lord, but he would have liked to know what it was.

"But there really was no other matter, was there?" she said slowly, more to herself than to anyone else. Her perplexed expression slowly began to grow brighter. "No, of course not. It couldn't have been, because at that time we hadn't, er, that is, I had never . . . oh, but Mr. Carrington, you weren't talking about me at all, were you?"

Carrington frowned. "No, we weren't, and I had no idea anyone else was present!"

"Forgive me, but I didn't mean to eavesdrop. I assumed you and Lord Rastmoor were talking about me," she said. "But you couldn't have been, could you? You must have been . . . Oh my, you were talking about Miss Graeley!"

Here Evaline clamped her mouth shut. It was obvious she'd said enough. Claudia turned an angry gaze on Carrington and would, no doubt, have jammed her fists into her hips if she hadn't actually needed to keep them balled in the thin fabric of the dust cover.

"I'm sorry, Claudia," Carrington said. "I never intended to discuss our personal matters, but Rastmoor confronted me. He had seen us together in London and had grown suspicious of our relationship. Lest he develop the wrong impression of your character, I felt compelled to inform him of the truth of our prior understanding. Sadly, though, there are additional elements to the situation of which you are not aware, my darling."

"Additional elements? Perhaps you'd best explain, dearest," Claudia said in that sickeningly sweet voice she used when she was thoroughly miffed.

Poor Mr. Carrington blushed beyond just his face and took a deep breath. "Very well. Your father was against our union because he cannot provide the dowry he's claimed for you all this time. He is, in a word, broke."

"Now see here!" Sir Victor protested.

"It's true," Carrington went on as Claudia's eyes got rounder and rounder. "Though I never cared about that. It seems, however, he was willing to deceive you with false accusations against me in the hopes of convincing you to marry Dashford, despite the man's dubious value as husband material."

"Now see here!" Dashford protested.

"But why would Papa do that?" Claudia asked, her dewy gaze going back and forth between her father and her lover. "He knows Dashy has no money, either."

"The Dashford estate is not nearly so depleted as his lordship has led everyone to believe," Carrington informed her. "Indeed, our firm has been involved with several of his accounts, and I can vouch for the fluid nature of the man's resources. Why he would choose to mislead everyone in this manner and give his poor mother so much pain and mental anguish, I have no idea."

Oh hell and damnation. Rastmoor had been right; Carrington knew. Bother. This was going to be a bit dicey. He had never meant for the truth to come out this way.

"What?" his mother exclaimed, glaring at him. "We're not on the brink of bankruptcy?"

Dashford sighed. "No, Mother, we aren't."

"You're not?" Evaline questioned. She glared, too. "But what about the creditors, the rumors, the man with only one eye?"

"All fabrications, I'm afraid," Dashford admitted. "I thought that if Claudia thought I was . . . well, if she came to believe I wasn't fit for polite society, she might, that is . . ."

"Oh, Dashy!" Claudia exclaimed. "You did all this just to get rid of me?"

Dashford felt like a naughty child caught sneaking biscuits. Damn, but what must Evaline think? He was afraid to look at her for fear of the scorn he might find in her eyes.

Claudia, too, was scowling at him. Her fury, however, shifted rather quickly from Dashford to her father. "Papa, you told me he loved me! It was your doing in the first place that we ended up betrothed, and you said I'd break his heart if I called it off."

"I only wanted what was best for you, Claudia," Sir Victor sputtered.

Claudia wasn't buying, though. "Dashy is my friend, Papa! I never wanted to marry him."

"You didn't?" Dashford asked.

"You certainly could have fooled all of us these past few days, my dear," her father said curtly. "Don't pretend you weren't doing all you could to snag him. I found the two of you together bright and early this morning, didn't I?"

Claudia lowered her eyes. "I'm sorry. It was only coincidence that we met up with each other in the hallway, Papa. I was up so early because . . . well, because I've been feeling rather ill in the mornings lately, and I didn't want anyone to find out. I'd been down to the pantry to pilfer some of those wonderful pickled quail eggs Cook served yesterday."

Carrington moved closer to her and reached his hand down to take one of hers in a loving, comforting gesture. Heartwarming as it was, Dashford would have rather they both kept their hands firmly clenched in the fabric that was now drooping uncomfortably low in areas it was supposed to be covering.

"Forgive me, Pomeroy," Claudia continued, gazing with devotion up at Mr. Carrington.

Pomeroy? The man had a name like Pomeroy? Dashford didn't know which would be worse, to be tagged for life with such a moniker or to be scrutinized by angry parents—naked—in a room as cold as this.

"I can't believe I was deceived by all those lies Papa told me," Claudia went on. "I thought you left me ruined and alone, so it seemed I had no choice but to bring Dashy up to scratch right away. When Papa saw me standing there with Dashy this morning I panicked and made it seem something had been going on. Oh, I've been so very confused lately!"

"It's all right, my dear," Carrington assured her. "Everything is sorted out now."

"No, it isn't!" Lady Dashford interjected. "Victor Graeley, if you knew your daughter was in love with another and you believed my son was a cad and a wastrel, why in heaven's name were you so eager to see them wed?"

Sir Victor frowned but didn't answer. He didn't need to.

"It's simple, Mother," Dashford replied. "He wanted the treasure."

"What treasure?" she asked.

"Loveland's treasure," Dashford explained. "Sir Victor believed the rumors that there was a treasure hidden away at Mrs. Gwin's home. He learned the intent was to give that house as a source of independent income to my future bride, whom he decided should be Claudia. Incidentally, in case any of you are still unsure, my future bride will most certainly be Miss Pinchley."

"Well, that's a relief," Lady Dashford said, much less surprised by this information than Dashford might have expected. "For a few minutes this morning I thought the girl was actually going to let her silly aunt force her into marrying that Bristol bloke."

"There's been entirely too much matrimonial scheming around here for my taste," Dashford said, making sure his mother recognized that he was aware of her own part in these machinations. "If you don't mind, Miss Pinchley will be marrying me, and Miss Graeley can marry whomever the hell else she wants. Sir Victor's just going to have to figure out some other way to resurrect his personal finances."

"Papa, is all this true? All along the only reason you wanted me to marry Dashy was so you could get your hands on some imaginary treasure?" Claudia asked.

Sir Victor shrugged. "It would have saved our family name, dearest. And you would have been a viscountess!"

"Pooh," Claudia said. "I'm ashamed of the family name! I wouldn't blame Pomeroy one bit if he decided to abandon me right here and now." She turned her huge blue eyes up at him. "You won't, will you?"

"Of course not, beloved," Carrington replied.

It was all so touching that Dashford thought he might choke. "Well, now it appears to be all sorted out."

"No, it isn't!" This time Sir Victor interjected. "You made a promise, Dashford."

"Surely he's released from that," Lady Dashford exclaimed. "You said you burned the betrothal. Besides, we've just found Claudia carrying on with another man! That betrothal cannot be binding now."

"Not that promise," Graeley said. "The other one, just this morning. As payment to allow him to break the betrothal, Dashford assured me I could have Loveland. He can marry all he likes, but the Pinchley chit won't get that house or anything that's in it. The property is mine!"

His mother glared up at him, and Dashford just shrugged. "Well, it was either that or marry Claudia."

"But, you can't sign away that property," his mother protested. "It isn't yours. I hold the title."

"True, you do, don't you?" Dashford sighed and turned to Sir Victor. "Sorry, old man. I guess she doesn't want to part with it."

"You said you would have no trouble getting her to agree, you ruddy bastard!"

"Watch your language, sir," Lady Dashford scolded. "You've no right to speak to my son that way. Besides, he's done you a favor. That property needs far more work to keep it standing up than it's surely worth. There's no treasure in there. Trust me, I know that for certain."

Dashford raised a hand. "Now, hold off. We just spent half the day there. You might be surprised to know the old place still harbors a few secrets. At least, it did."

He took a nice deep breath and let the pause heighten suspense. Everyone gazed intently on him, waiting for some grand revelation. Well, not everyone. Evaline merely rolled her eyes at his drama. She was amused, though; he could tell.

He was just about to tell the story when someone approached from behind.

"I say, I thought I might find the two of you out here!"

It was Rastmoor. The man's sense of timing was uncanny. Now everyone shifted their attention to him.

He'd ridden up on horseback but now left the animal and was coming toward the group in the doorway. At first all he must have been able to see was Dashford and Evaline, but as he drew nearer and could see inside the grotto, his eyes grew large.

"What, ho! By God, is this an orgy and no one saw fit to invite me?"

"Down boy," Dashford said. "We're simply here to wish Miss Graeley and Mr. Carrington happy."

"Is that so?" Laughing, Rastmoor leaned past Evaline and pretended to tip his hat—neither he nor Dashford had been wearing one all day—into the room. "Many fine felicitations to you both. But I say, Carrington, aren't you a bit underdressed for the occasion?"

"Not the particular occasion we found them in," Dashford informed him.

Rastmoor howled with laughter. Lady Dashford cleared her throat, and Claudia wiggled deeper under the dust cover.

"Perhaps we should resume this conversation indoors—with everyone fully clothed," Lady Dashford suggested.

"No," Sir Victor fumed. "Dashford's hiding something, and I want to know what it is."

"Papa, please!" Claudia whined.

The poor thing, she did seem to be turning a fair shade of blue. Indeed, the cold, damp air filled the place. No doubt after all this time, Carrington probably didn't need to work so hard at covering himself. Between the embarrassment of a growing audience and the chilled grotto interior, any object of a rather sensitive nature was likely to be minuscule by this point. God, how Dashford didn't envy either of them. He was finding it rather amusing, though.

"Spill it, Dashford," Sir Victor said. "You found something in that old house, and I want to know what it is!"

"You told him about the box you found behind the wall?" Rastmoor asked.

"Not yet I hadn't, but thank you, Anthony."

"Oh. Sorry, old chap."

"You did find something!" Sir Victor insisted.

Dashford sighed. "I did find something, Gracley, but it legally belongs to Evaline. After all, she is to be my wife." Until Evaline felt comfortable with things, he was not about to force her into revealing her relationship to Mrs. Gwin. That would come with time. For right now, he wanted to assure her ownership of her rightful inheritance.

He glanced at her for permission, and she nodded. "Go ahead."

Chapter Twenty

The man couldn't just pull out that little box and open it, could he? No, that would be too easy. He had to draw out the suspense and make Sir Victor think he had something to look forward to. Sir Victor wasn't going to be happy when he learned the truth. Evaline gritted her teeth and waited for the explosion. She loved Dashford completely, but he surely did have a flair for the dramatic.

He drew the box slowly out of his pocket. He held it gingerly, carefully, as if he knew it contained the rarest treasure of all time. Oh, why was he doing this? Sir Victor was not going to be pleased.

"What is it, man?" Sir Victor asked.

"It's a box," Rastmoor replied.

"A jewel box, from the looks of it," Sir Victor said. "You found it in a wall?"

"Indeed," Dashford said. "In a secret hiding place."

"Now, Randolf, there's no reason to believe a treasure is inside," his mother said.

"Of course there is," Dashford assure them. "I already checked."

Lady Dashford looked confused. "Are you certain?"

"But of course, Mother."

Sir Victor was about out of patience, it seemed. "Go on, man, open it!"

"What, you're not enjoying the anticipation?" Dashford asked.

"By God, I'll open it," Sir Victor nearly shouted. "It should be mine, anyway!"

Sir Victor grabbed the box from Dashford's hand. He pried the lid off quickly before Dashford could snatch it back and exposed the little leather bag inside. With a greedy grin, Sir Victor yanked the bag out and pulled the strings open.

"What is this?" he asked.

"Careful, man!" Dashford ordered.

Almost ruthlessly, Sir Victor poured the contents of the bag into his large hand. Dashford and Rastmoor were like two little boys delighting in their mischief. Evaline watched Sir Victor's face as it furrowed in disgust.

"Sand?" he asked, glaring at Dashford. "You stole the treasure and replaced it with sand?"

"Did I? Oh, how thoughtless of me," Dashford said.

"It's not sand, you dolt," Lady Dashford said. "It's strawberry seeds. Dashford, that was a cruel trick."

"Oh, but I thought after the way he lied to his own daughter and tried to trap me into . . . wait a moment," Dashford said, stopping himself and turning a suspicious eye on his mother. "Exactly how do you know these are strawberry seeds? You aren't standing close enough to see them."

Now everyone turned to Lady Dashford. She smiled sheepishly. "Fine. I'll tell you. Before he died, your father and I found the box, that secret Loveland treasure."

"You were the ones who ripped the box open and put everything back in the compartment?" Dashford asked, incredulous.

"Well, we had gone over there to look for something your father recalled might be in Mrs. Gwin's library, and, well, we found the treasure."

"Bah!" Sir Victor growled.

"Oh, be careful with them!" Evaline cried, reaching to stay Sir Victor's hand when it appeared he would toss the seeds onto the ground. "They might still grow!"

"What exactly were you looking for in Mrs. Gwin's library, Mother?" Dashford asked. "It didn't by any chance happen to have a clue in it as to the whereabouts of the treasure, did it?"

Evaline paused from helping a reluctant Sir Victor scrape the seeds back into the little bag. She glanced up at the knowing grin on Dashford's face and the nervous twitch on Lady Dashford's. Oh good heavens. Dashford's parents had been consulting Sir Cocksure? Evaline suddenly found herself fighting back another wave of giggles.

"You're telling me this is the treasure? The *real* treasure?" Sir Victor grumbled.

"It is," Dashford replied. "At least as far as my grandfather was concerned. He believed strawberries brought Mrs. Gwin to Loveland. I'm fairly convinced, though, there may have been more to it than just the man's, er, strawberries."

With a warm smile, Dashford retrieved the treasure from Sir Victor and handed it to Evaline. "I believe this belongs to you."

"Thank you," she said.

She wrapped her fingers around the box, making sure to contact Dashford's skin wherever she could. He responded by closing his hand over hers. She really wasn't sure how long they stood like that, their hands embracing over the box and their eyes locked in silent communication. All she knew was that she found it quite annoying when Lord Rastmoor interrupted.

"Well, that's bloody anticlimactic," he quipped.

"And I say I've been duped," Sir Victor grumbled. "We had an agreement, Dashford."

"Really, Papa," Claudia said sharply. "You were going to sell me off for a bag of strawberry seeds? Honestly."

"Never you fear, my love," Carrington said. "You're worth all the jewels in the world to me."

Claudia batted her eyes some more and beamed up at him. It was quite disgusting, actually, and Evaline hoped she didn't appear such a twit when she happened to look up at Dashford. He smiled back at her, and she felt her insides go to jelly. Yes, she probably looked as much a twit as Claudia. All right, she probably looked worse. Claudia, at least, didn't have the added benefit of river muck and cobwebs plastered all over her.

"All right, it's time we let these two get some clothes

back on," Lady Dashford said loudly. "And let these two get out of theirs. Heavens, what a sight you are, Randolf! Come now. Everyone back to the house."

"I will not be treated this way! Dashford, you owe me!" Sir Victor stormed.

"Oh, give it a rest, Victor," the dowager cut him off, marshaling the group with the determination of a collie dog. "Come along and we'll see if there is any luncheon yet edible while I inform my people that Randolf managed to survive his drowning incident today. I swear poor Mrs. Kendall was ready to bring out the black wreaths already."

"Luncheon sounds good," Lord Rastmoor said. "All this rescuing business leaves a chap bloody ravenous, you know."

The group was herded out onto the shady lawn between grotto and lake, and Lady Dashford pulled the door closed behind them. A pair of birds overhead rustled and flew away as Sir Victor's gruff voice hollered out some unpleasant warnings and oaths to his daughter and future son-in-law still inside. Other than that, though, Evaline couldn't shake this wonderful feeling of well-being that settled over her.

The lake, the trees, the cool spring air—it was all lovely. The sun was still feebly poking through the clouds, and the sleepy atmosphere of early afternoon surrounded them. Dashford came up beside Evaline and quietly slid his hand around hers. Indeed, he looked a sight, but it was a wonderful sight. They'd survived that dreadful cellar and made it back to discover things were not nearly so bleak as she'd feared. Things were, in fact, wonderful.

"Come, Victor," her ladyship was saying. "I daresay your daughter can dress herself. Escort me up to the house before this damp air has entirely ruined my gown. Randolf, you should bring your lady, too. It cannot be healthy for her in those wet clothes."

Dashford grinned. "I rather like her in wet clothes, Mother."

"Impertinent creature," the dowager said, knocking Sir Victor with her knuckles until he offered her his arm. "Stop your larking and come with us."

"I'll get the horse," Dashford said, still grinning, and

leaned in to whisper into Evaline's ear. "I rather like you out of wet clothes, too."

She tried hard not to react, but of course her face was heating and her blood raced. The man was incorrigible. He was actually laughing as he left her and headed back around the side of the grotto.

Lord Rastmoor had his closer horse untethered and was already mounted when the door to the grotto opened and Mr. Carrington escorted a remarkably composed Claudia out to join them. Evaline was surprised. Either Mr. Carrington had a surprising talent for dressing ladies, or there was a very good reason why Claudia hugged her wool shawl so tightly around her. All the same, she appeared quite the picture of modesty now, with the exception of a few hairpins out of place.

"Hurry, Randolf," Lady Dashford called. "Everyone's waiting."

"My mount has his tail all snarled up in a bramble," he called back.

Evaline frowned. The poor creature. She hadn't realized they'd secured him so close to such an obstacle. Hopefully he hadn't been suffering from it long.

"You all go on ahead," he said, poking his head around the corner of the grotto. "Perhaps if Miss Pinchley comes, she can steady the horse while I untangle him."

"Of course," she said, hurrying to join him.

Lady Dashford sighed. "Oh, very well. But do hurry. The servants are surely in a quandary about our absence. I don't know how Cook will react when she's forced to reheat everything yet again."

Sir Victor made some further unpleasant remarks to his daughter and future son-in-law, but Evaline ignored them all as she hurried around the grotto to do what she could to help Dashford's horse. She stopped in her tracks when she found the huge animal happily chewing leaves and very clearly not entangled. But how did . . . oh, of course she understood. She whirled around to face Dashford.

He was right there behind her, grinning again.

"I may have exaggerated the bit about the brambles," he said. "But I assure you, I do need your help."

"Oh, do you have something tangled up, sir?"

"Most definitely," he replied. "And it's getting deuced uncomfortable."

She tried not laugh at him, but it was a bit obvious the man did, indeed, have a growing problem. Heavens, had they not taken care of that same problem merely an hour ago? And now his mother and several others were nearby! What on earth was she getting herself into with this man?

"Here, I've got a knife!" Lord Rastmoor said, riding into view.

"Good God, man," Dashford said, stepping cleverly behind Evaline. "We don't need a knife."

Rastmoor glanced at the horse then back at Dashford. The man was no fool and obviously assessed the situation in an instant. He clucked his tongue and shook his head.

"You're determined in this, Dash, aren't you?" he asked.

"I am," Dashford said firmly, placing his hands on Evaline's shoulders.

She wasn't quite certain what was passing between the two men, but it seemed significant enough that she held her tongue. When Rastmoor's eyes fell on her, she shrank back a little. He stared a moment then shook his head again. This time, however, she detected a smile.

"Then I suppose I ought to go catch up to the others and tell them you're taking the other way around, straight toward the stables," he said. "And of course you'll go directly to your rooms to change, so it might be a good while before you turn up for the meal."

"Precisely," Dashford said.

Rastmoor just chuckled. "And they say men rule the world. Ha!"

With that, he turned his horse and went trotting off in the direction the others had gone. Sir Victor could still be heard railing about something, but it was clear they were well on their way back toward the house. Evaline turned to face Dashford.

He opened his mouth as if to speak but then apparently thought better of it. Instead, he swept Evaline into his arms and captured her in a heated kiss. She yielded instantly. She forgot they were wet and bedraggled, forgot they were

standing in the woods, and forgot his mother and former
fiancée were merely yards away. She felt his desire flowing
through him and knew it matched her own. Whatever flaw
had caused Grandmamma to be such a wayward woman,
Evaline knew she'd certainly inherited it in spades.
Truthfully, she couldn't have been more grateful.

"I believe the grotto is available," Dashford said, fire
dancing in his eyes. "Pity you didn't think to bring Sir
Cocksure along with you today, just in case we run out of
ideas."

"I doubt we'll need him."

Of course, she was right.

Epilogue

"But Anthony, do you really have to leave so soon? The breakfast is just beginning," Evaline asked their friend, pushing the little halo of violets and cherry blossoms back onto her head. The dratted thing had been slipping off all morning, and she could only imagine how her hair looked by now. It didn't help that the moment their ceremony was over Dashford practically ravished her in the vestry as they waited for the rector to come and sign the book.

"They're expecting me," Lord Rastmoor replied. "When I got Mother's letter, I sent word I'd be here through the wedding, but I promised to leave as soon as possible after."

"I'm sure things will be fine when you get there," Dashford said, standing beside Evaline. "Your cousin has nothing to gain by dredging up this old feud again."

"It worked for him before," Rastmoor said.

He looked weary, as if the mere idea of traveling home to deal with family issues had already taken a heavy toll. Evaline supposed she shouldn't be surprised. Dashford had explained to her about Rastmoor's cousin, Cedrick Fitzgelder, and his horrible claims to have information that would damage Rastmoor's family. Moreover, the girl Rastmoor had been set to marry three years ago ended up spurning him only to go off and marry Fitzgelder. She died shortly thereafter in childbirth, so it was no wonder their friend was not looking forward to revisiting these issues.

"Take care, Anthony," Evaline said. "And you're always welcome here; you know that."

"Oh, I'll be back," he said with forced cheerfulness. "Hell, I might have to bring my whole family. If Fitzgelder has his way, we'll be homeless."

"It won't happen," Dashford assured him. "He just likes to make life difficult. Tell your mother and sister not to worry. Then tell Fitzgelder he can go to hell."

"I'll do that." Rastmoor smiled with the first hint of real sentiment.

Another of their wedding guests approached the threesome and clapped Rastmoor on the back. It was Dashford's friend, a striking young earl named Lindley. Evaline doubted she'd ever get used to being in such company.

"Leaving so soon, are you, Rastmoor?" Lindley asked.

"Family matters." Rastmoor sighed.

Lindley nodded. Apparently he understood. "Pity. Who's going to keep me entertained now that Dashford's out of the game? I daresay there's a dearth of excitement in this rustic place."

"You might be surprised, Lindley," Dashford said with a quick wink to Evaline.

Lindley looked hopeful. "Oh? All the more reason to stay and enjoy the festivities then, eh, Rastmoor?"

"Sorry," Rastmoor said. "My mother's expecting me in London."

Lindley shrugged. "London, you say? Well, that might be promising. Care for a bit of company on the way there?"

"Too kind," Rastmoor replied. "But you only arrived last night; I'm sure the last thing you want is to head out on these roads again. I'm not much company right now, anyway, I'm afraid. Fitzgelder's been at it again."

Lindley frowned. "Your bloody cousin? Oh, pardon the expression, Lady Dashford."

It took Evaline half a moment to realize he'd referred to her. Heavens, so she was a lady now, was she? That would take some getting used to.

The carriage Rastmoor had hired clattered up the drive,

ready to convey him—via a rather roundabout detour due to the failed bridge—to the nearest posting house. Pity he hadn't his own carriage for traveling; this one looked less than promising. The poor man was, no doubt, in for an uncomfortable journey.

"By God, man," Lindley said, his face displaying an elegant disgust. "You can't possibly mean to travel in this!"

"I rode out with Dash," Rastmoor explained. "So I had to hire one for the return."

Lindley turned a stormy glare on Dashford. "Haven't you got something at least civilized to offer the poor man? Honestly, Dashford!"

Dashford simply laughed. "I offered, but this was Rastmoor's choice. I can't help it if the man has a death wish."

"By all means, Rastmoor," Lindley said, "send this back to its dung heap and travel with me. I'll have my phaeton brought around, and we can leave straightaway."

It appeared Lindley would not take no for an answer, although Rastmoor made a concerted effort. Evaline had the distinct impression he'd rather have walked back to London than be stuck with the overly fussy Lord Lindley. In the end, though, Lindley won, and servants were sent to ready his gleaming new phaeton.

More and more guests were arriving for the wedding breakfast, and Evaline was forced to take her attentions from Rastmoor's dilemma to greet them. She congratulated and embraced until she felt her arms must be bruised, but she couldn't deny it was a good feeling. And Dashford was right there beside her the whole time, which made it all much more than simply bearable.

At last Lindley's carriage rolled up. It was indeed a fine conveyance—a far sight better than the dogcart Rastmoor had hired. Lindley took charge of Rastmoor's bags, directing the servants in their placement, quite obviously convinced the footmen had no clue how to accomplish such a thing on their own. Evaline certainly was not envious of the hours Rastmoor would soon be spending in Lindley's company.

"Good-bye, Anthony," she said, giving their friend a heartfelt hug. "And thank you for everything."

Despite the rocky start, she had come to care for Dashford's dear comrade. She knew the man's unhappy past made him leery of romantic entanglements, so it was quite an honor when he agreed to stand up with Dashford at the wedding. Once things settled in, she'd have to see about finding Rastmoor a worthy wife so he could know the same happiness she and Dashford had found. Yes, that would certainly be her next project.

"Thank you, my lady Dashford," Rastmoor replied with unexpected warmth. "And don't worry. Wherever she is, I'll deliver your message to your cousin."

Evaline nodded. She had felt most uncomfortable sharing details of her family history with Rastmoor, but Dashford assured her he would be sensitive. He'd been right. Rastmoor truly did seem eager to help.

So far, all attempts at locating Sophie had failed. No one at Sophie's previous address would talk with the investigators she had hired, and there were simply no other clues. It was as if the girl merely evaporated, and Evaline was desperate to understand why. Dashford assured her they would travel to London once he had things under control here with his flooded farmlands and town, but she knew that would be several weeks at least. Right now, Rastmoor was her best hope for finding Sophie.

"Thank you, Anthony," she said, giving him her warmest smile.

"What's this?" Lindley asked, finally done defending his carriage from the frightful, baggage-wielding footmen. "The dazzling lady Dashford has a cousin?"

Evaline cringed. She'd rather not have to bring any more of Dashford's friends into their confidence. The fewer people who knew Sophie's secrets, the better. As it was, she hadn't exactly told Rastmoor the full extent of Sophie's situation. She wasn't entirely sure Rastmoor would willingly volunteer to hunt for a wayward Sophie *and* a fatherless infant. Certainly she was loath to share any of these details with Lindley.

But Dashford handled things smoothly. "Her cousin, Sophie, has been out of touch these past few months. Rastmoor is going to help us locate her."

"Quite so," Rastmoor assured them. "Miss Darshaw is bound to turn up somewhere."

Lindley frowned. "Darshaw? Sophie Darshaw, you say?" He fluffed his starched cravat. "Now, this might be simple coincidence, but I do believe I met such a person in London."

Evaline couldn't help but gape. "You met her? Sophie Darshaw? Are you certain?"

"Yes, I'm quite certain. Young, with blond hair about the color of yours?"

Evaline was nearly beside herself. "Yes! That could be her!"

This was almost too good to be true. Lord Lindley knew of Sophie's whereabouts? A miracle! Then again, perhaps it was not so miraculous. If Lindley was one of Dashford's gaming cronies, there was no telling where he might have run across poor Sophie, or in what situation! She cringed to think of the implications.

"We were not well acquainted," Lindley went on, to her relief. "Although the young miss did favor you, now that I think about it, Lady Dashford. Something around the eyes, I think. Her name is no longer Darshaw, however."

This was news to Evaline. "What? She's changed her name?"

"It's Clemmons now, if I recall correctly," Lindley said, his brow furrowing. "I believe she and her husband were traveling for their honeymoon."

"Husband!"

Now this was astonishing. Sophie had a husband? Truly, truly miraculous. Oh, but how she hoped this might indeed be her Sophie.

"He's an actor," Lindley went on. "I know little more, I'm afraid."

An actor? Well, that did not bode well for Sophie's future. But a husband! That was indeed encouraging. She turned excitedly to Dashford.

"Perhaps that's why no one could find her; she has a new name!"

"Indeed. This does seem to change things," Dashford replied.

"I'll find her," Rastmoor said firmly. "And we'll see what sort of fellow this husband of hers really is."

"Thank you, Anthony," Evaline said.

Yes, Rastmoor could surely be trusted to handle things for them. She reached up on tiptoe to kiss his cheek. He pretended to be immune, but she knew him well enough now to know better. Anthony Rastmoor was not nearly so cold as the man he portrayed.

Dashford and his friends made fine show of giving each other manly slaps on the back, then finally it was time for Rastmoor and Lindley to leave. Evaline bid them a fond farewell, and Rastmoor followed Lindley up into the striking phaeton.

Dashford called after them, "Take care."

"Indeed we will!" Lindley called back. "It's a long ride to London. There's no telling what might happen along the way."

Rastmoor simply laughed at the thought. "Honestly, Lindley, what could happen?"

Lindley tapped his horses into action, and the phaeton glided away. Evaline tried to ignore the niggling apprehension behind her smile. Could things possibly have worked out satisfactorily for Sophie? It was almost too much to hope for.

Dashford moved closer and squeezed her tightly. She squeezed him back. The footmen had gone off, and the guests now waited indoors. For all intents and purposes, Evaline and Dashford were alone. Cook would no doubt scold them for delaying the breakfast, but for now it was good to just stand in the quiet, basking in the glow that came with a wedding day. Evaline sighed and leaned against her husband. He was warm and solid beside her. It was good to finally have someone to lean on.

"I hope Sophie is as happy with her new husband as I am with mine."

"And why wouldn't she be?" Dashford asked with a casual shrug of his broad shoulders. "If she's half as adorable as you, the gentleman must make a complete cake of himself for her."

Evaline smiled. "Well, that's as it should be."

She tipped her face up toward his as Dashford leaned in for a kiss. They were interrupted, of course, by Lady

Dashford's appearance to remind them everyone was waiting and stomachs were rumbling. Evaline drew away from her husband and laughed.

"I suppose we ought to be used to that." He gave a wearied sigh and smiled back at her, lacing his fingers with hers and leading her back toward the house. Their *home*, rather. A home full of love, laughter, and all the freedom Evaline could ever want. And, of course, a rather private little garden around back that would look quite lovely in the moonlight tonight.

TURN THE PAGE FOR A PREVIEW OF
THE NEXT HISTORICAL ROMANCE

Damsel in Disguise

BY SUSAN GEE HEINO
COMING SUMMER 2010 FROM BERKLEY SENSATION!

Chapter One

Julia St. Clement had never tried to eat soup through a mustache before. It was dashed difficult, she found. No wonder the awful things had gone out of favor with modern men. Three days now she'd hidden behind the blasted thing and already she felt weak and malnourished from struggling to strain any decent sustenance through it. Why ever had she let Papa talk her into this dreadful disguise?

Because she'd had no other choice—that was why. Papa had whacked off her long dark hair, fashioned a sorry little mustache from a lock of it, and threw a pack of clothing at her.

"Change quickly, *ma cherie*!" he'd ordered. "Fitzgelder will know my face if he sees me, but now he'll never recognize you."

And it was true. The man they both feared—for good reason—had been completely deceived. Papa was safe to flee, and Julia had faced Fitzgelder alone. They'd been properly introduced and the foul little man had no suspicion his new friend Alexander Clemmons was as much a sham as his shabby facial hair. This bloody mustache, it seemed, had saved Papa's life.

And now, God willing, it would save a few others. Hopefully Julia's would be one of them. Provided, of course, she didn't succumb to starvation first.

"You've got soup on your whiskers," her pretend-wife, Sophie, announced with a girlish giggle.

"Of course I do," Julia grumbled. "I've got soup on my chin, soup in my cravat, soup everywhere but in my mouth. Blast this disgusting mustache!"

"But you look quite dashing, you know, Miss St. Clement," Sophie said as she daintily spooned plenty of soup safely into her own mouth. "Really, it's a pity mustaches aren't more the style."

"I feel wretched and I look worse," Julia assured her. "It's a monstrous thing and Papa will never hear the end of it when we finally meet up with him again."

"*If* we meet up with him," Sophie corrected, her sweet voice wavering. "The coachman has been so slow, miss. What if Mr. Fitzgelder catches us?"

"He won't. Surely that locket you stole from him isn't so important he'd come chasing us all the way out here."

"I didn't steal it!" the girl insisted for at least the dozenth time. "When he attacked me it must have torn off in the struggle and fallen into my apron."

"Little that will matter to him, will it? But I doubt he'll be looking for you, Sophie. That locket is the least of Fitzgelder's worries just now. He's got bigger things on his mind, I'm afraid."

"Such as killing your friend, you mean."

Julia shushed her. They were sitting off alone in the crowded common room of the posting house, but still it couldn't hurt to be cautious. There was no telling who might be listening in. Fitzgelder had men out and about and they could be anywhere right now. The room was quite full of strangers, not all of them respectable looking.

"Anthony won't be killed if I can help it," Julia muttered under her breath.

Sophie gave a dreamy sigh. "He must be very special to you."

Lord, she'd quickly disabuse the girl of that deranged notion. "The man is a selfish lout who doesn't have an honest breath in his body," she announced. "He very nearly deserves to be murdered."

Sophie wasn't swayed. "Then why have we spent the last three days traveling all the way out here to warn him?"

"I said *nearly*," Julia had to admit. "No one deserves what Fitzgelder has planned for him; murdered on the highway by cutthroats and left there to rot."

Sophie shuddered, momentarily forgetting her soup. "Are you sure we shouldn't just find the local magistrate and tell him? I'm not too keen on all this cutthroat business."

"I told you to wait back in London, didn't I?"

Now the girl was offended. "What? And leave you to come out here alone? I couldn't do that, Miss Clement! You saved my life."

"Well, I certainly didn't save you from Fitzgelder just so his hired thugs could do you in on the road," Julia said and stared longingly at the two shriveled potatoes in her bowl. "It's getting dark. I think we should let the mail coach go on without us and spend the night here."

"Here? But surely we're getting close to—what's that little town where your gentleman friend is staying?"

"Lack Wooton. He's at a wedding near there and we've not yet passed through Warwick. As bad as these roads are, it's bound to be another full day's travel."

Sophie sighed. "Well, I suppose we ought to stay here, then. I just hope, for the sake of that selfish lout you want to rescue, we get there in time."

"So do I, Sophie," Julia agreed, making another brave go at the soup. "So do I."

Almost as irritating as this blasted mustache was the worry that Fitzgelder's men had already passed them and accomplished their goal. True, she and Anthony Rastmoor had not parted on the best of terms, but she'd give anything right now to see that he was alive and well. If he could just walk through that door safe and sound, she'd . . . well, she'd be very relieved.

Then she'd knock him on his arse and ask what in the hell he'd been thinking three years ago when he'd wagered—and lost—her at the gaming table. Good God, as if she was some piece of chattel he could own and barter at will! Well, he'd owned her, all right—owned her heart and soul—right up until that night when Fitzgelder showed up waving Anthony's vowels and claiming that *he* was her fiancé now. As if such a thing could be legally binding. Fitzgelder knew it could not.

But it was the fact that Anthony had done such a thing, even as an angry jest, that had broken Julia's heart. She knew what it meant. Anthony had found out the truth about Julia's identity and wanted no part of such a wife.

Indeed, Anthony Rastmoor simply had to remain alive. If Fitzgelder's men got to him first, how would Julia ever get her revenge?

"IT'S BROKEN," ANTHONY, LORD RASTMOOR, SAID as he inspected the underside of their carriage.

"Damn," his companion, the Earl of Lindley, fumed. "I just bought this curricle three weeks ago. Quite a piece, don't you think?"

"I think you got taken." Rastmoor dusted the dirt off his hands and trousers. "Most of the higher quality conveyances have axles that actually attach to the wheels."

"It certainly was doing that when I bought the blasted thing," Lindley said, fairly diving onto his hands and knees to crawl under the carriage. "Are you saying there's been shoddy workmanship here?"

Rastmoor was perfectly content to let his elegant friend get muddy. It was, after all, Lindley's carriage. He should have been the one down there investigating in the first place, although what Lindley would have investigated Rastmoor couldn't say. The stylish earl likely wouldn't have known the difference between a broken axle and a hay rake. Still, Rastmoor was happy enough not to be the only one with dirt on his knees.

Lindley swore and Rastmoor had to chuckle. While most men might let out a string of colorful words over the condition of the axle, Lindley was more likely upset over what he'd just done to his clothes. He probably wouldn't even notice it was some very shoddy workmanship, indeed, that put them in this predicament.

In fact, it hardly looked like workmanship at all. No, if Rastmoor didn't know better, he might even wonder if the damage to Lindley's carriage was intentional. But that was ridiculous. Who would tamper with Lindley's carriage? Unless of course . . .

But that was ridiculous, too. Surely dear cousin Fitzgelder would not stoop to something like this, would he? No, this had to be merely an accident.

Damn, but it was rather coincidental, wasn't it? Mother sent a message warning he'd best get himself to London for some unnamed trouble Fitzgelder was stirring up, and now something so unusual as this threatened to delay him. Could it be mere coincidence? He wanted to believe so, but somehow he just couldn't.

What was Fitzgelder about, this time? The terms of Grandfather's will had been well settled these two years. Surely his cousin couldn't think to dredge all that up again, could he? Then again, Rastmoor had learned the hard way not to put anything past Cedrick Fitzgelder.

The horses fidgeted nervously, so Rastmoor went to calm them.

"What rotten luck," Lindley said finally, uttering a few more oaths and crawling out from under his carriage. "I don't suppose you have a spare axle or whatever you said that was?"

"No, I don't," Rastmoor said. "But if you have some straps or the like we might be able to bind the thing well enough to get it back to that posting house we just passed. We won't be riding, though."

Lindley bit his lip and glanced around at the dusky trees lining the road on either side of them. "That's slow going, isn't it?"

"I suppose, but with that axle broken we're done for the night, I'm afraid."

"Yes, it appears that way, but I'm not sure my cattle are up for pulling dead weight. Even if we bind it, that axle won't turn very well, will it?"

So Lindley did have some basic understanding of the mechanics of the thing. Well, he couldn't very well blame the man for not wanting to overtax his horses. The only thing finer than Lindley's wardrobe was his stables, and these two goers were as good as they got. It would be a shame for such proud horseflesh to be dragging a lame curricle all the way to that posting house.

"All right, help me loose them, then. We'll walk the

horses and send someone back to get your precious curricle."

Lindley agreed, then noticed his muddied condition. "Bother. My valet will have my hide over these trousers."

Oh, not the valet, again. Rastmoor rolled his eyes. "I don't see how you abide the man. From what you say he sounds like a ruddy tyrant."

Lindley smiled. "That he is, but I assure you I'd never make it without him. Which reminds me."

He left Rastmoor with the horses and went around to the back of the carriage. He dug through a box stowed there.

"Ahem, but we unharness the horses up at this end," Rastmoor called.

"Yes, but the weapons are back here."

"Weapons?"

"Here, take this," Lindley called out, tossing Rastmoor a lethal little pistol.

"What's this?" Rastmoor asked.

"It's a pistol," Lindley informed.

"I know it's a pistol. What in God's name is it for?"

"For shooting anyone who might come out of those trees after us." Lindley glanced at said trees and shuddered. "You never know what sort of persons are about these days, and it's very nearly dark out."

"Good grief. Is it loaded?"

"Of course. What bloody use would it be empty?"

Rastmoor shook his head, but he accepted the pistol and slipped it into his pocket. He was a bit taken aback when Lindley casually tucked his own pistol into the front of his trousers. This image of the always elegant Lindley with a pistol wedged at his waist was more than a bit humorous.

"What is it?" Lindley asked.

"Aren't you worried that will ruin the lines of your tailoring?" Rastmoor asked, not bothering to hide his smirk. "Whatever will your valet think?"

"Should a highwayman leap out after us, I would prefer to have my weapon where I can get at it," Lindley said, stepping up to help with the horses. "A few wrinkles can always be ironed out. Blood, my valet tells me, is a bit more dicey."

"I'm sure it is," Rastmoor had to agree.

No highwaymen did leap out, though, and they pushed

and pulled until the curricle was safely out of the roadway. Leading Lindley's fine horses, the men headed off to the posting house. The evening was dreary and still, yet not nearly so dreary as the day two months ago when Rastmoor had traveled this same road.

He'd been traveling with his friend Dashford on the way to what was supposed to have been a quiet house party. Some house party, though. There were floods and fiancées and fiascos until the bloody thing ended with Dashford's wedding. Rastmoor still wasn't sure how he felt about that.

The whole concept of matrimony hadn't exactly worked out very well for him, and to be honest, he was still not convinced any man ought to put much stock in the institution. From what Rastmoor had seen so far, women were an untrustworthy lot. He hoped Dash wouldn't have to learn that the hard way.

Rastmoor sighed as they plodded along. Damn, but with Dashford trussed up and married now Rastmoor would likely have to settle for Lindley's persnickety company more often. Oh well. For a game here or there at the club or a visit to the races, no one could fault Lindley's sportsmanship or his overall entertainment value. But if Rastmoor had to have one more discussion about where to find the best gloves or which bloody knot would look best in his cravat . . . Honestly, what could Dashford have been thinking to go and get leg shackled?

"You know what I'm thinking?" Lindley said after they'd walked in silence quite a while, the horses plodding nervously along behind them.

He hated to imagine. "No. What?"

"There'll likely be women at this posting house."

"Probably so."

"That suits me just fine. With luck there'll be a couple for both of us. Which do you prefer, the blondes or the brunettes?"

"The ones who do their job and disappear before daylight."

"I reckon that'll be all of them," Lindley declared with a hopeful laugh. "I think I'd favor a blonde tonight. Unless of course there's only one available and blonde is your preference, then naturally I would—"

"No, thank you. Have any woman you want. I think I'll just sleep tonight."

"What? But you've been stuck up there at Hartwood for nearly two months, and I saw the sort of guests they had—not exactly fresh and accommodating, as they say. Surely now that you're getting out and about again you'd want to prime the old pump handle, if you know what I mean."

"I know what you mean, damn it," Rastmoor grumbled. "But I'm not interested, all right? Good luck to you and your pump handle, but I'd rather sleep. Alone."

Lindley frowned as if that was a foreign concept. "Alone? But you're not ill, are you?"

"No. I'm fine."

"You don't sound fine. You sound—blue deviled. My God, but you can't possibly still be pining after that girl? That little French actress of yours—St. Clem, or something, wasn't it?"

"St. Clement," Rastmoor corrected before he caught himself. The last thing in the world he wanted was to discuss Julia right now. "And I'm not pining. I'm just not interested in some dirty whore at a posting house, all right?"

Lindley gave a slow whistle. "You *are* still pining! Dash it all, Rastmoor, that was years ago. And didn't she end up marrying your cousin, or something?"

"Yes."

By God, what would it take to not have this conversation? Was he going to have to use that pistol on Lindley?

"That's right, and then she died in childbed, didn't she?" Lindley went on.

Rastmoor gritted his teeth. "That's what I heard."

Oh, he'd heard the story, all right. Then he'd gone and got roaring drunk. Dashford lost his father at that same time and the two of them were roaring drunk together. Things hadn't gone so well for them after that, as he recalled.

Eventually Dashford pulled himself together and Rastmoor had simply learned to pretend. He supposed, in a way, it had been easier for Dash. He'd been mourning a devoted father, a man who left behind fond memories and warm emotions. Rastmoor, however, had been grieving something altogether different.

When Julia St. Clement died all she left behind were bitter wounds and heartbreak. It was hard enough knowing she'd left him for another man, but with time he might have recovered from that. It cut deeper than that, though. Julia left him a scar that would never go away. The whore may have died in Fitzgelder's bed, but the child she'd taken to the grave with her had been Rastmoor's. She'd carried *his* child and still left him for another, passing the child off as Fitzgelder's.

How did a man ever recover from that?

"I CAN'T WAIT TO SEE THIS LORD RASTMOOR'S face when he meets you again," Sophie was saying as they finished their supper.

Julia cringed. "Hopefully that will never happen. With luck we'll find he's safely at Lord Dashford's home and I can simply send a warning message. He'll find out what Fitzgelder is about and you and I can be off to meet Papa."

"You don't want to see him again?"

"Heavens no!"

"We've come all this way and you're not even going to see the man?"

"Exactly."

Sophie was downcast. "That's so sad. I was hoping the two of you might…"

"Sorry, Sophie. That only happens in novels."

It was a shame to disappoint the poor girl, but better she get such foolishness out of her mind now before she started expecting grand romance for her own life. Indeed, women like them should harbor no such hopes—Julia had learned that the hard way. Perhaps the truth would come easier for Sophie.

"We'll be done with this before you know it," Julia went on, hoping her light tone and warm smile would both encourage and distract her young friend. "Then we'll find Papa and you'll become a part of our troupe. You're quite a hand at sewing, but perhaps we can coax you into acting, as well."

"Acting? Oh, I'm sure I could never be so very good at that. All those lines I'd have to memorize!"

"You've been playacting the part of a blushing bride for three days now and so far the audience seems quite enthralled," Julia said, sweeping her arm wide to indicate the patrons of the posting house, a few of whom had traveled this last leg of the journey on the mail coach with them.

Sophie looked around the dim room and frowned. "I believe our audience would be no less enthralled were I simply a chicken tucked under your arm. They've hardly taken note of us at all."

"There, you see? You've played your part to perfection. Who's to say you might not make a memorable Juliet or Ophelia or—"

"Lord Lindley!" Sophie said suddenly.

"Lord Lindley? I don't believe we have any scripts with Lor—"

And then Julia glanced up to realize what Sophie meant. The doorway was filled with the elegant form of a man they had briefly met in London just as they were making their hasty escape. Lord Lindley—a good friend and confidante of the evil Fitzgelder.

Sophie's eyes were huge and terrified, and Julia wanted to slide under the table. Good heavens, if Lindley recognized them he'd notify Fitzgelder of their whereabouts! They had to hide, to get out of here this very instant.

But there was nowhere they could go; nowhere in the room to hide and Lindley was standing in the only exit. They were trapped. Julia's pulse pounded and she struggled to think up some scheme to protect themselves. What could she do? Where could they . . .

Suddenly all coherent thought ceased.

A familiar, broad-shouldered form appeared behind Lindley. Julia's lungs contracted, and the air rushed out of them in a gasp. Around her, the world disappeared and she was aware of only one thing: Anthony Rastmoor was still alive.

Thank God she wasn't too late! Fitzgelder's men hadn't succeeded in their plan. Anthony still lived and breathed and wore that smile of half-amusement, half-boredom she'd come to know so well three years ago. Three long, painful years ago.

He was alive, and he was beautiful. And he was cold.

When his gaze fell on her she recoiled, both inwardly and out. The chill that emanated in his hazel eyes was as unfamiliar as the image that had been greeting her in the mirror since she and Sophie had taken up this masquerade. Indeed, the Anthony Rastmoor who followed Lindley into the poorly lit common room was a man much changed from the man who had taken Julia's virtue—as well as her heart.

His gaze didn't last long on her, though. Quickly it moved on, as if she were of little importance to anyone. This surprised her more than even the fact she was seeing him again. How could she be struggling for air, feeling as if the universe itself would collapse around her, and yet his gaze simply swept over her as if she'd been nothing more than furniture? It was unthinkably hurtful.

Then his gaze did linger, but not on her. She had to physically turn her head to see what he was seeing. The air swept back into her lungs and burned like fire.

He was gazing at Sophie.

Her brain began functioning again. Mostly her thoughts were torn, though. Should she gouge out the man's eyes or grab up a dull knife and castrate him here? God, but how he was staring at Sophie! The nerve of him!

Funny, Julia had never contemplated how fetching the girl must appear to those of the male persuasion. Yes, Sophie was pretty, she supposed. Gentlemen would notice that, of course. But, by God, what was that charming expression forming on Sophie's fresh, youthful face? Why, the little tart was actually smiling at Anthony!

Julia's stomach roiled and she put an involuntary hand up to her mouth. Damn, but there was soup in the mustache there. She hated the itchy thing all the more. Of course Anthony Rastmoor would not look at her in the same way he was ogling Sophie—soup-stained gentlemen were hardly his type. Gullible little misses like Sophie were. Just like Julia had been, once.

"Why, Mr. and Mrs. Clemmons," Lindley said, noticing them and coming their way.

Julia had given the false name at the spur of the moment as they were leaving London. It had seemed convenient to use as they'd traveled, and now she was glad they had. No one would think it amiss to see the quiet Clemmons couple being greeted by an old acquaintance here and no awkward explanations would have to be given at mistaken names.

Anthony, too, would likely not recognize the name.

Or maybe it didn't really matter. He'd likely forgotten her altogether, judging by the way his attention was now given entirely to her companion. Indeed, why should he so much as spare a second glance to Julia's severe haircut and soupy mustache while Sophie was sitting there in front of him, all blonde and dreamy and feminine? Damn his eyes.

"How odd to run into you here," Lord Lindley said when he reached their table. "I had no idea you were traveling this way else I would have invited you to share my carriage."

He, too, had his eye on Sophie. What pigs these men were. Didn't they realize Sophie was supposed to be a married woman? How dare they stare like this! If it kept on Julia feared she'd end up having to call at least one of them out or risk exposing herself as a fraud. What husband could sit calmly while virtual strangers drooled over his wife? Shame on them. How on earth had Julia ever thought Anthony Rastmoor to be a decent, worthwhile human being?

"We had a rather sudden change of plan," Sophie was saying. "Didn't we, Mr. Clemmons?"

Julia cleared her throat. "Er, yes. We came this way rather spur of the moment." She worked at keeping her voice low and hoped Anthony might not recognize it.

She needn't have worried. His focus was all on Sophie, to the point the poor girl must have noticed and was finally starting to appear uncomfortable.

"Forgive me," Lindley said, at least trying to tear his eyes from Sophie and act respectably. "Everyone has not been introduced. Lord Rastmoor, this is Mr. Alexander Clemmons and his lovely wife, Mrs. Sophie Clemmons. We met a few days ago in London."

Rastmoor made a polite bow and allowed Julia a quick nod before turning his attention back to Sophie. It had been highly unnecessary for Lindley to recall Sophie's first name, but obviously he had. Sophie was looking decidedly anxious now. The girl might be too pretty for her own good, but at least she appeared to have some sense. She knew enough not to trust the flattery of blackguards.

"How do you do," Julia said, not pausing long enough for Rastmoor to speak before directing her next question to Lindley. "Will you gentlemen be staying for the night here?"

Lindley sent a quick look toward his partner and Rastmoor gave the reply. His voice sliced Julia to the heart. Odd that a voice could have so much power.

"We're undecided as yet, Mr. Clemmons. Will you be staying?"

Julia fixed her eyes firmly on her soup bowl. *Mr. Clemmons.* He still hadn't recognized her. Somehow that hurt far more than it should have.

"We haven't entirely decided that, my lord," Julia replied. It was true, too. If she found the men would be here, she'd simply leave a note for Rastmoor with the innkeeper then get herself and Sophie back on the road and far away from the lusty lords.

But Sophie had her own ideas. She smiled brightly for the men. "The roads have been so very difficult, though. I do truly dread getting back in that coach to be jostled along to the next posting house. Perhaps if Mr. Clemmons knew some of his gentlemen friends were to be staying here tonight I could stand a better chance of convincing him."

Julia gaped at her friend. What was she doing? Now that Lindley was here, they needed to leave, not settle in for the night! Maybe Sophie didn't have so much sense, after all.

Lord Lindley gave a rumbling chuckle and turned his gaze onto Julia. "Shame on you, Mr. Clemmons, forcing your young bride to travel under these conditions."

His attention was short-lived. He turned his focus—and a disgustingly warm smile—back on Sophie. "Rest assured, Mrs. Clemmons, if it will gain you a few hours respite from the torment of travel, Rastmoor and I will do our best to persuade your husband to obtain a room for the night. In fact"—here Lindley smiled at Rastmoor who gave a slight nod—"I'll go see to making arrangements with the proprietor. Don't worry, Clemmons, tonight will be at my expense."

Lindley made a showy bow then went off in the direction

the innkeeper had last been seen. Blast, what had Sophie done? It was true the small purse Julia had on her at the time of their departure was growing a bit thin right now, but certainly she couldn't allow Lindley to assume their expenses. Even more certainly, she couldn't spend the night under the same roof as Anthony Rastmoor! What if the man tried to engage her in conversation? How long could she expect her disguise to hold out if Rastmoor ever did decide to take his eyes off Sophie long enough to question Mr. Clemmons's bizarre mustache and feminine voice?

But so far Rastmoor hadn't reached that point. He was still staring at Sophie and smiling in delight as he called out to Lindley. "See about getting us a private dining room, as well. I'm sure the Clemmonses will wish to join us in a quiet supper."

Oh Lord. What next?

Lindley nodded and disappeared through the doorway toward the front entrance area. Julia glanced nervously at Sophie. The girl just batted her wide blue eyes and shrugged. Well, Julia would just have to find a way to get them out of this.

"There's no need for a private room, sir," she protested. "Mrs. Clemmons and I have just finished our meal, as you can see, and now we'd like—"

"Oh, but dearest," Sophie interrupted, innocent and darling. "Surely that little bowl of soup was barely enough for a strapping man such as yourself. Why not join your friend Rastmoor over a hearty meal?"

Ah, so *that* was Sophie's angle. The chit was meddling. Julia would put a quick end to that. And just what on earth did the little hussy mean by calling Julia "strapping"?

"I assure you, my precious, that soup was quite adequate for my frame," Julia said. "We have no need to remain here any longer. I simply need to give a note to our innkeeper, if you recall." Now she gave Sophie a glare that should have wiped the pink smile from her rosebud lips. It didn't.

"What's our hurry, dear? Surely you can think of *something* interesting to discuss with these fine gentlemen," Sophie suggested.

"No, actually, I'm sure I can't," Julia assured her.

"Fear not, Clemmons," Rastmoor said, leaning casually against a nearby table and leering down at Sophie. "I'm sure we'll find plenty to occupy our time. In fact, a private room will be just what we need. There is a particular matter I'm certain you'll be most eager to discuss."

Now that erased the pink smile. Sophie slid a nervous glance at Julia. What was Rastmoor hinting at with that glinting eye and ominous tone? Had he found them out? Preventing any hasty escape Julia may have contrived, Lindley returned with the proprietor.

"Yer in luck," the older man said with an eager grin. "I got a nice room just for ye and the wife'll bring a good, healthy stew."

Julia tried to demur, but Lindley gracefully swooped in to loop Sophie's hand through his arm and assist her up from her chair. When Julia glanced over at Rastmoor she found him, at last, looking her way.

"Come, Clemmons," he said. "I doubt you'll want to miss this."

Indeed, from the way he spoke she was fairly certain she *did* want to miss it, whatever *it* was. She was fairly certain, too, he was not about to let her. Helpless, she followed Anthony Rastmoor across the hallway into a private dining room.

About the Author

Susan Gee Heino has worn steel-toed boots, done legal research, held a real estate license, and worked as a caterer, theatre director, youth director, and administrative assistant. Only writing has been able to hold her interest year after year. When her children arrived, she shifted focus from plays to romance. In 2008 she was awarded RWA's Golden Heart for Best Regency Historical.

After growing up in Michigan, Illinois, Indiana, and Kentucky, Susan now resides in Ohio with her husband and two children. Her writing days are frequently interrupted by the variety of furry, finned, and feathered critters that share her life. Visit her online at www.SusanGH.com.

Enter the rich world of historical romance with Berkley Books.

Lynn Kurland

Patricia Potter

Betina Krahn

Jodi Thomas

Anne Gracie

Love is timeless.

penguin.com

M9G0907

Enter the tantalizing world
of
paranormal romance
MaryJanice Davidson
Laurell K. Hamilton
Christine Feehan
Emma Holly
Angela Knight
Rebecca York
Eileen Wilks
Berkley authors
take you to a whole new realm
penguin.com